Hostages for Life

BY
ILONA ZWOLSKA
FREYA LINDVIK
OTTO LARSEN

ISBN: 979-8-9930167-7-1

First edition

Quotation and Scripture Acknowledgment

Disclaimer

This is a work of fiction inspired by historical events and the authors' personal and family history. To protect the privacy of individuals and to enhance the narrative, certain names, characters, identifying details, and events have been altered, fictionalized, or imagined.

Some characters are composites, and dialogue and timelines have been created or modified.

While grounded in historical reality, this work does not claim to present events exactly as they occurred.

Any resemblance to persons, living or deceased, beyond documented historical figures, is coincidental or used fictitiously.

In matters involving historical, political, diplomatic, or governmental contexts, certain portrayals, perspectives, institutions, and interpretations have been adapted, condensed, or reimagined for narrative purposes and should not be understood as literal, factual, or complete representations of actual persons, organizations, or events.

The authors expressly disclaim any intent to portray factual assertions about any identifiable individual, living or deceased, or any specific government, agency, or institution, and no such portrayal should be interpreted as a statement of actual conduct, affiliation, or intent.

This work is presented solely as a literary narrative and not as a factual record, memoir, testimony, or historical documentation.

Epigraphs

"Love and compassion are necessities, not luxuries. Without them, humanity cannot survive."

— The Dalai Lama

"Hath not a Jew eyes? Hath not a Jew hands, organs, dimensions, senses, affections, passions?"

— William Shakespeare
The Merchant of Venice, Act 3, Scene 1

"Blessed be the LORD, for he has wondrously shown his steadfast love to me when I was in a besieged city."

— Psalm 31:21 (ESV)

Table of Contents

Part One

Perilous Journey

Chapter 1

U.S. Consulate General Frankfurt, West Germany September 1983

A Turning Point

Catherine was driven to the American Consulate in Frankfurt in a police car and dropped off not far from the entrance to the compound, nestled among thick, towering trees. She carried a cabin-size bag filled with summer dresses and family pictures.

Emotionally drained and physically exhausted, she struggled to walk down the long driveway in the hot summer sun. Each step felt heavier than the last. When she got closer to the building, the sight of the American flag flying outside stirred in her a sudden, fragile sense of relief. She stopped walking, her eyes fixed on the flag as it moved slowly in the warm wind, as if confirming that she had finally reached a place where someone might listen. She approached the front door and was met by uniformed American military guards. In her best English, she said, "My name is Catherine Yampolsky. I am a Soviet citizen, born to an American father. My father, George, entered the Soviet Union in 1936. I want to talk to the American Consul."

Both guards hesitated, looking at her with suspicion and curiosity. They spoke to each other in low tones that she could not hear, their eyes occasionally returning to her as if measuring the gravity of her words, and then one guard opened the door and disappeared behind it. The remaining guard stood firmly in front of the door. Hungry, tired, and frightened, she forced herself to stand politely while she waited for whatever decision might determine her fate.

After a few minutes, the second guard reappeared, whispering something inaudible to his compatriot. The second guard very politely asked her to follow them into the building. They opened the door and gestured for Catherine to cross the threshold into the building. She immediately felt the cool, almost perfumed air of the building wash over her overheated skin.

They took her to the entrance of an elevator and slowly and methodically pressed the button. Almost immediately, the elevator door slid open. Again, the person who appeared to be the senior guard on duty courteously gestured for her to enter. After she stepped into the elevator, both guards entered with her and positioned themselves on each side of her. Catherine became acutely aware of their presence, the quiet authority of their uniforms and the narrow space between them making her feel as though she were already under careful supervision.

Another button was pressed, and the elevator began to descend. Catherine looked up at the elevator display and saw the numbers slowly changing: 1 … B1. She wondered how far inside the building they intended to take her, the small, illuminated symbols glowing softly above the door as the elevator carried her farther from the bright summer sunlight outside. When the elevator stopped, the doors automatically opened.

One of the guards stepped out into a long corridor and motioned for Catherine to exit the elevator. She followed his directions, desperately hoping the journey would soon end and she could sit and relax. The second guard followed, and they slowly walked down the corridor in a single file, moving in perfect step as if there was a strange magnetism between the three of them. The sound of their footsteps echoed faintly along the polished floor. She walked with them until they reached the second door on the left.

The guard on her right side opened the door and entered, gesturing for her to follow. She saw a large room dominated by a polished wooden desk with many chairs lined against the walls. The first guard walked to one of the chairs, slightly turning it towards her and motioning for her to sit. He returned to the door and spoke a few hushed words to the second guard, who exited the room quietly, closing the door behind him. The first guard positioned himself in front of the door, facing Catherine with the composed stillness of a sentry on duty.

As she sat, her eyes wandered across the wall, and she saw a framed picture of Ronald Reagan, the President of the United States. To the right of the picture of the president, there was a framed American flag. Catherine found herself studying the two images in silence, sensing that the quiet room, the guarded corridor outside, and the long journey that had brought her there were all somehow bound to the power represented on that wall. The two symbols seemed to radiate an almost solemn authority in the quiet room.

It seemed like hours passed although it was probably only minutes. She tried to be patient, knowing she was on the last leg of a similar perilous journey that her grandparents had embarked upon many years ago—only going the opposite direction—in September of 1936, a lifetime to many.

While waiting for an American official to see her in person, Catherine went into a deep reverie, pondering her family's voyage and wondering why they had left America to go to Russia ... and why her grandfather had been so idealistic about Russia—the country where she was eventually born. The past and the present seemed to fold into one another as she sat silently in the guarded room, suspended between two worlds.

Chapter 2

From the American Dream to Soviet Realities

On September 12, 1936, Ethelyn Gertrude White, known by her married name Yampolsky, embarked on a journey that would forever alter the course of her life. Alongside her husband Nikifor and their four children – Natalie, Eleanor, Eugene, and the youngest, George, who would later become the father of Catherine – they boarded the ocean liner Georgic, bound from New York to London, the first leg of their ominous journey to the Soviet Union. The massive liner rose high above the crowded pier, its white hull gleaming and its tall funnels releasing slow plumes of smoke as passengers and dockworkers moved along the gangways below.

Ethelyn, a petite woman with grey eyes and dark blond hair neatly tied in a bun, appeared much younger than her actual age. Despite her youthful appearance, the strain of the journey had taken its toll. Her skin had paled, a clear sign of her exhaustion and nervousness. Standing on the deck, she gazed out at the slate blue expanse of the ocean, lost in thoughts about the life she was leaving behind and the uncertain future that awaited them. A cool Atlantic breeze brushed lightly across the deck as the ship slowly prepared to leave the harbor. The emotional farewell to her native Boston weighed heavily on her mind, the fear of never seeing her homeland again haunting her as they headed towards the Soviet Union.

She had taken precautions, carrying the birth certificates of her children and her own in a hidden pocket. Her leather satchel held personal treasures: a Holy Bible, an American history book, and cherished family pictures. From time to time her hand instinctively rested on the satchel, as if reassuring herself that the most precious pieces of her past were still safely with her.

As the ship began its slow departure, Ethelyn stood on the deck, capturing the last glimpses of the Statue of Liberty – a beacon of hope at the entrance of New York Harbor. The great statue stood solemnly against the morning sky, its torch raised high above the harbor waters. Both she and Nikifor gazed back at the iconic symbol with a mixture of doubt and nostalgia. Overcome with emotion, Ethelyn turned away to hide her tears, while Nikifor tried to reassure her that they could return to America if things went awry.

Nikifor, clad in a suit and a raincoat, with a wide-brimmed hat shielding him from the salty wind, was filled with a mix of elation and agitation. The wind tugged gently at the brim of his hat as he stood beside the rail. He was returning to his homeland to contribute to the socialist cause he had long championed, driven by the motto, "From each according to his ability, to each according to his needs." This mantra was both his guiding principle and obsession, rooted in his deep-seated quest for justice. Yet, deep down, he felt he was tempting fate, which had been kind to him so far. Undertaking this monumental move across the ocean, he sought a better life for his family, lured by the promises of employment, healthcare, rent-free living, and paid vacations. But amidst these hopes, he dared not ponder what other costs this journey might entail, driven by dire circumstances and a belief that he had no other choice.

Ethelyn, who grew up in the Presbyterian faith in Somerville, Massachusetts, had pursued higher education, culminating in a career as a professor of English literature at a local university. Nikifor, on the other hand, was the owner of a small lumber business. Together, they had built a life in their home in Rochester, New York, built through years of hard work and perseverance.

However, with the onset of the Great Depression in 1929, their once-stable life was plunged into turmoil. For seven years, they struggled to hold on to their home, battling the relentless tide of economic hardship. With each passing year, uncertainty tightened its grip, eroding what little security remained. But by 1936, the struggle had become untenable, and they were ultimately forced to sell their home for a fraction of its worth.

During these challenging times, Soviet propaganda offered a contrasting vision—a utopian society where jobs were plentiful, life was depicted as thriving, and food was abundant. This carefully crafted image of prosperity and stability began to take hold of Nikifor's imagination, stirring in him the hope of a better life for his family in his ancestral homeland. Posters, pamphlets, and glowing reports circulated widely, portraying the Soviet Union as a land of opportunity and renewal. He came to believe he could play a role in building a more just society, convinced that such a move would bring not only personal fulfillment, but also a secure and prosperous future for his children.

Amidst these hopes and aspirations, Nikifor stood on the deck of the Georgic, surrounded by his family. Despite the uncertainty and the daunting nature of their journey, he found some solace in the immediate comforts the voyage offered. For the duration of their sea travel, they would enjoy regular meals - breakfast, lunch, and dinner - served in the ship's elegant dining hall, where white tablecloths, polished silverware, and wide windows overlooking the open ocean created a brief illusion of comfort and stability. It was a small but significant consolation, a temporary respite that allowed them to momentarily forget the hardships of the past and the uncertainties of the future.

In 1936, America was still in the grip of the Great Depression. Across cities and small towns alike, economic hardship shaped the daily lives of millions. Breadlines and relief stations became a common sight, as families struggled to secure even the most basic necessities. Parents, driven by desperation, sometimes made the unthinkable choice to send their children to relatives—or even to strangers—hoping to give them a better chance of survival. Many felt abandoned by institutions meant to protect them, left to endure uncertainty and quiet despair. The streets filled with the unemployed and the homeless, men and women standing in long, silent lines for a bowl of soup or a piece of bread, their dignity worn thin by circumstance. Outside soup kitchens and charity halls, weary faces bore witness to a nation still searching for its way out of darkness.

Amidst this bleak backdrop, Nikifor placed his hopes in the Soviet Union. Reports and reviews painted a picture of a society making remarkable progress. In contrast to the struggles in America, the Soviet Union reportedly had no unemployment or homelessness. Natalie, their twenty-one-year-old daughter, had recently suffered from a car accident, leaving her with broken ribs but also a settlement of twenty-five thousand dollars from the insurance company. Nikifor faced a critical decision - his children needed higher education, security, and the prosperity that typically accompanies well-paying jobs. Soviet newspapers and the *Amtorg*[2] agency portrayed life in the Soviet Union in glowing terms, depicting it as a workers' paradise with beautiful, light-filled factories, seven-hour workdays, and clean air. Photographs and articles circulating in newspapers and pamphlets showed smiling workers and modern industrial buildings, reinforcing the promise of a prosperous socialist future. Socialism was being presented not as a mere dream but as a fairy tale come true.

After much deliberation, Nikifor made the fateful decision to relocate his family to Russia, his birthplace. Through Maxim Litvinov, the Soviet Commissar for Foreign Affairs, assurances had been conveyed that Americans relocating to the Soviet Union would retain their passports and legal protections. With this assurance, Ethelyn, a native-born American, accompanied by her children, followed Nikifor into an uncertain future. The decision weighed heavily on the family; yet the promise of stability and opportunity seemed, for a time, to outweigh the fears that lingered beneath the surface. For weeks, the family immersed themselves in laborious preparations, readying for the arduous journey that lay ahead.

The *Georgic* first sailed to London, docking in Great Britain in 1936. Eugene and Eleanor, in their late teens, were deemed old enough to travel separately with Natalie, apart from their parents. Ethelyn, Nikifor, and George then boarded the ocean liner Lithuania, which sailed from Great Britain to the ports of Gothenburg, Riga, and finally to Leningrad (St. Petersburg). The long voyage carried them steadily across the gray northern waters, each port marking another step toward the uncertain future awaiting them in the Soviet Union.

On the deck of the Lithuania liner, the family stood dressed in their finest attire, mingling and smiling with fellow travelers – engineers, workers, teachers, all bound for the Soviet Union. These Americans were not just moving; they were bringing with them equipment and various tools, purchased with their life savings, as gifts to the Soviet people, symbolizing their commitment and hope for their new life in the Soviet Union. Crates and carefully packed boxes stood nearby on the deck, tangible proof of the faith many of these travelers placed in the promises of the socialist experiment.

As the ship approached the harbor of *Leningrad*, a wave of emotions engulfed its passengers. The Yampolsky family, like others on board, were greeted with the vibrant and unfamiliar sounds of the bustling port. Steam whistles echoed across the water while dockworkers shouted instructions from the crowded piers. Towering posters came into view, their slogans resonating with the spirit of the Soviet Union: "Proletariat of all countries unite!" and "Long live the Communist Party - the mind, honor, and conscience of our times! Stalin is the leader of all nations!"

The passengers, poised to disembark into this new world, were a mix of excitement and nervous anticipation. American women stood out in their lovely summer dresses and wide-brimmed straw hats, while the men donned suits and hats, reflecting the era's fashion. Against the backdrop of red banners and Soviet symbols, their American clothing seemed almost strikingly out of place.

Ethelyn clutched her travel bag, which held not only her essentials but also cherished items: a dress patterned with tiny flowers, a reminder of her first date with Nikifor, and a sweater she had knitted for George, who was prone to feeling cold. Her fingers tightened slightly around the bag's handle, as if the familiar objects inside might anchor her to the life she had left behind. Nikifor, carrying the responsibility of his family's journey, held a leather briefcase containing their American passports.

As they made their way towards the port, they were greeted by banners and slogans, a vivid introduction to their new home. Nikifor, returning to his homeland after years abroad, was visibly moved. His heart raced with a mix of nostalgia and excitement as he stepped off the liner, the first passenger to set foot on Soviet soil. For a brief instant he paused on the gangway, taking in the unfamiliar sights and sounds before him.

"Long live my fatherland!" he exclaimed, his voice blending with the crowd's buzz.

They were soon approached by a man in a trench coat speaking English. "Hello, comrades! Welcome to the port of Leningrad, the cradle of the revolution!" he announced, introducing himself as Peter Brown, a journalist, likely an American. He spoke with energetic enthusiasm, his notebook already in hand as if eager to record the moment. His words, however, were soon drowned out by the sounds of an orchestra and the bustling noise of the harbor.

Their arrival also attracted the attention of stern-looking men in leather jackets, adorned with caps bearing the hammer and sickle emblem. Their watchful eyes moved methodically across the arriving passengers. "Welcome to the Soviet Union," one of them said, his expression devoid of warmth. The journalist's attempts to converse were quickly overshadowed by the men's presence, and the loudspeakers and the harbor's ambient noise swallowed the rest of his words.

Thus, the Yampolsky family, along with their fellow passengers, stepped into the Soviet Union, their faces a mixture of hope and apprehension, unaware of the profound changes and challenges that awaited them in this new chapter of their lives. Behind them the ship's gangway creaked softly as more passengers followed, each carrying their own hopes, doubts, and dreams into the unfamiliar landscape before them.

Chapter 3

From Ocean Liner to Soviet Soil

As they disembarked, a young man in a *militsiya* uniform addressed the crowd, his voice sharp and authoritative. Standing rigidly near the gangway, his dark uniform and polished boots immediately commanded attention. Speaking in Russian, he instructed, "Fellow citizens, you must hand over your passports for registration now. Please prepare your American passports and give them to Comrade Smirnov for registration. You can reclaim them in Moscow at the local registration office."

The families, somewhat bewildered but compliant, began gathering their passports to hand over as they passed by Comrade Smirnov. A small table had been placed nearby where the official stood waiting, methodically collecting the documents one by one. Many, unfamiliar with Russian, looked to Nikifor for guidance, their anxiety palpable.

"Fellow passengers, we are at the port of Leningrad," the *militsioner*[1] announced into the loudspeaker. His voice crackled through the metal speaker mounted above the dock, echoing across the crowded harbor. Nikifor, assuming the role of an impromptu leader due to his fluency in Russian, stood at the forefront, trying to reassure the anxious travelers. Ethelyn, gripped by fear at the surrender of their passports, was visibly disturbed. Beside her, young George clung tightly to her hand, his usual smile replaced by a look of distress.

Ethelyn, with a protective instinct, kept the birth certificates of her children and her own securely in a hidden pocket, close to her heart. Her hand instinctively moved toward the pocket, as if confirming that the precious papers were still safely there.

"Your passports, fellow citizens!" the official demanded, his tone brooking no resistance. "Your passports, citizens!" he repeated louder, as the Americans reluctantly handed over their passports to the Soviet official. One by one the small blue booklets disappeared into a growing stack on the registration table.

Amidst the exhaustion, shock, and mounting fear, murmurs spread among the Americans:

"Do you know when and where we can get our passports back?"

"What if we don't?"

"Where are they taking them?"

"Can we ever return?"

Nikifor, overwhelmed and pale, struggled to find words. For a moment he looked from one anxious face to another, sensing the weight of their fears. Finally, he managed to say, "Do not worry. You will be able to collect your passports from the local *militsiya* units. Everything will work out in time."

***

As they made their way out of the port onto a large square overlooking the grand city of Leningrad, Nikifor glanced back at Ethelyn, who was seeking direction and reassurance. George, visibly shaken, trembled uncontrollably. The confusion and shock were palpable, especially for those like George, who did not understand Russian and could only sense the disorientation and fear in those around them. The reality of their new life in the Soviet Union was beginning to dawn on them, laden with uncertainty and apprehension. Around them the square buzzed with hurried footsteps, distant voices, and the rumble of carts and vehicles moving through the busy port district.

By late September, the brisk, salty winds from the Baltic Sea swept through Leningrad, intensifying the sense of unfamiliarity for Ethelyn and her family. The cacophony of the bustling city was almost deafening, leaving Nikifor momentarily disoriented as he surveyed his surroundings. With only a few American dollars left, he was unsure of where and how to exchange them for Russian rubles. Clutching a precious silver cigarette case gifted by Ethelyn's father, he contemplated using a cigarette lighter as a potential bribe or bargaining tool to navigate their immediate needs. The unfamiliar language, the cold wind, and the constant movement of strangers made the vast city feel overwhelming and strangely distant.

The family, burdened with three bulky suitcases and additional bundles, stood wearied and emotionally drained from their initial experiences at the port. Faced with this daunting new reality, they decided to avoid any confrontations, especially with the militsiya, sensing the futility of such disputes. Every official uniform they encountered seemed to deepen their unease. Ethelyn, anxious and overwhelmed, sought reassurance from Nikifor.
"What are they saying?" she asked nervously.

"They're just trying to intimidate us into compliance," he replied, struggling to maintain a facade of calm.

Ethelyn, visibly exhausted, lamented their situation. At fifty-five, with Nikifor seven years her senior, the ordeal felt particularly taxing.
"Let's just cooperate so we can move on and get some rest," she suggested, her hand resting on her husband's arm.

"You're right, darling," Nikifor agreed, his voice laced with fatigue.

Their turn for a taxi arrived, a welcome relief amid the chaos. As they loaded their belongings, the taxi driver shouted over the din, "Hey, comrade! Where to?"

"Train station!" Nikifor responded loudly.

The family settled into the taxi, with Ethelyn, despite her weariness, peering out the window at the changing landscapes of Leningrad. The taxi wound its way past the embankments of the Neva River, over bridges, and past historical landmarks. The wide river reflected the gray northern sky as the vehicle rattled along the stone embankments. Ethelyn's eyes lingered on the grandeur of St. Paul's Cathedral and the Winter Palace, captivated by the architectural beauty of St. Petersburg, a city that held a majestic charm despite their circumstances.

Just as she allowed her eyes to close, seeking a momentary escape, the taxi driver announced their arrival. "This is the railway station, you have arrived."

With that, the Yampolsky family braced themselves for the next leg of their journey, their hearts heavy with a mix of exhaustion, apprehension, and the faint glimmer of hope that lay in the unknown.

Nikifor fumbled for his cigarette lighter which was hidden deep inside his inner pocket. His tired fingers searched anxiously through the lining of his coat.
"I have a cigarette lighter to offer for our ride to the station, and I will be glad if you accept it."

He continued speaking in his tired cracking voice.
"You see, we just arrived in Leningrad. Still, we must travel to Moscow. I don't have any rubles on me."

He paused for a second, still holding a cigarette lighter in his hand.

"What is your name, Comrade?" the driver asked.

"Nikifor," he answered with an effort as he could hardly stand on his feet and swayed from sheer exhaustion.

"Where are you traveling from?" asked the driver still thinking over the offer which could be a lucrative deal if he could sell it for a profit.

"From the far north," he replied deciding it would be safer not to tell the truth.

"So, you are saying you traveled from far away." The driver looked at the pale faces of Ethelyn and George who were huddled together.
"It must have been a long journey. Good luck to you, Comrade. You will have to stand in line for a long time to get train tickets to Moscow. Good luck to you. The cigarette lighter will be a nice thing to have. I will be able to exchange it for food at the *Torgsyn*[3] store," said the driver at last.

"Thank you, comrade." His voice was cracking both from fatigue and nervous energy, knowing they still had to get to Moskva where they could stay with Comrade Shklovsky, his old friend. The thought of reaching Moscow and finding familiar help gave him a small measure of strength. He desperately needed help from his friends in Moscow, so he was willing to part with valuable things in exchange for traveling to Moscow—the capital of the Soviet Union with many foreign embassies and foreign trade offices seeking to establish business contacts with the Soviet Union.

Parents with George by their side were now standing in front of the noisy train station. Crowds of travelers moved in and out beneath the high arches of the station entrance, their voices echoing across the wide stone forecourt. Nikifor took his wife by the hand and led her inside the train station then he proceeded to a large hall and finally located a chair standing by the wall. He sat his wife and his younger son down.

"George," he said. "You must not leave your mother's side until I return with tickets. Do you understand?"

"Yes, Father." George nodded. A sudden sense of responsibility seemed to steady him. Feelings of importance took over his feelings of tiredness and he stood little straighter.

***

Nikifor looked through the train schedule on the wall. He had only a little more than one hour before the next train would leave, but the train station was filled with people who had been waiting in line for weeks to buy a ticket to Moscow, sleeping on benches and chairs in their weariness. Some passengers sat wrapped in coats and blankets, their tired faces illuminated by the dim station lights, while others dozed upright against their luggage. Perhaps he could get the tickets through the management of the station. In the bustling train station, Nikifor navigated his way through the crowd until he found a corridor leading to various offices. The noise of voices, footsteps, and distant train whistles echoed through the cavernous hall behind him. Spotting a door marked 'Station Director, Comrade Korneev,' he knocked timidly and entered upon hearing an invitation. The man behind the desk, rugged and middle-aged, looked up in surprise. Stacks of papers and railway documents were scattered across the desk in front of him. "Hello, my name is Nikifor—" Nikifor began, only to be cut off by the gruff station director.

"What brings you here, citizen?" Korneev asked, his demeanor uninviting.

Nikifor, feeling the weight of desperation, pleaded for help. "Comrade Director, please, I need tickets for tonight's train to Moscow for my wife, son, and myself."

Korneev seemed indifferent, dismissing the request with a wave of his hand. His expression suggested that such pleas were far from unusual. Nikifor, however, persisted, explaining their weariness from the long journey. He stood firm, despite having no documents or rubles to offer. Korneev, sizing up Nikifor, saw an opportunity for a transaction. His eyes lingered briefly on Nikifor's worn coat and exhausted face. "Why should you get priority?" he questioned.

With a sudden realization, Nikifor offered his old army watch as a trade for the tickets. The watch, though modest, carried the quiet dignity of something long treasured. Korneev considered the offer and agreed, explaining the tickets would be for standing room only on a train arriving that night. He also warned that payment for the tickets would be expected upon their arrival in Moscow, subtly reminding Nikifor of his influential connections.

Nikifor, relieved and grateful, accepted the tickets and the terms. As he left Korneev's office, he silently thanked the Lord for this small mercy, feeling a burden lift from his shoulders. The station corridor seemed slightly less oppressive as he stepped back into the crowded hall. With the precious tickets in hand, he made his way back to where he had left Ethelyn and George.

Finding them in the corner, Ethelyn waved him over. George, sleepy, his eyes half-closed, smiled at the sight of his father. Nikifor's heart swelled with relief, knowing that they were one step closer to safety and a new life, whatever it may bring. Each small step was a significant stride towards their future, and for now, that was enough to keep them going.

"I have the tickets!" Nikifor exclaimed with a triumphant tone, revealing the train pass to Ethelyn. However, noticing the glares of other passengers, he quickly subdued his excitement and motioned his family to move quietly. "Let's get going. The train's already here. We need to get to the platform," he urged, his voice tinged with urgency as they navigated through the crowded station.

As they made their way, Nikifor reassured them, "We'll be in Moscow by tomorrow morning. I'll try to get us some tea and food on the train. It'll be better there." Ethelyn, ever resourceful, whispered about the biscuits she had saved from the ship, emphasizing the need to conserve their resources.

The platform was bustling with anxious travelers. Steam drifted through the cold air as the locomotive waited under the dim platform lamps. Nikifor, Ethelyn, and George pushed through the crowd towards the conductor, who was managing the boarding process with a stern demeanor. Holding out the tickets and the station director's note, Nikifor gained the conductor's acknowledgment. "Fellow citizens, please, make way for three people!" the conductor announced, allowing them to board the train.

Once on the train, they quickly found their way to a lower berth near a small window, providing them a respite from the crowd's stench. George, exhausted, fell asleep on his mother's lap. Despite the ordeal, they had secured their passage to Moscow. As the train began its journey, the rhythmic motion of the wheels provided a monotonous yet comforting backdrop. Outside the window the dark countryside slipped past in silence. The train attendant served them hot tea in metal holders, accompanied by lumps of sugar. Nikifor relaxed, knowing it was only a matter of hours before they reached Moscow and met with Comrade Shklovsky, an old friend who had offered to host them initially.

The next morning, as they disembarked in Moscow, the crisp autumn air greeted them, along with uplifting songs playing on the radio. The vast station bustled with early-morning travelers and porters moving briskly along the platforms. Their spirits lifted, they walked down the platform to meet Comrade Shklovsky, who helped them with their luggage and led them to his apartment.

In the heart of Moscow, they anticipated new opportunities to meet people, make friends, and perhaps find the stability that had eluded them for so long. Despite the city's housing shortage, they felt a cautious sense of relief. Soon after, their other children arrived, reuniting the little family in their temporary home. Once again, the small household was whole. In this new and unfamiliar city, they began to navigate their way through the challenges before them, holding quietly to the belief that the sacrifices of their journey would one day justify the risks they had taken.

Chapter 4

Beneath the Red Sky

In 1936, the family found solace in a new flat, attempting to acclimate to the astonishing cultural differences they encountered. Life in Moscow unfolded before them with a mixture of fascination and unease. George, a bright child, and his mother, Ethelyn, began exploring their surroundings, including the vibrant city center, the iconic Red Square, and the Kremlin. The vast cobblestones of Red Square stretched before them beneath the looming red walls of the Kremlin, while soldiers, workers, and hurried pedestrians moved across the square with purposeful strides. George's keen intellect led him to rapidly pick up the Russian language.

Soon after, they were fortunate to secure a room in a communal apartment on Arbat Street, thanks to a friend. The famous old street, lined with narrow buildings and small shops, bustled with life from early morning until late at night. This marked the beginning of their journey to gather their previously shipped furniture, now stored in a local warehouse.

Their rented space was modest: a small, square room with an iron bed, an aged sofa, and an armchair draped in faded tapestry. The window overlooked a courtyard, which gave off a mix of chemical and other pungent smells during the sweltering Indian summer. Laundry lines stretched between the surrounding buildings, and voices echoed through the enclosed courtyard throughout the day. Despite this, the location was agreeable and safe, offering them a sense of privacy they craved.

One day, George's father, Nikifor, glanced at his watch and addressed Ethelyn, "I'm off to a meeting at the international club. They've posted job listings; I'm hopeful to find something."

Ethelyn, visibly anxious, responded while gazing at their dwindling bread supply, "I do hope you find work soon."

"Don't worry, Ethelyn. George will be back shortly," Nikifor reassured her, adding, "Don't wait up for me; I have a key."

On the way to the club, Nikifor encountered David Bell, a fellow member of the international community. As they walked together, Nikifor inquired about David's family, aware of their struggles in adapting to their new environment.

David, with a hint of sorrow in his eyes, replied, "We're managing, but it's been incredibly challenging for all of us."

Together, they left the park, heading towards Gorky Street. The wide avenue, one of Moscow's main thoroughfares, was crowded with pedestrians moving past government buildings and dimly lit shop windows. They passed nearly empty storefronts and a long queue of people, all hoping to purchase what little was available.

"How are things going for your sister Bertha and her husband, Solomon?" Nikifor inquired.

David exhaled deeply before responding, "It's been tough. Bertha is on edge. The Soviet militsiya were not welcoming to newcomers. They face constant scrutiny and harassment. Solomon, a talented violinist, has even brought a Stradivarius as a last resort to sell if their financial situation worsens. I never imagined Bertha and

Solomon would endure such harsh treatment. It's distressing how the authorities are targeting newcomers."

Nikifor silently pondered whether his family could avoid such scrutiny and clung quietly to the hope that their situation might unfold differently.

Continuing their journey from Red Square, Nikifor and David approached the central telegraph building, recognizable by its towering clock. The massive structure dominated the square, its clock visible from far down the street. They veered into a narrow alley leading to the club, a hub for recent international arrivals. This space, designated for the foreign club, was a melting pot of ideologies, often filled with proponents of the burgeoning socialist system.

Upon arrival, Nikifor and David, both in dire need of employment, exchanged pleasantries and began their separate searches. Nikifor quickly spotted a job listing that seemed ideal. He copied the details carefully onto a scrap of paper and slipped it into his pocket. He then joined the club's meeting.

There, he struck up a conversation with Michael, a middle-aged man who had moved from New York with his wife, Gabriella, a year ago.

"How have you been adjusting to the new life?" Nikifor asked him, seeking comfort and hoping to hear that the government would provide for all their needs.

"I find it very troublesome," Michael sighed. "I had hoped for decent medical care at no cost for me and my wife. Instead, doctors are readily dispensing aspirin, claiming it's a new panacea for every ailment in the world. And we are very upset that nothing is as it should be."

"Is that so?" Nikifor asked cautiously, not wanting to believe it, as he would have to acknowledge his own poor judgment. "Listen, maybe things are not so gloomy. The authorities promised us free lodging. But how does one find a vacant apartment when there seems to be a housing shortage?"

"Forget about any freebies," Michael said. "The Communist Party members get the best apartments in the city. It's all about who they know and the connections they have. Don't hold any hope of getting a decent place to live in Moscow. You could move to the outskirts and maybe rent a room in a shantytown. Nothing fancy. And then it will cost you a pretty penny," Michael replied.

"By the way, have you heard anything about how to claim our American passports taken away at registration?" questioned Nikifor.

"We've written to the Soviet authorities here, went directly to the local *militsiya* stations, to no avail. 'No' is all we've heard. We've tried so many times to get in touch with the American Embassy. They want to stay out of this mess and keep silent. Maybe there's nothing that the American officials can do about it. Once we were issued Soviet passports, the Soviets claimed we were no longer considered American citizens. And we might never get our US passports back," clarified Michael with deep sadness.

Nikifor was perturbed. "What do you mean they won't give our passports back? It was a deal that we were free to come and go as we wished," he said.

"Wake up. We live in a dictatorship led by a ruthless leader, Stalin. It's he who decides who will live and who will die. This so-called fair society is ruled with an iron fist and indoctrinates all with communist ideology."

Another man within hearing spoke up. "If you don't comply, they will take you out with a bullet in the back of your head. Their Secret Services, the so-called *NKVD*[4] forces, carry out raids in the morning to take out any dissenters. If there were an exodus, we would leave at a moment's notice. But I have a gut feeling the door has closed off forever. They will keep us hostages forever..." Michael shook his head, clearly distressed. "It's time for me to go home," he said. "I don't want Gabriella to get worried about me." Michael shook Nikifor's hand and walked away with his head down.

Nikifor and David mingled with the crowd, anticipating a Russian language learning session. "Maybe we'll finally receive our 'Learn Russian in a Few Weeks' textbooks," David murmured. Their absence had impeded their learning, but Nikifor, with his basic Russian, had become a makeshift tutor for his friends, though he too felt the pinch of lacking educational materials.

"Textbook or not," David mused, "I suspect mastering Russian will take me years, not weeks." Nikifor understood the immense challenge of fluency in such a complex language, especially as they embarked on their new life in the Soviet Union. Despite the hardships, the weekly meeting attendees remained optimistic, believing in a brighter future once communism was fully established.

At the gathering, Nikifor held a glass of tea in a decorative metal holder and picked at the hard pretzel from a large dish, attempting to soften them in the hot tea for his worn-out teeth. The samovar hissed gently as steam rose into the dimly lit room. The hostess served tea from a samovar, offering cups of strong brew and a few hard sugar lumps. The modest refreshments fell short of the lavish meal they had been promised.

Trying to keep spirits high, Nikifor reminded everyone of their fortune to be in Moscow, a cultural hub, rather than in a remote provincial city. Eventually, he stepped up to the podium, sharing his insights on learning Russian, drawn from his own experience with English. "Don't fret over word order," he advised, "Focus on pronunciation and practice with friends." He encouraged them with a promise of progress within a year.

The evening took a lighter turn when a stranger, exuding confidence, whisked Nikifor onto the dance floor, proclaiming, "Everything will be okay!" Laughter and music filled the hall as couples began to dance. They spent the rest of the evening dancing to the tunes of Russian music, enjoying a moment of joy amidst their struggles.

On his way home through Moscow's older streets, Nikifor hoped Ethelyn wouldn't worry about his prolonged absence. The narrow streets were dimly lit, the yellow glow of scattered streetlamps falling unevenly across the worn cobblestones. As he neared his apartment, a sudden unease overcame him. The night air felt unusually still, and the distant echo of footsteps made him instinctively glance over his shoulder. He sensed a figure in a dark overcoat and hat, lurking in the shadows, possibly a state official. The man appeared motionless beneath a streetlamp, his face obscured by the brim of his hat. With a quickened pace,

Nikifor crossed the street, entered his building, and ascended the stairs with renewed vigor, his mind racing with thoughts of the mysterious observer.

Nikifor ascended the staircase, its walls scrawled with graffiti. The stairwell smelled faintly of damp plaster and stale tobacco. Fumbling for his keys in the dark, he quietly opened the door to the communal area of the apartment on the second floor of the old building. He tiptoed through the narrow, cluttered hallway, careful not to disturb the basins and junk scattered on the floor. A single weak bulb flickered overhead, casting long shadows along the corridor. Gently opening his own door to avoid waking Ethelyn and George, Nikifor found Ethelyn sitting in the corner, looking frightened.

"Nikifor, is that you?" she whispered.

"Yes, it's me, Ethelyn. Why do you sound so alarmed?" he asked.

Ethelyn stood and glided across the room, embracing Nikifor tightly. "I was afraid I'd never see you again," she confessed.

Nikifor smiled sadly. "Silly, don't you know I love you," he reassured her as they headed to bed. George was curled up in the corner, sleeping on a small couch covered by his mother's long scarf. The faint glow from the courtyard window illuminated the quiet room. Nikifor had hoped they would be more settled by now.

He thought of a Russian folktale about a knight at a crossroads: If you go to the right, you will lose your horse; if you go to the left, you'll lose your life. If you go straight ahead, you will lose both. Nikifor felt trapped in a no-win situation, regardless of the path he chose. The thought lingered in his mind long after the room had fallen silent.

The next morning, Nikifor reviewed the paper he had taken from the wall and headed to the address, only to discover it was a position for a building caretaker. Though beneath him, it would put bread on the table.

Nikifor soon realized that Moscow, brimming with paranoia and suspicion towards foreigners, was a stern city. Foreign accents drew attention, and unfamiliar faces were often met with guarded glances. An American cultural center had been set up in the city's heart for new foreign workers to learn basic Russian and socialize. The newspapers and radio stations, constantly playing patriotic songs like "Life has become better! Life has become more joyful!" were part of a campaign to indoctrinate the masses with communist ideology. The cheerful slogans echoed through loudspeakers in public squares and factories alike.

One day, Nikifor found himself on a bustling street in the city center near the House of Soviets' Colony Hall, amidst chaos. Government prosecutors were accusing the so-called Trotskyite anti-government circle of plotting to assassinate high-level party officials and engage in sabotage. A group of foreign journalists was gathered at the entrance. Officers pushed the crowd back as loudspeakers crackled with official announcements. Suddenly, he saw a crowd of pro-government demonstrators chanting, "Death to the enemies of the people!" Nikifor stood frozen, overcome with fear. The chant echoed through the square like a thunderous wave. From then on, he never felt safe. A sense of invisible surveillance seemed to follow him everywhere he went. An iron curtain had descended, sealing the country from the rest of the world, with no escape from the grim fate awaiting Nikifor and his family.

November proved to be exceptionally cold. The family huddled in their small, rented room, which was bitterly cold despite the gurgling heater by the window. Thin frost formed along the inside edges of the windowpane during the night. The rent was straining their meager finances.

The family endured harsh conditions, suffering from cold, lack of comfort, and privacy. The extreme stress weakened them, and they all succumbed to severe colds, battling high fevers, coughs, and the looming threat of pneumonia. Nikifor scoured local pharmacies for medicine, only to find that outpatient clinics were swamped, leaving patients waiting for hours to see an overworked doctor who offered little help. The medications, while affordable, were hardly effective; sometimes, only vitamins were available.

Nikifor often reflected on their life back in America, contrasting it with the challenges they faced in Moscow. Memories of warmer kitchens and familiar streets in America returned to him during the long winter nights. Despite working as a caretaker, a far cry from his engineering career in America, he maintained hope that this was just a temporary setback. Yet he couldn't fully admit to himself the irreversible impact of his decision on his family. Their American dollars, their only lifeline, had dwindled to a meager amount, which Nikifor conserved for the upcoming harsh winter.

A month passed in these severe winter conditions, with the family still reeling from illness and stress. Relief came when a distant relative of Nikifor's, a geologist heading on an expedition to the far north, offered them his modest Moscow apartment for the duration of his absence. To them, the one-bedroom apartment with a living room felt palatial. It was freshly painted, simply furnished, and had two separate beds in the bedroom, with Ethelyn and Nikifor in one and the girls in the other, while Eugene and George slept on blankets on the floor. The apartment also boasted a kitchen with a gas stove, a separate bath, and toilet facilities.

Nikifor marveled at how his relative had secured such an incredible living space. Gratefully accepting this rent-free arrangement, he was able to save a little money that month. He visited the *Torgsyn* commissary to buy quality food like cheese and various sausages, helping the family regain their strength.

The tranquil warmth of the apartment was a lifesaver, helping them endure the worst of the winter. Avoiding illness was crucial, as hospitals were poorly equipped. Nikifor's relative cautioned them to self-manage their health as best as they could, noting that while the healthcare system could handle common colds, it was inadequate for more serious issues. When the month ended, they faced the daunting task of finding another room in a communal apartment, a challenge compounded by overcrowding. Fortunately, they received news that their relative's mining expedition was extended, allowing them to stay a few more months until the harsh winter abated.

With the arrival of spring, Nikifor set out to find a new accommodation. He managed to secure a room in another communal apartment. It was a modest space with a dirty window, covered in thick soot, overlooking a makeshift playground in the courtyard. Children's voices echoed faintly from below as they played among broken benches and rusted swings. The room, furnished with a square table, an old sofa draped in threadbare fabric, and boxes used as a makeshift desk and seating, was their new home.

Daily, Nikifor spent hours hunting for necessities. Many items were scarce, labelled as "deficit," and hard to obtain. He often stood in long lines for milk, only to return empty-handed.

One day, Ethelyn, anxious to contribute, asked, "Should I go out and try to find milk? Maybe I'll have better luck."

Nikifor gently refused, "No, my dear, I wouldn't expose you to the dangers outside. It's not safe in our district. Stay here."

Ethelyn, expressing her frustration, said, "I'm sorry I can't help more. I'm just too scared and my Russian isn't good enough."

Nikifor reassured her, "Don't worry, I'll take care of everything."

The country turned out to be full of stark contrasts. While a small circle of privileged Communist Party members and government apparatchiks enjoyed the best food and exclusive privileges reserved strictly for them, most of the working class appeared worn and exhausted, dressed in rags and subsisting on what could only be described as scraps. Long lines formed outside bakeries and shops at dawn, as ordinary citizens waited patiently for whatever small portion of food might become available that day.

Farmers in the rural areas faced even more dire circumstances. Unlike city dwellers, they were not even permitted to possess internal passports, which effectively bound them to the collective farms where they labored. Their earnings were not paid in rubles; instead, their work was measured in so-called "labor days," an abstract accounting of effort recorded by the collective farm administration. Compensation came in the form of payment units, typically a bag of grain or another food item distributed after the harvest, often barely sufficient for survival. The land they worked did not belong to them but to the state, and every harvest was carefully controlled and rationed by government authorities. As a result, farmers lived in abject poverty, and their life expectancy was tragically short.

A few brave individuals dared to rebel against this oppressive system, voicing their anger in quiet whispers or acts of resistance, only to meet with either disappearance or violence. Rumors circulated in villages and cities alike about arrests that took place before dawn, when men were quietly taken away and never seen again. The rest, however, resigned themselves to a life of silent toil and hardship, learning to lower their voices, avert their eyes, and endure the heavy weight of a system that allowed little room for dissent.

Chapter 5

The Journey of Transformation

The summer of 1937 was a season of struggle for Nikifor's family, with his modest earnings barely making ends meet. The optimism that had once accompanied their arrival in Moscow had slowly faded into a routine of quiet endurance. Life in the city remained stagnant—neither particularly bad nor good. Days passed in a gray monotony of work, queues, and uncertainty. Before they realized it, another bitter winter had enveloped them.

On a blustery February day, along with hundreds of other Muscovites, Nikifor hurried to a tramway stop. The wind swept across the streets in sharp gusts, driving snow along the pavement like drifting sand. The crowd was frantic, pushing and shoving to board the tram first. Clutching his leather briefcase, filled with reference letters and important documents, close to his chest, Nikifor navigated through the chaos. He was dressed in a long American-made gray wool coat with a wing beaver collar and a fur hat, his attire standing out against the worn coats and patched garments of the surrounding crowd. His destination was the local militsiya unit to reclaim his family's passports, hoping to maintain their US citizenship for their safety and security. The daily grind of long lines and the struggle to board public transport had become a routine he had reluctantly accepted.

After managing to board the tram and securing a spot amidst the crush of people, Nikifor disembarked, took a moment to gather himself, and checked his belongings. His breath rose in white clouds in the freezing air as he stepped onto the snow-covered pavement. Confidently, he walked towards the district militsiya unit.

Upon arriving at the militsiya building, Nikifor was met with the stern gaze of a puffy-eyed official guarding the entrance.

“Good morning, Comrade!” Nikifor greeted, trying to maintain a friendly demeanor.

“Your documents!” the *militsioner* demanded gruffly.

Nervously, Nikifor opened his briefcase. His hands trembled slightly as he spoke, “I have an appointment with Captain Ivanov.”

The official, with a puffy face and narrow eyes, briefly scrutinized Nikifor’s Soviet documents before motioning him to follow. They traversed a long corridor, lined with heavy wooden doors and a worn carpet runner leading to Captain Ivanov’s office. The corridor smelled faintly of tobacco smoke and damp wool coats, and the sound of distant typewriters echoed behind the closed doors. After a couple of knocks, the official opened the door, ushering Nikifor into the room where Captain Ivanov sat behind a large dark mahogany desk.

A gigantic marble ashtray in the corner of the desk stood perfectly clean, without any cigarette stubs, serving more as decoration than for use. Portraits of Stalin and his henchmen were hanging on the wall, and a huge red flag was standing in the corner. In the portrait, Stalin, the head of the Soviet government, was staring across the space with a vigilant look. The portrait was polished, and no one could see the pockmarks all over Stalin’s face. A slogan written beneath Stalin’s portrait read: “The greatest genius of all times and peoples, Comrade Stalin!" Nikifor noticed all the minute details around him with the alertness of a man who understood the language and the danger hidden behind such symbols. Something had radically changed in the society which he had known and loved as a younger man.

"Captain Ivanov, I have a citizen to see you!" reported the *militsioner* in a harsh tone of voice. As soon as he said it, he turned and slammed the door shut behind Nikifor.

"Good morning, Comrade Ivanov!" started Nikifor, trying to sound amicable and energetic.

"Good morning, Yampolsky Nikifor," replied Captain Ivanov.

Well, so far so good, thought Nikifor, knowing only too well how powerful this *militsioner* could be. Nikifor had come to pick up their American passports after the so-called registration and prolonged waiting time which allegedly had happened due to bureaucratic delays. The night before, he had barely slept, tossing and turning while imagining every possible outcome of this meeting. Nikifor did not sleep the whole night before, turning and tossing, wondering what would happen in the local militsiya office when left in a one-on-one meeting with a Soviet official. Captain Ivanov looked at Nikifor with a stern gaze. Nikifor stepped slightly back as if trying to hide from a very dangerous man.

"Comrade Yampolsky, where are you from?" asked Captain Ivanov.

"I have arrived from New York with my family to help build communism a few months ago, but originally I am from Belorussia," replied Nikifor.

"So why did you come to see me?" asked Captain Ivanov with a mocking sneer, as though he had already decided the visit was a pointless formality.

Nikifor started stammering. His heart was racing, and he felt a dull pain on the left side of his forehead. He wiped his forehead with his hand, trying to calm down sufficiently to explain to the captain why he had come over to the militsiya unit.

"I came here to get a residency stamp in our papers. We were told by the officials to hand over our American passports for registration at the port of Leningrad upon our arrival. The man in charge instructed us to pick up our passports at the local unit once we got our registration stamps."

As Nikifor mentioned "American passports," Captain Ivanov's gaze sharpened, piercing through him. Nikifor barely finished his sentence when the captain sternly unraveled the mystery of the missing American passports.

"Comrade Yampolsky, you and your family are now proud citizens of the Soviet Union. You no longer require your American passports," Captain Ivanov declared, pausing as if expecting Nikifor to respond. When Nikifor remained silent, the captain continued.

"Your wife, formerly Ethelyn Gertrude White, will be known as Etalina Urkovna Yampolsky. George, your youngest, will be Georgy Nikiforovich Yampolsky. Natalie, already bearing a Russian name, will be Natalia Nikiforovna Yampolsky. Eugene will be Evgeniy Nikiforovich Yampolsky, and Eleanor will keep her first name. Soviet passports with these new names will be issued to you soon."

Captain Ivanov stood, locking his gaze with Nikifor's ashen face.

"The matter is closed!" he barked.

Approaching the door, Captain Ivanov flung it open for Nikifor, who hesitated before stepping out. The door slammed shut behind him with a resounding thud.

Leaning against the wall for support, Nikifor slowly navigated through the building whose decisions silently dictated the fate of millions of Soviet citizens. Once outside, he gazed skyward, as if searching for answers. He wandered aimlessly through the streets, surrounded by a somber crowd cloaked in black and dusted with snow. Their faces were downcast; no smiles broke the gloom.

Nikifor was no stranger to harsh winters, but this one seemed exceptionally brutal. The wind howled, snowflakes pelted his face, and his thick brows turned white with frost. Clutching his heart, he felt an unfamiliar pain and shortness of breath. Despite the dull headache and growing despair, Nikifor whispered to himself, "Everything changes in life. Today is gray and bleak, without hope. But tomorrow could be better. I must retain hope."

Nikifor, reeling from his encounter at the militsiya, aimlessly wandered through the city center. As he crossed Gorky Street, passing the Central Telegraph building, he noticed a large, silent crowd gathered in front of a store window. The freezing air was thick with steam from their breath as they shifted from foot to foot, covering their mouths to retain warmth.

Men braced against the cold in old, padded jackets, fur hats, and felt boots with rubber tops, while women wrapped their faces in scarves, known as babushkas, to fend off the bitter frost. These were desperate Muscovites, many from the suburbs, scouring for any sustenance they could gather.

The promises of lavish parties, free food, and accommodations—a life purportedly surpassing anything in America—now seemed painfully distant, overshadowed by the endless lines for bread, pungent herring, slabs of meat, frozen codfish bricks, soap, and other necessities, queues that stretched for hours and slowly wore down even the youngest spirits.

Meanwhile, George was at home, grappling with deep culture shock. As a sensitive boy, he felt increasingly alienated in the harsh Moscow environment. The unfamiliar rhythms of Soviet life weighed heavily on him, making even the simplest daily moments feel unsettling and strange. Their communal apartment was always bustling. The communal kitchen, with its tables once white but now chipped and discolored, revealing dark wood underneath, was a hub of constant activity. Russian songs and party leader speeches blared from the radio, accompanied by brazen swearing and the gurgling of heaters. The air often smelled of boiled cabbage, kerosene, and damp wool coats hung to dry. With only four gas units on a single stove for all tenants, tensions often ran high. Arguments flared regularly as neighbors fought over cooking time, banging pots and shouting across the narrow room.

George, tall and thin, wrapped himself in an old American sweater, a relic from his past life, knitted by his mother. The soft wool had faded with wear, but to George it still carried the warmth and familiarity of home. He found solace in its familiar embrace, shielding himself both physically and emotionally from the grim reality surrounding him. The frequent moves and the ever-changing environments had toughened George in some ways, helping him develop a certain detachment. He observed the world around him quietly, absorbing everything without always revealing his thoughts. His primary focus was on mastering Russian, a task at which he excelled, learning fifty new words each day. His English accent was almost imperceptible, a testament to his adaptability in these challenging circumstances.

Often, George would sit quietly by the frost-covered window, tracing the ice that formed on the inside, watching his breath fog the glass in the cold apartment, his mind wandering back to their home in Rochester, New York. That house had been a haven of warmth and comfort. Its wooden floors creaked softly in winter, and the kitchen was always filled with the comforting smells of baked bread and warm meals. He yearned for his old friends and the joyous times they shared, sledding down snowy slopes in winter, and basking in the cozy warmth of his home. Summers and autumns were marked by bowls of fresh fruit always gracing the table.

George, naturally cheerful, had sun-kissed blond hair, bright blue eyes, and an athletic build. He was not only highly intelligent and kind but also had a passion for astronomy and classical music. On clear evenings in America, he had loved standing in the yard and studying the stars, imagining distant worlds beyond the reach of human troubles. An accomplished tennis player, he had won first place in junior tournaments in his region. His Sundays were spent at the local Presbyterian Church. He devoured books on science, astronomy, and physics, wrote essays, and practiced the violin. Those quiet routines had once given structure and meaning to his young life. All these facets of George's life were now part of a distant past.

Now George found himself in Moscow, caught amid the Soviet government's growing campaign of fear against its own citizens. The whispers he overheard in hallways, the anxious faces of neighbors, and the constant propaganda on the radio all hinted at dangers he was only beginning to understand. His world had transformed dramatically, leaving him in a reality far removed from the one he once knew and cherished.

Chapter 6

Twilight Whispers

George meandered through the bustling central streets of Moscow, making his way along *Gorky Street* and past the Central Telegraph Office. The evening crowds moved in restless currents around him, their footsteps echoing across the broad pavement. He crossed the street and slipped into a narrow alley leading toward *Gertsen Street*. Moving quickly, he soon emerged at *Nikitskie Vorota*—the historic *Nikitsky Gate* district. Winding through a labyrinth of alleys and boulevards, he eventually arrived at the square of the three railway stations. It was early evening, and the area was abuzz with people hurrying to and from the stations. Porters shouted, vendors called out to passing travelers, and the distant whistle of departing trains cut through the murmur of the crowd. The night air was pleasantly warm, the pavement still holding the day's heat, softening beneath his steps.

Curiosity about the city drew George towards the stations. He crossed the square and entered a massive building echoing with the hustle and bustle of travelers. The loudspeakers' announcements intertwined with the distant rumbling of trains. The cavernous hall seemed to breathe with movement—boots striking the stone floor, suitcases dragging, voices blending into a constant roar. Wandering further, George reached a quieter section of the station. To his shock, he noticed a train with barred windows, behind which silent faces peered out. The faces were pale and expressionless, pressed close to the iron bars as if searching the platform for one last glimpse of freedom. It was a haunting sight – these were the trains destined for Siberia's forced labor camps.

Among the recent American arrivals in Moscow, horrific stories circulated. One particularly chilling tale that George couldn't shake off involved a friend's uncle sent to Siberia. The story recounted a bitterly cold day when the uncle saw a bird flying in the clear blue sky, only for its wings to freeze mid-flight, causing it to plummet to the ground, dead. The image of the frozen bird falling silently from the sky had lodged itself in George's imagination like a dark omen. This haunting image was now etched in George's mind.

Rooted to the spot, George stared at the silent faces in the train before a rush of helplessness propelled him to flee the station. He hurried through the station's exit, quickly diverting into a side street away from the square. The noise of the station faded behind him as he moved deeper into the darker streets of the district. He sped through the dark alleyways, guided only by intermittent streams of light from house windows. His footsteps echoed sharply against the stone walls as he hurried past shadowed doorways and silent courtyards. Finally, he arrived at the three-story building where his family resided – a place he loathed, yet there remained a hopeful belief that they would soon move to a better neighborhood.

Many similar dilapidated buildings, relics from before the October Revolution of 1917, dotted the outskirts of Moscow. Neglected and poorly maintained, they were rapidly deteriorating under the extreme Moscow climate: sweltering summers and freezing winters. The house where George's family lived was concealed behind trees with withered crowns, hidden behind a crumbling, tilted wooden fence. The crooked boards creaked faintly in the evening breeze. As George neared the decrepit building, he paused to calm his racing heart and glanced around, a habitual check to ensure no one was following him. The courtyard stood silent except for the distant clatter of a tram passing somewhere beyond the buildings. The staircase's stale air, a nauseating mix of human waste and boiled cabbage, greeted him as he ascended. At the sound of his mother's light footsteps, George began to relax.

Ethelyn opened the door with a worried look.

"George! Why are you so late? I was so worried!"

"Sorry, I'm okay," George muttered, avoiding her gaze, and went to sit by the window.

Noticing George's disturbed silence, Nikifor and Ethelyn sat at the table and began writing on a piece of paper, fearful of being overheard. Even the thin walls seemed to listen in such apartments, where a careless word could travel farther than intended. In this oppressive atmosphere, being overheard could cost them their freedom, or worse, their lives.

Nikifor scribbled:
"Many Americans have vanished after leaving the American Embassy. Arrested on Moscow's streets. Their fates unknown."

Ethelyn wrote in response:
"We must avoid trouble. Living on the outskirts, or even in the suburbs, far from central streets and the embassy, is safest. No more discussions on such matters. We focus on survival and cling to hope for a better future."

They consciously avoided "dangerous subjects" in their daily conversations, a survival tactic swiftly learned in Soviet society. Nikifor silently took the paper, struck a match, and watched as the words turned to ashes – a necessary precaution to ensure no incriminating evidence about the American Embassy remained, preventing any risk of interrogation or imprisonment.

For a few moments they watched the ashes curl and darken in the flame, until the last fragile fragment of paper vanished into smoke—along with the words they dared not speak aloud.

Chapter 7

The Aftermath of Conviction

Time passed, and Nikifor settled into his bleak routine. The days blended into one another, marked by long hours of work and the quiet tension that had become part of everyday life. A few months later, at the beginning of his workday, Nikifor was called into the office by one of his regular bosses, Ivan Serdyukov, the head of the maintenance office, an overweight man in his early sixties.

"Hello, Comrade Yampolsky," began Ivan in his monotone voice. "Nikifor—everyone is to attend the meeting today at 11 a.m. in the main hall. Clear?" Ivan stated in his raspy voice. He dabbed his damp forehead with a crumpled handkerchief and shuffled the papers on his desk with slow, indifferent movements. Nikifor nodded in agreement and mumbled something in response before leaving the office.

The hall was slowly filling with plumbers, carpenters, and caretakers. Heavy boots scraped against the wooden floor as men took their seats. The murmur of street noise from outside and the buzz of conversations started to spread throughout the hall. Nikifor scanned the room and spotted an empty chair at the back of the large square room, still unoccupied. He chose to sit at the end of the row, right by the door. From there he could see the entire hall — and, if necessary, leave quickly.

On the stage, behind a long rectangular table covered with a green woolen tablecloth, members of the city regional party committee were ready to begin the meeting. Initially, Nikifor was unsure of what was happening, but he was conscious that it would be wise not to show his ignorance by asking why the meeting was scheduled for today and why it was so crucial to attend.

The meeting started half an hour late, and a grey-haired bureaucrat — a government official and party member — was ready to address the audience. As usual, he scanned the crowd as if he were about to deliver a verdict. Petr Osokin, like most of the men representing the district committee of the Communist Party, was in his early sixties. His narrow eyes moved slowly across the room, lingering on faces as though memorizing them.

He took the stage, casting a menacing glance around, which by itself spelled nothing good for the workers gathered in the hall.

"Good afternoon, dear comrades! Today, we have very important issues to discuss — our great achievements in building socialism and a new book by our great leader Stalin, the genius of all times and the leader of all peoples. This, and only this, will bring us closer to achieving our main goal on the path to communism!"

The audience began to applaud. People stood up, clapping as loudly as they could for five minutes. The sound of hundreds of hands striking together echoed sharply against the high walls of the hall. Only when Petr Osokin raised his hand to silence the crowd did the attendees obediently follow his command.

Another comrade from the committee, Comrade Krutikov Stepan, sitting at the table, then took the floor and energetically listed the great achievements of the Communist Party and the Soviet people under the leadership of the great Stalin, leading the Soviet people to full victory — to communism. He then delivered a fiery speech about the enemies of the people and the intensification of the class struggle as stated by the great leader of all peoples, Comrade Stalin.

Plumbers, carpenters, and all types of handymen applauded loudly at each mention of Stalin's name. Several men rose to their feet automatically, as though driven by instinct rather than conviction. They stood up from their places and continued with an ovation for several minutes.

When the speech by the grey-haired Comrade Krutikov, adorned with the Order of Lenin, concluded, the head of the district Communist Party's regional committee, the rotund and completely bald Sergey Simkin, took the stage.

Rising from his seat and clearing his throat several times, he began:

"Today we need to discuss the personal case of Comrade Sidorov Viktor. He has been serving as a caretaker in our district for six months. In this regard, we must address the recent arrest and exposure of his father, Sidorov Afanasy, as an enemy of the people, a spy, a saboteur, and a wrecker — in short, a deplorable figure."

"You have all read about it in the newspapers *Pravda* (Truth) and *Trud* (Labor). The father is a traitor with ties to the traitor Trotsky. Such individuals are venomous snakes, poised to threaten and destroy our harmonious society with their Trotskyist ideologies."

Simkin paused dramatically before continuing.

"Dear comrades, Komsomol members, and Communist Party members, I speak to you. You bear a significant responsibility to always remain vigilant, both at home and at work, to protect our Communist society's healthy body from the perpetual threat of undermining our efforts to build a communist society. You must purge our healthy society of secret foes and double-dealers who have craftily infiltrated our ranks."

Comrade Simkin, now noticeably flushed and sweating profusely, dabbed his face with a handkerchief, then took a sip of water.

After some initial stammering, he called out to the man seated in the last row.

"Comrade Sidorov, approach the podium and explain how you failed to notice anything amiss while living under the same roof as your father, a heinous enemy of the people. You must denounce your father, a traitor, and an enemy of the people!"

A hush fell over the auditorium.

The audience, comprised of simple blue-collar workers, sat in silence, casting furtive glances around.

Comrade Sidorov, a slight man, coughed into his handkerchief and slowly made his way to the podium.

Standing silently on the podium, the son of the arrested man dared not meet the gaze of his coworkers. After coughing several times into his handkerchief, stained with dark red blood, he struggled to straighten up before the gathered crowd.

The *NKVD*[3] officer then pressed the accused to disclose how his father had allegedly spied for a foreign nation.

After clearing his throat several times and scanning the crowd for any sign of support or kindness — finding none — Comrade Sidorov began, his voice wheezing as if gasping for air:

"Comrade Sidorov Afanasy is my father, and he is a good man. He never betrayed the Communist Party. In fact, during the October Revolution, he was guarding trains loaded with wheat and soap. He never took anything for himself or our family."

"He knew Lenin and took part in the revolution but was born deaf and uneducated, unable to read. He's been a handyman, earning his living through his skills. I stand by my father, a good man and a communist."

The party functionary on the podium glared at the audience, then menacingly at the son of the arrested man.

"You're suggesting our esteemed organs have erred. That's not possible. It only means you're oblivious. You and your father are our secret adversaries, and you've been caught."

"We know you and your father plotted sabotage. You're neither a Komsomol member nor a party member; hence, you're dismissed today. You've lost your prestigious position as a Soviet worker because you're an enemy."

The son looked out over the assembly of plumbers, carpenters, and caretakers and spoke softly:

"I hope my father will be absolved of all charges, for he is an honest man, truly devoted to Comrades Lenin and Stalin. He has dedicated his life to the revolution. He's also disabled with a heart condition. I'm battling tuberculosis, and my days are numbered."

"I need my job to survive. I reside in a warm boiler room, which greatly aids me during winter."

The man at the podium, glaring at Viktor, announced:

"The workers of this district will vote!"

He then surveyed the crowd menacingly.

"Who supports the firing of Comrade Sidorov?"

Hands began to rise.

Within minutes, it seemed the entire auditorium concurred with the district party committee's decision.

One by one, arms lifted across the hall, until the raised hands formed a silent forest of fear and obedience.

As the raised hands formed a forest of betrayal and fear, a wave of despair washed over the hall, marking the cruel culmination of an orchestrated charade.

The victim stood, a solitary figure against a tide of judgment, his frail body a stark testament to the harrowing trials he endured. His voice, a mere whisper against the clamor of injustice, resonated with a poignant plea for understanding and compassion, yet was met with a wall of silence.

The room, once filled with the camaraderie of workers united by toil, now echoed with the hollow sound of complicity.

Nikifor remained seated, bowing his head, until someone forced his hand up, warning:

"Don't be a fool. You'll be arrested if you don't raise your hand."

Nikifor, his hand reluctantly raised, embodied the internal struggle of many present — the battle between self-preservation and the gnawing sense of injustice.

His heart raced, pounding against his chest as if seeking escape from the moral quandary that ensnared him.

The finality of the vote struck like a thunderbolt, sealing the fate of a man condemned not for deeds but for blood ties to an accused.

The air grew thick with tension, heavy with the weight of unspoken guilt and shattered solidarity.

In that moment, the hall transformed into a somber theater of human frailty, where fear overshadowed truth, and loyalty was sacrificed on the altar of survival.

The verdict, delivered without evidence or empathy, exemplified the tragic absurdity of the times — an era where innocence was irrelevant, and the mere shadow of suspicion could demolish lives.

As Comrade Sidorov returned to his seat, navigating through a sea of averted gazes, the silence spoke volumes.

Not a single voice rose in protest. Only the dull echo of hands still trembling from the vote lingered in the heavy air of the hall.

Chapter 8

The Young Love Affair

"Love and compassion are necessities, not luxuries. Without them, humanity cannot survive."
— The Dalai Lama

In the middle of all the adversity and despite the many obstacles in his way, George was enrolled in an Anglo-American school, an exclusive institution that catered to foreign diplomats and Soviet elites, where all subjects were taught in English. However, the school was shut down after many of its teachers were arrested, a development that shocked many of the students and families connected to the school, forcing George to continue his education at a working people's school for adults.

During this time, Nikifor, Ethelyn, George, Natalie, Eleanor, and Eugene frequently relocated, renting rooms for brief periods. Their lives unfolded through a series of temporary homes, each move bringing uncertainty and disruption. For a while, they lived near the *Pushkinskaya* station in Moscow. George's daily commute to school was arduous, involving an hour-long journey on a slow train that rattled through the outskirts of the city before reaching the crowded urban districts. It was a period marked by constant challenges, from the struggle to purchase schoolbooks to enduring long queues for essential items like rubber tops for winter boots, especially since ration cards were discontinued and everything was difficult to obtain.

One day, while walking and reading in the school hallway, George accidentally bumped into a girl with cornflower blue eyes and long, braided chestnut hair. The sudden collision startled them both, and a few loose papers slipped from George's hands onto the floor. The instant he saw her, he thought, "I am so in love. I will never forget these blue eyes." Snapping out of his daydream, he quickly apologized to her. The girl, Sonya, blushed a deep crimson and hurried away, her braid swaying behind her as she disappeared down the corridor.

Days later, they crossed paths again. This time, Sonya and George walked home together in silence, occasionally glancing at the ground. The late afternoon light stretched long shadows across the pavement as they walked side by side. When Sonya's hand brushed against his, George felt an unfamiliar warmth envelop him. It was his first encounter with love, and he didn't fully understand the emotions stirring within him.

She told him stories of her family, of her father's paintings, of the old traditions her mother lovingly preserved, and though she never said the words outright, George came to understand that Sonya was Jewish. It was something quietly present between them, understood without needing to be spoken aloud.

As they passed each other in the school corridors, their eyes would lock, and soon Sonya could greet him with a smile without blushing. Before long, they were sharing secrets and passing notes. George and Sonya would see each other secretly in school as often as possible and every time they reached a dark hallway, they would quickly kiss each other. One day as George kissed Sonya, he felt her soft breast against his hard chest and in that sudden closeness he realized with certainty that she was the one he wished to marry. Because their little affair turned into something warm, sensuous, and beautiful.

"How soon may I ask your parents for your hand in marriage?" he asked.

"Come tonight for dinner," she suggested.

George met with her parents, Raisa and Anatoly, to ask for Sonya's hand in marriage. Their modest apartment was warmly lit, and the table was set with tea and simple food prepared for the evening meal. The parents agreed and Sonya and George were betrothed to each other to be formally married when they would both come of age. George was only seventeen, and Sonya was a few months older.

Their young love, though filled with the innocence and intensity of first affection, was set against the backdrop of a challenging and uncertain era. Yet, in each other, George and Sonya found a sense of solace and connection that transcended the difficulties of their daily lives.

For George, those quiet moments with Sonya became a fragile sanctuary—brief flashes of light in a world that seemed to be growing darker with each passing day.

Chapter 9

The Unyielding Silence of Moscow

Ethelyn's life in Moscow was marked by isolation and a growing sense of despair. Unable to master the challenging Russian language and wary of the potential risks her English accent might pose; she found herself increasingly confined to their home. The unfamiliar sounds of the language around her felt like an impenetrable wall, separating her from the world outside. Her social interactions were limited, and she relied on books from a foreign language library frequented by Americans to fill her days. The scriptures became her refuge, offering solace in times of uncertainty and loneliness.

Ethelyn also began to pour her emotions into writing a diary and letters. The act of writing became a quiet ritual, a way of preserving her thoughts in a world where speaking freely was no longer safe. She hoped these letters would eventually reach her relatives in America, trusting that Nikifor might find someone with diplomatic immunity brave enough to smuggle them out of the Soviet Union.

Her outings were rare, typically brief walks with Nikifor. Most of her time was spent watching the world from her window, overlooking a narrow street lined with brick buildings and a tramway line. The slow rumble of passing trams and the distant clatter of metal wheels on the tracks became the soundtrack of her long days. But even from this vantage point, Ethelyn couldn't escape the pervasive sense of isolation. Rumors circulating among the American community in Moscow about compatriots disappearing added to her distress. The apparent inaction of the American embassy only intensified her feeling of abandonment.

As the new year approached, Ethelyn's emotional burden became unbearable. One chilly morning, overcome with desperation, she experienced a panic attack. Her breathing became shallow as waves of fear swept over her. Seeking relief, she opened a small windowpane to let in some fresh air. The songs of a goldfinch and sparrows broke through her despair, reminding her that spring was near. Their fragile chirping floated through the cold morning air, delicate yet persistent. The simple, joyful sounds of the birds momentarily calmed her troubled mind.

In these moments of quietude, Ethelyn's thoughts drifted back to her earlier days in Massachusetts. She reminisced about a cherished gray taffeta dress and a matching hat adorned with small gray feathers. Memories of meeting her best friend, Emily, in a cozy Boston coffee shop where they shared laughter over hot chocolate came flooding back. She could almost hear the clink of porcelain cups and the soft murmur of conversations around them. She longed for those carefree days, wondering if such times would ever return.

Ethelyn's mind then wandered to her childhood home in Somerville, Massachusetts. She remembered the familiar streets, the wooden houses, and the comforting rhythm of life she had once taken for granted. The nostalgia was overwhelming, and the pain of contrasting her past life in America with her present circumstances was almost too much to bear. In her room, Ethelyn paced, grappling with the stark reality of her situation, her heart aching for a past that seemed irretrievably lost.

After completing her morning ritual in the communal kitchen, Ethelyn's feelings of alienation and despair deepened. The clatter of dishes, the murmured conversations in Russian, and the watchful glances of neighbors only heightened her discomfort. The simple act of avoiding her neighbors to evade language barriers was a constant reminder of her isolation. Despite being in the Soviet Union for four years, she felt no closer to adapting or understanding the culture around her. Her dislike for Russia grew with each passing day, fueled by the somber faces and dreary crowds she encountered during outings with Nikifor.

Emotionally exhausted and overwhelmed with worry, Ethelyn felt an urgent need to connect with her family in America. She believed that establishing communication with her cousin Helen might provide some solace and potentially help in formulating an exit strategy from the Soviet Union. Seated at the kitchen table, she began to pen a letter, pouring out her heart about the difficulties they faced, the shock of their forced Soviet citizenship, and the unending quest to retrieve their American passports.

In her letter, Ethelyn candidly expressed her concerns and the emotional toll of their situation. Yet she refrained from burdening Nikifor with her deepest fears, understanding his desire to remain hopeful about the future in the Soviet Union. She wrote of the relatively better conditions in Moscow compared to the provinces and her intention to stay connected with Helen as a witness to their plight. She planned to include a family photograph with the letter, hoping it would serve as a tangible connection to their life in the Soviet Union.

Despite feeling a sense of relief after writing the letter, Ethelyn was acutely aware of the risks involved. The possibility that her correspondence could fall into the hands of the *NKVD* secret services was a constant threat. The very act of sending a letter abroad carried the weight of danger. But the need to reach out, to break the silence and isolation, outweighed her fears.

For Ethelyn, writing that letter was more than an attempt to contact family—it was a quiet act of defiance against the suffocating silence that had settled over their lives in Moscow.

***

Standing by the window, Ethelyn looked out onto the busy street, watching people go about their daily routines. Trams rattled along the tracks, their metal wheels screeching against the rails, while pedestrians hurried past in heavy coats, collars turned up against the chill. The weight of desperation clung to her, a relentless shadow that followed her every move. In that moment, staring out into the bustling street of Moscow, Ethelyn felt the full extent of her isolation in a foreign land, far from the familiar comforts of her past life in America.

"Back home I was somebody," Ethelyn mused to herself, her thoughts drifting to the life she had left behind. She missed her connections, her relatives, and her fulfilling career as a teacher. The transition to life in the Soviet Union had been jarring, thrusting her into an environment where she felt invisible, disconnected from a society wary of foreigners. "I understand their suspicion," she thought, acknowledging her own cautious approach toward the locals. Despite this, she remained steadfast, staying calm for her family's sake, finding strength in her prayers and thoughts.

In the early evening, as Nikifor returned to their rented room, Ethelyn rose from her chair by the window. Nikifor, visibly tired yet carrying a sense of excitement, embraced her warmly. His coat smelled faintly of cold winter air and the smoke of the city streets. "You must see what I bought for you at the commissary," he said, his eyes gleaming with anticipation.

Ethelyn's curiosity piqued as she opened the string bag. The sight of imported cheese from Denmark, Italian salami, Ceylon black tea, Swiss dark chocolate, and fresh white bread brought a genuine smile to her face for the first time in a while. The luxury of these fine foods momentarily displaced the room's usual odors of valerian root and mothballs. Nikifor, she learned, had exchanged his last valuable possession, a cherished Swiss pocket watch gifted by his father, for this assortment of delicacies.

As they unwrapped the food, the room filled with tantalizing aromas, creating a small oasis of comfort in their otherwise stark existence. The sharp scent of salami and the rich fragrance of freshly cut bread seemed almost miraculous in a place where scarcity ruled everyday life. They hugged each other, sharing a moment of joy in their hardships. Nikifor then took the tea kettle to the communal kitchen, only to be met with the suspicious gaze of their neighbor Boris.

Boris, a product of the Soviet regime, resided in what used to be a spacious apartment belonging to a Russian merchant who had fled during the revolution. The flat's original owners had been displaced; their rooms appropriated by government workers like Boris. The once elegant apartment had long since been divided into cramped communal quarters, its high ceilings and carved moldings now bearing the scars of neglect. In this new Soviet reality, the complexities of their living situation were a constant reminder of the dramatic shifts in society and the personal losses they entailed.

For Ethelyn and Nikifor, these small moments of happiness, like savoring the luxury foods Nikifor had brought, were rare but vital reprieves from the daily struggles of adapting to a life so far removed from what they had once known and cherished.

In the communal kitchen, the tension between Nikifor and Boris, the government employee, was palpable. Boris, a coarse, illiterate man prone to swearing, filled the room with the heavy odor of his cigarette smoke. A thin gray haze hovered beneath the ceiling as the smoke curled lazily through the dim light of the bare bulb. Nikifor, maintaining a polite distance, responded minimally to Boris's attempts at conversation about the weather, a safe yet superficial topic in Russia.

Nikifor found the lack of privacy in Moscow suffocating. His adaptability and belief in his ability to adjust to any situation were the only things keeping him going. As he took the boiling pot off the stove, he couldn't help but notice Boris's hostile gaze. Boris's hissed threats about the militsiya and taking over Nikifor's room were a chilling reminder of the precariousness of their situation. The hostility and suspicion they faced, particularly because of Ethelyn's American background, were constant sources of anxiety.

Returning to their room with the pot of hot water, Nikifor found Ethelyn setting the table. Upon asking about George, Ethelyn's response carried a tinge of sadness. George had been increasingly absent, spending his time with Sonya and working overtime at various places. Nikifor expressed his concern about George not being more present to help at home, but Ethelyn, ever protective, defended their son's actions.

Their daily life had become a series of small, tense interactions, underscored by the looming threat of surveillance and the hostility of their neighbors. Even the thin walls seemed to listen. Each day brought new challenges as they navigated this hostile environment, clinging to the few moments of family togetherness they could salvage. For Ethelyn, each day in this foreign land deepened her yearning for the life and connections she had left behind in America. The sense of alienation and the strain of constantly being on guard weighed heavily on her, making every day a battle for emotional survival.

"George is finding his own way," Ethelyn defended their son. "He's diligent in his studies and even finds time to indulge in English literature." She mentioned George's recent interest in Charlotte Brontë's *Jane Eyre*, a book that brought her a sense of familiarity and comfort amidst the foreignness of their life in Moscow.

Nikifor, weary from the day's ordeals and not wanting to argue further, simply nodded. He was more focused on the prospect of enjoying the rare luxury of a good meal. As they sat down to eat, they said grace, grateful for the small blessings like the comforting cup of hot tea and the imported delicacies they were about to savor. For a moment, the harsh world outside their door seemed to fade, replaced by the fragile warmth of family gathered around a modest table.

***

After dinner, Ethelyn handed Nikifor her unsealed letter. He read it carefully, his eyes filling with tears as he absorbed her words. The thin paper trembled slightly in his hands as he reached the final lines. Standing up, he moved closer to her. "I've been thinking about doing the same," he whispered. "I'll find a way to send it. I'll do everything in my power to make sure it reaches our relatives in America."

Despite a couple of years in Moscow, they still felt like strangers in a foreign land. The lack of communication with their family in America and the absence of their American passports left them feeling trapped and isolated. The city around them seemed vast and impenetrable, its rhythms and rules forever foreign to them. This letter, their tentative lifeline to their past and to a hope for change, held immense importance.

As winter set in Moscow, Nikifor found himself wandering the city streets, lost in thought. He visited Red Square, observing the Kremlin's imposing walls and the frozen expanse of the Moscow River. A bitter wind swept across the square, carrying with it the distant echo of boots on cobblestones. The city, with its historical monuments and vibrant cultural life, offered brief moments of distraction.

Standing outside the Bolshoi Theatre, watching diplomats and their elegantly dressed spouses, Nikifor contemplated his next move. Women in fur-lined coats and men in polished evening shoes stepped from black government cars beneath the glowing theatre lights. The lively chatter and the allure of the theater's grandeur momentarily liberated him from his burdens. The idea of contacting a foreigner at the Bolshoi struck him – a risky but potentially fruitful endeavor. The thought of navigating such delicate interactions felt akin to walking a tightrope above Moscow's skyline, each step fraught with potential danger but also a chance for liberation.

One step and he could fall into an abyss. The faint glow of streetlamps cast long shadows across the pavement. A large hammer and sickle drawn on one of the wooden stands reminded him of being cautious in his actions, and he turned instead and went home.

The very next day, Nikifor got up early and went to the kitchen. It was still empty. The silence of the early morning hour felt almost unnatural in the crowded communal apartment. He went to the sink and washed up. Then he put on the tea kettle and waited patiently until it started boiling. As soon as the neighbors started to appear in the kitchen, he hurried back to his room.

Ethelyn was still asleep, covered by a well-worn shawl. Her breathing was soft and steady, a rare moment of peace amid the uncertainty of their lives. Nikifor counted his rubles and a few remaining dollars. Money was dwindling fast, and he was not making enough to cover the basic expenses. He was going to try again.

He put on his American coat with a beaver collar and went out. Nikifor walked fast down the boulevard, reaching the tramway just in time. He got on the tramway, paying a three-kopek fare for his ride. It was only a half hour's ride to the center. The tram rattled forward, its windows fogged with the breath of passengers pressed shoulder to shoulder.

He got off at the stop and walked fast to the Bolshoi. He wanted one ticket for the world-famous ballet *Swan Lake* with the leading ballerina Galina Ulanova. It was his chance to meet someone who would be willing to take Ethelyn's letter.

Nikifor stood for a minute or two in the square looking at the Bolshoi Theatre. Its grand columns rose into the gray winter sky, illuminated by pale electric lamps. The area was not busy with traffic or pedestrians.

When he entered the lobby of the Bolshoi, he saw a tired-looking saleswoman sitting inside the ticket booth.

"Good morning," said Nikifor and tried to smile at the cashier.

The cashier looked indifferently at Nikifor and greeted him: "Good morning," with lips pressed, not attempting to smile back.

"I want one ticket for *Swan Lake* for tonight with Galina Ulanova," Nikifor said, speaking English so he could pass for an Englishman working at the embassy.

The cashier looked through a stack of tickets and picked one.

"I have only one ticket left for tonight in the last balcony row!" said the cashier in English with a heavy Russian accent. "What embassy are you from?" asked the salesperson suddenly and suspiciously.

Nikifor unabashedly answered, "I serve at the British Embassy!"

"This ticket is only five dollars for you, since you work at the embassy," the salesclerk said a little friendlier.

Nikifor paid her. The crisp foreign bills disappeared quickly into the drawer. At least he had a ticket now—the first step. He returned home to wait for the show.

Nikifor had taken two days off from work as a caretaker in the local maintenance office, saying that his wife was sick and he had to take care of her. By early evening, Nikifor stood in front of the Bolshoi. There were already people waiting to buy tickets from the bystanders who were scalping.

Nikifor, upon entering the grand Bolshoi Theatre, was momentarily swept away by its lavish interior. The plush burgundy seats, mahogany paneling, opulent chandeliers, and gold figurines transported him into a world far removed from his daily struggles. The warm glow of the chandeliers reflected across the polished balconies like scattered stars. As he settled into his seat, the curtain rose, and the hall was filled with the enchanting music of Tchaikovsky. The ballet, with its graceful dancers in shimmering costumes, captivated him completely, providing a brief escape from his troubles.

During the intermission, Nikifor stood up and mingled in the crowded buffet area, observing the well-dressed patrons. Without money for refreshments, he remained a spectator in the corner. His attention was caught by a man who seemed to be watching him intently from the souvenir line. The man's eyes lingered a moment too long.

Feeling a surge of suspicion, Nikifor quickly decided to leave the theatre to avoid any potential confrontation or risk.

After the second act commenced, he discreetly exited the Bolshoi and made his way to the metro station. The cold night air struck his face as he stepped back onto the quiet street. The possibility of finding someone to deliver his letter to America seemed increasingly dangerous and unattainable.

Gripped by a sudden fear of the letter being discovered, Nikifor destroyed it, tearing it into unrecognizable pieces. The small fragments of paper fluttered briefly in the winter wind before disappearing into the darkness. He made a silent vow not to tell Ethelyn about this decision, sparing her the additional disappointment and worry.

The burden of their situation, the constant surveillance, and the limitations imposed on their freedom weighed heavily on Nikifor as he traveled back to his rental room. The fleeting moments of beauty and normalcy at the Bolshoi Theatre seemed like a distant dream, overshadowed by the harsh reality of their life in Moscow.

For Nikifor and Ethelyn, each day was a test of endurance, a continual struggle to maintain hope in the face of overwhelming challenges. And in the silent streets of Moscow, hope itself had become something fragile—something that could vanish as quickly as a torn letter carried away by the wind.

Chapter 10

A Date of Infamy

The tranquil moments spent in *Aleksandrovsky* Garden were a stark contrast to the usual daily life in Moscow. Amidst the serenity of the park, with its statues, lovely trees, and a pond graced by swans, Nikifor and Ethelyn experienced a rare sense of peace. The soft rustle of leaves and the distant laughter of children created an illusion of normal life that felt almost unreal to them. The sunny summer days in Moscow brought some respite as they, like other city dwellers, tried to capture fleeting moments of normalcy and relaxation.

Finding a bench in the shade at the park's entrance, they settled down, Nikifor buying Ethelyn an ice cream as a small treat. The sweet, cold taste lingered pleasantly in the warm summer air. In these moments, the impending tensions of a world on the brink of war seemed distant. The tranquility of the park offered them a temporary escape from the oppressive atmosphere of their rental room and the constant struggles of their life in the Soviet Union.

However, the return to their room that evening brought them back to reality. The sounds of drunken voices from a nearby apartment and the meager dinner of Russian rye bread and dried-out sausage served as stark reminders of their grim circumstances. Ethelyn quickly succumbed to sleep, exhausted by the day's emotional toll, while Nikifor stood by the window, drawing a sliver of hope from the summer night's scents before retiring to bed.

Their brief respite was shattered the next morning. On the 22nd of June 1941, the early rays of sunlight were replaced by the booming voice of Comrade Levitan, the Soviet Union's eminent radio announcer, echoing through the streets. Nikifor and Ethelyn rushed to the window, startled by the announcement that reverberated from every direction. From open windows, street loudspeakers, and communal radios, the same grave voice filled the morning air.

"Attention, Attention! All radio stations of the Soviet Union are working! Citizens of the Soviet Union, men and women—The German Armed Forces perfidiously attacked the Soviet Union today at 4 a.m. without the declaration of war."

This chilling announcement marked a turning point, signaling the beginning of a new and terrifying chapter in their lives. The Soviet Union, which had been their home for the past five years, was now thrust into the throes of World War II. For Nikifor and Ethelyn, already struggling to navigate the complexities of life in a foreign land, this new development brought with it an overwhelming sense of dread and uncertainty about what the future held.

The ominous announcement from Comrade Levitan shattered the illusion of peace and tranquility for Nikifor and Ethelyn. The streets outside their window bore witness to the shock and fear gripping the citizens of the Soviet Union as the reality of war set in. People gathered in small clusters, whispering anxiously, their faces pale with disbelief.

Ethelyn's question, "What will we do?" hung heavily in the air. Nikifor, overwhelmed and realizing their vulnerability and lack of influence in these events, replied somberly, "We can do nothing. We just must wait." The sense of powerlessness was palpable.

The non-aggression pact, once a symbol of an uneasy peace between Germany and the Soviet Union, was now rendered meaningless. The pleasant exchanges between Ribbentrop and Stalin during the signing in 1939 entering a fearful alliance seemed a distant memory considering the treacherous invasion by Germany. Operation Barbarossa marked the beginning of a brutal conflict on Soviet soil.

As Foreign Minister Molotov's speech echoed across the nation, declaring the start of the Great Patriotic War against the fascist invaders, the Soviet people were called to action. Stalin, however, remained silent, leaving Levitan's deep voice to resonate through the loudspeakers, rallying the citizens:

"Our cause is just. The enemy will be crushed. We will win the war."

In this turmoil, George, being of foreign origin and only eighteen, was spared from military conscription. His sisters, Eleanor, 24, and Natalie, 26, contributed by teaching English to military interpreters, a crucial role in the war effort. Eugene, at 22, was sent to a munitions factory in the far north, a testament to the widespread mobilization of resources and people. George found employment in a steel factory, working near open furnaces – the searing heat and deafening clang of metal marking a harsh new chapter in his young life. Sonya, entwined in her own family obligations, stood ready to support them in these dire times.

For the Yampolsky family, life had taken yet another drastic turn. The outbreak of war added layers of complexity and danger to their already challenging existence in the Soviet Union. Each family member found themselves adapting to new roles, contributing to the war effort in whatever ways they could, their personal aspirations and desires overshadowed by the overwhelming demands of a nation at war.

In Moscow, the long shadow of war had fallen across every street, every home, and every fragile hope for the future.

Chapter 11

Veiled Fortitude

As Catherine sat quietly in the corridor, waiting to be called in, the distant echo of footsteps and muffled voices faded into the background. Her thoughts drifted away from the present moment and returned to the memories of her mother, Sonya Hazzan, and the turbulent years that had shaped her family's fate.

Sonya's life was deeply affected by the outbreak of World War II. What had once been ordinary days filled with study, work, and youthful hopes quickly transformed into a life overshadowed by fear and uncertainty. Her days became consumed with worry for her loved ones, who were quickly drafted and sent to the front lines.

Amidst the chaos, Sonya and George, Catherine's father, tried to cherish every moment they had together, even as their plans for marriage had to be put on hold. Every meeting between them carried the quiet awareness that it might be their last for a long time. Their bond was strong, a connection that seemed destined to endure through the trials of the time.

Sonya and her brother, Lazar Hazzan, had experienced suffering from an early age, born in the Jewish ghetto in Belorussia during a period rife with turmoil, hunger, and the brutalities of the revolution. Childhood unfolded in narrow streets shadowed by poverty and fear, where survival itself was often uncertain. Their father, Anatoly Hazzan, a talented artist, had managed to move the family to Moscow with assistance from Comrade

Lunacharsky, who recognized and nurtured young talent. For a moment, the family believed that Moscow might offer them a future shaped by art rather than hardship. Sonya harbored aspirations of furthering her artistic abilities and gaining recognition for her skills, just like her father and brother. She spent long evenings sketching quietly by lamplight, dreaming of a life devoted to beauty and creation rather than survival.

Lazar, like his father, was a gifted painter and sculptor, known for his beautiful landscapes and portraits. His canvases captured wide rivers, quiet villages, and the golden light of summer fields—images of a peaceful world that seemed increasingly distant. The family had once seen a future full of promise, but the war altered their course irreparably.

On June 22, 1941, Lazar was conscripted into the army at the age of twenty-four. Sent to the front with minimal equipment, he bravely defended his homeland against the invaders. Like thousands of other young men, he marched eastward with little more than a rifle and the determination to survive.

Unfortunately, he was captured and spent years in a German concentration camp, enduring unimaginable torment as one of the countless Jewish prisoners caught in the Nazis' ruthless purge. Behind barbed wire and watchtowers, life became a daily struggle against starvation, disease, and despair. Stripped of his name and dignity, he survived only through sheer will until his liberation by American forces in 1944.

However, the suffering did not end with his liberation. Instead of being celebrated as a hero upon his return to the Soviet Union, Lazar found himself subjected to further persecution under Stalin's regime, which harbored deep-seated anti-Semitic sentiments. Branded with suspicion and deemed a traitor simply for having been imprisoned by the enemy, he was unjustly arrested and condemned to yet another camp. The homeland he had fought for now treated him as an enemy.

Eventually, he was declared missing in action, his fate swallowed by the shadows of history. No grave, no farewell—only silence.

These harrowing experiences profoundly impacted Sonya's life and the lives of her family members. The war and its aftermath left indelible marks, shaping the narrative of their family history that Catherine would carry with her. For Sonya, the loss of her brother was not merely a personal tragedy but a wound that never truly healed. The resilience and endurance of her family, especially in the face of such adversity, were a testament to their strength and the unbreakable bonds that held them together.

And as Catherine sat waiting, these memories rose within her like distant echoes—reminders that the quiet strength she carried within herself had been forged through the suffering and courage of those who came before her.

Chapter 12

Fragile Hope

George and Sonya's marriage, although a beacon of love and hope amidst the chaos, was not without its challenges. With no place of their own, they shuttled between rented rooms in Moscow and stays with friends. Suitcases remained half-packed beneath narrow beds, ready for the next inevitable move. George, balancing work at the steel factory with part-time studies at the Foreign Language Institute, was determined and focused. Sonya, too, pursued her passion by enrolling in the School of Architecture, attending classes during the day. George's diligence paid off as he earned his Diploma as a Translator and Teacher of Foreign Languages in just one year.

Their lives were a whirlwind of activity and hardship. Long working hours, nightly studies, and the constant threat of air raids that forced them to seek shelter in metro stations marked their days and nights. Sirens would pierce the darkness without warning, sending crowds rushing down endless staircases into the cavernous underground stations where families huddled together beneath dim lights and peeling posters. Despite these hardships, their love and companionship provided the strength they needed to endure the realities of wartime living — rationed food, cramped living conditions, and the constant fear for their safety.

In December 1944, amidst the turmoil, Sonya became pregnant. This news brought a glimmer of hope and joy to their strained lives. For the first time in months, George allowed himself to imagine a future beyond war. With Sonya nurturing a new life within her, they looked forward to the birth of their child, a symbol of new beginnings and a better future.

As 1945 dawned, George and Sonya managed to secure a small flat on Gertsen Street. The building, while modest, offered them some stability. It was a sturdy brick structure with a foreboding back alley and a courtyard filled with trucks, their engines often rumbling through the night as supplies were moved for the war effort, a stark reminder of the ongoing conflict and scarcity that surrounded them.

During these times, American aid in the form of lend-lease supplies like cans of beef stew occasionally reached them, providing much-needed relief. The unfamiliar English labels on the cans seemed like small relics from a distant world. However, such instances were rare, and often, they struggled to find enough food. Families like theirs survived by sharing whatever little they had, even if it meant dividing a single slice of bread into four meager portions.

1945 brought with it a sense of change, a feeling that the end of the Great Patriotic War was near. The defeat of Nazi Germany in May marked a turning point, yet the daily struggles persisted. It was during one of these days, while carrying slices of bread sent by Sonya's parents to share with Nikifor and Ethelyn, that George felt a distinct shift in the air. The streets seemed quieter, as though the city itself was cautiously exhaling after years of relentless strain. The hardships and sacrifices of the war years were beginning to give way to a new era, one that held the promise of peace and the hope of rebuilding their lives amidst the ruins of a world that had been forever altered.

In the quietude of the night, George and Nikifor's conversation, laden with the weight of their shared struggles, unfolded in subdued whispers. The small room was dimly lit by a single lamp whose yellow glow cast long shadows across the worn wooden floor. The atmosphere in the room was heavy with a mixture of hope and apprehension. Ethelyn's early retirement to bed underscored the toll that the prolonged stress and uncertainty had taken on her.

"How are you and Sonya doing?" Nikifor asked with a deep, sad sigh.

Nikifor's inquiry reflected not just concern for his son and daughter-in-law but also the broader anxiety about their collective future.

"We are surviving. How is Mom?" George's response was a testament to the resilience they had all been forced to muster. His concern for his mother, Ethelyn, indicated the tight-knit nature of their family, each member acutely aware of the others' hardships.

"We are coping as best as we can. We should be patient and kind to each other. The war will soon be over, and it will bring about changes," Nikifor continued.

Nikifor's remark encapsulated their coping strategy amid the turmoil. His hopeful note about the impending end of the war and potential changes carried a dual sense of longing and dread. The prospect of change, while potentially harboring positive developments, also held the risk of further upheaval.

Their cautious conversation, held in hushed tones to avoid the prying ears of neighbors, was a daily reality in a city where distrust and fear of surveillance had become ingrained. Even the thin walls of their apartment seemed capable of carrying whispers into unwanted ears. The moonlight streaming through the reinforced windows served as a stark reminder of the city's scars from the bombings and the fragility of their security.

As George departed, the silent acknowledgement of imminent change hung heavily between father and son. The uncertainty of what these changes might bring — whether relief or further challenges — added to the already burdensome emotional landscape they navigated daily. George's heavy heart as he left the apartment was not just for the immediate struggles they faced but also for the unknown future that lay ahead for them all.

Outside, the night air of Moscow felt unusually still, as though the war-torn city itself was waiting — waiting for the fragile promise of peace to finally arrive.

Chapter 13

A Prophetic Encounter

In the early spring of 1945, as the war neared its end, Moscow remained gripped by the harshness of winter. Gray snow lingered along the streets, hardened into icy ridges where thousands of boots had passed. The biting cold and persistent hunger shaped the daily lives of its citizens. Food, scarce and rationed, was distributed via a card system, with each person's share determined by their registered address. Life under Stalin's regime was oppressive, with citizens treated more like state property than individuals. The court system functioned more as an extension of the state's repressive machinery than as a protector of rights.

In this environment, personal freedoms were non-existent, and private property was a concept relegated to the most personal of belongings. Apartments, kitchens, and even bathrooms were communal, and people's words were constantly monitored. Even casual conversations were guarded, spoken in lowered voices behind closed doors. The move from socialism to communism was marked by increased surveillance and control over every aspect of daily life.

George, amidst these trying conditions, regularly visited his parents by tramway. Nikifor, once a robust and hopeful man, had suffered a minor stroke, a physical manifestation of his disillusionment with the ideals he once fervently believed in. The toll of realizing the grim reality of the system he had once championed was evident in his now silver-white hair and the weariness in his intense blue eyes.

Late in the evening, with few passengers around, George traveled on the tramway, acutely aware of the pervasive danger. The tram rattled through the darkened streets, its interior dimly lit by a single flickering bulb. The *NKVD*, the feared state security organization, had unrestrained power to monitor and arrest citizens without due process. George's journey was laden with the fear and caution that had become second nature to him and his family.

As George approached his parents' rental in a dilapidated wooden house, his childhood fear of the dark resurfaced. The street was nearly deserted, the wind carrying faint echoes from distant factories. The eerie shadows cast by streetlights heightened his anxiety. Rounding the corner to the building, his steps quickened, driven by a mix of fear and urgency.

Knocking on the door, George was greeted by Ethelyn.

"Hi, Mom. How are you?" he asked, his voice carrying a mix of concern and relief.

"Hi, Georgie. We are managing. Come in quickly, it's cold outside."

Ethelyn's response, though simple, revealed the quiet exhaustion of a woman who had endured years of uncertainty. It served as yet another indicator of how the family was coping in these challenging times, at the cusp of a post-war world that held both the promise of change and the uncertainty of what that change might bring.

Another knock at the door suddenly echoed through the small room.

Everyone froze.

"Who could that be?" George whispered fearfully.

The unexpected visitor at the door in the dead of night brought a wave of fear and apprehension to the Yampolsky family. In those times, a knock could signify the dreaded arrival of the *NKVD*.

George's cautious query was met with the feeble voice of an old woman, a pitiful figure ravaged by the harsh realities of the war.

George, upon receiving a nod from Nikifor, hesitantly opened the door to find the old woman standing there, an embodiment of the suffering that had engulfed many lives in Moscow. Her clothes hung loosely from her frail frame, and snow clung to the hem of her worn coat. Homelessness and hunger were rampant in the city, with many like her roaming the outskirts in search of aid.

"Please, help me. My house burned down in the fire. My family is all gone. I am dying from hunger," she begged for anything to keep her afloat.

Her plea for help, born from desperation and loss, struck a chord of empathy in the family.

George, moved by her plight, quickly brought the last two pieces of bread from their table.

As he handed them to her, he silently uttered a prayer, invoking divine protection for the destitute woman.

"Lord Jesus, our Savior, please help this woman."

Her gratitude was palpable as she clutched the bread with trembling hands.

"Thank you… thank you, kind people," she murmured.

The room fell silent.

Then suddenly, the woman's tone shifted.

Her voice dropped to a hushed, almost mystical whisper.

"Your daughter will be born soon, and she will change your family's destiny. She will bring joy where there has been sorrow. The war will be almost over by then. After the war… in about eight years from now… there will be earth-shattering changes."

Her words hung in the air like an echo from another world.

With a deep bow and a chant-like mumble, she slowly disappeared into the night, vanishing as mysteriously as she had appeared.

Closing the door behind her, George, Nikifor, and Ethelyn stood silently for a moment.

Then together they whispered a prayer:

"Thank you, Lord. Amen."

Their simultaneous prayer of gratitude was a testament to their enduring faith amidst adversity.

The moment was interrupted by the sudden sound of Comrade Levitan's voice emanating from the radio.

His deep, commanding voice filled the room:

"The Soviet Army, together with coalition forces, is defeating fascism. Victory is near!"

After years of hardship, loss, and fear, the prospect of victory and the end of the war was a beacon of light in the dark tunnel of their struggles.

This news, combined with the mysterious woman's prophecy, left the Yampolsky family contemplating the future with a renewed sense of possibility and cautious optimism.

For the first time in many years, hope did not feel like a fragile illusion—but like something that might truly arrive.

Chapter 14

A Cycle of Joy and Sorrow

April 20th marked a transformative day in the lives of Sonya and George. That night, Sonya experienced a dream of profound symbolism — a radiant white dove descending gently toward her, carrying a small child in its wings, a dream that foretold the imminent arrival of their daughter. Her dream was abruptly interrupted by the onset of labor pains, plunging both her and George into a flurry of action and anxiety.

With no transportation available in the war-ravaged streets of Moscow and the maternity hospital reachable only on foot, Sonya and George embarked on the arduous journey. The streets were quiet and cold beneath the dim glow of streetlamps, the city still scarred by years of war. Sonya, enduring waves of intense pain, had to pause frequently, sitting on the sidewalk until she could muster the strength to continue. George, by her side, offered words of encouragement, trying to assuage her fears with assurances that everything would be alright and that they would soon be returning home with their baby.

Upon reaching the maternity hospital, a nurse in traditional white attire greeted them. After helping Sonya inside, she turned to George, informing him that he would have to wait outside.

"We will take care of your wife. Only medical staff and expectant mothers are allowed entry," the nurse told the anxious future father.

The doors closed behind Sonya, leaving George alone with his thoughts and anticipation.

Outside, the world slowly came to life as Muscovites began their daily routines. George observed the mix of people around him — civilians hurrying to work and military men, perhaps still processing their survival through the horrors of war, now carrying a semblance of giddy relief in these final days of conflict.

As George waited in front of the imposing structure of the maternity hospital, the early morning sun brought a long-awaited warmth. Pale sunlight crept across the hospital's stone façade, slowly dissolving the lingering chill of the night. The hospital, with its fortress-like appearance, stood as a stark reminder of the harsh realities outside its walls.

Finally, the wait ended with joyous news.

A nurse appeared at one of the small windows, calling out to George with the heartening announcement:

"George, you have a daughter. Your baby daughter and the mother are doing well!"

This proclamation brought a profound sense of relief and happiness to George. For a moment, the exhaustion of the war years seemed to lift from his shoulders. The birth of his daughter, a symbol of new life and hope, seemed to herald a new beginning for their family, a bright spot amid the surrounding turmoil.

The birth of Catherine was not just a personal milestone for Sonya and George but a beacon of hope in a time of immense hardship and uncertainty. As George stood outside the hospital, the realization of becoming a father in such challenging times was both daunting and uplifting, marking the start of a new chapter in their lives.

In a burst of elation, George hurried to his in-laws' home, eager to share the news of his daughter's birth. His announcement, brimming with joy, was a moment of celebration for the family. The following day, his heart swelled with emotion as he saw Sonya at the hospital window, cradling their newborn daughter, Catherine, wrapped in white fabric — a tiny bundle of life held gently against the glass, symbolizing hope and renewal amidst the backdrop of war.

May 1945 ushered in not only the brightness of spring but also the jubilation of Germany's capitulation and the end of the Second World War. Across Europe, people rejoiced in their newfound freedom, and Moscow was no exception. The city's heart, Red Square, became a hub of celebration, with the public gathering to sing and dance, reveling in the victory over fascism.

Crowds flooded the streets waving red banners, soldiers embraced strangers, and music echoed across the squares as church bells and factory sirens rang in unison.

Sonya, George, and baby Catherine returned to their home, now brimming with relatives and friends ready to celebrate. The table was laden with lend-lease food, including American beef stew and potato salad, centered around a bottle of vodka — a true feast in those times of scarcity. In Sonya's arms, Catherine slept peacefully, oblivious to the significance of the occasion.

The mood was elevated further when Raisa brought out a letter from Anatoly, Sonya's father, who was still on the battlefield. George read the letter aloud, its words conveying Anatoly's pride and congratulations on the birth of their daughter. His wishes for Catherine to find her place in life resonated with everyone in the room, moving many to tears.

However, the joyous atmosphere was abruptly interrupted by the sound of the doorbell.

Raisa, with a glimmer of hope, rushed to the door, perhaps expecting her son Lazar, who had been missing since the war.

Instead, she was greeted by a man in military uniform. Introducing himself as Sergey Ivanov, he asked quietly to speak with her.

The sudden appearance of a military officer, especially during such a time of celebration, brought an instant wave of anxiety. The laughter in the room faded instantly, replaced by a heavy silence.

"You have a letter from the military detachment where Lazar served. I am very sorry, but your son is missing in action," the young soldier said with sorrow in his voice.

The moment the military officer handed the letter to Raisa, the atmosphere in the room shifted from celebration to grief. The words *missing in action*, a phrase all too common during these tumultuous times, struck Raisa with an overwhelming sense of loss.

The page, bearing the stark, impersonal notification, became a symbol of the ultimate sacrifice made by countless families during the war. As Raisa grappled with the reality of never seeing her son Lazar again, her sorrow was palpable. The memories of Lazar, embodied in the portraits he left behind, became treasured remnants of a life cut short by the brutality of war.

His portrait of Raisa, a testament to his talent, now served as a poignant reminder of what had been lost — the youthful woman captured in the painting standing in painful contrast to the grieving mother before them.

"Oh, dear Raisa," cried Ethelyn, and the others surrounded her with the only thing they had to offer—their compassion and love.

Ethelyn's cry of consolation and the surrounding family's attempts to offer comfort highlighted the shared nature of their suffering. In times of war, grief was a collective experience, with each loss reverberating through the community.

"So much evil," Nikifor mumbled, and the other men nodded in agreement.

"And so much yet to come," George added quietly, knowing that Stalin, the communist dictator, had one goal: to keep the entire nation gripped by fear so that no one would dare challenge his rule.

Nikifor's somber reflection on the evil they had witnessed, and George's foreboding addition about the fear instilled by Stalin, underscored the broader context of their personal tragedy. The Stalinist regime, marked by terror and repression, had left a deep scar on the Soviet people.

The loss of Lazar was not just a personal tragedy for the Hazzan family; it was a stark reminder of the countless lives disrupted and destroyed by the war and the oppressive political climate. In this moment of profound sorrow, the family's unity in the face of adversity was a source of strength. Their ability to come together, to share in each other's pain and offer support, was a symbol of the resilience of the human spirit in the darkest of times. Outside, Moscow celebrated victory. Inside the small apartment, the war had claimed yet another quiet casualty.

Chapter 15

A Journey from Blossoms to Frost

As the seasons turned, Catherine's presence brought a glimmer of joy to her parents amidst the continued challenges of post-war life. The autumn, with its vibrant colors and crisp air, offered a temporary escape from the harsh realities they faced. Catherine, now beginning to toddle uncertainly along the pathways of Moscow's small parks, delighted in reaching for the falling leaves that drifted gently from the trees. Her tiny hands grasped at the air, chasing the golden leaves as they spiraled downward, becoming a source of light and happiness for Sonya and George.

Their living conditions, however, remained difficult. They had moved to a small, dimly lit room that, while quiet, was inadequately heated. The communal living arrangements were far from ideal, with one bathroom shared among twenty tenants and a kitchen that was a constant battleground for space and resources. The narrow corridors of the building carried the constant echo of footsteps, whispered arguments, and the clatter of pots from the overcrowded kitchen.

Despite these challenges, the family tried to make the room their own. Sonya and George brought in what few furnishings they could gather, including a cherished gramophone and a typewriter, their most treasured possessions, symbols of their aspirations and pastimes. In the evenings, when electricity flickered weakly through the single hanging bulb, the gramophone would sometimes fill the small room with faint music — a fragile reminder of a more hopeful world beyond their walls.

George's dream of working for a publishing house remained unfulfilled, as everyday survival took precedence. The scarcity of necessities was a constant struggle. Grocery stores offered limited choices, often just basic items like soap and herring. Sonya's daily excursions to the *gastronome*, a local supermarket, were a testament to her determination to provide for her family, even if it meant standing in long lines for meager offerings of meat or vegetables. Often, she would stand for hours in the cold, clutching her ration card, uncertain whether anything would remain by the time she reached the counter.

Sonya's efforts in the kitchen, despite the limited resources and communal tensions, were a labor of love. She endeavored to prove her culinary skills to George, but the lack of variety in ingredients and the crowded conditions of the shared kitchen made cooking a challenging and often disheartening task. The smell of boiled cabbage and burnt porridge lingered constantly in the air, mixing with the sharp odor of kerosene from the stoves.

In these trying times, Sonya and George's resilience and love for each other and for Catherine shone through. They faced each day with a determination to make the best of their situation, finding solace in small joys and in the hope that better days were ahead. Catherine, oblivious to the hardships around her, continued to be a beacon of joy and a reminder of the simple pleasures of life.

Her laughter, bright and spontaneous, sometimes echoed through the narrow stairwell, startling the weary neighbors who had long forgotten such sounds of innocence.

In the post-war landscape of Moscow, life was a daily battle for survival, with the city becoming a magnet for those in search of better opportunities. The influx of people from the suburbs, each day vying for scarce resources, exemplified the struggle faced by ordinary citizens. Long hours spent in queues for necessities became a common sight, with the fortunate few managing to secure enough to get by.

Lines formed before dawn outside bakeries and shops, silent rows of people wrapped in worn coats, each hoping that the supplies would not run out before their turn arrived.

The political climate under Stalin's regime only compounded these hardships. The pervasive fear of repression, with the KGB and *militsiya* exerting tight control over the populace, left many living in a state of constant anxiety. The possibility of midnight arrests and the need to keep belongings ready for a quick departure were grim realities of the time.

Many families slept lightly, always listening for the sound of heavy footsteps on the stairwell — the sound that so often preceded a knock in the night.

Amidst this challenging environment, George's health deteriorated. The development of tuberculosis, a disease rampant in the stressful and unhygienic conditions of post-war Moscow, was a severe blow. Natalie, his elder sister, also struggled with her health, battling asthma and symptoms akin to tuberculosis. Their illnesses further isolated them from family and loved ones, adding layers of emotional distress to their physical suffering.

Sonya, while trying to care for her husband and daughter, found herself grappling with the additional challenge of keeping George isolated to prevent the spread of his illness. Even within the small room, distance became necessary — a heartbreaking separation measured only in a few steps. The separation within their own home added a poignant layer of frustration and sadness to their already difficult lives.

In these dire circumstances, the introduction of penicillin, a groundbreaking medical discovery, offered a glimmer of hope. This new drug, although not easily accessible, provided a lifeline for many like George and Natalie, battling life-threatening conditions. Whispers about the miraculous medicine spread quietly among doctors and patients alike, and for families it carried the fragile promise that survival might still be possible.

Their survival, against the backdrop of such adversity, was a testament to the crucial role of emerging medical treatments.

The Yampolsky family's experience during this time was reflective of the broader struggle faced by countless Soviet citizens. Amidst political oppression, economic hardship, and the lingering effects of a devastating war, their story was one of endurance and hope.

Yet beneath the quiet determination of their daily lives lay an unspoken truth: the long winter of fear that had settled over the Soviet Union was far from over.

Chapter 16

Light in the Depth of Turmoil

The year 1946 marked a harrowing period in Soviet history, characterized by a fresh wave of arrests and detentions. Although the war had ended, the shadow of fear across the Soviet Union had only deepened. This time, the crackdown extended beyond Soviet citizens, ensnaring foreigners as well. The notorious nature of these imprisonments was heightened by the abduction of individuals from foreign streets for show trials in Moscow, reflecting the far-reaching and ruthless nature of Stalin's regime.

In the post-war period, the sight of soldiers returning from the front, many severely disabled and forced to beg on the streets of Moscow, was a stark and heartbreaking reminder of the war's devastating toll on the Soviet people. Along the city's boulevards and near railway stations, wounded veterans gathered in silence, their uniforms worn and their faces hollow with exhaustion. Many of them moved on makeshift wooden platforms mounted on small wheels because their legs had been amputated in battle. They pushed themselves slowly across the cold pavement with their hands, their metal cups rattling softly as they asked passersby for coins or bread.

These wounded men, once hailed as heroes, soon became an uncomfortable sight for the authorities. In a chilling display of cruelty, Stalin ordered these disabled veterans to be rounded up and removed from Moscow. They were deported to remote places such as the *Valaam and Solovetsky Islands,* where many faced almost certain death due to harsh conditions, hunger, and the complete absence of medical care. Within weeks, the familiar figures that had once lined the streets of Moscow vanished, as if they had never existed.

Stalin's order to exterminate "enemies of the people"—and even their families—deepened the terror that gripped Soviet society. Every citizen knew that a careless word, a jealous neighbor, or a single anonymous accusation could destroy an entire family overnight. Meanwhile, Communist Party members enjoyed a relatively privileged existence with access to better apartments, improved food rations, and rare vacation opportunities. Yet even these elites lived in constant fear of arbitrary arrest and persecution, as no one was truly safe from the regime's unpredictable and merciless power.

Amid the fear that surrounded them, George and Sonya experienced a moment of unexpected joy when they adopted their niece, Maria, after her mother tragically died in childbirth. They welcomed the fragile child into their family as their own, wrapping her carefully in blankets and carrying her into their already crowded home.

Her arrival brought new warmth into their small apartment, and she soon became a sister to Catherine. The two girls, unaware of the grim realities unfolding around them, found happiness in each other's company. They spent their days chasing each other through the narrow corridor, whispering secrets, and inventing games in the small corners of the communal courtyard. Their laughter, bright and spontaneous, sometimes echoed through the stairwell, offering a rare reminder that innocence could still exist even in the darkest of times.

Life in their communal apartment was difficult. Shared kitchens and bathrooms, thin walls, and constant proximity bred suspicion and quiet despair among the tenants. Conversations were whispered, doors were closed carefully, and neighbors watched one another with guarded eyes. In such places, trust was rare and silence was often the safest protection.

The bathroom, with its crude provisions and the ever-present risk of being accused over something as trivial as a missing roll of toilet paper, was a daily reminder that privacy did not exist. Even the smallest disagreements could quickly escalate into dangerous accusations.

Sonya understood that childhood innocence would not protect her daughters forever. As she watched Catherine and Maria playing together on the worn wooden floor, a quiet worry lingered in her heart. Sooner or later, they would face the same world she did—a world of fear, scarcity, and careful silence, where survival required vigilance and happiness rarely lasted.

Yet in the fragile glow of the small lamp that lit their room each evening, Sonya held onto a single quiet hope—that somehow, against all odds, her daughters might grow up in a world kinder than the one she had known.

Chapter 17

The Unseen Grip of Fear

The summer of 1948 in Moscow brought with it not only the warmth and greenery of the season but also the palpable tension of a city living under the tightening grip of Stalin's regime. Sonya, seizing a rare moment of calm, took her daughters, Catherine and Maria, to a nearby park. As she sat on a wooden bench reading while the children played nearby, the serenity of the park—with its quiet pond, swaying willow trees, and gentle rustling of leaves—offered a brief respite from the hardships of their daily life.

Children's laughter floated across the grass, and for a short while the world seemed almost ordinary. Catherine and Maria chased each other along the gravel paths, their small shoes scattering dust as they ran. Dragonflies skimmed the surface of the pond, and the warm air carried the faint scent of summer flowers. For Sonya, these peaceful moments felt fragile but precious. However, this tranquil interlude was short-lived.

As they were leaving the park, Sonya and her daughters suddenly witnessed a disturbing incident that shattered their momentary calm. Near the central telegraph tower, a man was abruptly seized by three individuals dressed in civilian clothes. The men moved with frightening efficiency. One grabbed the man's arms, another forced his head down, while the third opened the door of a dark automobile waiting at the curb. Within seconds, the man was shoved inside the vehicle.

The car door slammed shut with a sharp metallic echo, and the vehicle sped away before anyone nearby could react.

The entire scene unfolded in plain view, yet no one intervened. People walking along the street quickly lowered their eyes and continued on their way, pretending they had seen nothing. Such silent obedience had become a survival instinct in Stalin's Soviet Union.

Catherine's reaction to the event was immediate. Her small body stiffened with fear before she burst into tears, clutching tightly at her mother's dress. Maria, frightened by her sister's panic and sensing the danger in the adults' silence, also began to sob.

The children's cries pierced the heavy stillness of the moment.

Sonya herself stood frozen for a second, her heart pounding as she realized what they had just witnessed. Scenes like this were whispered about constantly—but seeing it unfold before her own eyes was something else entirely. Quickly regaining her composure, she gathered the girls into her arms and hurried them away from the street. Her only response was a whispered prayer.

"Lord, protect us," she murmured under her breath as she walked quickly, urging the girls to stay close beside her.

The incident became even more terrifying when Sonya later learned that the man who had been taken was their neighbor—a man they knew personally and who had once shared friendly conversations in the courtyard. The news spread quietly among the residents of their building, each tenant speaking in cautious whispers behind closed doors. The arrest brought the terror even closer to home.

It served as a grim reminder that no one was safe from the secret services' arbitrary and ruthless actions. A friendly neighbor could vanish overnight. A colleague might suddenly stop coming to work. Entire families sometimes disappeared without explanation.

This climate of fear and uncertainty permeated every aspect of life in Stalin's Soviet Union. Neighbors watched one another carefully. Conversations were measured and cautious. Even children were sometimes warned not to repeat anything they heard at home. For Sonya and her family, these events underscored the precariousness of their existence. The constant threat of arrest and the pervasive atmosphere of suspicion and paranoia were a daily reality, casting a shadow over their lives.

They had learned to live quietly, to avoid attention, and to trust only those closest to them.

Yet even in the quiet of their small apartment that evening, as Catherine and Maria slept peacefully, Sonya could not forget the sound of the car door slamming shut—an echo of the unseen grip of fear that ruled their world.

Chapter 18

Last Quest

In a desperate effort to resolve the long-standing issue of their confiscated American passports, Nikifor, now in his late sixties, made the bold decision to approach the Soviet Ministry of Foreign Affairs directly. For years he had carried this burden in silence, but time was slipping away, and the thought of leaving his family trapped in the Soviet system weighed heavily on him. He was driven by urgency and a quiet determination to free his family from the regime's hold. Despite his fear and the risks involved, he knew he had to exhaust every possible avenue to reclaim their passports and secure a better future for those he loved.

As Nikifor approached the Ministry building, he slowed his pace. The structure rose above him, massive and severe, its stone façade darkened by time. The tall windows reflected the pale Moscow sky like cold mirrors. He felt suddenly small beneath it. Somewhere inside, his family's fate would be decided.

At the entrance, a *militsioner* blocked his way. Nikifor forced a polite smile and handed over his Soviet passport. His hands trembled despite his effort to steady them. The officer examined the document in silence, his expression unreadable. Nikifor stood motionless, waiting.

After what felt like a long time, another man appeared, dressed in civilian clothes. He spoke quietly and motioned for Nikifor to follow.

Inside, a long red runner stretched down the corridor. Officials passed without looking at him, their footsteps muted against the carpet. No one spoke. The silence inside the building felt heavy and deliberate, as though every movement was being watched. Nikifor walked behind the man, deeper into the building, each step carrying him farther from the life he had known.

The corridors seemed endless. Doors lined the walls, all closed. Everything moved with quiet precision, as if nothing here were accidental. Each step reminded him of the risk he was taking. Reclaiming their American passports was more than a bureaucratic matter. It was the final hope he carried for his family—the last thread tying them to the life they had once known.

The man escorting him stopped at a wide door with a brass nameplate: Comrade I. I. Alexeev. He knocked lightly, then opened the door and motioned Nikifor inside.

Nikifor stepped into the office of Ivan Alexeev, gripped by both fear and resolve. The room was austere. Behind the desk hung a large portrait of Stalin, his gaze inescapable. The dictator's dark eyes seemed to follow every movement in the room. It was a stark reminder of the power that ruled their lives—and how easily his fate could be decided here.

Will this mission be the end of me? Nikifor thought to himself. *Should I have spared myself the humiliation and the punishment?*

"Hello, Citizen Yampolsky," the official addressed Nikifor while looking through a black leather folder filled with documents. "What brought you here, Comrade Nikifor?"

Despite the overwhelming anxiety pressing against his chest, Nikifor found the strength to speak.

"Comrade Alexeev, I want to know what happened to my family's American passports. We were told by the State Department before leaving for the Soviet Union that we could keep our passports and travel freely. My wife, Ethelyn Gertrude White, is an American, and she wishes to return home along with our children."

Nikifor spoke in a hushed tone.

His plea to Comrade Alexeev was his last chance to reclaim their American passports—the only proof of the life that had been taken from them, and perhaps the only path back. His voice faltered at first, weakened by fear, but it steadied as he spoke of the assurances they had received from the U.S. State Department before their departure.

Insisting on their right to return to America—especially for his wife, Ethelyn—was a dangerous step in a place where such requests could carry consequences.

"Our identities were changed without our consent," he continued quietly. "New Soviet passports were issued to us under unfamiliar names. Please… let us return to our homeland."

Alexeev's reaction was difficult to read. For a moment, he said nothing. The room fell into an uneasy silence broken only by the faint rustle of papers on the desk. Something in his expression shifted, and Nikifor allowed himself the faintest trace of hope.

He stood there, an aging man with little left but his resolve, asking not only for the return of their passports, but for the restoration of their names—and the life they had lost.

What would happen next was uncertain. But he knew he could not remain silent any longer.

Then the official cut him short.

"Congratulations," he said coldly. "Your family now has Soviet passports. You will help build socialism."

Nikifor stood frozen. The words did not seem real. For a moment the room seemed to tilt around him, as if the ground beneath his feet had shifted.

He murmured, "Thank you," though he did not recognize his own voice.

He turned and walked toward the door.

He opened the heavy door and stepped into the corridor, trying to steady himself. A dull pressure throbbed in his temples. He moved slowly down the staircase, one hand trailing along the wall for support. The red carpet beneath his feet blurred before his eyes.

His only thought was to get home.

Outside, the summer light was blinding.

He stepped onto the pavement and looked up at the sky, as if searching for something beyond reach. For a moment the noise of the street faded, and the world around him seemed strangely distant. His face drained of color. Then he fell. People gathered, but it was already too late.

Nikifor lay on the pavement before the Ministry building—the place where his last hope had ended. The building stood above him, silent and indifferent, its stone walls unmoved by the life that had just slipped away beneath them. He would never see his home again.

When Nikifor's body was taken to the morgue, his personal belongings were returned without ceremony. His papers, folded and impersonal, were handed to his widow, Ethelyn.

He was buried several days later.

At the graveside, a Russian Orthodox priest spoke softly of eternal peace and the soul's journey beyond suffering. His quiet prayers rose into the cool air, mingling with the distant sounds of the city.

Dressed in black, his family and friends stood in silence. One by one, they stepped forward and cast a handful of earth onto the coffin.

The sound of soil striking wood was final. Ethelyn did not move for a long time.

Nikifor had given everything he could for his family. Now they were left to go on without him.

And the hope he had carried into that building—the hope of returning home—was buried with him.

Chapter 19

The Perpetual Wanderers

The death of Nikifor left Ethelyn enveloped in a profound sense of loss and isolation. The man who had once been her companion, her protector, and her link to hope was suddenly gone. Her grief manifested in increased seclusion and introspection, as she struggled to comprehend the harsh reality of life without her partner. The sorrow of her situation was compounded by the ongoing uncertainty and instability that marked their lives in the Soviet Union.

In the aftermath of Nikifor's funeral, Ethelyn, accompanied by her daughter Eleanor and grandson Eugene, embarked on a nomadic existence, constantly moving from one residence to another in the outskirts of Moscow. Their life became a quiet migration through forgotten neighborhoods and decaying houses. This continual relocation to the suburbs of Moscow was a strategy to evade the ever-watchful eyes of the *militsiya*. Their frequent moves, carrying their few possessions—including their treasured piano—became a routine born out of necessity for survival.

The piano, a cherished link to their past life in Rochester, New York, held special significance for Ethelyn and her family. It was not just a musical instrument but a symbol of happier times and a connection to their American roots. Whenever its lid was opened, the faint scent of polished wood seemed to carry memories from another world—one of warm living rooms, familiar voices, and a life that had once felt secure. The presence of the piano, with its beautiful reddish-brown polish, helped recreate a fragile semblance of the comfort and elegance they once enjoyed. It was a piece of their old world, a reminder of their identity and heritage amidst the turmoil and displacement they faced.

Eleanor, sharing her mother's musical talent, found solace in playing the piano and singing, offering brief moments of joy and normalcy in their otherwise challenging lives. On quiet evenings, the soft sound of music would drift through the small wooden houses of the neighborhood, startling neighbors who were unaccustomed to hearing such melodies in a place ruled by fear and hardship. The family's attachment to their personal belongings—such as the piano, the round table, and the threadbare sofa, along with treasured napkins and silverware—was a testament to their resilience and their determination to preserve their sense of self.

The places they moved to, often dilapidated summer houses on the outskirts of the city, were far from ideal. Many of the houses leaned slightly from age and neglect, their wooden walls warped by years of harsh winters. Yet Eleanor's efforts to make each new residence clean and welcoming reflected their enduring spirit and the importance of maintaining dignity and hope in the face of adversity. Despite the bleakness of their surroundings, they clung to their faith and to each other, finding strength in their family bond and their memories of a life once lived.

For Ethelyn, the ordeal transformed her physically and emotionally. Her hair turned completely white, and her actions—such as her repetitive pacing and constant cleaning—became outward expressions of her deep-seated anxiety and her unyielding hope for a safer future. Often, she would walk slowly from one corner of the room to the other, as if searching for something she had lost and could not recover. The family's current abode, sandwiched between industrial workshops and lit by dim streetlights, might have appeared barely livable to others, but for Ethelyn and her family it was a refuge—a place where they could at least attempt to hold onto fragments of their past and the faint glimmer of hope for a better tomorrow.

Eleanor's daily journey through the foreboding forest and the desolate streets to and from work epitomized the pervasive sense of danger and fear that characterized life in the Soviet Union during Stalin's reign. The narrow dirt paths she walked were often empty, swallowed by shadows from the surrounding trees. The empty, darkened roads were a constant reminder of the risks ordinary citizens faced every day. The solitude and vulnerability she experienced on these treks symbolized the broader isolation and anxiety that permeated Soviet society at the time.

The ever-present sounds of the nearby railway station and the relentless broadcasting of Soviet propaganda added to the oppressive atmosphere. Stalin's speeches, a constant reminder of the regime's tight control, echoed through the streets, reinforcing the state's presence in every aspect of life. Loudspeakers mounted on poles crackled to life at regular intervals, their metallic voices cutting through the quiet of the evening. The broadcasts, coupled with the playing of popular Soviet songs, created a surreal juxtaposition of forced celebration and omnipresent state surveillance.

The newspapers in the Soviet Union served as yet another instrument of the state's propaganda machine. Front-page articles about trials and the exposure of so-called political enemies fed into the culture of fear and suspicion. These media reports dehumanized the accused, labeling them as "deplorables"—spies, enemies, saboteurs—and justified their harsh punishments, whether execution or exile to the *gulag*[5]. The use of these terms in state propaganda was a deliberate effort to instill paranoia and validate the government's repressive actions.

The gulag system, with its forced labor camps and unbearable conditions—particularly in the brutal Siberian mines—was a grim reality for countless people. Stories about prisoners freezing in the snow or collapsing from exhaustion circulated quietly among the population, whispered only behind closed doors. The inhumane treatment of prisoners and the extreme cold they endured were emblematic of the cruelty and heartlessness of the regime. This system of forced labor and punishment revealed the true despotism of communism, leaving no doubt about the regime's disregard for human life and dignity.

For Eleanor, Ethelyn, and their family—as well as for the entire Soviet populace—life was a constant struggle against an all-encompassing state apparatus that sought to control and suppress. Despite the pervasive dread and oppression, people clung to a faint hope for a better future.

And so, the Yampolsky family continued to move from place to place, carrying their few possessions—and the quiet hope that somewhere beyond the shadows of fear, a different life might still be waiting for them.

Chapter 20

Satin Blue Slippers

Catherine's journey home from her ballet class through the icy, wind-swept streets of Moscow vividly illustrated the challenging conditions that children in the post-war Soviet Union often faced. She was rather small for her age of five, but sturdy. Wrapped in a white woolen hat and a thin coat far too light for the biting winter air, she carefully maneuvered between patches of ice and slush. From a distance she might have looked like a small bundle of cloth waddling through the snow, stubbornly pushing forward against the cold wind.

Her little legs moved quickly as her hands searched for an opening in her garments, a tiny place where she could tuck her fingers to protect them from the freezing air. She carried a bulky bag nearly as large as herself, and her small, resilient figure swayed with every strong gust of wind that swept down the street. As Catherine approached the apartment building, her little legs moved even faster, her breath rising in small clouds of frost, battling the sharp cold of the Moscow winter.

The building itself bore the scars of wartime artillery fire, yet it still stood solidly, its thick walls weathered but enduring. Dark marks from shrapnel pocked the façade like silent reminders of the war that had only recently ended. The intermittently functioning elevator and the missing chair in the entrance hall were small but telling details, reflecting the constant compromises and adjustments that were part of everyday life in such communal living spaces.

The elevator seemed to be working this afternoon. Catherine stood still for a moment, trying to catch her breath and warm herself before her frozen little hands could emerge from the bundle of clothing that protected her from the cold. While she strained to reach the button for the third floor, she could feel the squishy snow seeping into her beaten-down shoes. The cold water crept slowly through the thin soles, sending a shiver up her legs. Seeing no neighbors nearby, she decided it would be faster to climb the stairs.

Catherine's struggle to reach the elevator button and her quick decision to take the stairs instead revealed her quiet resourcefulness—an adaptability shaped by the demanding circumstances of her upbringing.

She climbed quickly to her floor and used her keys to get inside. The door handle to her family's home was more accessible than the elevator button, yet it posed its own challenge as her small hands slipped repeatedly from the cold metal. But at last, the handle turned under her determined grip, and she pushed the door open.

She was home. With relief, she happily kicked off her dirty winter felt boots and left them at the front entrance. Her arrival at home—shedding her layers of cold, damp clothing and tiptoeing quietly through the room—revealed a child already wise beyond her years. She knew how to move carefully so as not to disturb her father, who sat deeply absorbed in his translation work.

George, her father, was immersed in his intellectual pursuits even in their modest living conditions. Papers covered the small desk near the window, and the faint smell of ink and old books filled the room. Though small, the room served as a sanctuary for the family—a place of warmth, peace, and relative comfort compared to the harsher realities of the communal flat.

Catherine began a silent game, sliding across the wooden floor as if she were skating on invisible ice, until she reached her father's chair. These small playful moments were reminders that even in difficult circumstances, childhood joy could still exist. George looked up from his work.

"Catherine! Are you ready for your English class?" he asked at just the right moment.

With a few careful hops, she climbed onto his warm but bony knee.

"Papa, can you tell me about the shoe store? Do they have beautiful slippers in America?" she asked, wiggling her cold toes. She sensed that time and repetition had softened the clarity of his memories, yet the stories about America remained her favorite.

Catherine's question about the shoe store was more than a child's curiosity. To her, America existed like a magical place—somewhere beyond the gray streets of Moscow, filled with colors and wonders she could only imagine.

"After your class is over, I will tell you another story from years past," he promised gently.

As George indulged his daughter with stories from another lifetime, it was evident that these memories were bittersweet for him. They were reminders of a past filled with promise—but also of what they had lost and left behind.

Yet for Catherine, these stories were magical.

Her innocent question about slippers in America was not simply about shoes—it was about the mystery and wonder of a world she had never seen. In her imagination, those slippers were delicate, shining, and soft, nothing like the worn boots she had just removed at the door.

The moment Catherine stood by the window, gazing out at the gray Moscow evening, was quietly poignant. Beyond the frost-covered glass, the streetlights flickered to life, casting pale circles of light onto the snow-covered pavement.

In her mind, she imagined herself wearing beautiful satin blue slippers.

In her imagination, she danced across bright wooden floors, far away from the cold streets and worn staircases of the communal building.

For George, sharing these stories was more than storytelling. It was a way of connecting Catherine to their family's past and preserving the memory of their American heritage. In a world that tried to erase their former lives, these quiet conversations kept their history alive.

Through these stories, he gave Catherine something precious—a sense that her life was part of something larger, a story that began long before the gray streets of Moscow.

And in Catherine's young imagination, those satin blue slippers shimmered like a promise of a different future.

Chapter 21

Blueprint for Escape

George's new job as an English teacher at an adult school represented a glimmer of stability and hope in the otherwise challenging daily life of his family. The ability to earn a slightly better income provided a small measure of security, crucial in a world where every day was a struggle for necessities.

However, the hardships of their life in post-war Moscow were still palpable. George's early morning routine was a daily battle against the harsh elements and a reminder of the family's ongoing struggle for survival. Before dawn each morning, he rose quietly in the dim light of the small apartment, careful not to wake the others. The cluttered room, filled with boxes of books and photographs from their life in America, served as a constant, melancholic reminder of a past that seemed both unreachable and deeply missed.

The presence of these boxes, while a source of quiet sadness for George, also symbolized the family's refusal to let go of their history and identity. These tangible fragments of their past life were not merely objects, but carriers of memories and a life once lived—holding the fragile promise that someday they might reclaim a part of what had been taken from them.

The innocence and adaptability of Catherine and Maria, happily playing in the corridor despite the grim surroundings and the neighbors' frequent quarrels, highlighted the resilience of children. Their laughter echoed down the narrow hallway, momentarily softening the harshness of the communal building. Their ability to find joy and normalcy in the simplest things stood in stark contrast to the worries and burdens carried by the adults around them.

George struggled each morning, battling coughs and shivering in the cold as he prepared to face another day. The lingering weakness in his lungs made every breath feel heavier in the bitter winter air. Circumstances were taking a heavy toll on his health and well-being. Yet despite this, his mind increasingly turned toward one urgent thought: escape.

He began to consider seeking help in the more westernized Soviet republics—the Baltic regions—where contact with foreigners was slightly more common and where, perhaps, some opportunity might emerge. The idea was dangerous, uncertain, and fragile, yet it was the only direction that seemed to offer even the faintest possibility of change. Like many others trapped within the Soviet system, George quietly nurtured the hope of finding a better life somewhere beyond the suffocating reach of Moscow.

In this environment of austerity and repression, George's continued perseverance demonstrated the remarkable capacity of the human spirit to adapt and endure.

One bitter morning on his way to work, George witnessed a disturbing scene at the tramway stop. It was a stark reminder of the brutal environment in which they lived. Two militsiya officers were dragging a man across the snow-covered pavement. The man struggled weakly, his coat torn and his face already bloodied. A small crowd stood nearby, silent and motionless. No one intervened.

The presence of the militsiya and their violent treatment of the civilian underscored the constant threat of arbitrary violence and persecution that hovered over every citizen. The man's blood stained the white snow, spreading slowly like dark ink across the frozen ground. It was not merely an act of violence—it was a warning to everyone watching.

George instinctively reached for his passport inside his coat pocket the moment he saw the militsiya. His fingers closed tightly around the small booklet, as if it were the only protection he possessed. Over the years, the habit had become automatic, driven by an ingrained fear and the instinct for self-preservation. The passport was more than a document. It was a fragile shield. A thin barrier between freedom and disappearance.

Just then, the tram arrived with a screech of metal against the rails. The sudden movement of passengers pushing toward the doors created a momentary distraction. George seized the opportunity. He stepped quickly onto the tram and managed to find an empty seat by the window. As the tram lurched forward, leaving the violent scene behind, he wiped the sweat from his brow. Despite the freezing air, his hands trembled. His heart was still racing—not from the cold, but from the realization of how close danger lived to every ordinary moment.

Outside the tram window, Moscow moved past in a blur of gray buildings, snow, and silent pedestrians. George stared ahead, deep in thought. He now understood something with painful clarity. Their situation was no longer sustainable. The dangers surrounding them were no longer distant possibilities—they were immediate and real. At any moment the same fate he had just witnessed could fall upon any one of them. This moment became a turning point for George. His resolve hardened. He would have to find a way out. Not tomorrow. Not someday. But soon.

For George, devising a plan for escape was no longer simply about leaving the Soviet Union. It was about something deeper: preserving the dignity of his family, protecting the future of his daughters, and keeping alive the fragile hope that somewhere beyond the gray horizon of Moscow, freedom might still exist.

Chapter 22

A Bridge Between Two Worlds

George, driven by a blend of hope and desperation, sought solace and support through the Baltic's Catholic network. For months the idea had quietly taken shape in his mind, growing stronger each day as life in Moscow became more unbearable.

The historical and cultural richness of Riga, with its blend of architectural styles and its significance as a Baltic hub, was overshadowed in his mind by the critical nature of his mission. To George, Riga was no longer simply a city—it had become a fragile doorway to possibility. The city's reputation for maintaining ties with the Catholic clergy provided a glimmer of hope in what seemed an increasingly desperate situation.

In the heart of the Soviet Union, the Baltics stood as a crossroads, welcoming citizens who yearned to explore Latvia, Lithuania, and Estonia. The region's Catholic heritage fostered a unique connection, bridging the gap between foreign clergy and local parishes, even amidst the constraints of the Soviet era. For people like George, these quiet networks represented something rare and precious: a faint channel of communication with the outside world.

George's quest was shrouded in secrecy; not even a whisper of his true destination reached the ears of those around him. The fewer people who knew, the safer his family would be. Earning a modest livelihood as a school educator and an English tutor, George navigated the delicate balance of private tutoring in a society where such practices—particularly in foreign languages—were viewed with suspicion. Yet his discreet and careful approach allowed him to remain largely unnoticed.

To Sonya, his beloved wife, George told a simple story—a routine visit to his friend David Bell, who lived in a provincial town far from Moscow's watchful eyes. The lie weighed heavily on him, yet he knew it was necessary. If the truth were discovered, the consequences for his family could be devastating.

Only to his elder sister Natalie, his trusted confidant and guide, did he reveal the truth. Her wisdom and quiet courage became the guiding light that pushed him forward.

"The beauty of the place will captivate you," Natalie assured him with a knowing smile.

But beneath her gentle words was a deeper understanding: this journey was far more than a visit. It was a risk that could change their family's destiny.

Amidst the bustling crowd at the train station, George's heart raced with nervous anticipation. The station hall was filled with the sound of footsteps, the rumble of luggage, and the distant echoes of announcements. Heavy winter coats brushed past one another as travelers hurried toward their platforms.

He made his way to the platform where the Riga-bound train awaited, its passengers queuing with suitcases and parcels in hand. The sharp whistle of the locomotive pierced the cold air, signaling departure.

Settling into his window seat, George welcomed the solitude. He avoided conversation with fellow travelers, pretending to sleep as the train began its steady rhythm along the rails. The clatter of wheels against the tracks created a hypnotic sound that filled the carriage.

Outside the window, the darkening landscape slowly unfolded. Quaint villages and endless stretches of snow-covered forests drifted past like scenes from a distant dream.

As the train moved deeper into the Baltic countryside, George climbed into the upper berth, grateful for the privacy it offered. Wrapped in his coat, he stared at the dim ceiling of the carriage for a long time before closing his eyes. His thoughts drifted to his family. To Sonya. To Catherine. To the fragile future he hoped to secure for them.

Eventually, exhaustion overtook him, and he slipped into a deep sleep—one he desperately needed for the long journey ahead.

When the train finally pulled into Riga, the crisp Baltic air greeted him as he stepped onto the platform. The setting sun cast long shadows across the station, painting the sky in soft shades of amber and gray. Gathering his briefcase, George joined the quiet stream of passengers exiting the station, stepping into the streets of the Latvian capital.

"Central Hotel," he instructed the taxi driver, his voice calm though his thoughts were racing.

George's first impressions of Riga were striking. The city carried an air of quiet elegance. Streets lined with graceful art nouveau buildings and fragments of medieval architecture stood in contrast to the rigid Soviet structures he had grown accustomed to in Moscow.

Tall spires pierced the evening sky, and the narrow cobblestone streets seemed to whisper stories from centuries past.

Yet beneath this beauty, George sensed something else—a subtle tension that reminded him he was still within the borders of the Soviet Union. For him, Riga was not simply a destination. It was the beginning of something far more dangerous—and perhaps far more hopeful.

***

This hotel in Riga was a respectable choice, offering anonymity and a central location. For a man traveling quietly and asking delicate questions, anonymity was a form of protection. As George arrived at his destination and checked into his room, he couldn't help but feel a wave of nostalgia, a strange mixture of comfort and melancholy washing over him, a stark contrast to the oppressive atmosphere he had left behind in Moscow. Situated in the heart of Riga, the hotel offered a splendid view of the city's Gothic-style architecture and cobblestone streets. Church spires pierced the pale winter sky, and narrow streets wound between ancient buildings that seemed untouched by the heavy hand of Soviet uniformity. The medieval charm left George quietly awe inspired.

His room, spacious with lofty ceilings, was tastefully appointed. A comfortable sofa adorned with vibrant tapestry, a well-appointed desk by the window, and a chair completed the ensemble. Soft afternoon light filtered through tall windows, illuminating the room with a warmth he had not felt in years. George could not believe that the bathroom boasted both hot and cold water, with plush white towels hanging from gleaming metal rails. Such small luxuries, almost unimaginable in Moscow, suddenly reminded him of the normal life he once knew.

The freedom and relative normalcy of life in Riga were both comforting and jarring. For a moment, he felt as if he had stepped into another country entirely—a place where breathing seemed easier and the walls did not listen.

After settling into his room, George planned his next steps. His priority was to contact the local Catholic clergy, hoping they could help or, at the very least, provide some guidance on how to proceed. He knew the risks involved in seeking help from foreign entities, but the potential rewards outweighed them. This was a long shot, but desperate times called for desperate measures. The thought of his wife and daughters strengthened his resolve. Failure was not an option.

That evening, George walked the streets of Riga, contemplating the city's complex history and its current role as a Soviet state with a distinctly different cultural and religious background. Lanterns flickered along the narrow streets, and the sound of distant church bells drifted softly through the cold evening air. The city seemed to be a bridge between two worlds, and George felt like he was standing on that precipice, searching for a path to a better future.

The next morning George hailed a cab and the taxi driver inquired, "Are you here to explore the enchanting sights of Riga?"

With a subtle nod, George acknowledged, and the driver proceeded to introduce him to the city's landmarks. The experience evoked a desire in George to linger in this captivating place. Every street corner seemed filled with history, every façade whispering stories from another century. However, his immediate concern was to seek assistance.

"Could you please direct me to a Catholic church nearby?" he inquired. To preempt further queries, he added, "A friend suggested I visit a local Catholic church." The taxi driver promptly gave him walking directions to the St. James's Cathedral and dropped him off in the city center.

The snow had already begun to fall, creating a serene winter landscape. Large, silent flakes drifted gently through the air, settling on rooftops and cobblestones like a soft white veil. He made his way to the St. James's Cathedral, also known as the Metropolitan Cathedral of Saint James the Greater. For a moment, he stood in admiration of its architectural grandeur, feeling a sense of transcendence. The towering structure seemed timeless, as if it had witnessed centuries of struggle and survival.

Snowflakes continued their gentle descent, and George attempted to brush them from his hat. A slight slip on the icy steps of the cathedral entrance served as a reminder of his purpose. He pushed open the massive door and entered.

Inside, the cathedral provided respite from the bustling city outside. The air was warm and filled with the faint scent of incense and old stone. George stood beneath the white arch, taking in the grandeur of this renowned place of worship. Colored light filtered through stained glass windows, casting soft reflections across the marble floor. Yet he couldn't afford to lose sight of his mission—seeking assistance from a Catholic priest.

A discreet check to ensure he wasn't being followed, his eyes scanning the quiet hall, and he proceeded. Locating an office door marked "Father Thomas," he knocked twice before hearing a soft, welcoming voice in English inviting him inside.

As he entered, he beheld a square room, where a beautiful Madonna statue adorned the priest's desk. In the subdued lighting, he found Father Thomas seated in a tall chair.

"Hello, my son," Father Thomas greeted George.

"Good afternoon, Father. My name is George Yampolsky," George began, his voice tinged with uncertainty. He paused momentarily, feeling uncertain about the correct approach. However, Father Thomas greeted him with a benevolent smile.

"Be seated, my son. What can I help you with today?" Father Thomas's words, though strained, conveyed an aura of reassurance, encouraging George to proceed.

Taking a deep breath, George spoke quietly, cautious of potential eavesdroppers.

"I need your help, Father Thomas. I was born in the United States, and my family came to the Soviet Union in 1936. We embarked on a long journey by boat from the United States."

George glanced up at the priest and continued.

"Upon our arrival in the Soviet Union, our American passports were confiscated for so-called registration, and we were issued Soviet passports with our names significantly altered."

He paused briefly, then added:

"We are now Soviet citizens, and we were left with no recourse. Many of our friends vanished without a trace, and we knew firsthand the peril of approaching the American Embassy, fearing immediate arrest and disappearance. Then the war engulfed the Soviet land, bringing chaos and suffering."

George cleared his throat with a few coughs, his voice growing steadier.

"Now, Father, I implore you to accept a letter from my mother and send it to America."

He paused again, exhaling heavily.

"We survived the war, and we yearn for our relatives to learn of our survival. We fervently seek their assistance to leave the Soviet Union with our children."

His gaze darkened, and for a moment, his hands trembled slightly.

"I have a wife who happens to be Jewish, and two daughters. Every day, I live with the gnawing fear that she will be taken from me—that the tides of hatred will sweep her away as they have so many others. The whisper of persecution grows louder, and with each passing day, the walls seem to close in. If we do not leave soon, I dread that it may be too late."

He pressed the papers into Father Thomas's hands.

"I hope to return to Riga in the summer with my family, provided I am not apprehended before then. By that time, you will bear good tidings from the other side. Our letters must reach Boston, where our family can formally request urgent assistance for all of us. It is our only means of salvation."

"May I read the letter, my son? I must ensure it contains no content that could endanger our church or involve propaganda against the Soviet government. Please understand the sensitivity of this matter," Father Thomas requested.

"Please, Father, I implore you to read my letter," George replied earnestly.

The priest accepted the precious pages, read them carefully, offered his blessing, and placed them in his leather briefcase.

"My son, fear not," Father Thomas assured him. "Is there anything else you wish to share?"

George sighed and replied, "Yes, Father, that is all."

"You will receive instructions," Father Thomas assured him.

With a prayer in his heart, George exited the room, traversing the cathedral's main hall as he marveled at the icons and statues. The candlelight flickered softly across the ancient walls, and for the first time in months he felt a fragile sense of hope.

***

It was already late, and the snowfall had ceased. Bright stars adorned the dark evening sky. George stayed the night at the hotel, and as he ascended to his room, he decided to rest. Despite his youth, his spirit was weary. The strain of secrecy and fear had begun to carve deep lines into his thoughts.

The next morning, George packed his suitcase and hailed a taxi to the main railway station. Upon entering the station, he made his way to the buffet where he enjoyed a cup of tea and a sandwich.

As he was about to leave, a dark-haired man approached his table.

"Excuse me, do you have a pencil?" the man inquired.

George nodded and extended his hand with a pencil, always prepared to jot down a hasty note of his whereabouts to leave with someone.

The man sat down, scribbled something on a piece of paper, and returned the pencil.

In a soft, pleasant voice, he spoke quietly,

"Meet Father Antonio at the St. James's Cathedral in June. Wishing you the best of luck."

The stranger then departed, glancing back to ensure he wasn't being followed.

George felt a surge of excitement and hope at those words. For the first time since leaving Moscow, the plan seemed real.

***

George blended into the crowds effortlessly. He could easily pass for a young Baltic resident—a well-dressed young man with a Nordic appearance, dark blond hair, blue eyes, and round glasses.

To anyone observing, he might appear as another cleric arriving in Riga.

When George boarded his train, he exchanged his trench coat for an old, padded jacket, prepared to return to Moscow.

"Farewell, magnificent city on the Baltic seacoast!"

The train slowly pulled away, and Riga disappeared behind a curtain of falling snow.

Hours later, the train arrived in Moscow, and the return to the city felt sobering. Moscow appeared cold at this time of year, and George found himself already missing the pleasant city of Riga.

In April, the earth was still covered in frozen slush and dirty snow. However, by May, trees began to bloom, their fresh leaves unfurling into bright green bundles.

George visited Natalie to obtain his birth certificate and recent family photographs taken in Moscow. He intended to bring them to his second meeting with the Catholic priest, both for the family in Boston and as evidence for American authorities, pleading for assistance in escaping the communist regime to the free world. It was nearly 3 p.m. when George stood in front of Natalie's communal apartment. He rang the bell twice and heard hurried footsteps approaching from behind the door. When Natalie opened the door, her expression was one of concern.

"George," she whispered, pulling him inside. "Mother says you took a letter of hers to Riga. Is that true? That is very dangerous."

George nodded and gestured for her to write her words. She nodded in understanding and fetched a paper napkin.

"Explain," she whispered.

Then, in a normal voice, she added, "I'll go make some tea with sandwiches."

While she prepared the tea, George wrote down what he needed from her and explained why it was essential. Natalie, who was a smoker, discreetly used her cigarette to burn the corner of the napkin to ashes, fearing it might incriminate them. They discussed the sights of Riga as she searched for some pictures and voiced her doubts about the situation. Finally, George had what he needed and bid farewell.

George knew he had to return to the Baltics with his family to meet the visiting Catholic cleric in June, as agreed. He felt that circumstances had boxed him into a corner, and he was particularly fearful for his wife and daughters.

After his first visit to Riga, the Baltics, George resolved to act and fervently hoped to find a way to change their fate. In the meantime, he delved into books on the history and geography of the region. He learned that the Soviet Baltic Republics were once sovereign Baltic countries, bordering Finland and near Scandinavian nations. He contemplated using the pretext of a summer vacation to meet the Catholic priest, even if it meant risking his life.

George was determined to locate his birth certificate among the personal belongings that the family had recovered following Nikifor's untimely passing after the infamous appointment at the Foreign Ministry. When he finally found his certificate, he breathed a sigh of relief.

George concealed his birth certificate in the same place where his mother, Ethelyn, used to keep it—in his inner pocket.

While examining the documents, George came across a family photo taken in Moscow in 1948, featuring all six of them together. In the picture, his elder brother Eugene stood by his side, a symbol of protection and kindness. As George gazed at the photograph, he couldn't help but reflect on the hardships they had endured during the Great Patriotic War—hunger, illness, cramped rentals infested with bedbugs, communal living, and the constant uncertainty of their future. What a strong and united family they were, the six of them, like a solid rock. Ethelyn never complained and always appeared composed. George couldn't fathom where she found the strength to cope with the dreadful reality they faced.

Only God knew how Ethelyn managed in those early years, unable to speak Russian and rarely venturing outside, mostly confined behind closed doors.

"Mama," George whispered to the photo. "Mama, what shall we do?"

It was the question that tormented him day and night.

"Daddy!"

George gazed sadly at his father in the picture as well.

"My father, a forward-thinking intellectual of his time, couldn't have been so wrong."

George realized that it was getting late and hurriedly left.

***

Time passed quickly, and finally, in June, George and Sonya packed their bags and headed to the train station for their journey to the Baltics. A lively voice echoed from the loudspeakers at the station: "Moscow – Riga train is departing from platform number one!"

The train began to move slowly away from the station. George looked relaxed and, at long last, he was smiling. They were ostensibly going on vacation to a small resort town by the Baltic Sea. A day and a night of travel awaited them before spending two days in Riga, Latvia, before departing for *Jurmala*, a beautiful town on the Baltic Sea coast about thirteen miles away. *Jurmala* was renowned for its white sandy beaches and pine forests. For the first time in many months, the journey ahead carried not only risk, but the faint shape of possibility.

The pleasant, rhythmic clatter of the moving train brought relaxation to George and Sonya, and the children soon fell asleep. When the train attendant knocked on the door, she greeted them with a cheerful, "Hello, bon appétit!" offering four cups of strong Ceylon tea, sugar lumps on a plate, and crunchy pretzels. The samovar-like warmth of the tea and the steady sway of the carriage created a brief illusion of comfort and safety. At the next stop, Sonya hurried to the platform to purchase items from local farmers' wives. They had buckets of sour pickles marinated in dill, garlic, and vinegar, hot boiled potatoes with skin on, green apples, bricks of warm and soft black bread, and freshly baked pirogis.

More women, wearing white headscarves with sun-darkened faces, deep wrinkles, and sleepy eyes, stood on the platform, selling fresh produce from their gardens. A woman's voice over the station loudspeakers announced, "Fellow passengers, the Moscow-Riga train is departing from platform number one!" The train whistle broke the monotonous hum of the provincial station, and Sonya rushed back to their train car, jumping onto the steps as the train slowly pulled away. She returned holding paper-wrapped bundles, cradled carefully in her arms, her blue eyes shining with joy. George and the two children sat on the lower benches, waiting for her, ready to enjoy the provisions she had acquired.

Sonya beamed with a smile and exclaimed, "Wait until I put everything on the table!" They enjoyed their lunch in a picnic-style manner, surrounded by the warmth of their family. It was a very early morning, the dawn of a new day, as the train continued its journey toward Riga. The young mother gazed at her family with immense love, cherishing this moment. For a few precious hours, the cramped railway compartment felt less like a place of transit and more like a small moving refuge.

Sometime later, their train pulled into Riga's main rail station. Riga had managed to retain the atmosphere of a Western resort area, unaffected by the changing tides of time and politics. "Dear fellow passengers, our train has arrived in the capital of Latvia, the city of Riga," announced a voice over the intercom. Passengers began to move slowly toward the exit.

Catherine walked briskly, eager to get off the train. Maria held her hand, both fatigued from waking up early. George led the way to a long line of weary passengers waiting for a taxi. The queue moved at a sluggish pace, and Sonya observed the unfamiliar surroundings with keen interest. The station seemed cleaner, quieter, and somehow lighter than Moscow, as though the very air carried a different rhythm.

Finally, a taxi pulled up to the curb, and the driver, a young man in his thirties, stepped out to assist them. "Central Hotel," George instructed as soon as they were all comfortably seated. The driver started the car and headed toward the grand hotel, not far from the central square. George settled the fare and proceeded to the hotel's reception to check in.

A hotel attendant promptly appeared and guided George and his family to their room. The room was impeccably clean, with a generously sized window that offered a beautiful view of the square. A tower with a large clock chimed every hour. George glanced around and was pleased to finally have a cozy room, modestly but comfortably furnished. The window was open, and the room was filled with the fresh sea breeze from the nearby Baltic Sea. The clean sheets, polished furniture, and salt-tinged air made the room feel almost unreal after the worn interiors of Moscow.

At five o'clock, George ordered room service, and a hotel waiter delivered a tray filled with a pot of hot tea, sweet petit fours, and savory appetizers featuring local cheese, sausage, and bowls of wild strawberries. As the sun set behind the trees, the clock on the tower struck seven in the evening.

George began organizing his papers, preparing for his meeting with the Catholic priest. However, he had no intention of disclosing his whereabouts to his wife. "Sonya, I'll be out for about an hour," he casually informed her. Sonya looked at George with a quizzical expression, but she knew better than to interrogate him when he was on a mission of sorts. "Please, don't worry and stay in the room until I return. Enjoy the comforts!" George said and hastily departed.

The early evening cast a dusky glow on the Baltic Sea coast as George closed the door behind him. He navigated through a long corridor to the main exit, moving quietly to avoid making any noise on his way to the back exit. Checking his inner pockets, he confirmed that all the letters and documents were securely in place. Everything was ready.

George clutched the two letters in his pocket, their weight a physical manifestation of his hopes and fears. He navigated the maze of Riga's streets, consulting a well-worn map under the fading sunlight. As dusk settled, he found himself drawn to an alleyway leading toward the imposing silhouette of the St. James's Cathedral. Every turn through the old city seemed to tighten the suspense within him.

The faint strains of an organ and the hushed voices of parishioners wafted from within, offering a sliver of solace amid his anxieties. Finally, after months of capricious Baltic weather, summer had arrived, its warm breeze carrying the intoxicating scents of pine and sweet berries. Hope bloomed in George's chest like a fragile flower as he approached the grand entrance of the cathedral.

He carried two missives in his coat's inner pocket. The first, penned by his mother Ethelyn, was a testament to their enduring familial bond. He intended to deliver it along with cherished family photographs. The second, penned in his own hand, was a desperate plea for assistance from American authorities, with a veiled request for covert communication channels through the Catholic Church. Those papers were more than letters; they were the family's last bridge to another world.

With a deep breath, George stepped into the cathedral's cool embrace. A hush descended upon him as he surveyed the hushed reverence of the space. His gaze landed on a figure approaching him – an elderly clergyman clad in a black cassock, his silver hair catching the fading light.

"My name is George—" he began, his voice tinged with apprehension.

The man nodded curtly, gesturing with a wrinkled hand for him to follow. "Father Antonio has been expecting you since his arrival," he whispered in hushed tones. "I will escort you to his chambers. Please, come with me."

George's apprehension morphed into curiosity as he followed the enigmatic cleric. Their procession led them to a secluded wing of the cathedral, finally culminating at a heavy oak door. The escort tapped twice, and a warm, baritone voice bade them enter. Pushing open the door, George found himself in a dimly lit room dominated by a statue of Saint Francis of Assisi, the patron saint of Italy.

Behind the desk, seated in a high-backed chair, was Father Antonio – a man of imposing stature with kind eyes that held a glint of mischief. The escort bowed and left, leaving George alone with the enigmatic priest.

George cleared his throat, nervously repeating his introduction. "Good evening, Father. My name is George. George Yampolsky. I met Father Thomas in February this year. He encouraged me to come back and meet with you..." He paused, gathering his courage, and then added, "and now I hope that God has listened to my prayers and sent a good omen – a favorable reply from the US authorities and a note from my family back home."

His voice trembled with a mixture of anticipation and dread, his heart pounding against his ribs like a trapped bird. He yearned for any sliver of hope, any indication that his desperate plea had reached their intended recipients.

Father Antonio regarded him with a silent intensity, his gaze seemingly boring into George's soul. Father Antonio's gaze, brimming with kindness and empathy, lingered on George. Without a word, he extended a letter.

This was it. The moment he had been waiting for, the culmination of months of agonizing uncertainty. As he tore open the envelope, a mixture of fear and elation coursed through him. This letter held the potential to change everything, to rewrite the narrative of his life and the lives of his loved ones. George opened it, his heart pounding as he scanned the lines.

But what message did it hold? Was it the answer to his desperate pleas, or another cruel twist of fate? The fate of his family, and his own freedom, hung precariously in the balance.

The simple message brought both elation and a twinge of sadness. "We are all well," it read, "living in Boston in our old home. It would be nice to have a picture of the whole family... You will find Father Antonio at the St. James's Cathedral. Please ask him to act as a go-between."

A relieved smile touched George's lips. At least he had brought the photograph.

Father Antonio, sensing his emotions, spoke. "George," he said, "I dedicate my life to aiding families in need. With God's help, some have achieved incredible escapes. But the iron curtain is more impenetrable than Orwellian darkest visions."

George understood. Risk coiled around him, even in the presence of a foreign priest like Father Antonio, whose visit to St. James strengthened ties with the Baltic Catholic church.

"Though I haven't received an official US response," Father Antonio continued, "do not lose hope. Persevere, and I will seek divine guidance."

Frustration flickered in George's eyes, but he persevered. "Father," he pleaded, "may I entrust you to carry my plea to the US government and relay messages to my family? We hope they'll petition for our extraction."

Father Antonio listened intently. "My son," he assured, "your words are sealed between God and me. I will carry your letters, keep you in my prayers, and do all in my power. The rest, my child, lies in His hands. God bless you, Amen."

The audience concluded, George handed over his letters, bowing his head in gratitude. The seed of hope, nourished by faith and courage, had been planted. This was just the beginning of their clandestine struggle, a dance between freedom and captivity where whispers across a divided world held the promise of a brighter dawn. When George stepped back into the summer night, the city felt changed—not safer, not kinder, but no longer entirely closed to hope.

Chapter 23

Summer Respite

The Baltic Sea's summer breeze brought a refreshing coolness, lifting George's spirits as he dreamt of possibilities, however distant they might seem. The salty air carried the scent of pine forests and warm sand, a rare sensation of freedom after the suffocating atmosphere of Moscow. Dreams, after all, are the essence of hope.

Returning to their room, George was greeted by a worried Sonya, her tears reflecting her unease in this unfamiliar land. The room was dimly lit by the fading evening sun, and for a moment George realized how fragile their fragile moment of safety truly was.

"Hush, Sonya," George comforted, sharing his evening escapades, and drawing parallels to the Great Lakes. His voice was calm, measured, careful. At the table, he silently conveyed the need for discretion and revealed a letter from his uncle in the United States. Sonya, unable to decipher the English words, understood its significance and origin. She studied George's face instead of the page, searching his expression for clues of hope or danger.

George then carefully penned a note explaining his correspondence with their American relatives and the letters he had sent—one from his mother and another to U.S. authorities. His pen moved slowly across the paper, each word chosen with deliberate care. Witnessing Sonya's understanding smile, George methodically burned the note, watching the small flame curl the fragile paper into ash, a gesture symbolizing both caution and closure.

"Tomorrow, we'll visit *Yurmala*," he announced with a sense of relief, envisioning a day of tranquility by the sea.

***

The summer in the Baltics became a rare and luminous chapter for the family.

Journeying to a coastal haven just thirteen miles from Riga, they embraced the gentle climate and the sea's rejuvenating embrace. The road to the resort wound through tall pine forests, their needles whispering softly in the coastal wind.

The sun's warmth blessed them with tanned skins and lifted spirits. For the first time in years, the weight of fear loosened its grip on their daily lives.

Simple pleasures like swimming, basking in the sun, and savoring market-fresh cottage cheese, sour cream, and wild strawberries colored their days with joy. Small wooden stalls near the beach displayed baskets of berries and jars of honey, while fishermen mended their nets along the shore.

Catherine and Maria, lost in childlike wonder, built sandcastles and chased the elusive, darting fish in the shallow waters, their laughter mingling with the steady rhythm of the Baltic waves. The girls ran barefoot across the warm sand, their carefree voices echoing through the quiet seaside air.

Sonya and George found their bond deepening in this idyllic setting. They often walked along the shoreline at sunset, speaking softly while the sky turned shades of gold and violet. Their smiles became a regular feature, reflecting a newfound closeness. For a moment in time, it almost felt as though life had returned to what it once might have been.

But as June faded into July, reality slowly beckoned. The school year loomed ahead, urging George and Sonya to gather their belongings for the journey back to Moscow. The peaceful rhythm of the Baltic coast began to give way to the familiar anxiety of returning home. The return journey was markedly different.

This time, the train was crowded and chaotic—a unified carriage packed with a diverse crowd, without the privacy of compartments. The air inside the wagon was thick with the scent of sweat, worn clothing, and fatigue.

Passengers crowded together shoulder to shoulder, their luggage stacked beneath benches and against the walls. Seeking respite, many gathered near the doors, where the pine-scented air rushing through the openings offered a brief escape as the train sped across the countryside.

Children cried, soldiers smoked near the corridor, and weary travelers leaned against the walls, exhausted by the long journey.

Finally, the conductor's announcement rang through the carriage:

"We are arriving in Moscow, the capital of the Soviet Union!"

A burst of patriotic music crackled through the loudspeakers.

As the train slowly edged into the station, the skyline of Moscow appeared once again—gray, imposing, and familiar.

It marked not only the end of their summer by the sea, but the return to a life shadowed by fear, terror, and deprivation.

The fragile dream of the Baltic summer faded behind them as the iron reality of Moscow closed in once more.

Chapter 24

Stalin's Final Crusade

"Hath not a Jew eyes? Hath not a Jew hands, organs, dimensions, senses, affections, passions?"
— William Shakespeare, The Merchant of Venice, Act 3, Scene 1

As the Soviet Union marched through the 1950s, Joseph Stalin's regime cast a dark shadow over its people, intensifying repressions and instilling fear. Across the vast country, an atmosphere of suspicion thickened like a gathering storm. Under Stalin's directive, a sinister campaign against "cosmopolitans"—a veiled reference to Jews—was launched by the Soviet media. Newspapers, radio broadcasts, and public speeches echoed with accusations and denunciations, turning neighbors into informants and ordinary citizens into targets. This era saw numerous Jews unjustly arrested on charges of espionage, subjected to torture, tried in secrecy, and executed.

1952 marked a year of heightened terror. The machinery of repression accelerated, grinding forward with ruthless precision. In a particularly egregious act, several highly skilled doctors from a prestigious Kremlin hospital were falsely accused of murdering Communist Party members. These medical professionals, dubbed "murderers in white coats," faced allegations of administering poison instead of treatment. The accusations spread quickly through newspapers and radio broadcasts, igniting fear and suspicion across the country. A grim plan was hatched for their public execution, intended to fuel animosity among the Russian populace toward these innocent doctors. However, a twist of fate—the unexpected death of Stalin—spared them from this cruel end.

Stalin's paranoia extended to grander, more horrific schemes. Behind the walls of the Kremlin, secret plans were quietly unfolding. He plotted the mass deportation of Jews from the European regions of the Soviet Union to the Jewish Autonomous District, a remote territory near the China–Russia border, with its administrative center in Birobidzhan, known for its harsh climate and crumbling infrastructure. In preparation for this inhumane act, Stalin's regime began compiling detailed records of Jewish citizens. Lists were drawn up in silence, family names catalogued with chilling efficiency. Simultaneously, construction companies were commissioned to erect barracks in the Far East, which resembled cattle hangars and lacked any form of heating, despite temperatures that plummeted to minus 40 degrees Celsius. These bleak wooden structures stood isolated in frozen wilderness, grim shelters for a population that had not yet arrived. Unheated train cars stood ready, ominous harbingers of the mass transport that awaited countless Jews. Railway sidings across the country quietly prepared for the movement of entire communities.

In Moscow, rumors circulated about apartments soon to be vacated and reassigned to Russian tenants under new lease agreements—a chilling testament to the scale of the planned expulsion. Whispers traveled through stairwells and communal kitchens, carried by fearful voices that barely dared to speak aloud.

Stalin's iron fist also struck hard within his prisons. He ordered brutal interrogations, demanding that captives confess to sabotaging the Soviet regime. Night after night, the echo of boots in prison corridors announced the arrival of interrogators. Many perished under relentless torture before they could even utter these forced confessions. The reign of terror had a clear objective: to cow the citizenry into a state of absolute obedience and silence, to ensure that fear would govern where law and justice had once stood. It was a strategy that cast a long and oppressive shadow across the Soviet Union.

Under that shadow, millions lived in quiet dread, uncertain whose door would be knocked upon next.

Chapter 25

A Chilling Summons in Moscow

November in Moscow brought with it a dreary transformation. Streets, once merely grimy, were now blanketed with a fresh layer of snow, covering the underlying dirt and slush. The city seemed quieter under the pale winter sky, yet the silence carried a heavy, uneasy weight. From her window, Sonya observed the gloom outside, a sight that mirrored the unease within her.

The day's routine was disrupted by an unsettling discovery: a letter from the militsiya addressed solely to Sonya. The envelope itself felt ominous in her hands. It was a summons demanding her presence at the local militsiya unit, laden with a dire warning.

"Citizeness Yampolsky Sonya must appear..." the letter stated, stipulating her attendance with a threat of criminal prosecution for noncompliance.

Panic set in. Her heart began to race as she reread the official words, each line tightening the knot of fear in her chest. With George at work and her children safely at her mother's, Sonya hurried to prepare herself, trying to suppress her growing anxiety.

But her identity as a Jew lingered at the back of her mind, a potential source of this unforeseen summons. The recent persecution of Jewish doctors in the Kremlin, a trial that had been sensationalized in the *Pravda* newspaper, echoed in her thoughts. The newspapers had shouted accusations, branding respected physicians as traitors. The Stalinist regime's propensity for public executions and show trials was no secret, and Sonya couldn't help but fear for her family's safety.

With a heavy heart, Sonya donned her modest coat and wrapped a gray knitted scarf around her head, babushka-style. Pulling on her felt boots, she braced herself for the cold outside and made her way to the tram.

Paying her fare, she squeezed into the packed vehicle, swaying with each jolt and turn. The tram rattled along the frozen rails, its metal wheels screeching against the winter track. The tram's frosty windows framed a monochrome world of snow and darkly clad passersby, ghost-like in their winter garb.

Upon reaching her stop, Sonya navigated through the crowd with a determination fueled by her anxiety. Her breath formed small clouds in the icy air as she walked quickly through the streets.

Despite the ominous message from the militsiya, she endeavored to maintain a semblance of hope. She reminded herself of her life as a good Soviet citizeness, her relatively secular Jewish practices, and her fortunate existence in Moscow, the heart of the Soviet Union.

The city's cultural jewels—the Bolshoi, the Pushkin Museum, the Tretyakov Gallery—flashed in her mind as symbols of the life she cherished. These memories felt like fragile proof that she belonged in the city she loved. Yet, as Sonya walked toward the militsiya unit, her attempt to stay positive was overshadowed by a nagging fear. The gray government building soon appeared ahead, stark and imposing against the winter sky. The uncertainty of what lay ahead gnawed at her, threatening the fragile peace of her ordinary life.

With every step toward the entrance, Sonya felt the invisible weight of the state pressing down upon her.

Chapter 26

A Name, An Identity, A Fear

The *militsiya* building, an unassuming three-story brick structure nestled in one of Moscow's central alleyways, stood as a silent sentinel. Its windows were dull and opaque, revealing nothing of the authority hidden behind them. Sonya approached the entrance, its door marred by scratches and patches of thick ice. The icy knob chilled her fingers as she pushed the heavy door open, stepping into a dimly lit interior shrouded in warm vapor.

Her heart pounding, Sonya made her way to the designated office, knocking three times before a stern voice summoned her inside. The *militsioner's* voice, harsh and unyielding, set her on edge. She scanned the room for a glass of water to moisten her dry lips but found none. The air felt thick and stale, pressing against her chest with suffocating weight.

"Comrade, good morning," she managed to say, her voice quivering despite her efforts to sound composed. She presented her passport, her hands betraying her with their uncontrollable tremor.

The gray-haired official, his face etched with deep wrinkles, inspected Sonya and her passport. His cold eyes moved slowly from the document to her face and back again, as though measuring every detail. His declaration that she must leave her passport and accept a temporary document sent a surge of fear through her. He noted her Belorussian last name, Yampolsky, and then, to her dismay, the line that revealed her Jewish heritage.

"Your patronymic is Anatolievna, but you are Jewish."

Sonya's heart sank as he told her he would change her patronymic to reflect her Jewish identity, from Anatolievna to Naftolievna, from her father's name, Naftali. The revelation that they knew her father's real name sent a wave of cold panic through her. It felt as if the walls of the small office had suddenly closed in around her.

"But... I am a good Soviet citizeness now," she hesitantly attempted to explain, hoping this might make them look upon her more favorably. "I-I-I am not a practicing Jew."

Her plea — that she was a loyal Soviet citizeness, not a practicing Jew — fell on deaf ears.

"It doesn't matter!" barked the head official.

"Are you Jewish on both sides?" he continued.

"Yes," Sonya answered mechanically. The word escaped her lips before she could stop it, sounding strangely hollow in the silent room.

"So, you are a pure Jew," he said, lowering his voice to a barely audible whisper. The room seemed suddenly smaller. Even the ticking of a clock somewhere in the corridor seemed unbearably loud.

"Is your husband Jewish?"

"No," Sonya replied, frozen in shock. Her mind raced ahead in terror. Would they come for him as well?

As the interrogation continued, Sonya's fear escalated. The mention of her husband's ethnicity and the issuance of a new identity document with the altered patronymic Sofia Naftolievna Yampolsky cemented the grim reality of her situation. With a few strokes of his pen, the official had rewritten her identity.

She left the militsiya building in a state of shock, the heavy door slamming shut behind her like a verdict. Her mind raced, unable to settle, circling the implications of what had just occurred.

Sonya's journey home was a blur, the frozen streets passing beneath her feet without shape or memory. Snow crunched beneath her boots, but the sound seemed distant, as though she were walking through a dream.

Her thoughts were consumed by the need to discuss this ominous development with her family, to speak it aloud before it swallowed her whole. The terror of what lay ahead was palpable, a living presence at her side, but she knew she couldn't succumb to fear.

With each step, she felt the weight of uncertainty pressing against her chest, the squeeze of her heart tightening with every breath, a painful reminder that she had just been seen — truly seen — and could never again return to the safety of invisibility.

In Stalin's Moscow, once the state marked you, there was no returning to anonymity.

Chapter 27

An Escape into Uncertainty

As the late afternoon sun cast its waning light over Moscow, Sonya ascended the stairs to their flat, her hand gripping the wooden banister for support. Each step felt heavier than the last, as though the weight of the day had settled into her bones. The creak of the front door echoed in the quiet hallway as she entered the space she shared with her family—a modest refuge that had always sheltered them from the world outside—a sanctuary that now felt precarious. Overwhelmed by the day's events, Sonya succumbed to tears, her shoulders trembling as the despair she had held back all afternoon finally broke through.

George arrived home later than usual, his greeting in the kitchen met with Sonya's silence and tear-streaked face. The familiar warmth of the kitchen stove could not soften the tension that filled the room. His repeated inquiries were met with her swaying form, unable to articulate the fear and uncertainty that gripped her. Finally, with a glass of tepid water as her momentary solace, Sonya revealed the day's harrowing experience.

She spoke of the indifferent interrogation, the confiscation of her passport, and the chilling alteration of her identity to mark her as a Jew. The words came slowly at first, halting and uneven, as though each sentence forced her to relive the moment once again. George listened intently, his response laced with the grim rumors circulating Moscow: *Stalin's plans to deport Jews from Moscow to the remote settlement region of Birobidzhan in the*

Soviet Far East, a policy that also conveniently relieved the capital's severe housing shortages.

He spoke quietly, but the gravity of his words hung heavily between them. His words painted a stark picture of a future where their home would be claimed by others, and they, cast out into exile.

In the quiet of their kitchen, George outlined a plan. He leaned forward across the small table, his voice low but resolute. He proposed they move to an isolated summer house owned by his friends, a temporary refuge in a hamlet with basic provisions. The urgency in his voice was palpable as he detailed their departure for the next morning—a journey by train followed by a trek through the forest.

Outside the kitchen window, the fading daylight deepened into the cold gray of evening, as though the city itself were closing around them.

His reassurance, "Do not be afraid! I am by your side," offered a flicker of hope in the enveloping darkness.

As he paused, George questioned when Sonya might receive her altered passport, a critical piece in their precarious situation. Sonya's nervous glance spoke volumes; the bureaucratic process, now expedited to mark the Jews of Moscow, would take days. Days they did not have.

George's instructions were clear and decisive: pack essentials, dress warmly, and prepare for an uncertain period of hiding. His mind was already racing ahead calculating the train schedules, the safest routes through the forest, and the supplies they would need to survive away from the city.

With a mixture of anger and fear fueling his actions, he left to gather provisions, the weight of their impending flight heavy on his shoulders.

In that moment, their kitchen—once a haven of familial warmth—became the backdrop for a decision that would alter the course of their lives.

The threat of persecution loomed large, propelling them into a future fraught with unknowns, their fate hinging on the fragile hope of finding safety in seclusion.

Beyond the apartment walls, Moscow carried on with its evening routines, unaware that within this small kitchen a family had just made the decision to disappear.

Chapter 28

Summer House

The Moscow winter, harsh and unyielding, had set in, painting the city streets with a blanket of crunching snow beneath a grey sky. The cold seemed to harden everything it touched—buildings, streets, even the faces of hurried passersby. For seven-year-old Catherine, the thought of leaving behind her warm room, her beloved dolls, and her cozy cot was daunting. But the pressing circumstances left her with no choice.

Early in the morning, Sonya and George, along with Catherine and her sister Maria, embarked on their journey to a summer house owned by one of George's friends. With only two weeks remaining in the year 1952, the family faced a three-hour train commute followed by a significant walk through a dense forest, a route that had to be traversed before nightfall.

Bundled in padded coats and layered in warm knits, scarves, and felt boots, the family set out. Their breath rose in pale clouds in the frozen air. George led the way, pulling the children on a small sled whenever the path allowed it. Their first leg of the journey was a tram ride to the city center. Upon disembarking, they faced a ten-minute walk through the snow-laden streets to the railway station, managing their sled, bags, and the tired children.

At the station, George exchanged crumpled rubles for four train tickets. They boarded the train, which was ready to depart, its engine puffing smoke into the cold air. The platform buzzed with hurried voices and the metallic clatter of luggage being dragged through snow. A brief interaction with the train conductor, a middle-aged woman in uniform, preceded the journey. As the train chugged into motion, the landscape of rural Moscow sped by, a blur of villages, shacks, and dilapidated fences.

Upon reaching their stop at *Ogorkovo* in the late afternoon, the family disembarked onto the snowy platform. George, shouldering a hefty suitcase secured with rope, and Sonya, pulling the sled with their daughters, began their trek through the forest. The half-hour walk, despite its relatively short distance, was arduous under the weight of their belongings and the biting cold.

With a mix of fear and determination, the family made their way through the snowy landscape, their journey marked by the silent hope of reaching the summer house before darkness enveloped the forest. The promise of Grandfather Frost and Miss Snow's arrival with New Year's gifts lingered in the children's minds, a fragile fairy-tale comfort against the stark reality of their flight.

"We will wait here for Grandfather Frost and Miss Snow," said Sonya with a reassuring smile. Her voice carried warmth she hoped the children would believe.

After they had traveled the distance, George suddenly realized he could not see the house. A flicker of panic rose in his chest. Darkness fell quickly upon the thick forest, where tall pine trees stood heavy with snow. The hamlet was nowhere in sight. Had he gone the wrong direction or taken a bad turn?

But then a crescent moon rose slowly above the horizon, casting a pale silver glow across the treetops.

"Daddy, I can see a house!" Catherine cried.

George followed her pointing finger and noticed the glimmer of moonlight reflecting off a distant roof. Relief washed over him like warmth returning to frozen hands. He sighed deeply.

The summer house was mostly obscured by tall pine trees and piles of sparkling white snow. George pulled the sled up to the door, which was secured with a large barn lock. He hurriedly pulled out his keys and opened the door.

The house was livable—but damp and freezing.

George knew the challenges that lay ahead. The summer house, devoid of electricity and not meant for winter habitation, would require them to find wood for the fireplace to stay warm. The absence of electricity and running water, coupled with the isolation of the deserted village, underscored the severity of their situation. However, the presence of an artesian well along the road offered a small consolation.

As the howl of a wolf echoed through the cold night—a haunting sound carried through the frozen forest—it served as a tangible reminder of their isolation and vulnerability. Sonya gathered thin wool blankets she had found in a closet. These would be their shield against the biting cold of the unheated house.

George looked around the room. He found some old newspapers, jammed them around the wood logs, then lit them. A small flame flickered, caught the paper, and soon a steady fire began to grow. Slowly, the icy room began to breathe again as warmth crept into the air.

With a quiet prayer of gratitude, George expressed relief for their safe arrival and the fragile comfort the fire provided. He decided against returning to Moscow that night, considering the danger posed by wolves and the late hour.

The reality of their situation was stark. The summer house, while a refuge from the immediate threats in Moscow, was far from comfortable or safe. With no nearby shops except for a tiny shack selling necessities, and the nearest doctor miles away, the challenges they faced were daunting.

As he lay in bed that night, George's thoughts were a whirlwind of plans and contingencies.

The next morning, he made an early trip back to Moscow to gather supplies and medicine, a journey made more difficult by the crowds of people from suburban towns doing the same.

Upon his return, George found some old antibiotics in the drawers, a small but crucial discovery for his daughters' health. Exhausted, he soon fell into a deep sleep, his body surrendering to the fatigue of constant vigilance.

The following morning George got up at 5 a.m. and hurried back to the train station. At the station he went straight to the large schedule board, boarded the train with other weary passengers, and found an empty seat next to the window.

A couple of hours later the train pulled into his stop.

If he walked quickly and stayed focused on the path, he could reach the hamlet before sunset.

The cold fogged his glasses, so George removed them and slipped them into his pocket, navigating the snowy path with blurred vision. The forest trail appeared as shifting shadows through the haze.

The journey back was treacherous. Snow obscured the path, and without his glasses the world around him dissolved into indistinct shapes. Yet within an hour he reached the house.

"Here I am," announced George, bursting in from the cold and slamming the door behind him.

He embraced Sonya tightly.

"How are the children?"

"The cold air has affected their lungs," she replied. "They've been coughing through the night."

"I'm sorry I wasn't here," George said regretfully. Then his face brightened as he remembered the medication.

"But I've brought some medicine!" he declared. "And some other necessities."

"I've given them something," Sonya informed him. "And they're feeling a bit better now."

George smiled.

"See," he said gently, "you've already overcome one challenge. Together, we can handle this. We'll be alright."

Sonya's relief at seeing George return was palpable. Her gratitude that he had brought medicine and other essentials was evident in her voice. She began quietly arranging the items George had brought, storing them carefully in the cupboards.

Sonya seemed to draw strength from her husband's presence, her anxiety visibly easing.

George's reassurance, combined with Sonya's quiet determination, strengthened their spirits. They were resolved to face the challenges ahead as a family.

As they settled into their new routine, the family slowly adapted to their rustic surroundings. Sonya's discovery of porcelain plates, a heavy iron frying pan perfect for cooking, and a box of candles felt like small victories against the bleakness of their situation. She eagerly showed these finds to George.

George's efforts to collect snow for water and Sonya's resourcefulness in the kitchen brought a fragile sense of normalcy.

Their days were marked by caution and simplicity. Evenings were spent beside the warm glow of the fireplace, the family huddled together for warmth and comfort, their days filled with stories and lessons for the children.

In the dim light of the summer house, George peered out the window, scanning the dark forest for signs of danger. The distant howls of wolves echoed through the night, a stark reminder of their vulnerability in this secluded refuge.

"Don't go outside at night," he cautioned Sonya, emphasizing the need for vigilance even during the day.

Then George went outside to gather buckets of clean white snow, placing them beside the fireplace where they melted into usable water.

Sonya opened a drawer where she had previously discovered some cutlery. Despite the threat of wolves outside, she felt a new confidence that they, as a family, could endure.

Every day Sonya ventured outside with the children for fresh air, always carrying a large stick in case they encountered a stray wolf.

At night, by the glow of the fireplace, she would light one of the candles. They had brought several books for the children, and together they read aloud, ensuring the girls' education continued.

Thus, they passed the winter quietly, one day following another, until the first signs of spring appeared.

One day, while Sonya was making potato soup in a pot hung over the fireplace, she suddenly heard the song of a bird—a herald of spring.

With the arrival of spring came rumors of Stalin's failing health, or perhaps even his death.

Knowing they needed to return to the city to check on their family and replenish their medicines, they realized it was time to leave their hidden refuge and return to Moscow.

Despite their sadness at leaving, they prepared to face whatever awaited them in the city.

Chapter 29

Deliverance

Back in Moscow, George and Sonya found themselves engulfed by a sea of people. The news of Stalin's sudden death had sent shockwaves through the city, with throngs of citizens flocking to witness the leader's body lying in state. The announcement had spread like wildfire through factories, tramcars, and apartment blocks, passing from whispered rumor to stunned confirmation. The early spring of 1953 was bitterly cold, the cobblestone streets slick with treacherous black ice, their frozen surfaces reflecting the dim gray sky like cracked mirrors, adding to the mounting chaos.

Crowds of mourners swelled spontaneously, their collective grief turning into a frenzied, disordered mass. People pushed forward blindly, driven by curiosity, duty, or fear of being seen as indifferent. Panic ensued as people were trampled in the confusion. Voices shouted, coats tore, and the dense crowd moved like a single uncontrollable wave. Sonya, carrying the quiet relief of being safe from deportation, longed for the tranquility they had found in the countryside. The memory of the silent forest and the small fire in the summer house suddenly felt like another world.

In their communal apartment, Sonya, Catherine, and Maria listened as Comrade Levitan announced Stalin's death on the radio. The familiar authoritative voice filled the small room with a gravity that seemed to freeze the air itself. Mournful music filled the room following the somber eulogy. The slow, solemn orchestral tones drifted through the thin walls of the apartment building, echoing from one room to another like a collective lament.

Tears of joy and relief flowed from Sonya's eyes, her fears of persecution fading away. She pressed her hands to her face, overwhelmed not by sorrow but by the sudden lifting of a weight she had carried for months. Meanwhile, neighbors wandered aimlessly through the corridor, lost in their own grief. Some whispered prayers, others stood silently by the radio in stunned disbelief. Sonya retreated to her room with her daughters, seeking a moment of solitude.

It was almost two hours later when George arrived.

"Sonya," he greeted her swiftly, sharing a hurried kiss. His face was pale from the cold and the tension in the streets.

"We need to go see your mother now."

They dressed quickly, navigating the labyrinth of alleys and side streets to avoid the swelling crowds. George instinctively chose the narrower lanes where the flow of people was thinner and movement still possible. The streets teemed with an uncontrolled flow of people, occasionally blocked by army trucks, creating dangerous bottlenecks.

The city was in disarray, with routes cordoned off and people desperately searching for ways out. George and Sonya held their children's hands tightly as they moved through the chaos. The girls clung to their parents, their small boots slipping slightly on the icy pavement.

Suddenly, the air was pierced by a cacophony of terrified screams echoing from the wider streets. The sound rolled through the city like a wave of alarm.

Militsiya on horseback struggled to maintain order, their horses slipping on the icy patches, further exacerbating the chaos around them. The animals reared nervously, their hooves striking the cobblestones as officers shouted commands that were quickly swallowed by the roar of the crowd.

The city, once familiar, now seemed like an unrecognizable labyrinth, its streets a reflection of the turmoil and uncertainty that lay in the wake of Stalin's passing. Every corner revealed new barriers, new streams of frightened citizens pressing forward without direction.

For George, Sonya, and their children, the journey through Moscow was not just a physical path but a passage through a moment of historical upheaval—a fragile crossing between fear and possibility. It marked the end of an era and the beginning of an uncertain future.

Chapter 30

A Reunion Amidst Turmoil

After a tense and harrowing journey through the chaotic streets of Moscow, Sonya and her family finally reached the home of George's in-laws. Their footsteps echoed softly against the frozen pavement as they approached the building, careful not to draw attention. They discreetly entered the building through a back door from a side street. The dim stairwell smelled faintly of coal smoke and damp wool coats. With a sense of urgency and relief, Sonya quickly warmed her numb hands together and rang the bell twice.

Anatoly, Sonya's father, greeted them with a simple yet heartfelt, "Well, finally you have arrived!" His voice carried both relief and fatigue. He ushered them through a long corridor into their room, where Raisa, Sonya's mother, awaited in the living room. The walls were adorned with Anatoly's artwork, a testament to his skill and passion. Even in the dim evening light, the paintings seemed to glow with quiet intensity. Despite the tremors in his hands, a result of wartime injuries, his paintings still echoed the beauty and depth of the Renaissance era.

Sonya admired her father's art, expressing her concerns for his well-being. Anatoly's canvases, often depicting scenes from Jewish ghettoes, conveyed a deep sense of loss and longing. Muted browns and shadowed figures filled the frames. The images of a sad violinist clutching his instrument spoke volumes about the pain and suffering endured under the shadow of persistent antisemitism.

"It is who I am," Anatoly responded stoically. "And no government can take that from me."

His voice was calm, yet firm, as if he had repeated those words to himself many times before.

Sonya acknowledged the risk he took, continuing to create art under such oppressive conditions. Anatoly's bittersweet smile conveyed his resolve, accepting the risks in exchange for the freedom to express himself through his art.

The room was filled with other works—landscapes and portraits—each deserving recognition in the art world. Yet, under Stalin's regime, with its profound hatred for Jews and an iron curtain isolating the Soviet Union, Anatoly's talents remained hidden, his art confined to the walls of his home. The paintings existed like quiet witnesses to a life that could never be publicly acknowledged.

As Sonya reflected on the suffering her father endured—his struggle with illness, harsh living conditions, and constant fear for his family's safety—she realized the full extent of communism's grip on the country. The family lived in perpetual uncertainty, waiting for a new leader to emerge.

Turning away from the poignant artworks, Sonya rejoined George and their daughters, who were conversing in subdued tones. Their voices barely rose above a whisper. In this household, speaking loudly was discouraged; they communicated in cryptic language understood only among themselves. Catherine and Maria sat by the window, observing the outside world, their small silhouettes framed by the frosted glass, when suddenly a loud buzz from the entrance door interrupted their quiet contemplation. Sonya, sensing the urgency, quickly made her way to the door.

In the dim light of their apartment, Dr. Verlene, a relative of Sonya's and a Jewish doctor who narrowly escaped execution, appeared at the door. Without a hat and looking exceptionally pale and distressed, he was a direct witness to the turmoil unfolding in Moscow. His coat was dusted with snow, and his eyes were red with exhaustion. The recent death of Stalin had fortuitously spared him and his colleagues from a horrific fate.

“Hello, Sonya,” he greeted softly, embracing her briefly before making his way through the corridor to the living room where Raisa sat, visibly fatigued.

Dr. Verlene removed his heavy black coat and sat down, a deep sigh escaping him. His shoulders slumped as though the weight of the entire day had finally caught up with him.

“May I get a glass of water?” he asked wearily.

Sonya quickly brought him a teapot, pouring lukewarm water into his glass. Dr. Verlene drank thirstily, his gaze shifting to the window.

“See all those trucks?” he said quietly, pointing toward the street; his voice laden with sadness.

“They're transporting bodies from the streets of Moscow.”

Dr. Verlene, who had operated in the trenches during the Great Patriotic War and now worked at the *Sklifosovsky* Hospital's trauma center, recounted the tragic events he had witnessed.

“Innocent people were trampled in the crowds,” he said, his voice breaking. “Hundreds… maybe more. I've spent hours trying to save as many lives as possible.”

His hands trembled as he spoke. Overwhelmed, he buried his face in his hands, tears streaming down his cheeks.

Amidst his grief, Dr. Verlene brought a message of relief.

"You are all safe now," he said quietly. "Jews will not be deported."

The words hung in the air like a fragile promise.

His eyes softened as he looked at the girls, managing a faint smile.

"How beautiful they both are," he remarked gently.

Before leaving for the hospital, he left some antibiotics for the family, a kind gesture in these trying times. He placed the small packet carefully on the table, as if it were something precious.

As night fell, George decided it was time to return to their own apartment. The girls, weary from the day's events, needed rest. Back in their home, George and Sonya tucked the children into bed. George gently kissed their foreheads before bidding them goodnight.

In the quiet of their apartment, the city finally seemed to fall silent beyond the frost-covered windows. The family drifted off to sleep, each lost in their own thoughts about the day's events and the uncertain future that lay ahead.

Chapter 31

The Voices of Suffering

March 1953 marked a pivotal moment in Soviet history as the reins of power shifted following Stalin's death. Across the vast Soviet Union, whispers spread from city to village, from factory floor to prison barracks, as people tried to grasp the meaning of this sudden change. This turn of events spared the Soviet people from another decade of his tyrannical rule. The feared deportation of Jews was averted, lifting a heavy burden off the nation's shoulders. Nikita Khrushchev ascended as the head of the Soviet government, and in a wave of change, political prisoners began to be released from the labor camps. For the first time in many years, faint hope began to circulate through a society long suffocated by fear.

The dusk had already enveloped Moscow in its soft gray blanket by the time George arrived at the apartment on Gertsen Street. Streetlamps flickered faintly along the sidewalks, casting long shadows across the melting patches of snow. Navigating through the heart of Moscow, he finally reached his destination, weighed down by fatigue. His heart warmed at the thought of the house where Sonya's parents lived, a pre-revolutionary building that still stood proudly, emanating warmth and quiet dignity.

Ascending the broad staircase, George opened the door. The long corridor was engulfed in darkness, but the living room door was slightly open, and a thin stream of yellow light spilled into the hallway.

Raisa, Sonya's mother, despite her fragile health, was seated at the table with her sister Sara, who had recently returned from a camp in the far north. Beside Raisa and Sara, two women were seated at a round table covered with a white tablecloth. Their gaunt figures and disheveled gray hair were silent witnesses to their past as political prisoners who had traversed the Urals to Moscow. They were part of small groups of recently released prisoners, still struggling to comprehend the fragile miracle of their freedom.

George paused for a moment at the threshold before entering the room.

"Hello!" Raisa warmly greeted him as she slowly rose from her chair.

"Good evening," George replied quietly.

"Join us," Raisa continued. "Here's a cup of tea and some sandwiches. Please, help yourself. This is my sister Sara and her two friends Tamara and Rosa, who have just returned from the camp."

"Hello, George," said Rosa, sitting next to Sara.

Her eyes were red and swollen, and her gaze drifted somewhere far beyond the room. George noticed her trembling hands and the slight shaking of her head, moving gently back and forth like a fragile porcelain figurine on a shelf. Rosa was hesitantly sipping tea before she looked up at Raisa, as if asking whether it was safe to speak in front of George. Raisa nodded firmly.

"George is one of us," she said softly. "You can feel safe in his presence."

Tears welled in Rosa's eyes. She took a deep breath and began to speak.

"I was arrested one summer day in 1936. I can't clearly remember what happened after my arrest. I've tried hard to erase it from my memory."

She paused.

"Before that, I lived like most Muscovites. I had a small room in a communal apartment. I had a life then. I could wake up at my own pace, drink a cup of tea, wash my face at the kitchen sink, and even apply bright red lipstick."

A faint, distant smile crossed her face.

"I looked good back then, when I was healthy and young. I worked as a schoolteacher and was proud of my job. I could walk through the streets of Moscow, visit parks. I had a boyfriend, a university student." Her voice trembled. "It was a good life. "She continued.

"One evening we were sitting on a bench when two plain-clothes agents approached us. They took Sergey aside. As I watched from a distance, my friend shouted: 'You have no right to arrest me!"

Her breathing grew uneven.

"Two more men came toward me and told me I was arrested for espionage."

"I tried to break free from their grip… but after that my memory becomes foggy."

She looked down at her hands.

“Some faces remain vivid in my memory, but most of it now seems blurred… as if it happened in another life.”

Her voice dropped lower.

“They wouldn’t let me sleep. The interrogators watched me constantly. Every time my head drooped, they struck me.”

“I was starving. They would sit at the table and eat smoked sausage sandwiches in front of me… smiling.”

A tear slid down her cheek.

“When I tried to steal a small piece of the sausage, the interrogator beat me until I lost consciousness.”

“I was delirious. I lost touch with reality. It felt as though I was losing my identity.”

“By that time, I had contracted typhoid fever.”

She wiped her eyes slowly.

“I remember being taken to the prison hospital… and then being transported north.”

“I remember being thrown onto a ship. I was freezing.”

“It was unbearable.”

“I think I lost consciousness… maybe even fell into a coma.”

"I went through hell."

She paused again.

"What saved me," she continued slowly, "was the belief that Stalin simply didn't know what was happening."

"If only I could write a letter to Comrade Stalin… he would free me."

She shook her head softly.

"I still remember my room in Moscow before my arrest. There was a window facing a willow tree and green grass in front of the house."

"The room had a round table, two chairs, and a sofa where I slept and read books."

Rosa fell silent and stared at her hands, which now resembled thin claws. Her fingers trembled uncontrollably before she finally began to cry.

The room fell into complete silence.

The small lamp hanging above the table cast a pale circle of light over the women.

George sat quietly, absorbing every word. He felt the weight of history pressing into the room. He resisted the urge to take notes, silently promising himself that these testimonies would one day reach the outside world. Tamara slowly raised her gaze from the cup of tea and the small pretzel that she could not eat because most of her teeth were gone. She sighed deeply before beginning.

“When I was arrested, I was a young woman,” she said quietly.

“My face was full of joy. I had all my teeth then.”

“I had a wonderful young man. He was a Red Guard. We were happy.”

“We walked together in the center of Moscow.”

Her voice faltered.

She wiped the corner of her eyes before continuing.

“Everything changed when Stalin began his purge against Trotsky’s supporters.”

“We were innocent.”

“Our only crime was believing in Trotsky.”

“My companion disappeared one day.”

“Two days later they arrested me.”

“I was taken to Lubyanka.”

“I was interrogated without explanation.”

“I was woken constantly and forced to sign documents.”

“Each time they woke me they poured cold water over my head.”

“I could not even read what I was signing.”

She shuddered slightly.

"But that was not the worst of it."

"There was unbearable noise… cruelty… things I cannot even describe."

"Then I contracted typhus."

"I survived because they sent me to the prison hospital."

"When I recovered, they sent me north."

"To a camp."

Her voice became barely audible.

"We were transported by boat."

"I lay there half dead from cold."

"I prayed for death."

"But somehow I survived."

She lifted her tear-filled eyes.

"I come from the mountains of Georgia, near the border with Iran… the same region where Stalin was born."

Tamara fell silent, wiping her face with a torn piece of cloth.

"We are free now," she said bitterly. "But we are banned from living within one hundred kilometers of Moscow."

"Freed… but never forgiven."

Sara, Raisa's sister, exchanged a weary glance with Raisa before beginning her own story.

"I was arrested because I supported Trotsky," she said quietly.

"During the revolution I served as a Red Guard."

"I supervised cargo trains carrying soap."

"Soap was essential to fight lice, typhus, and cholera."

"I never stole a single bar."

"Our loyalty was absolute—to the revolution, to Lenin, to Trotsky."

"At that time, we knew almost nothing about Stalin."

"We believed anyone in Lenin's circle must be trustworthy."

Her voice grew bitter.

"How wrong we were."

The dim light from the lampshade cast soft shadows across the women's-tired faces as they continued to speak.

They understood, perhaps instinctively, that they had a sacred duty—to bear witness to the cruelty of the system that had nearly destroyed them. George listened with intense concentration, committing every detail to memory. He was already planning how these stories could be carried beyond Soviet borders—perhaps through the Catholic network in the Baltics.

As the testimonies unfolded, a powerful tapestry of suffering and endurance emerged. These were not merely individual stories of pain. They were fragments of a collective memory belonging to an entire generation that had endured one of the darkest chapters of the twentieth century. George knew that their voices must not be silenced. And he silently vowed that one day the world would hear them.

Chapter 32

Conversations of Change

The next day, George set out to visit his elder sister, Natalie, who resided in a cramped communal apartment notorious for its lack of privacy. The long corridor outside her room was lined with worn doors, each leading to another family's fragile world. The faint smells of boiled cabbage, coal smoke, and cheap soap lingered in the air. Voices carried easily through the thin walls, a constant reminder that in such apartments no conversation was ever truly private. Upon his arrival, Natalie promptly opened the door, revealing a small room where she was busy translating articles for an emerging publishing house. Papers were spread across the table in neat piles, a dictionary open beside her, and a small lamp cast a pool of warm light over the desk.

"Hello, George. How are you?" she greeted him warmly, ushering him inside. "And how are Sonya and the girls?"

"We're all fine," George replied as he settled in. He removed his coat slowly, brushing off a few lingering droplets of melted snow. "But I came to seek your insights. You have a deep understanding of current events. I'm hoping you can help me make sense of everything."

In the confines of Natalie's modest room, they engaged in a subdued conversation about politics, the shifting landscape of the world, and George's uncertainties about the future. Their voices remained deliberately low, instinctively cautious in a building where neighbors might be listening through the walls.

Natalie, always perceptive, leaned back in her chair and studied her brother for a moment before speaking.

"There's a lot happening right now," she observed quietly. Her fingers rested thoughtfully on the pages she had been translating. "The country is changing faster than most people realize."

She lowered her voice even further.

"I think we'll soon see the possibility of open correspondence with our relatives in the United States."

This prospect visibly brightened George's mood.

"Do you think there's a chance we might be able to leave?" he asked, the idea sparking a fragile hope within him. For a moment, he allowed himself to imagine a life beyond the borders of the Soviet Union.

Natalie responded with a thoughtful shrug.

"There's a growing demand for change," she said quietly. "People in Moscow and beyond are yearning for a better life—the freedom to travel, to speak openly, to breathe."

She glanced briefly toward the door, lowering her voice to a whisper.

"I believe the Warsaw Pact countries will eventually crumble."

George looked at her with surprise.

"There's a palpable discontent in Warsaw, Budapest, and other places under communist rule," Natalie continued softly.

"Something is brewing in those closed-off societies. You can feel it in the air."

She paused, choosing her words carefully.

"People have lived too long under fear. That kind of pressure doesn't disappear—it builds. And one day it breaks."

George listened intently, absorbing every word.

Natalie continued, almost to herself.

"It may not happen tomorrow… or even next year. But history is moving beneath the surface."

George left Natalie's apartment feeling uplifted by her insights and quiet confidence. As he stepped back into the narrow corridor, the sounds of everyday life resumed around him—distant arguments, the clatter of dishes, footsteps echoing across the worn wooden floorboards.

As he walked home through the chilly Moscow streets, he pondered her words.

Above him, the gray sky stretched endlessly over the city, and for the first time in many months he felt something unfamiliar stirring inside him—cautious hope.

Natalie's foresight painted a picture of significant change, a prophecy that, unbeknownst to them, would only come to fruition years later. But for George, even the possibility of such transformation offered a glimmer of light in an otherwise uncertain time.

Chapter 33

New Year's Eve at the Kremlin

New Year's Eve in Moscow, 1953, was a time of celebration, a stark contrast to the political and social upheavals of the past year. After months of uncertainty and whispered rumors following Stalin's death, the city seemed eager to breathe again. The city, adorned with festive decorations, brimmed with an air of anticipation and hope. Strings of lights shimmered along the main boulevards, and fir trees decorated with red stars stood proudly in public squares.

The authorities, in a rare gesture, allowed groups of commoners to tour the Kremlin, showcasing its architectural wonders to the public. For many Muscovites, the Kremlin had long stood like a distant fortress of power—visible from afar yet unreachable. Muscovites, especially those with the necessary privileges, flocked to *GUM*, the central department store, eyeing luxurious fur coats and preparing for grand celebrations. Behind its vast glass windows, displays of crystal, velvet dresses, and polished leather shoes glittered beneath the bright store lights.

December 25th dawned bitterly cold, with occasional sun rays glittering off the pristine snow, adding a magical touch to the festive atmosphere. The snow sparkled like scattered diamonds across the rooftops and sidewalks. Catherine and Maria, both talented ballet students, were chosen to perform in *The Nutcracker* at the Kremlin, a great honor for any aspiring dancer.

Their instructor, Galina, a retired ballerina, dedicated her life to training schoolchildren in the art of ballet. For this special occasion, she adorned herself with an old silver fox collar, a treasured memento from her performing days.

Catherine and Maria's parents, unable to attend the performance, waited anxiously outside the Kremlin's imposing gates. They stood among clusters of other parents and teachers, their breath forming pale clouds in the freezing air. The setting was awe-inspiring: from the majestic *Spassky Tower* with its enormous clock to the grandeur of the Kremlin cathedrals, the Red Army soldiers stood in ceremonial guard, adding to the solemnity of the occasion. Their boots struck the frozen ground with rhythmic precision as they shifted positions.

As the young performers approached the Kremlin gates, they were greeted by a stern colonel in a long gray wool coat adorned with golden insignia, his head covered by a Persian lamb fur hat. His tall figure stood immobile against the crimson walls of the fortress. For many, the Kremlin had always been a distant, almost untouchable relic of power, its gates rarely open to ordinary citizens.

"Citizeness, your documents, please!" the colonel demanded, his voice sharp and official, his gaze cold and unyielding.

Galina, with a practiced calm born of years on the stage, presented a black leather folder containing the names and addresses of the young dancers. The children stood silently behind her, clutching their small dance bags and watching the exchange with wide, curious eyes.

The colonel scrutinized the documents meticulously, his thorough inspection heightening the tension. The cold wind rustled the papers slightly as he turned each page with deliberate care. After a seemingly interminable wait, he returned the documents with a brief nod of approval.

"Good, Comrade. You are cleared to enter," he declared.

Relief washed over Galina as she ushered the children through the gates.

"Follow me quietly," she instructed in a soft but firm voice. "We are entering the Kremlin!"

With a mixture of pride and quiet awe, she led the young dancers into the heart of Russian power.

For Catherine and Maria, passing through the gates felt like stepping into a fairy tale. The massive red walls seemed to rise endlessly above them, and the golden domes of the cathedrals shimmered against the pale winter sky. The opulence and grandeur of the Kremlin's palaces left them wide-eyed with wonder.

They were about to dance in a hall where the legendary Olga Lepeshinskaya once performed—an honor that filled them with a mixture of excitement and nervous anticipation.

Galina gathered the girls before they entered the backstage corridor.

"Remember," she said quietly, adjusting one of their ribbons, "you are standing on a stage where the greatest ballerinas once danced. Hold your heads high."

Her words carried both encouragement and reverence.

The backstage halls buzzed softly with activity—the rustle of costumes, the faint tuning of instruments from the orchestra pit, and the quiet murmurs of stage assistants preparing for the performance.

As the curtains prepared to rise on their performance of *The Nutcracker*, the young dancers adjusted their slippers and smoothed their costumes. The warm glow of the stage lights filtered through the curtain, casting golden reflections across the polished floor.

Beyond the curtain, the orchestra began the opening notes of Tchaikovsky's familiar score.

The young dancers readied themselves, their hearts beating quickly.

Unaware of the watchful eyes of history upon them, they stepped forward toward the stage.

This New Year's Eve marked not just the end of a year—but the beginning of a new era, one filled with possibilities and change.

Chapter 34

A Night of Enchantment

The performance night of *The Nutcracker* at the Kremlin was filled with anticipation and magic, especially for Catherine and Maria. The vast palace corridors hummed with quiet excitement as young performers hurried past in colorful costumes, their soft slippers whispering across the polished floors.

After being escorted to the dressing room by Galina, the girls donned their pristine white tutus and satin ballet slippers. The dressing room glowed under bright mirrors framed with warm lights, reflecting rows of delicate costumes hanging neatly along the walls. Galina meticulously checked the fit and tied the slippers securely around their ankles.

"Stand still for a moment," she said gently, tightening the ribbons with practiced precision. Her hands moved with the calm confidence of someone who had spent a lifetime in the theater.

The young dancers, brimming with excitement, were then led quietly to their positions behind the stage curtains.

The orchestra began assembling in the pit below the stage. Musicians adjusted their instruments, the soft tuning of violins and the low murmur of cellos drifting upward into the wings. The conductor stepped forward, straightening his tuxedo jacket and lifting his baton as he prepared for the performance.

When the curtains opened, the stage burst into life, bathed in brilliant golden lights that illuminated the dancers and captivated the audience.

The viewers, dressed in their finest satins, lace gowns, and luxurious fur coats, radiated an air of elegance and quiet prestige. Crystal chandeliers glimmered above the hall, scattering light across the richly decorated balconies.

From behind the curtains, the children peeked cautiously at the audience, their eyes wide with wonder.

"Look how many people," Maria whispered, barely containing her excitement.

As the conductor tapped his baton, the first enchanting notes of Tchaikovsky's music filled the air, signaling the beginning of the magical performance.

The ballet unfolded like a living fairy tale. The orchestra's melodies flowed through the hall as dancers glided across the stage in graceful harmony. The children performed their parts with care and determination, their movements following the rhythm of the music and the unfolding story.

The chase between the children and the mouse character became one of the evening's highlights. Laughter rippled softly through the audience as the scene unfolded, drawing everyone deeper into the fantastical world of *The Nutcracker*.

For Catherine and Maria, the stage lights felt dazzling and warm, and the music seemed to carry them effortlessly from step to step. In those moments, the outside world—with its fears and uncertainties—disappeared completely.

When the final scene concluded, the audience rose to their feet in a standing ovation. Applause thundered through the hall like a rolling wave. The dancers bowed together as the orchestra played its final triumphant notes.

Galina quickly ushered the girls off the stage and back toward the dressing room.

"Well done, my little ballerinas," she said proudly. Her voice trembled slightly with emotion.

The excitement backstage was palpable as the children hurried to change out of their costumes. Laughter filled the room as ribbons were untied, slippers slipped off, and warm coats pulled on. They dressed quickly, making sure they were bundled up for the cold Moscow night awaiting them outside.

When they exited the Kremlin gates, Catherine and Maria were greeted by a woman comrade distributing small bags of candy to the young performers.

"Happy New Year," she said kindly, handing them each a brightly wrapped parcel.

The girls' delight was immediate.

Their chatter became ceaseless as they walked toward their parents, filled with vivid descriptions of the performance and their favorite moments.

"The mouse almost caught me!" Catherine exclaimed excitedly.

"And the orchestra was so loud!" Maria added breathlessly.

Sonya and George listened with pride and quiet joy, smiling at their daughters' happiness. For a moment, the hardships of the past year seemed distant and unreal.

New Year celebrations held a special significance for Soviet citizens. Families gathered for festive meals, hopeful that the coming year might bring relief from the hardships of the past.

Across Moscow, beautifully decorated pine trees stood in homes and public halls, adorned with lights and handmade paper ornaments. These celebrations carried no religious meaning; instead, they centered around joyful figures such as Grandfather Frost and Miss Snow, who brought gifts and laughter to children throughout the country.

For Catherine and Maria, the night at the Kremlin was more than just a ballet performance.

It was a moment of wonder—a brief glimpse into a world of music, beauty, and dreams.

And as the New Year approached, it carried with it the quiet promise of new beginnings and brighter days ahead.

Chapter 35

A Festive Gathering

The New Year celebrations, though devoid of public fanfare, were deeply rooted in family traditions. George, Sonya, and their daughters joined Ethelyn and Eleanor for a festive dinner in their new residence, a splendid building awarded to Eleanor for her role as an English radio presenter for Radio Moscow. The building's grandeur, complete with a concierge standing quietly in the foyer, spoke of the esteem in which Eleanor was held—a small island of privilege in a city governed by silence and restraint. Outside, the winter night wrapped the streets of Moscow in stillness, the snow absorbing the distant sounds of the city.

Inside, Eleanor had set up a charming little pine tree adorned with homemade ornaments. Tiny stars cut from paper, delicate strings of glass beads, and hand-painted wooden figures hung from the branches, each fragile shape catching the soft glow of lamplight, symbolizing the joy and warmth of the season.

The dinner table was a testament to Eleanor's culinary skills, featuring a traditional American apple pie baked in her new oven and a sumptuous plump chicken, its golden skin glistening like a promise fulfilled. The spread was rich and varied, with blintzes, potato pancakes, braised carrots, turnips, halva, and fresh oranges—luxuries that, in another life, might have seemed ordinary. The warm aromas of roasted chicken and baked apples filled the apartment, creating a rare atmosphere of comfort.

The centerpiece was a large bowl of potato salad, believed to bring good luck in the coming year.

The family gathered around the table, drawn not only by hunger but by the rare permission to feel whole.

George, embracing the festive spirit, wished everyone a Merry Christmas and a Happy New Year, his voice steady, though his eyes betrayed the weight of years survived. For a moment, the worries of the outside world seemed suspended.

Ethelyn, moved by the occasion, had a tear in her eye as she reminisced about Nikifor. His absence seemed almost tangible, as though an empty chair stood quietly among them.

The atmosphere deepened when George began reading passages from the Bible in a soft, reverent tone. The room grew still as his voice moved gently through the quiet apartment, his words rising into the room, carrying with them something older than fear—something that could not be confiscated, censored, or erased.

After the meal, the family gathered under the tree to exchange gifts. The sight of the tree, with its green boughs, was a reminder of the spring yet to come, of seasons that arrived regardless of borders or decrees.

The joy of unwrapping presents was evident. Wrappings rustled softly as small gifts passed from hand to hand, each member of the family beaming with happiness, their laughter brief, bright, and quietly defiant.

The children danced around the tree, holding hands. Their small footsteps tapped rhythmically against the wooden floor.

Meanwhile, the adults gathered near the piano. Eleanor gently lifted the lid and began to play.

At first their voices were soft—almost cautious—but gradually the Christmas carols grew stronger. The melodies floated through the apartment, filling the room with warmth that seemed to push back the long shadows of recent years.

It was a rare indulgence, overlooked by the authorities in a brief concession to freedom and enjoyment—as if even the State, for one night, had turned its face away.

As the evening ended, George and his family prepared to leave. The women busied themselves with cleaning up, ensuring Ethelyn wouldn't have to deal with the aftermath of the gathering.

Parting wishes of joy and good fortune were exchanged at the door. Their embraces lingered longer than usual, as if each person understood how fragile such moments truly were.

The door closed softly behind them. The tree lights remained, flickering quietly in the empty room. Their small flames reflected gently in the window glass. Holding their silent vigil against the dark.

* * *

Catherine was jolted back to reality, finding herself in the embassy's waiting room. The murmur of distant voices and the muted rustle of papers replaced the warmth of memory. Fluorescent lights hummed faintly above her; their sterile brightness far removed from the soft lamplight of the past. She stretched her limbs, her body heavy, as though she had traveled not across a room but across decades. A lingering drowsiness clung to her as she reflected on the immense changes the world had undergone since that memorable New Year. For a moment she remained still, suspended between who she had been and who she was becoming. The memory of the small pine tree, the music, and the voices of her family faded slowly like the final notes of a distant song.

Behind her, the door to that life had already closed forever.

Part Two

Trap for Eternity

Chapter 36

A Portal into the New World

Catherine drifted back into memory.

She was twelve years old, standing in the middle of something she did not yet fully understand—the Sixth World Festival of Youth and Students in Moscow.

The city felt transformed. Everywhere she looked, there were colors, music, and faces unlike any she had seen before. Young people had come from all over the world. They laughed in unfamiliar languages, wore bright clothes, and moved with an ease that fascinated her.

It was 1957. Nikita Khrushchev had begun to open the Soviet Union, if only slightly, after the long years of Stalin's isolation. For the first time, Moscow welcomed foreigners not as enemies, but as guests.

To Catherine, it felt like the world had suddenly arrived at her doorstep.

At *Luzhniki* Stadium, newly built for the occasion, a great emblem hung above the crowds—a five-petal flower, each petal a different color, each representing a continent. It was meant to symbolize unity. Catherine stared at it for a long time.

The streets overflowed with celebration. Students rode through Moscow in decorated trucks, waving and singing. New Hungarian buses carried visitors through the city. Music filled the squares. The Central Square drew crowds so large Catherine could barely see beyond the sea of people. Even the Kremlin, once distant and forbidden, opened its gates. Everywhere she heard the same words: For Peace and Friendship. Something had shifted. Even at twelve, she could feel it. After the festival ended, Moscow did not seem quite the same.

What stayed with Catherine most was not the speeches or the slogans, but the people—especially the girls. They wore skirts that moved when they walked. Their hair fell freely around their shoulders. They looked unafraid.

She wanted to look like them. One evening, she gathered her courage.

"I want blue jeans," she told her father. "Or at least a skirt like theirs."

George looked at her carefully.

"No," he said.

His answer was quiet, but final. Catherine felt the familiar wall between them—the wall she could not yet name.

"Why do you have to be so afraid all the time?" she asked.

He did not answer. She said nothing more, but something inside her had already begun to change. One day, she promised herself, she would choose her own life.

***

In 1959, Moscow witnessed something few had imagined possible—the American National Exhibition in Sokolniki Park.

For six weeks, the Americans built an entire world inside the park. They spent millions of dollars constructing pavilions filled with things most Soviet citizens had never seen: modern kitchens, sleek automobiles, televisions, and household appliances designed to make life easier. Crowds lined up for hours to enter. For many, it was their first glimpse beyond the Iron Curtain. Catherine walked among them, carried forward by curiosity.

Women gathered around washing machines and electric mixers, studying them closely, whispering to one another. Men stood near polished automobiles, running their hands along the smooth metal as if touching something unreal. Everywhere she looked, there was movement, color, possibility. At one pavilion, Catherine was handed a small paper cup.

"Pepsi-Cola," the man said.

She hesitated, then took a sip. The taste was sharp and sweet. She had never experienced anything like it.

Nearby, a large crowd gathered around a cosmetics display. At its center stood Helena Rubinstein. She was elegant and composed, dressed in a white suit trimmed in black, her presence alone commanding attention. Catherine had never seen a woman like her. Rubinstein spoke calmly, inviting two volunteers forward. Makeup artists began their work as the crowd watched in silence. Catherine leaned forward, barely breathing. She imagined what it would feel like to sit in that chair, to be transformed before everyone's eyes. But she knew her father would never allow it.

When the women were handed mirrors, their faces filled with astonishment. The crowd responded with applause. Rubinstein smiled.

“Beauty,” she said, “is power.”

The words lingered in Catherine’s mind. For the first time, she understood that beauty could be more than appearance. It could be freedom. The exhibition revealed other American products as well. Cigarettes, cosmetics, clothing, and appliances—all symbols of a life that seemed distant and unattainable. Catherine moved through the exhibits slowly, absorbing everything. By the time she returned home, she felt both exhausted and restless. That night, she lay awake in bed. She thought of the women she had seen. Their confidence. Their ease. She thought of the taste of Pepsi. She thought of the world beyond Moscow. Something inside her had shifted again. The exhibition had shown her not just objects, but possibilities. And she could not forget them.

Chapter 37

Ethelyn's Passing

In 1972, the phone rang with news that would change everything.

George answered. Catherine watched his face as he listened.

"My dear Georgie," his sister Eleanor said gently, "Mother passed away in her sleep."

For a moment, he did not speak. When he lowered the receiver, Catherine understood. Ethelyn was gone. The loss settled quietly over the family. They traveled to New Jerusalem for the burial, a peaceful place several hours from Moscow. It was there, far from the city where Ethelyn had spent most of her life, that they said goodbye. The priest opened his book and began to read.

"Ethylin Gertrude White, born in Somerville, Massachusetts, in 1881…"

Catherine felt a sudden stillness. She had never heard that name before. Ethylin. To her, she had always been Ethelyn. The priest continued.

"She married Nikifor Yampolsky, and together they raised four children. In 1936, she followed her husband and family to Moscow, where she lived the remainder of her life…"

Somerville, Massachusetts. The words lingered in Catherine's mind. America had always existed in her family's story, yet it felt distant—almost unreal. A place that belonged to another version of her grandmother. One by one, the family stepped forward to pray. Catherine stood beside her father. She wished she had asked her grandmother more questions. About America. About the life she had left behind. About who she had been before Moscow. Now she never could.

As the service ended, Catherine understood that something had closed forever. Ethelyn was gone. And with her, a part of their past.

Yet something remained. A question. And Catherine knew that question would stay with her.

Chapter 38

At the Junction of Fate and Concealed Realities

In 1972, Catherine faced an uncertain future. She had finished her studies, but the path ahead was unclear. Then, one morning, the phone rang. It was Boris Tondorf from the Foreign Trade Academy. He knew her mother, Sonya, from an art class. His voice was warm, but cautious.

"There may be a position for you," he said. "Teaching English."

Catherine felt her heart quicken. The Academy was one of the most prestigious institutions in Moscow. Its graduates would represent the Soviet Union abroad. But Boris hesitated.

"There is something you must understand," he continued. "Your background… it could create problems."

She knew exactly what he meant. Her mother was Jewish. For years, the family had hidden it.

"And your American roots," he added quietly. "They will watch you more closely than others."

Catherine said nothing.

"You must be careful," Boris said. "Officially, you are Belorussian. Like your grandfather."

"I understand," she replied.

Despite the warning, he encouraged her to come for an interview the next morning. After the call ended, Catherine sat in silence. This was the opportunity she had hoped for. And the risk she had always feared.

The Academy building rose before her the next morning, solid and imposing. Inside, an elderly woman led her to the office.

Three men sat behind a polished desk. Above them hung a portrait of Leonid Brezhnev.

Boris was among them. They asked about her education. Her English. Her family. Catherine answered carefully. She had rehearsed every word. When it was over, Boris escorted her into a faculty meeting. The room was filled with teachers. He introduced her.

Catherine stood.

"My name is Catherine Yampolsky," she said. "I was born in Moscow. I graduated from the Foreign Language Institute."

Her voice remained steady. She did not say anything more. Others were introduced as well. One woman had returned from Canada. Another had studied abroad. Catherine listened closely.

These were people who had seen the world she had only imagined. For the first time, she felt she might be stepping into that world herself. Her first day of teaching came soon after. She dressed carefully, choosing her best suit. Boris greeted her and handed her a class list.

"You will be teaching three postgraduate students," he said.

She walked to the classroom and opened the door. Three young men stood as she entered. They wore dark suits and white shirts. Their posture was formal, disciplined. They watched her closely. Catherine realized they were studying her, just as she was studying them. She took her place at the front of the room. For years, she had been the one waiting. Now, she had crossed the threshold. Her new life had begun.

Chapter 39

An Unexpected Offer

Catherine began her first class by greeting the students in Russian. Alejandro, seated by the window, raised his hand.

"May we conduct the class in English?" he asked.

She hesitated only a moment.

"Of course," she replied, switching effortlessly.

She introduced herself, then asked each of them to speak. Alejandro answered with confidence, his accent noticeable but his vocabulary strong. The others followed. Catherine listened closely, correcting their pronunciation, guiding them gently. They were intelligent. Disciplined. And they were watching her just as carefully. When the class ended, the students gathered their things and left. All except Alejandro. He lingered at the door, then turned back.

"Would you like a ride home?" he asked. "I live in the Southwest District. I believe we are neighbors."

Catherine froze. Few people owned cars. It was a privilege reserved for the well-connected.

"I… thank you," she said carefully. "But we must be discreet."

He nodded.

"My car is nearby. I'll wait for you."

She finished gathering her papers, aware of how exposed she suddenly felt.

Outside, a silver *Moskvich*[6] idled on the side street.

Alejandro stood beside it, wearing a leather jacket. He opened the passenger door. Catherine hesitated, then sat down. Music filled the car—Edith Piaf. The scent of cologne and tobacco lingered in the air. Nothing about this felt ordinary. As they drove, she gave him her address. He smiled slightly.

"I know," he said. "I live across from you."

She turned toward him, surprised. He said nothing more. They drove the rest of the way in silence. When they reached her building, Catherine stepped out quickly.

"Thank you," she said.

He nodded. Inside her apartment, she leaned against the door. Her heart was still racing. She did not know why Alejandro had offered the ride. Kindness, perhaps. Or something else.

In her world, nothing was ever simple. And nothing was without consequence.

Chapter 40

Privilege and Pretense

Catherine's days quickly fell into a routine. She arrived at the Academy before eight each morning, nodding to the guard as she entered. Inside, everything felt ordered, controlled. Different from the world outside. Her students were already waiting when she entered the classroom. Alejandro. Anatoly. Sergey. They stood to greet her.

Their suits were perfectly pressed. Their hair neatly cut. They carried themselves with quiet confidence, as if their futures had already been decided.

Catherine began the lesson. They listened to BBC recordings. Translated newspaper articles. Practiced pronunciation. They worked hard. But there was something else about them. A certainty. A protection she did not share.

They would travel abroad. Represent the Soviet Union. Live lives closed to most citizens. Catherine understood what that meant. She chose her words carefully. Always.

That evening, darkness had already fallen when she left the building. The cold air stung her face.

She pulled her coat tighter and started toward the street.

"Catherine."

She turned. Alejandro sat behind the wheel of his car.

“I’ve been waiting,” he said.

He opened the passenger door.

“I brought something for you.”

She hesitated, then sat down. He pressed a button. Music filled the car.

The Beatles. Catherine felt her breath catch. Western music was difficult to find. Dangerous, even. She listened in silence. For a moment, the Academy, the watchful eyes, the careful words—all of it faded. There was only the music.

Alejandro glanced at her.

“They’re very popular,” he said.

She nodded.

“Yes,” she replied softly.

She did not tell him what it meant to hear them here. In his car. In Moscow. In that moment, she understood how close and how far another world truly was.

Chapter 41

An Enigmatic Encounter

Catherine sat quietly in the passenger seat as the car moved through the dark streets. Warm air filled the interior. The scent of cologne lingered. The Beatles played softly. She watched the city pass outside the window, half-listening, half-lost in her own thoughts. Alejandro said little. When he stopped in front of her building, he turned toward her.

"We're here," he said.

"Thank you," Catherine replied. "You're very kind."

He hesitated.

"May I call you sometime?"

The question caught her off guard. Telephones were never private. In a communal apartment, anyone could answer. Still, she reached into her bag and found a scrap of paper. She wrote the number.

"If someone else answers," she said carefully, "ask for Catherine." He smiled.

"I will."

She stepped out of the car and closed the door behind her. Alejandro remained where he was, watching her. She did not look back. Inside the building, she climbed the stairs slowly. Only when she reached her apartment did she allow herself to breathe. She had crossed a line. It was a small thing. A telephone number. Yet she understood what it meant.

In Moscow, nothing personal was ever entirely private. And nothing happened without consequence.

Chapter 42

The Door Begins to Open

In May 1972, Moscow prepared for the arrival of U.S. President Richard Nixon. Catherine watched the broadcast on television early that morning. Nixon and his wife descended the steps of their plane at Vnukovo Airport. Soviet officials waited below. Flags waved. Cameras lingered on every gesture. It felt unreal. An American president in Moscow. She turned off the television reluctantly and left for work.

The city had been transformed overnight. Streets were swept clean. Police stood at every major corner. Even the air felt different—tense, watchful. At the Academy, security was tighter than usual. An official checked her passport before allowing her inside. When she reached her classroom, two men in plain clothes were already waiting.

"American visitors will be in the building today," one of them said. "For security reasons, you are to remain here."

They took seats in the back of the room. They watched everything. Catherine said nothing. She understood. Even a moment like this—one that spoke of peace—required surveillance. At home, the visit stirred something else. Hope. It was not spoken openly. It never was. But Catherine saw it in her father.

One afternoon, George went to visit his sister, Natalie. They sat at her kitchen table, their voices low.

"The Helsinki agreement…" George said carefully. "Do you think it could change anything for us?"

Natalie hesitated.

"It might," she said. "Some people are talking about exit visas. About visiting family abroad."

George leaned forward.

"America," he whispered.

He had not said the word in years. Natalie studied him.

"It will not be easy," she said. "There will be applications. Questions. Waiting."

George nodded. He understood waiting. He had been waiting most of his life. Still, something had shifted. For the first time, the possibility did not feel impossible. They sat in silence for a moment. Neither of them dared to say more. Hope, in their world, was dangerous. But it was alive. And once awakened, it could not easily be silenced.

Chapter 43

The Price of Freedom

In the months that followed, hope no longer lived only in whispers. It entered their home.

One evening, Catherine sat with her parents at the kitchen table. The familiar scent of her mother's beet soup filled the apartment. Outside, darkness pressed against the windows. Her father was unusually quiet. Finally, he rose.

"Catherine," he said. "Come with me."

She followed him into the next room. He closed the door. For a moment, he said nothing.

Then, quietly:

"Your mother and I have decided. We are going to apply for exit visas."

Catherine stared at him.

"To America?"

He nodded. The word hung between them. Her heart began to race.

"But… my work. The Academy," she said. "If they find out—"

He understood.

"We have already contacted our relatives," he said. "Through priests in the Baltics."

This was no longer a dream. It was real.

"You know what this means," she said. "They will watch us. They may take everything."

George did not look away.

"We cannot remain here forever," he said.

Catherine felt the ground beneath her shift. All her life, America had been memory. Story. Possibility. Now it was becoming a decision. A risk.

"And if they refuse?" she asked.

He did not answer. He did not need to. Refusal carried its own punishment. Silence filled the room. She thought of her work. Her students. The fragile life she had built. And she thought of her grandmother. Ethylin. America. Nothing would remain untouched.

"This will change everything," she said softly.

George nodded.

"Yes."

Neither of them spoke again. They both understood. Once the door began to open, it could never truly be closed again.

Chapter 44

A Fork in the Path

In the days that followed, Catherine moved through her routines as if nothing had changed. But everything had. One evening, she sat with her father again at the kitchen table. The same table where he had told her of their decision. She studied his face. He looked older.

"Dad," she said quietly, "I keep thinking about what will happen. If you leave… everything here could disappear for me." George nodded. He had expected this.

"I know," he said. "We are asking a great deal of you. More than I ever wished." He hesitated.

"America is where I was born," he said. "It is the only place where I was free. I want to see it again… before I die."

His voice was calm, but she heard the truth beneath it. This was not only hope. It was necessity. He looked at her.

"My dream is that one day, you will follow us."

Catherine lowered her eyes. She thought of her classroom. Her students. Her fragile place inside a system that could erase her without warning.

"I want you to be happy," she said. "You, Mama… Aunt Natalie. Maybe it will be easier for her. She has already lived her life."

George reached for her hand. Neither of them spoke for a while. For the first time, Catherine understood that their lives were beginning to separate.

Not because of love. But because of history. They were standing at the same doorway—

and preparing to walk through it in different directions.

Chapter 45

The Illusion of Escape

In the weeks after her parents' decision, Catherine lingered longer at the Academy. Work gave her refuge from thought. One evening, she stayed late to finish her annual report. By the time she stepped outside, dusk had settled over the empty streets.

"Catherine!"

She turned. Alejandro leaned against his silver car, smiling.

"Good evening," he said. "You look exhausted. Let me take you home."

She hesitated only a moment before slipping into the passenger seat. The car smelled faintly of cigarettes and French cologne. He turned on the radio. Music filled the silence. For a while, neither spoke. Then Alejandro glanced at her.

"Tell me something," he said. "How do you see your future here?"

The question was quiet—but dangerous. Catherine felt her pulse quicken. Cars could be listened to. People could disappear for less. She forced a light laugh.

"At this rate," she said playfully, "I should probably marry someone like you."

She paused, letting the joke settle.

"But since you're already married," she added, "I suppose I'll have to keep looking."

Alejandro smiled, watching her carefully.

"And what would make you happy?"

She turned toward the window.

"A passionate love affair," she said.

It was safer than telling the truth. Alejandro laughed softly and turned the music up. They drove the rest of the way in silence. When he pulled up in front of her building, she thanked him and stepped out quickly, the night air cold against her face. Inside her apartment, the silence returned. She realized that with Alejandro, she was no longer certain who was asking the questions—or why. That night, Catherine cried. Not for Alejandro. Not even for her parents. But for herself. For the life that was closing around her. In the morning, she woke with a single thought: Bulgaria. The Black Sea. Even that small freedom felt distant.

At the Academy, she stood outside Comrade Tondorf's office, steadying herself before knocking.

"Come in," he called.

He looked irritated, distracted. She spoke quickly, before she could lose her nerve.

"I wanted to ask if I could apply for a visa. To Bulgaria. Just for vacation."

The change in his face was immediate. His eyes hardened.

"A visa?" he repeated.

He stood.

"Have you lost your mind?"

His voice rose.

"You have a position here. A future. And you want to throw it away for this nonsense?"

Catherine said nothing.

"You could lose everything," he continued. "Your job. Your reputation. You would never work again. Do you understand?"

He leaned closer.

"And don't even think about marrying a foreigner. I have seen too many young women ruin their lives chasing fantasies."

The words struck deeper than she expected. He lowered his voice.

"I am telling you this because I respect your family. Do not make this mistake."

The conversation was over. Catherine left his office without speaking. In the corridor, she stopped. Her hands were shaking. Even Bulgaria was forbidden. Even a vacation.

Freedom, she realized, was not measured in distance—but in permission. And she had none.

Chapter 46

The Courage to Seek More

Catherine left Comrade Tondorf's office in a daze. His warning still rang in her ears. You could be fired. You could lose everything. She walked slowly down the corridor, past the familiar doors and bulletin boards, barely seeing them. Until now, her life had followed a narrow, predictable path. Study. Work. Obey. Survive. But something had shifted. Her father had applied for an exit visa. He had dared to hope.

For the first time, Catherine allowed herself to wonder if she could hope too. She knew what it would mean. Endless forms. Interviews. Questions about her loyalty. Questions about her family. Questions designed to trap her. And always, the silent presence behind it all — the KGB. She understood the risk. Still, the thought refused to leave her. Freedom. Even the possibility of it felt dangerous.

Later that day, she attended a mandatory faculty meeting. The rector stood at the podium, his voice steady and rehearsed, praising the superiority of Soviet society. He spoke of the failures of the capitalist world — unemployment, inequality, insecurity — and contrasted them with the protections enjoyed by Soviet citizens. Catherine listened quietly, her hands folded in her lap. Then he mentioned vacations. Every teacher, he reminded them, was entitled to a month of paid leave. Rest was not a privilege, he said. It was a right. A right. The word lingered in her mind. Perhaps she could apply for a visa under that pretext. A vacation.

Nothing more. Nothing suspicious. She kept her face calm, betraying nothing. But inside, a decision was forming.

She did not know where it would lead.

She only knew she could no longer ignore the question that had begun to haunt her:

What if another life was possible?

Chapter 47

The First Crack in the Wall

The faculty meeting grew tense as the rector's voice hardened. He warned of "*renegades*" — citizens who betrayed their homeland in pursuit of selfish dreams abroad. His words hung in the air like a threat. No one moved. No one spoke. Agreement was expected. Agreement was survival.

Then Lisa Ivanov took the podium. Her platinum hair and red lipstick set her apart from the other lecturers. She stood rigid, her expression severe, and began describing her recent trip to New York. Her voice dripped with contempt. She spoke of filth. Of unbearable heat. Of homelessness. Of human misery on every corner. Catherine listened, her stomach tightening.

This was not the America she had heard about at home. Her father had spoken of wide streets and possibility. Her grandmother had spoken of dignity. Of belonging. Lisa's America sounded like a warning. Catherine wondered: Was Lisa lying — or had she simply learned which version of the truth was safe to tell?

The lights dimmed. A documentary flickered onto the screen. Crowds filled New York sidewalks. People hurried toward subway entrances. Cars streamed through avenues lined with towering buildings. The narrator's voice condemned capitalism. But Catherine saw something else.

The people were well dressed. They moved with purpose. The city felt alive. Even the disorder seemed… free. She leaned forward, absorbing every detail. The film was meant to discourage her. Instead, it ignited something she could no longer suppress. *I will be there one day,* she thought. The realization frightened her. But it also felt like truth. Her chance came sooner than she expected.

Soon after, Catherine was summoned before a committee to review her application for a travel visa to Bulgaria. It would be her first trip beyond Soviet borders.

Comrade Tondorf sat at the center of the table. Two female officials flanked him, their faces unreadable.

"This is a serious responsibility," Tondorf began. "You will represent the Soviet Union abroad."

Catherine nodded, careful to remain calm. They questioned her reading habits. Her political views. Her loyalty. She answered as she had been taught. She read *Pravda*-Truth. She supported Soviet ideals. She had traveled only within the USSR. Every word was chosen carefully. Every word was watched. At last, the interview ended. She was dismissed without explanation. The waiting was unbearable. A week later, the telephone rang. It was Tondorf.

Catherine gripped the receiver, unable to speak. He told her that he had personally supported her application. He had argued for her reliability. Her loyalty. His voice softened.

"You must justify our trust," he said.

After she hung up, Catherine sat motionless. Her visa to Bulgaria was no longer just a vacation. It was a test. A test of loyalty. A test of obedience. A test of whether she belonged to the system —or to herself.

And for the first time, Catherine understood something with absolute clarity:

The door had opened.

But it could close forever.

Chapter 48

Permission to Leave

Three days later, Catherine stood before another committee. Three men sat behind a wide desk. Balding heads. Tobacco. Cologne. They smiled, but their eyes did not. The chairman began without introduction.

"Your English is excellent. How did you acquire it?"

Catherine had prepared for this moment.

"My father taught me from childhood," she said calmly. "I later graduated from the Foreign Language Institute. I now teach post-graduate students to serve our country."

Every word mattered. The men exchanged glances. They understood her value. At last, the rector checked his watch.

"You are approved for a twenty-day tourist trip to Bulgaria," he said. "Pending medical clearance."

Good luck. The words echoed in her mind long after she left the building.

Back home, Catherine stood before the mirror. She wore a light silk dress. Her hair pulled back neatly. She looked composed. But inside, something had shifted. Bulgaria was not America. It was not freedom. But it was outside. For the first time in her life, she would cross a border. She stepped into the street beneath a heavy summer sky, feeling both exhilaration and fear.

The next day, Comrade Tondorf summoned her. He stood alone in an empty classroom, his breathing labored. Without greeting, he handed her the character reference.

"I helped you," he said.

His voice was tight.

"But I would not go, if I were you."

He looked at her with something like anger — or fear.

"You are a Soviet citizen. The state educated you. Fed you. Protected your family. Do not forget that."

Catherine said nothing. The letter in her hands was official. Stamped. Signed. It described her as disciplined, politically reliable, worthy of travel. It was also a warning. Travel was never just travel. It was a test.

Her final obstacle was the medical examination. At a distant government clinic, she submitted to every procedure without question. Blood tests. Physical examination. Even a hearing test. She sat inside a soundproof booth, listening for faint tones, wondering what they truly wanted to measure. Loyalty? Fear? Intent? She followed every instruction. Compliance was survival.

When she stepped back onto the street, it was finished. Nothing stood between her and departure now. For years, her life had been confined within invisible walls. Now, for the first time, one of those walls had opened. Only slightly. Only briefly. But enough.

As she walked home, she imagined the Black Sea.

Foreign air.

Foreign voices.

Foreign possibility.

It was only Bulgaria.

But to Catherine, it felt like the edge of another world.

Chapter 49

The Invitation

The letter came from Vilnius. George recognized the foreign stamps immediately. He opened it carefully, his hands unsteady. Inside was a name he had not seen in decades. Watkins. Family. Alive. In America. He read the letter twice, scarcely breathing. An official invitation might follow. If it did, everything could change. Or everything could collapse. The phone call came two days later. The voice spoke English first. Then broken Russian. They agreed to meet.

Bolshoi Theatre square. By the fountain. Public. Neutral. Dangerous. Before hanging up, the caller described himself. Gray trench coat. Hat. George understood the risk.

In Moscow, meeting a foreigner was never just a meeting. It was exposure. It was surveillance. It was consequence. But it was also hope. He said yes. George arrived early. He stood beside the fountain, forcing himself to remain still. Every passerby felt like a witness. Every uniform felt like a threat. Then he saw him. The coat. The hat. The hesitation. The man approached slowly.

"George?"

The English was unmistakable. George nodded. Tim Watkins. Family. From Boston. They did not embrace. Not here. Not in public. They walked without speaking. They did not talk until they reached Natalie's apartment. Inside, the door closed quickly behind them. For a moment, no one moved. Then Tim spoke.

English. Natalie covered her mouth. She had not heard her native language spoken freely in decades. He told them everything. The family had searched for them. For years. They had never stopped. Then Tim reached into his coat. He removed two envelopes. Official. Heavy. He placed them on the table. Invitations. From the United States. Signed. Authorized. Real.

George stared at them. He did not touch them. Not yet. He was afraid they might disappear. Memories returned without warning.

Lake Ontario. Snow. Christmas lights. Freedom. A life that had ended in 1936. A life that might still exist. Natalie began to cry quietly. George picked up the envelope at last.

His name was written in English. He traced the letters with his finger.

He had not seen his name written this way in most of his adult life.

For a moment, no one spoke. Outside, Moscow continued as always.

Inside, everything had changed.

Chapter 50

The Application

George and Natalie worked in silence. The typewriter keys struck the paper one letter at a time.

Each word mattered. Each mistake could destroy everything.

The applications lay between them on the table — thin sheets of paper that carried the weight of their lives. Exit visa. United States. Family. Freedom. Or punishment.

George had taken the subway that morning, surrounded by the same gray faces he had seen for decades. No one spoke. No one looked at one another. Everyone understood the rules of survival.

Natalie's Khrushchev-era apartment offered a brief refuge. The curtains were drawn. The radio was off. Even here, they kept their voices low. They knew the risk. People who asked to leave were no longer trusted. Some lost their jobs. Some lost their homes. Some disappeared. Still, they continued. Their father had come to the Soviet Union believing in justice. They would leave it in search of truth. When the last page was finished, George placed it carefully on the stack. He looked at his Soviet passport beside it. Two identities. Two futures. One decision. He did not speak. Neither did Natalie. They did not need to. They both understood. There was no turning back. The call came three days later. The voice was formal. Controlled. A meeting at the Ministry of Foreign Affairs. George repeated the words slowly after hanging up. Ministry. Foreign Affairs.

He felt his chest tighten. He reached for his heart medication. This was not routine. Nothing about this was routine. He did not sleep that night. By morning, exhaustion had settled into his bones. Still, he dressed carefully. He chose his best jacket. He checked his documents twice.

Outside, Moscow moved as it always had. Inside, George felt the ground shifting beneath him.

The guard at the entrance examined his passport without expression. For a moment, George thought he might be turned away. Or detained. Or questioned. Instead, the guard returned it.

"You may proceed."

The words brought no relief. Only deeper uncertainty. Inside, the corridors were silent. Red carpet stretched ahead of him. Doors closed behind him. An official walked several steps ahead, never turning around. George followed.

He had no choice. He felt suddenly very old. All his life, he had obeyed.

Worked. Waited. Survived.

Now he was here. Asking permission to leave. Asking permission to be free.

He understood, with absolute clarity, that this meeting could decide everything.

Chapter 51

The Warning

The door closed behind him with a sharp, final sound. George did not turn around. He heard the lock engage. He was alone.

Sergey Petrov sat across from him, already watching. A black leather folder lay open on the desk. George recognized his own name on the paper inside. Petrov did not look up immediately. He let the silence settle. Then he spoke.

“Comrade Yampolsky.”

His voice was calm. Measured.

“You have submitted an application to visit the United States.” It was not a question. George swallowed.

“Yes.” Petrov nodded slightly. “A serious decision.” He turned a page. “You understand what it means.”

George did not answer. Petrov continued.

“You have lived here most of your life.” Another page.

“You have worked.” Pause.

“You have raised your family here.”

He looked up now.

"Your daughters are respected citizens."

The words lingered. George understood. This was not about travel. This was about loyalty. Petrov closed the folder.

"You must remember," he said quietly, "it is a privilege to be a Soviet citizen."

George felt his hands trembling in his lap.

"You carry a Soviet passport."

Petrov leaned forward slightly.

"It would be unfortunate if anyone questioned your loyalty."

Silence filled the room again. George forced himself to speak.

"I have always been loyal."

Petrov watched him for a long moment. Then he nodded once.

"Our meeting is finished."

He gestured toward the door. George stood. His legs felt unsteady. He did not trust himself to speak again. He left. The corridor seemed longer than before. He walked slowly. No one stopped him. No one spoke to him. Outside, the sunlight was blinding. He stood on the steps, unable to move. His chest tightened. He reached into his pocket. His fingers fumbled with the small glass vial. He swallowed the pill dry. He told himself to breathe. He walked without direction. Away from the building. Away from the warning.

The sky above Moscow was clear. Bright. Indifferent. He reached the park and sat down on a wooden bench. For a moment, nothing happened. Then the pain returned. Stronger. Crushing. It spread across his chest and into his jaw. His vision dimmed. He tried to stand. He could not. He understood, in that moment, that his body was failing him. Years of fear. Years of silence. Years of waiting. He collapsed onto the ground. The trees above him blurred. The sky faded.

Then there was nothing.

Chapter 52

The Fragility of Hope

The hospital smelled of antiseptic and exhaustion. Catherine walked quickly down the corridor, afraid of what she might find. Her mother was asleep in the chair beside the bed. George lay motionless, his face pale against the white pillow. For a moment, Catherine could not move. Then his eyes opened.

"Catherine," he whispered. She took his hand carefully.

"Dad, I'm here." His fingers tightened weakly around hers.

"I frightened you." She forced herself to smile.

"You just need to rest." He studied her face. As if trying to memorize it. She did not tell him about Natalie's visa. Not now. Not while his heart was still fighting.

"One step at a time," he murmured. "Yes," she said.

One step at a time. Outside, night had already fallen. Catherine walked home alone. The city moved around her, unchanged. At home, she opened the old photo album. She had not looked at it in years. Her father as a child. Standing on a wooden porch. America. Sunlight. Confidence. A boy who belonged somewhere. She turned the page. Another photograph. Older now. Serious. Already carrying something invisible. Already leaving something behind. She touched the edge of the photograph. This was who he had been. Before Moscow. Before fear. Before permission was required for every dream. She realized, with sudden clarity, that her father had lived his entire life between two worlds. One remembered. One endured. And now, when he had finally reached for the first one again, his body had broken.

She closed the album slowly. For the first time, she understood the cost. Not just of leaving. But of staying.

Chapter 53

The Telegram

The telephone rang late. Catherine knew, even before answering, that something had happened.

"Aunt Natalie?" Her aunt's voice was unrecognizable.

"You must come. Immediately." A pause.

"Your father is stable." Then, quieter: "Eugene is dead." The line went silent.

Outside, rain was falling hard. Catherine stood on the curb, soaked within seconds. A taxi stopped. She gave the address. They drove without speaking. Natalie opened the door before Catherine knocked. She looked smaller. Older. Without a word, she handed Catherine the telegram. Catherine read it slowly. Sudden fall. Pronounced dead. Hospital. No further explanation. No witnesses. No details. Only conclusion.

"He applied for his exit visa," Natalie said. Her voice was barely audible.

Catherine did not answer. Outside, thunder rolled. Natalie leaned closer.

"Do you think…" She hesitated.

"…they could do something like that?"

Catherine felt the question enter her body like ice. She wanted to say no. She could not. Instead, she took her aunt's hand. Natalie's fingers were cold.

Later, on the bus home, Catherine watched the embassies pass by. Poland. Hungary. France. The United States. Each one stood behind guarded gates. Lit. Untouchable. Possible. She pressed her hand against the glass. And for the first time, she understood:

Freedom was not only distant. It was dangerous.

Chapter 54

The Choice

Catherine returned to the Academy the next morning. The corridors were quiet. Too quiet.

When she entered Comrade Tondorf's office, he did not look at her.

"Dean Luchkin wants to see you," he said.

Immediately. His door was heavy. She hesitated before knocking.

"Come in."

Dean Luchkin sat behind his desk, a thick folder open before him. He gestured to the chair.

"Sit." She obeyed. He studied her for a long moment. Then: "You must make a decision."

His voice was calm.

"Your father and your aunt have chosen a path hostile to the Soviet state."

He paused.

"If you support them, your career is finished."

Another pause.

"You will be dismissed."

Silence.

"Or" he continued, "you may dissociate yourself from them." His eyes did not leave her face.

"In that case, your position may be preserved." He leaned back.

"You are either with us." A beat. "Or against us."

Catherine said nothing. Her hands were cold. She knew her answer. But she did not speak it.

Luchkin closed the folder.

"Very well." His voice hardened. "I demand your resignation."

The words fell without emotion. Without appeal. Without mercy. Catherine stood. Her heart was beating so violently she thought he must hear it.

"I must inform you," she said.

Her voice was barely steady.

"I am pregnant."

Luchkin froze.

"Pregnant?" She nodded.

By law, he could not dismiss her. His face darkened. “Who is the father?” She did not answer.

“Who is the father?” he repeated. Tears filled her eyes. She let them. Silence stretched between them. Finally, he spoke again.

“I will consult the rector.”

A pause.

“You may go.”

Outside, Catherine did not stop walking. She left the building. Boarded the bus. Sat by the window. Embassies passed in silence. Behind their gates, another world existed. Untouchable. She pressed her hand against her stomach. She did not know yet whether the child existed.

But she knew this: It had already saved her.

Chapter 55

The Ultimatum

Comrade Tondorf called her early the next morning. His voice was strained.

"Come immediately." He did not say why. He did not need to. His office smelled of tobacco and anxiety. He did not invite her to sit. "Your father's visa application," he said, his voice trembling with anger, "has implicated your entire family." He leaned forward. "You must resign." The words hung in the air. "This is the minimal consequence." Catherine felt the floor tilt beneath her.

"I have done nothing wrong," she said quietly. "My work—"

"Your work no longer matters." His breathing was labored. "Our institution cannot be associated with traitors." The word struck her like a slap. Traitors. She forced herself to remain calm.

"I am pregnant."

He froze. For a moment, uncertainty flickered across his face. Then it vanished. "It will not save you." His voice dropped.

"You do not understand what is happening."

She understood perfectly. Her family had crossed an invisible line. And now the system was closing around them. She left his office without another word. Outside, the morning air felt thin.

For the first time in her life, she understood: Her future no longer belonged to her.

That evening, she stood alone at her window.

And began, for the first time, to consider escape.

Chapter 56

The Edge of Desperation

Moscow glittered outside her window. Cold. Distant. Untouchable. Inside the apartment, everything felt temporary. Fragile. Her father lay in recovery. Her uncle was dead. Her family was under suspicion. And she was next. Her hand moved unconsciously to her stomach. Her protection. Her lie. Or perhaps her truth. She did not know which anymore. Only that it was the only thing standing between her and destruction.

She thought of the others. Those who had applied for exit visas. Those who had disappeared. Those who had been imprisoned. Those who had escaped. Israel. America. Names that no longer sounded like geography. They sounded like survival.

Across the street, the diplomatic towers rose into the night. Foreign lights. Foreign lives. Foreign freedom. She watched the windows. Somewhere inside them, people lived without permission. Without fear. Without asking the state for the right to breathe. A dangerous thought entered her mind.

What if they could help her?

What if they were her way out?

She did not move. She stood there a long time. Listening to her own heartbeat. Understanding, at last: She had reached the edge. And there was no way back.

Chapter 57

Charting a New Course

In the weeks that followed, Catherine's life in Moscow became as unpredictable as the city's weather. Moments of fragile calm were quickly swallowed by gathering clouds of uncertainty. Though she remained at the Academy, she understood the protection of her supposed pregnancy was only temporary. Her position had already been quietly diminished.

She was reassigned to evening classes.

The change was not accidental.

Her new students were older—factory workers, clerks, and laborers who came after long shifts, carrying exhaustion in their eyes and quiet determination in their notebooks. They were not the privileged elite of the daytime faculty. Yet Catherine found unexpected solace among them. Their longing for something more—for dignity, for possibility—mirrored her own.

Still, the message from the Academy was unmistakable: she was being pushed toward the margins.

Toward disappearance.

Amid this tightening noose, Catherine decided she could no longer postpone.

She would seek a way out.

One gray afternoon, her heart pounding beneath her coat, she approached the Central Synagogue of Moscow. The building stood modestly against the street, neither welcoming nor forbidding—simply waiting.

Inside, the air was heavy with candle smoke and whispered prayers.

Hope lived here quietly. A young cleric stood near the entrance, his yarmulke slightly askew, his expression cautious but kind.

"Shalom," Catherine said softly.

"Shalom," he replied. "How may I help you?"

For a moment, her voice failed her. Then she spoke. She told him about her mother. About her Jewish lineage. About her family. About her need to leave. He listened carefully, asking questions in a low voice, writing notes with deliberate precision. Each answer felt like a confession—and a liberation. Finally, he stopped writing.

"You will return on September twentieth," he said.

The date hung in the air like a fragile promise.

As she turned to leave, he added quietly,

"We will see each other in Jerusalem next year."

Outside, the Moscow air felt different.

The streets were the same. The gray buildings unchanged.

But something inside her had shifted.

For the first time, Catherine was no longer simply enduring her life.

She was moving toward another one.

Chapter 58

A Fragile Sanctuary

As Catherine stepped out of the synagogue, the air felt heavier than before. Inside, every whisper had carried meaning. Every glance had carried risk. Hope lived there—but so did fear. She knew the *KGB* watched such places. It was impossible to prove, yet impossible to doubt. Even sacred walls could not guarantee safety. Faith offered comfort. It did not offer protection.

Her decision to seek an invitation from Israel had set something irreversible in motion. She was no longer simply enduring her life. She was resisting it. She knew the stories. Years of waiting. Careers destroyed. Families harassed. Lives reduced to quiet punishment for the crime of wanting to leave. She also knew she could not turn back.

As she walked, memories surfaced—her grandparents' stories of the ghetto, of hunger, of survival balanced on chance. They had endured the unendurable and lived. Their courage moved beside her now. Her feet carried her toward the *Ukraine* Hotel.

The towering Stalinist building rose above the Moscow River like a monument to another world. Its illuminated windows shimmered with promise and exclusion. Inside, warmth and luxury replaced the gray austerity of the streets.

"Passport."

The concierge's voice was sharp, practiced. Catherine handed it over, feeling once again the familiar reduction of her identity to a document—something to be inspected, judged, controlled. She waited. The lobby glowed with polished marble, chandeliers, and foreign voices. Western guests moved freely, laughing, smoking, existing without fear. It felt unreal.

As a Soviet citizen, she was permitted to enter—but not to belong. She could not shop in the currency stores. Could not dine freely. Could not speak openly. Freedom existed here, but behind invisible glass.

Still, she watched.

Several Soviet women moved confidently among the foreigners, elegant and self-assured. They laughed easily, untouched by the hesitation Catherine felt in her own body.

How did they live like this?

How did they cross that invisible line?

No one explained.

No one needed to.

Catherine walked slowly toward the hotel spa, her pulse unsteady.

She had entered a borderland.

Not yet free.

But no longer entirely contained.

Chapter 59

Unexpected Allies

As Catherine stepped out of the *Ukraine* Hotel, she saw Alejandro's car pulling up to the curb. He spotted her immediately and gestured for her to get in. For a moment, she hesitated. Then she opened the door and slid into the passenger seat. The warmth inside the car wrapped around her, shutting out the cold Moscow night. They drove in silence.

"So," Alejandro said finally, his voice quiet but deliberate, "how are you really doing?"

Catherine kept her eyes on the passing streetlights.

"It's been difficult," she said. "At the Academy. With my family. Everything." Alejandro nodded. "I've heard they're putting pressure on you."

She gave a faint smile. "Pressure is one word for it."

He glanced at her.

"You don't deserve this, Catherine. You're one of the best teachers there." His words unsettled her. Not because she doubted them. Because kindness had become dangerous. As they approached her building, he slowed the car. "If there's anything I can do," he said, "tell me."

She turned to him.

“I will,” she said softly.

She stepped out and watched his car disappear into the night. For the first time in weeks, she did not feel entirely alone. The next evening, Catherine stood before her class. Teaching had become her refuge—the only place where her voice still belonged to her. Yet even here, her thoughts drifted to the folded letter hidden in her purse.

Israel. The word itself felt like oxygen. After class, as she gathered her papers, one of her students approached her. Dmitry.

“May I walk you to the bus?” he asked.

She hesitated, then nodded. They rode together in silence. Finally, he spoke.

“There may be a position for you,” he said. “At the International Exhibition.”

She turned to him sharply.

“What kind of position?”

“Interpreter.”

Her pulse quickened. Interpreter. It meant foreigners. It meant access. It meant risk.

“I know it’s sudden,” he continued. “But they need someone with your English. You would be perfect.”

Perfect. Or exposed. She studied his face, searching for motive.

"Why are you helping me?" He met her gaze calmly.

"Because you deserve the opportunity."

The bus slowed. Her stop. She stood.

"I will think about it," she said.

Outside, the night air felt different. Not freer. But open. For months, every door had been closing. Now, unexpectedly, two had opened. She did not know which one to trust. She only knew she could not remain where she was. For the first time, escape no longer felt like a dream. It felt like a decision.

Chapter 60

Intersecting Worlds

As dawn broke, Catherine entered a world she had only glimpsed from a distance.

The exhibition pavilion stretched before her like an aircraft hangar, vast and humming with life. Television screens flickered with foreign programs. Tables overflowed with unfamiliar foods — peanut butter, oat biscuits, scones, almonds. The air carried the scent of coffee, cigarette smoke, and expensive perfume. It did not feel like Moscow.

Comrade Pospelov moved confidently through the crowd, introducing her to exhibitors from Britain, Canada, and beyond. English flowed freely here, uninterrupted by suspicion or ideology. For the first time in her life, Catherine was not explaining the Soviet Union to others. She was helping the Soviet Union understand the world.

"Miss Yampolsky," Pospelov said, gesturing toward a tall man in shirtsleeves. "This is Mr. John Walters."

Walters smiled warmly.

"Pleased to meet you, Catherine. We've been looking forward to working with you."

His voice carried none of the caution she was used to hearing. Only ease.

Only assumption of freedom.

By evening, Catherine was exhausted.

Dmitry met her afterward.

“Well?” he asked. “How was it?”

She hesitated, searching for words.

“It felt,” she said finally, “like stepping into another life.”

He smiled. “I thought it might.”

The days that followed blurred together. Catherine moved between two worlds. By day, she stood beneath bright pavilion lights, interpreting discussions of aircraft systems and navigation equipment. Soviet engineers listened intently, asking careful questions. Military officers watched everything. Watched her. By night, she returned to the Academy, where the corridors smelled of chalk and state control. She belonged to both worlds. And to neither.

One afternoon, Colonel Savchenko, a senior military officer, approached her after a presentation.

“Your work today was excellent,” he said. Walters nodded in agreement. “Exceptionally handled.”

Their praise warmed her. But it also frightened her. Because she understood what it meant to be noticed.

In the Soviet Union, visibility was never neutral.

On the bus ride home, Catherine watched the city pass in silence.

Her father lay recovering from his heart attack. Her aunt was preparing to leave.

Her own future hung in uncertainty. And yet, for the first time, she felt something unfamiliar growing inside her. Not hope. Not yet. Possibility.

She understood now that the world was larger than she had been allowed to believe.

And she had stepped into it. There would be no returning unchanged.

Chapter 61

From Moscow to Freedom

"Blessed be the LORD, for he has wondrously shown his steadfast love to me when I was in a besieged city."
— Psalm 31:21 (ESV)

Natalie walked slowly through the Moscow streets, as if memorizing them.

Her black wool coat, trimmed with brown mink, rested lightly on her shoulders. She had bought it only weeks before from a secondhand shop, an indulgence she could scarcely afford. Today, it no longer felt like extravagance. It felt like armor. The city moved around her as it always had — gray apartment blocks, crowded sidewalks, the distant onion domes of old churches. Yet everything seemed altered. Or perhaps it was she who had changed. The taxi carried her past the Kremlin walls and Saint Basil's Cathedral; their familiar outlines etched against the pale morning sky. For decades, these monuments had stood as silent witnesses to her life — her youth, her endurance, her waiting. Now they belonged to someone else.

Natalie clutched her purse tightly in her lap. Her suitcase rested in the trunk behind her, carrying the small fragments of a life she was permitted to take — photographs, letters, a few personal items that had escaped confiscation. The rest remained behind, dissolved into memory. She thought of George. Her dear brother. She saw his tired face, his failing heart, his quiet courage. Leaving him behind was the deepest wound of all. She could not save him.

Perhaps, by leaving, she could save Catherine. The taxi slowed. Sheremetyevo Airport rose before her — vast, impersonal, final. A gust of cold air met her as she stepped onto the pavement. She did not hesitate.

Inside, the familiar rituals unfolded without emotion. Passport. Inspection. Waiting. For decades, this small booklet had bound her to one life. Today, it was releasing her from it. The officer stamped the page. The sound was quiet. Irrevocable.

Natalie inclined her head in silent acknowledgment and walked forward, each step carrying her farther from the only world she had known for forty years. She did not allow herself to look back. At the boarding gate, she paused only once. Not from doubt. From understanding. She was not merely leaving a country. She was leaving a system designed to outlast her. And she had survived it.

Inside the aircraft, Natalie settled into her seat and folded her hands in her lap. Around her, strangers spoke softly, their lives continuing along paths she would never know. The engines roared to life. She felt the vibration beneath her feet. A trembling. Not of fear. Of crossing.

As the plane lifted from the runway, Moscow receded into abstraction — streets dissolving into lines, buildings into shadows, memory into distance. She pressed her forehead lightly against the window. She had survived. The interrogations. The silences. The endless waiting. All the years of believing she might never leave.

Tears gathered in her eyes but did not fall. This was not sorrow alone. It was release. When the seatbelt light dimmed, Natalie reached into her handbag and removed her Bible. The pages fell open easily. Psalm 31. She closed her eyes.

Moscow had been her prison. But it had also been her proving ground. Above the clouds, there were no borders. No permissions. No watchers. Only sky. She thought of her parents, their decision long ago that had carried them across an ocean into a different fate. She thought of Catherine, still standing within the system she herself had escaped. She understood now that freedom carried its own burden. She was not merely traveling to America. She was reclaiming the life that had been interrupted. She was crossing from survival into possibility. She did not know what awaited her. But for the first time in forty years, the future belonged to her.

Natalie closed her eyes and breathed deeply. Somewhere below, Moscow continued without her. Ahead lay a country she remembered more in feeling than in fact. A country that might still accept her. A country that might still be home. As the aircraft carried her westward, Natalie whispered a silent farewell. Not only to a place. But to the woman she had been inside it.

Chapter 62

American Reawakening

Natalie felt the moment before she understood it. The words hung above the terminal entrance:

'WELCOME TO THE UNITED STATES'

She stopped walking. For a brief instant, she could not breathe. This was not arrival. This was return.

At the Customs desk, she handed over her passport. The officer examined it, then looked up at her.

"Purpose of your visit?" Natalie hesitated. Forty years could not be explained in a sentence.

"I'm returning home," she said quietly.

The officer studied her face, as if sensing the weight behind the words. He stamped the passport and handed it back.

"Welcome home."

The words entered her like air after drowning. She walked forward, no longer watched, no longer stopped. Free. Outside, New York roared around her — traffic, voices, neon light, motion without permission. It was overwhelming. It was alive. She hailed a taxi.

"Where to?" the driver asked.

She hesitated.

“The nearest police precinct.”

She needed someone official. Someone real. Someone who could tell her she existed again.

The officer listened patiently. He did not question her. He did not doubt her. He helped her. He lifted her suitcase himself.

“Come on,” he said gently. “We’ll get you settled.”

As they drove through the city, Natalie watched everything. The light. The movement. The abundance. They stopped at a drive-through window.

“Three Big Macs, two fries, two large Cokes,” the officer said casually.

Natalie stared in disbelief. Food. Immediate. Plentiful. Unrestricted.

“Help yourself,” he said, smiling. “You’ll get used to it.”

She knew she never would. Not completely. Not after Moscow.

He took her to a small hotel.

“I’ll meet you in the morning,” he said.

His kindness felt unreal. She sat alone in the room. No surveillance. No listening walls. No fear of midnight knocks. She lay down fully clothed. Freedom was exhausting. The next morning, she saw America clearly for the first time. Food laid out without ration. People moving without permission. Voices without fear.

She carried extra bread back to her room without thinking. Scarcity lived inside her still.

At the First Presbyterian Church, she prayed. Not for herself. For those left behind. For George. For Catherine.

In the hotel lobby, a man approached.

"David O'Connell. U.S. State Department."

He shook her hand.

"We're here to help you."

Help. The word still sounded foreign.

At the INS office, she was fingerprinted. Photographed. Documented. Recognized. Each step restored something taken decades earlier.

Mr. Ringer spoke gently.

"Your citizenship reinstatement has been approved."

She did not respond. She could not. Forty stolen years had just been acknowledged.

"You'll soon take the oath," he added.

Oath. Belonging. Identity. Restored. That evening, Natalie stood beside the Hudson River. The wind was sharp. Alive. Real. She held her Soviet passport in her hands. Red. Official. Oppressive. It had defined her. Contained her. Denied her. She stared at it one last time.

Then threw it into the dark water. It floated briefly. Then disappeared. Just like that. She was no longer owned. She breathed deeply. The air filled her lungs without permission. For the first time in forty years. She belonged only to herself.

Back in her hotel room, she opened her new American passport. Her photograph stared back at her. Older. Marked. Alive. She touched it gently. Proof. She lay down. Outside, New York moved endlessly. Inside, Natalie was finally still.

She had crossed. She had survived. She was home.

Chapter 63

Under Moscow's Cold Gaze

On the other side of the world, winter had already claimed Moscow.

Snow fell in fine, relentless sheets, dulling sound, softening edges, concealing nothing.

Catherine moved quickly through the frozen streets, her rabbit-fur collar drawn tightly around her neck. Her high-heeled boots struck the pavement with measured urgency as she hurried toward the subway, then the bus that would carry her to the exhibition hall.

The exhibition still felt unreal to her.

Inside, warmth, light, and foreign voices created the illusion of another country — a place where men and women in tailored suits spoke openly beside displays of Western machines and inventions. Televisions flickered. Foreign cigarettes burned. Perfume lingered in the air.

But the illusion never lasted. The watchers were always there. Men who did not belong to any delegation. Men who never smiled.

Only visitors cleared by the Ministry were permitted entry. Everyone else remained outside. Including freedom.

By the end of the day, Catherine was exhausted. Interpreting for engineers from the Foreign Trade Ministry required precision, vigilance, and restraint. Every word mattered.

Every word could be remembered. Every word could be used.

That night at the Academy, the atmosphere had changed. Her students avoided her eyes. Their laughter was gone. Their caution spoke louder than questions. Someone had warned them. Someone had decided she was no longer safe.

She finished the lesson, dismissed the class, and stepped outside into the night.

The wind struck her immediately. Sharp. Punishing. The bus stop glowed faintly ahead. She walked faster.

A car pulled beside her.

"Catherine."

Alejandro's voice.

He leaned across the seat and opened the door.

"Do you need a ride?"

She hesitated only a moment before climbing in. Warmth enveloped her. Safety. Temporary. She exhaled.

"Alejandro… I'm so tired."

He drove without speaking at first. Then gently: "How is your family?"

Catherine stared ahead.

"Complicated."

He nodded. "I heard your aunt left."

The words hung between them.

"Yes," she said quietly. "She's gone."

Gone. Free. The word existed, but not for her.

"And the Academy?"

She gave a faint, humorless smile.

"I live under a microscope."

Alejandro tightened his grip on the wheel.

"If I can help…"

She looked at him. Kindness had become something fragile. Dangerous.

"Maybe," she said.

Snow drifted across the windshield. The city passed in silence. Gray. Endless. Watching. He stopped in front of her building.

"Take care of yourself, Catherine."

She stepped out into the cold. The warmth vanished instantly. She watched his car disappear. Then turned toward the entrance. The building loomed above her. Silent. Immovable. Unforgiving.

She stood there for a moment longer.

Gathering strength. Preparing. Tomorrow would come.

And Moscow would still be watching.

Chapter 64

Gifts of Hope

The final days of the exhibition passed in a blur of motion and farewell. Foreign delegates packed crates. Contracts were signed. Displays dismantled. Conversations shifted from possibility to departure. The world was leaving Moscow. And leaving Catherine behind. She worked quietly at her station, aware that something in her life had changed, though she could not yet name it.

Mr. Wilson, the exhibition manager, approached her that afternoon carrying a small parcel wrapped in bright paper and tied with a red ribbon.

"Hello, Catherine," he said warmly. "How are you?"

"I'm well, thank you," she replied automatically. He extended the package.

"I have a present for you. Merry Christmas — and a happy new year to you and your family. Your professionalism has been instrumental in our success here. This is my way of saying thank you."

She froze. Christmas. The word itself felt forbidden. She remembered Comrade Tondorf's warnings. No religion. No Western sentiment. No deviation. Yet here it was. Wrapped in ribbon. Offered freely. "Thank you," she said softly. She hesitated only a moment. "And… Merry Christmas to you."

The words left her lips before she could stop them. Mr. Wilson smiled.

"I hope someday you'll see Europe during Christmas," he said gently. "It's magical."

Magical. She clutched the gift after he left. It was not the object that mattered. It was what it represented. A world where such gestures were ordinary. A world where she could belong.

For the first time in years, she allowed herself to imagine it. Freedom.

The next day, snow fell steadily over Moscow. Catherine stood at the curb, raising her hand to hail a taxi. She never saw the car until it was already upon her.

A white *Moskvich.*

Swerving. Accelerating. Heading directly at her. Time fractured. She jumped. The car missed her by inches. Its tires screamed against ice as it veered back onto the street and disappeared.

Gone. No license plate. No witnesses. No explanation. Only intention. She stood frozen. Her heart pounding violently. Around her, people moved away. No one spoke. No one intervened. No one would help. She understood why.

In Moscow, accidents were rarely accidents. She descended into the subway. Into the crowd. Into anonymity. But safety no longer existed. As the train pulled forward, her reflection trembled in the darkened window. They were warning her. Or they had already decided. The Israeli invitation surfaced in her mind. Israel. Escape. Exile. Risk. If she applied, she could become a *refusenik*[7]. She could lose everything. If she stayed—She might lose her life. Her fabricated pregnancy would soon be exposed. Her position at the Academy was ending. Her protection was ending. Her time was ending.

She understood now. This was no longer a question. It was a decision.

Ride out the storm. Swim. Or sink.

She lifted her chin. She would apply. Whatever came next.

Chapter 65

Pilgrims of the Modern Age

The familiar voice of the subway announcer broke Catherine's thoughts. She had only half an hour before class. She gathered her papers and climbed the worn stone steps to the Academy, her breath still visible in the cold corridor air. Her four students were already waiting. They rose as she entered.

"Hello, Comrades."

"Hello, Comrades," she replied, forcing warmth into her voice.

She was suddenly aware this might be her final lecture here.

She opened her father's book.

"Today," she said, "we will study American history."

The word America changed the room.

Her students leaned forward.

She began.

"In 1620, a group of English settlers crossed the Atlantic Ocean aboard a ship called the Mayflower. They were fleeing religious persecution. They sought a place where they could live freely."

She spoke of fear. Of exile. Of uncertainty. She spoke of the Mayflower Compact. A government created not by decree—— but by agreement. Equal men. Equal voices.

Equal rights. She saw something awaken behind her students' eyes.

"What was the Mayflower Compact?" she asked.

Vadim answered immediately.

"A voluntary agreement to govern themselves."

She nodded. Yes. Voluntary. Not imposed. Chosen. As the lecture ended, silence filled the room. No one hurried to leave. They understood. Freedom was not given. It was taken.

When they were gone, Catherine remained alone. Her hand rested on the worn cover of her father's book. The Pilgrims had crossed an ocean. She needed only to cross a border. Yet the distance felt greater.

That evening, Catherine sat alone in her apartment. The room felt smaller than ever. She knew what must come next. To leave the Soviet Union, she would first have to resign. To resign, she would have to return to the Academy. Face them. Comrade Kaganov. Comrade Tondorf. Declare her intention. Declare her disloyalty. The Departure Sign-off sheet. The final document. The final act. Once signed, her life would change instantly. She would become a refusenik. An outcast. She could lose her job. Her home. Her safety. Her future. She could be arrested. Or worse. She understood this. She understood all of it. Yet something inside her had already crossed the ocean. She thought of the Pilgrims. They had stepped into the unknown. Not because it was safe—but because it was necessary. Catherine stood. Walked to the window.

Moscow stretched before her. Gray. Silent. Watching. She no longer belonged to it. She belonged to the future. She whispered the words aloud. "I will apply." The decision did not free her. But it gave her power. Her journey had begun.

Chapter 66

Twilight Celebrations

The early evening air was sharp with winter as Catherine stepped into the Academy for what she knew might be one of her final days.

The corridors felt different now. Quieter. Watching. At the cashier's window, the elderly woman handed her salary in a plain envelope. The rubles felt heavier than usual. Not because of their value. Because of what they represented. An ending. She moved next to the commissary line.

Teachers waited patiently for their weekly privileges.

When her turn came, she accepted what was available: A small chicken. Two cans of green peas. Latvian sardines. A jar of Indian coffee. And, almost ceremonially, a bottle of Soviet champagne. Fragments of a life she was about to leave behind. Groceries in hand, she walked toward her classroom.

Her students were already waiting.

"Good evening, Comrades," she said.

Her voice was steady. Stronger than she felt. Tonight, she spoke of holidays. Of Grandfather Frost. Of Thanksgiving. Of traditions born in freedom. Her students listened intently. As if they understood this lesson was not in the curriculum. It was a farewell. When the class ended, she lingered.

"Remember," she told them softly, "holidays remind us that light exists, even in darkness."

She turned off the lights. Closed the door. Perhaps for the last time. Outside, twilight had settled over Moscow. The sky burned faintly violet above the snow-covered streets. She adjusted her bags and stepped into the cold.

A familiar beep sounded behind her. Alejandro. He leaned across the passenger seat and opened the door.

"Looks like you could use a hero."

She laughed.

"My knight in shining armor."

Inside the car, warmth surrounded her.

"So," he asked gently, "how was today?"

She stared out the window.

"It felt like a farewell."

He nodded.

"I'm here, Catherine. Whatever happens."

His words settled inside her. Not as rescue. But as witness. When they reached her building, he helped carry her bags. She paused before stepping out.

"Thank you, Alejandro."

"For everything." He smiled. "Your life is just beginning." She stepped into the cold. But she was no longer afraid of it. Because now she was walking toward something. Not away.

Chapter 67

A Quiet Supper

As the clock edged toward midnight and the dawn of 1979, the Yampolsky household in Moscow glowed with the fragile warmth of New Year's Eve. Inside their small apartment, the yellow light of a single lamp softened the peeling wallpaper and worn furniture, creating the illusion of safety. Beyond the thick windows, winter pressed against the city with merciless indifference.

At the center of the modest table, a roasted chicken rested like a quiet triumph, its aroma filling the room with a rare sense of abundance. Sonya, Catherine's mother, had spent the day preparing thin, delicate layers of pastry for the traditional Napoleon cake, spreading each with sweet cream made from boiled condensed milk—a treasured luxury reserved for special occasions.

A bottle of Soviet champagne stood chilling by the window, its label boldly proclaiming itself the finest in the world. Catherine studied it silently, wondering if such claims could survive beyond the borders of the country that had printed them.

Nearby, a large bowl of potato salad and Sonya's hand-made cabbage and potato pies completed the meal. The familiar smells wrapped around them like a memory—comforting, steady, and heartbreakingly finite.

They gathered at the table, their faces softened by candlelight. For a moment, they were not citizens under surveillance, not suspects in their own country, but simply a family.

Glasses were raised.

"To the New Year."

The words carried more than ritual. They carried absence.

To Aunt Natalie, now across an ocean. To those lost. To those who might never leave.

The champagne fizzed weakly as they drank.

Inside their apartment, with its heavy walls and aging sofa bed, peace felt possible—even if only for an evening.

Yet beneath the celebration lay an unspoken truth.

Everything was changing.

For Catherine, the coming year was not simply another turning of the calendar. It was a crossing.

A threshold between obedience and escape.

Between safety and freedom. Between the life she had endured—

and the life she was preparing to risk everything to claim.

Chapter 68

The Farewell

January 5 marked a decisive fracture in Catherine's life.

She walked into the Academy knowing she would never truly belong to it again. The corridor buzzed with clerks and instructors lining up to sign salary slips and collect their vacation pay. A rare wage increase had been announced—a small concession from the State, offered as proof of its supposed benevolence.

Catherine joined the line. When her turn came, she accepted the envelope in silence. The rubles inside felt strangely weightless. This would be the last salary the Soviet Union would ever pay her. She folded the envelope carefully and slipped it into her bag.

Then she took out her resignation letter. She had rewritten it three times. Each word had been chosen with surgical caution. She walked down the corridor to Comrade Luchkin's office. The secretary glanced up.

"Would you like to see Comrade Luchkin?"

"I won't take long," Catherine replied.

She stepped inside. The office smelled of paper and dust. She placed the letter on his desk.

"Here is the letter you requested."

She did not wait for permission. She turned and walked out. She had just severed herself from the system. Outside, the Moscow air cut through her thin coat. Her next destination was unavoidable. The *militsiya.* The building crouched among gray apartment blocks like a concrete sentry. Inside, citizens waited in silence. A young woman applied for travel to Bulgaria. A nervous couple clutched their documents like lifelines. Catherine watched.

Each face carried the same question: Would the State allow them to leave? When her turn came, she stepped forward.

"I am applying for an exit visa to Israel." The official barely looked up.

"The clearance sheet is missing." Her voice was flat.

"Your application cannot proceed without the sign-off from your workplace."

The First Department. The words hung in the air like a sentence. The First Department was not merely bureaucratic. It was the Academy's internal security organ. Its function was surveillance. Its authority absolute. Its personnel often former *KGB*. To obtain their signature was to place herself fully within their grasp. She returned to the Academy. To Comrade Luchkin. He read her request. His face tightened. He picked up the phone.

"Comrade Ivanov… Yes. Citizeness Yampolsky has applied for an exit visa." Pause.

"To Israel." He hung up.

"Report to the First Department."

Sergey Ivanov's office was small. Airless. Final.

He held her biography in his hands. Thirty-four years old. Interpreter. Family in America. Requesting exit to Israel. He studied her.

In another era, the solution would have been simple. A gun. A single bullet. A quiet administrative correction. The system had never hesitated before.

But this was no longer 1936. The world was listening now. Radio Liberty. Voice of America. Radio Freedom. Their broadcasts crossed Soviet borders every night, carrying stories of dissidents, refuseniks, disappearances.

The '*Helsinki Accords*' had changed the rules. If Catherine vanished, questions would follow. Her American connections made her dangerous. Not because she was powerful. But because she was visible.

Ivanov understood something else. Sometimes it was safer for the State to let such people go. To export the problem. To remove the contagion. He signed.

"I am approving your clearance." He looked at her one last time.

"The road you have chosen will not be easy."

She nodded. She knew. Two days later, in minus thirty-seven degrees Celsius, Catherine returned to the *militsiya*. This time she carried the signatures. The stamps. The proof of her separation from Soviet life. Ahead of her, a woman wept openly. Two years waiting. A husband broken by interrogation. A child beaten at school.

"Why are you keeping us here?"

The officer did not look up.

"My responsibility is paperwork." Nothing more. Nothing less. Catherine stepped forward. The officer examined her documents. Paused. Stamped. Signed.

"Your application has been accepted."

Just like that. Her life as a Soviet citizen ended. Not with an arrest. Not with a bullet. But with a stamp. She stepped outside into the frozen air. For the first time, she understood what she had become. Not citizen. Not employee. Not protected.

She was now something else. A refusenik. Marked. Exposed.

Irreversible. Freedom had begun.

And it had cost everything.

Chapter 69

The Cold Verdict

As the new year dawned, whispers circulated among those awaiting their fate, creating an atmosphere fraught with uncertainty and fear. The rumor that refuseniks, those denied exit visas, might be imprisoned during the upcoming Summer Olympic Games in Moscow loomed large over Catherine. This palpable threat intensified her resolve. She had to act swiftly, decisively.

Throughout the difficult year, Catherine's father, George, had been her steadfast support, translating scientific texts to help sustain her financially. Sonya, her mother, contributed what she could from her modest earnings as a building decorator, while Maria, her sister, occasionally chipped in with the little extra she had from child support and alimony. The rumors about the Soviet regime's harsh treatment of *refuseniks*—viewed as traitors and outside the protection of any law—echoed ominously in Catherine's ears. She could very well be among their number if her application were rejected, a possibility that seemed all too real.

Then, on a bitterly cold day, a postcard arrived from *OVIR*—the Soviet Office of Visas and Registrations, summoning her to headquarters on January 21. Stepping into the building, Catherine was assaulted by the oppressive heat and the acrid mix of body odor and dust. She navigated the corridor, her eyes adjusting to the dim light, and joined the queue at the specified desk. Ahead of her, an elderly couple stood, the man reassuring his visibly anxious partner, "Calm down. We'll get the exit visa." They exuded the air of the intellectual elite, a vestige of a middle class rapidly disappearing under Soviet rule.

Catherine tried to dismiss the persistent rumor that those summoned by postcard were destined for refusal. The vulnerability of *refuseniks*, their fates hanging precariously in the balance, was a constant reminder of the regime's cruelty. The couple ahead of her soon exited the office, the woman in tears, the man red-faced with anger and muttering curses. Fear clutched at Catherine's heart as she contemplated the potential denial of her visa and the consequent impossibility of challenging the implacable communist system.

Yet, as she awaited her turn, a sliver of hope flickered within her. "Not refused yet," she thought, clinging to the possibility of a positive outcome.

The gruff voice from inside the office broke the tense silence, "Next person in line, come in!"

Inside, a balding middle-aged man with a thick neck glared at her from behind the counter, his demeanor devoid of any courtesy. "Your full name, citizeness?" he demanded abruptly. Trembling, Catherine replied, "Catherine Yampolsky."

The man's eyes bore into hers with a chilling intensity. "Citizeness Yampolsky," he declared with undisguised hostility, "you will never set foot on foreign soil. Dismissed."

Catherine did not remember leaving the room. In the corridor, the same heavy air pressed against her lungs.

Somewhere behind her, another voice called,

"Next person."

She stepped outside into the freezing Moscow air. The door closed behind her.

And for the first time, she understood—she was no longer trying to leave the country.

She was trapped inside it.

Part Three

Ticket to Freedom

Chapter 70

Moscow's Mysteries Unveiled

On a damp, overcast day in March 1980, Alfred Fuchs found himself in the heart of Moscow, battling the chilly gusts sweeping in from the Moskva River. The wind curled through the wide avenues and along the stone embankments, carrying with it the sharp scent of melting snow and coal smoke from distant chimneys. As he navigated the bustling streets, Alfred's path led him to the Rossiya Hotel, an edifice of modernity starkly contrasting with the ancient grandeur of the neighboring Red Square. Its massive concrete structure loomed over the riverbank like a monument to Soviet ambition, while beyond it the onion domes of St. Basil's Cathedral glowed faintly through the gray sky.

Seeking refuge and a bit of solitude, Alfred made his way to the hotel's restaurant. He paused briefly in the lobby, shaking a few droplets of damp snow from his coat before stepping inside. The marble floors echoed softly under the footsteps of travelers and uniformed attendants moving briskly through the hall. The sparse crowd inside afforded him the quiet he craved. A few businessmen sat scattered at distant tables, speaking in low voices, while a pair of foreign tourists studied a guidebook near the entrance.

Settling into a window-facing seat, he perused a simple menu, eventually opting for a steaming bowl of beet soup, borsch, adorned with a dollop of sour cream and accompanied by a savory meat pie. Outside the window, the muted rhythm of Moscow life unfolded - pedestrians wrapped in thick coats hurried along the sidewalk while a trolleybus rattled slowly past, its wires crackling faintly overhead.

Contentedly rubbing his hands together, Alfred signaled for a shot of Stolichnaya vodka. The waiter approached silently, placing the small glass before him with professional precision. The warmth of the alcohol and the familiar tune of "Sailor" by Werner Scharfenberger and Fini Busch playing in his mind lifted his spirits, stirring a sense of readiness and resolve within him. The melody echoed gently in his memory, like a distant radio playing somewhere far away.

As he hummed the melody, Alfred contemplated his surroundings and the opportunities that Moscow might present. He watched the slow drift of snowflakes beyond the restaurant window and studied the passing figures on the street with quiet curiosity. The city had evolved since his last visit, and he sensed potential for advantageous business dealings, influential connections, and a path into the elite circles of Soviet society. In a place where power was rarely visible but always present, Alfred believed that patience—and the right acquaintances—could open many doors.

After leaving a generous tip, Alfred stepped out into the crisp Moscow air, his spirits buoyed by the light snowfall and the vibrant city life around him. Streetlights had begun to glow softly against the falling snow, illuminating the broad avenues with a pale golden shimmer. "Hello, Moscow!" he exclaimed, his mood romanticized by the scene unfolding before him.

With a deep breath of the frosty air and a wave to hail a cab, Alfred continued his journey, slightly tipsy but filled with a mellow optimism, back to the comfort of his room at the National Hotel. As the taxi pulled away into the evening traffic, the Kremlin walls appeared briefly in the distance, their red bricks darkened by the gathering twilight—silent witnesses to the countless stories unfolding within the city.

Chapter 71

Snowfall Serendipity

Alfred Fuchs strolled through the grand lobby of the National Hotel, slipping a few Deutsche Marks into the doorman's hand in a smooth, practiced motion. The heavy revolving doors sighed shut behind him as the warmth of the lobby wrapped around him, carrying faint scents of polished wood, tobacco smoke, and strong Russian tea. Inside his room, he poured himself a glass of scotch and settled into a chair by the window, his mind preoccupied with the upcoming meeting with Gunter Huber. As the company president, Huber held the key to Alfred's future endeavors, particularly concerning the imminent summer Olympic Games in Moscow—a significant opportunity for their West German enterprise.

Outside, the heavy snowfall blanketed Moscow, yet the city's inhabitants moved with their usual vigor. Through the tall window Alfred watched bundled figures crossing the wide avenues below, their footsteps leaving brief impressions in the powdery snow before being erased by the wind. Alfred admired the Soviets' resourcefulness and their ability to think creatively. His thoughts then shifted to Gunter Huber, an acquaintance from Frankfurt. Alfred pondered the motives behind Huber's decision to involve him in Moscow's affairs. He was confident that Huber sought to expand their company's influence and outmaneuver foreign competitors. Still, Alfred's precise role in this strategy remained shrouded in ambiguity.

The challenge ahead involved navigating a complex network of Soviet officials, each with distinct personalities and agendas. Faces, titles, and ministries floated through Alfred's mind like pieces of a complicated chessboard. Alfred questioned what they might expect from him. Lacking access to sensitive information or government secrets, he wondered about the true nature of his assignment. Could it be that Huber wanted him for something more clandestine, like a mule?

Herr Alfred Fuchs, a prominent businessman from Frankfurt am Main, led a life shrouded in discretion. Renowned for his shrewd dealings, he balanced his time between his primary residence in the bustling port city of Frankfurt and his cozy ski chalet in St. Moritz. His love for adventure often led him to the Swiss Alps, where he would cruise in his sleek black Rolls-Royce. The car's polished body reflected the snowy peaks like a mirror as he wound his way through mountain roads that curved above frozen valleys.

In St. Moritz, Alfred's preferred haunt was the opulent casino, where fortune and chance intertwined. Crystal chandeliers glowed above the gaming tables, casting golden reflections across polished marble floors while the quiet murmur of gamblers filled the air. On one memorable occasion, a mysterious woman with raven-black hair, clad in a striking red dress, whispered two numbers to him, "Nineteen in black, and twenty-five in red." As quickly as she appeared, she vanished, leaving Alfred intrigued. He placed his bets on the enigmatic numbers, and luck was on his side. To his astonishment, he found himself holding winnings of 50,000.00 CHF.

Riding the wave of his good fortune, Alfred then ventured to the baccarat table. There, his winning streak continued, and he skillfully amassed an additional 75,000.00 CHF. The soft clatter of chips, the rustle of silk gowns, and the restrained excitement of the crowd surrounded him as the cards turned in his favor. With a total windfall of 125,000.00 CHF, Alfred heeded his sister's sage advice—when fortune smiles upon you, make a graceful exit. Quietly, he cashed in his chips and retreated to the sanctuary of his room, his heart racing with the exhilaration of the night's success.

In the privacy of his room, Alfred reflected on the evening's events. Outside the balcony doors, the snow-covered mountains shimmered under the pale light of the moon. The thrill of the casino, the allure of chance, and the sudden twist of fate all contributed to the tapestry of his adventurous life. As he savored his victory, he couldn't help but wonder about the enigmatic woman in red. Was she a harbinger of luck, or merely a fleeting shadow in the grand game of chance? Whatever the answer, Alfred knew that nights like these were what made life truly exhilarating.

Alfred's days were steeped in luxury and leisure, a routine he cherished deeply. Each day, he would arise at 1 p.m., embarking on a relaxed stroll to the hotel's main street, where he eagerly anticipated a lavish breakfast. The quiet alpine streets would still be wrapped in morning mist as shopkeepers slowly raised their shutters. The familiar voice of the friendly waitress would greet him, "What will you have, sir?"

Alfred, with a taste for the finer things in life, would reply with his usual order. "Two eggs Benedict, please, and make sure all the condiments accompany it," he'd say. "And, of course, a steaming pot of coffee. Kindly ask the cook to preheat the pot before pouring the coffee. Oh, and I'll have Norwegian rolls on the side."

"Would you like cream and sugar with that?" the waitress would inquire.

"Absolutely," Alfred would respond. "Sugar cubes, if you please, and cream. Oh, and don't forget the morning newspaper," he'd add as an afterthought, ensuring his breakfast experience was nothing short of perfect.

Alfred reveled in the Italian art of *dolce far niente*—the sweetness of doing nothing.

He found immense pleasure in the simple things, whether it was savoring his breakfast, enjoying a nightcap of Grappa on his chalet's veranda on a serene evening, or gazing at the starlit sky and spotting the Pleiades constellation. The crisp mountain air would shimmer with cold, and the distant sound of church bells from the valley would drift upward through the darkness. His evenings would end with a contented yawn, and he'd retire to his bed draped in satin sheets, where dreams of the enigmatic lady in red often visited him.

Alfred's life was a tapestry of international travel, filled with intrigue and an insatiable hunger for new adventures and opportunities. Now, as he embarked on his latest journey in Moscow, he was eager to discover what this new chapter would bring, ready to embrace whatever adventures lay ahead in this intriguing and mysterious city.

As he sipped his scotch and gazed out at the wintry Moscow scene, Alfred braced himself for the complexities and uncertainties of his new venture. Beyond the window, the Kremlin towers glowed faintly through the falling snow, their red stars shining dimly in the gray sky. With his skills and acumen, he was ready to dive into the high-stakes game of international business and intrigue, where fortunes were made and lost on the turn of a card or the roll of a dice.

On a chilly afternoon in Moscow, with only the occasional snowflake drifting past the windows, Alfred Fuchs found himself intrigued by the city's offerings. He wrapped himself up against the cold and set out to explore, heading toward the famed GUM department store to browse for souvenirs. The Red Square, dusted in snow, lent an air of enchantment to his walk. The vast cobblestones stretched before him like a frozen sea, while the crimson Kremlin walls rose solemnly against the winter sky. People bustled around him, bundled in their warm shearling coats and fur hats, a stark contrast to his own attire.

Approaching GUM, Alfred paused to admire the window displays, reflecting on the upcoming Olympic Games and the vibrant energy of the city. Inside the glass displays, lacquered boxes, porcelain figurines, and brightly painted folk crafts glimmered beneath warm yellow lights. As he entered, his attention was captured by an elegantly dressed woman, her blond hair gracefully framing her face, strolling through Red Square amidst the swirling snowflakes.

Their paths converged unknowingly as both Alfred and the woman, Catherine, headed toward the same souvenir shop. When Catherine paused to adjust her stocking, Alfred was instantly charmed and felt compelled to meet her. For a moment he hesitated, studying the quiet confidence in her posture before speaking. "Madam, are you by any chance lost and may I assist you?" he inquired with a warm smile.

"No, I am not lost," Catherine replied, her voice conveying a quiet confidence.

"Well, I am," Alfred confessed playfully. "I'm trying to find souvenirs to send to some friends and family, but I'm lost as to what I should get."

"If you want some help, I am happy to assist you. My name is Catherine," she offered, and they began selecting items together.

"What is that doll there?" Alfred asked, pointing to a colorful item.

"It is a *Matryoshka* doll," Catherine explained, demonstrating how it opened to reveal smaller dolls nested inside. "How perfect it will be for my sister!" Alfred exclaimed.

After a while, Alfred proposed, "Madam, I do not want to be presumptuous, but may I offer you a light dinner with me this afternoon?"

"Yes," Catherine agreed, "this will be most pleasant."

They left the store and caught a taxi to a fine French restaurant at the National Hotel. The taxi slid carefully over the icy streets as the golden lights of Moscow reflected off the snow-covered avenues. The restaurant's grandeur and intimacy captivated them both. "Madame," the maître d' inquired, "where would you like to be seated?"

"In an intimate corner," Catherine requested, "where we will have a view of the musicians playing the balalaika." As she removed her elegant fur coat, Alfred couldn't help but admire her beauty.

Catherine gazed at him and, lowering her eyes, she said, "The food here must be very delicious. Please, order whatever you wish."

Then they began to order the sumptuous food. The waiter came up. He set the table with fine white linen napkins and lovely golden silverware. First, the waiter brought escargots, and they were delightful. Next, he brought a hot borscht soup.

Alfred asked Catherine, “May I take the liberty of ordering the main course?” Then he told the waiter that they would like to have Supreme de volaille à la Kiev, commonly known as Chicken Kiev. The meal was delightful and was followed by a rich dessert of souffle dripping in chocolate. Soft music drifted through the room as other diners spoke quietly at nearby tables, the clink of crystal glasses echoing faintly.

Over dinner, they exchanged stories. As the evening grew darker, Catherine noted, “I must be getting home.”

“I never want this evening to end, Catherine,” Alfred replied softly.

“Where are you from, Alfred?” she inquired.

“I am from Frankfurt, I was born and raised in Rothenberg ob. der Tauber, a town in Middle Franconia, the Franconia region of Bavaria. I had seven siblings, and my father was a college professor. Overall, I had a secure childhood. Although I do remember there were food shortages and occasionally some cash problems.” he shared, recounting his upbringing and family background. “By the way, a friend of mine has an office in Moscow on Commanders’ Street. Do you know the neighborhood?”

“Yes,” Catherine said. “I live right across the street. Your tower faces the high-rise where I live. From what I know, businessmen live over there.”

Alfred, speaking English with a distinct German accent, offered, "I will be honored to have lunch with you in our office. I work for this company," and handed her his business card.

"Thank you," Catherine responded, giving him her number. "If you wish, give me a call sometime."

After settling the bill, Alfred escorted Catherine outside and hailed a cab for them. When they reached her destination, he tenderly kissed her hand and said, "Catherine, until we meet again. Auf Wiedersehen." With that, they parted ways, each carrying the memory of a delightful and unexpected encounter.

Catherine gently lowered her beautiful blue eyes and softly spoke, "We shall meet again." Her words carried a hint of anticipation as the taxi conveyed Alfred Fuchs to his high-rise office/apartment on a hill, a prominent structure in Moscow's skyline. The building, painted in stark white, was accompanied by two similar towers, all housing accredited foreigners and showcasing Moscow's attempt at modernity. Their illuminated windows glowed against the dark winter sky like watchful sentinels overlooking the vast Soviet capital.

As Alfred entered, he was greeted by Vasyli Ivanov, the lone Soviet guard stationed at the main entrance. The vestibule smelled faintly of damp wool coats and floor polish, and the echo of Alfred's footsteps carried softly across the marble floor. "Good afternoon, Herr Alfred Fuchs!" Vasyli called out.

"Good afternoon, Comrade," Alfred replied in his carefully practiced Russian. He paused for a moment, removing his leather gloves with deliberate calm. "Comrade, I have something for your family, a small gesture from the Gunther Huber's firm." He extended a plastic bag filled with select items from the hard currency birch tree store, known for its exclusive merchandise available only to a privileged few.

Vasyli's face flushed with a mix of surprise and gratitude as he accepted the bag. For a brief second, he glanced toward the corridor behind him, as if instinctively checking that no superior officer was watching. "Danke—thank you!" he managed, revealing his familiarity with a foreign tongue. Alfred nodded and headed towards the elevator. The old metal elevator doors clanged shut with a heavy sound, slowly lifting him upward through the silent building.

Reflecting on his experiences in Moscow, Alfred mused over the necessity of small gifts in smoothing interactions in the Soviet system. In this country, gestures carried meanings far beyond their modest appearance. It might have been a form of bribery, but it was an accepted practice that eased daily life. He felt content with the progress of their business endeavors, bolstered by the generous distribution of gifts.

Herr Fuchs enjoyed the privileges extended to foreigners in Moscow, frequenting fine restaurants, attending performances at the Bolshoi Theatre, and partaking in the city's luxurious offerings. Evenings in the Bolshoi's velvet halls, where chandeliers glowed above audiences dressed in fur and silk, offered a glimpse of elegance that seemed almost detached from the gray austerity of the city outside. These social events, though seemingly innocent, provided additional advantages for conducting business on behalf of numerous German enterprises keen on exploring the Soviet market.

As he entered the office of the company, a sense of relief washed over him, easing the day's minor frustrations, and reminding him of the freedoms and comforts of European life he dearly missed. Here, behind these closed doors, the atmosphere felt different—quieter, freer, almost insulated from the invisible watchfulness that permeated the city. Alfred Fuchs settled into his role, navigating the complexities of German Soviet business relations with a keen eye on the opportunities that lay ahead.

Alfred Fuchs smoothly removed his coat, placing it with care on the hanger. He straightened the sleeves with a meticulous gesture, a habit born from years of disciplined routine. He then proceeded to the bar, pouring himself a generous serving of whisky. Settling into a plush leather armchair, he took a moment to appreciate the well-appointed and comfortable surroundings of the office. The space, designed to host guests from West Germany and Switzerland, offered a private and inviting atmosphere, a stark contrast to the closely monitored hotels frequented by foreigners in Moscow. The air in the headquarters of Herr Gunther Huber's company carried a sophisticated blend of scents, combining the freshness of cleanliness with the allure of expensive perfume. A faint trace of polished wood and imported tobacco lingered in the background, completing the atmosphere of discreet luxury.

Alfred walked into the living room, where a dark brown leather sofa and a coffee table created a warm and welcoming setting. A tall lamp cast a soft amber glow across the carpet, leaving the corners of the room in gentle shadow. The office was quiet, with only him present. As darkness fell and the chill of the evening grew more pronounced, he sat down to address some remaining work tasks. Outside the large window, the lights of Moscow flickered to life one by one, illuminating the vast city beneath the winter sky. Yet his thoughts kept drifting back to the stunning blond woman with black silk stockings he had met earlier. Drawn to the window, he gazed towards the building where she resided and softly uttered, "Tomorrow." Imagining their next encounter, he envisioned it as two meteorites colliding, two bright trajectories crossing unexpectedly in the dark expanse of a vast and complicated world, a thought that brought a knowing smile to his lips.

***

Meanwhile, Catherine sat in her chair, lost in contemplation. The small apartment was quiet around her, the faint hum of distant traffic filtering through the frosted windowpanes. A dim lamp cast a warm circle of light across the table, leaving the corners of the room in soft shadow. She gently tapped her finger against her cheek, pondering the possibilities that lay ahead. Her gaze drifted toward the window, where the winter evening pressed silently against the glass. Snowflakes moved lazily through the air, dissolving into the darkness of the Moscow night.

"Could he be the one?" she mused to herself. The words lingered in the stillness of the room, almost as if she were afraid someone might overhear them. "Could he be my escape route out of the Soviet Union?" Her heart quickened at the thought, a quiet rhythm echoing in the silence.

The idea of seeing Alfred again filled her with a mixture of excitement and apprehension. She remembered the warmth of the restaurant, the soft glow of candlelight on the table, and the way Alfred had looked at her with an unfamiliar openness—something rarely seen in a country where strangers often guarded their thoughts. She knew that any decision she made would significantly impact her future. Here, in Moscow, every step carried consequences, every choice could open or close doors that might never appear again.

As she weighed her options, the prospect of a new beginning outside the confines of the Soviet Union lingered in her mind, urging her to consider the possibilities that lay with this chance encounter. Beyond the walls of her apartment stretched a vast world she had only imagined—cities she had never seen, freedoms she had only heard whispered about, and a life that might exist somewhere beyond the invisible borders that surrounded her.

For a long moment she remained still, listening to the quiet of the room, as if the future itself were waiting for her answer.

Chapter 72

An Unexpected Encounter

Catherine strolled down her street, wrapped in thoughts, the winter air crisp against her cheeks and the faint crunch of snow beneath her boots marking her slow, deliberate steps, when she heard a familiar voice call out her name. "Catherine," Alfred exclaimed with surprise, his voice rising above the muted sounds of the busy Moscow street, "I cannot believe it is you. What are you doing in this district?"

She turned to him with a smile, brushing a loose strand of hair from her face as the cold wind stirred her coat, gesturing towards the surrounding buildings. "I have been looking for a position. And there seem to be a lot of offices in this area."

"It just happens that in my office there is a position available. I know you will fit in so well there. Have you ever done any secretarial duties?" Alfred asked, hope evident in his voice. His eyes lingered on her with an expression that blended professional interest with unmistakable admiration.

Catherine replied confidently, "I am an interpreter, and I can answer the phone, and I can do any filing work that you would need." She looked up at him, her eyes conveying both eagerness and a hint of vulnerability. For a moment the bustle of the street seemed to fade around them, leaving only the quiet intensity of their conversation. "Could I be useful to you in this way?"

"Will tomorrow morning be too soon?" Alfred inquired, already imagining her as part of his team.

"Oh, no, I will be there at whatever time you request," Catherine assured him, her voice filled with anticipation. A faint glow of excitement spread across her face, as though a door she had long hoped might open had suddenly appeared before her.

"Excellent. And meanwhile, could we have supper again?" he suggested, eager to spend more time with her.

"Oh, I would love it," she responded, her heart fluttering at the prospect of another evening together. Her smile carried a mixture of warmth and curiosity, as if she herself were surprised by how quickly their connection had deepened.

Alfred led Catherine to another restaurant, where they enjoyed a delightful dinner, lost in each other's gaze. Soft music drifted through the room while candlelight flickered gently across the white tablecloths. The food seemed secondary to the deepening connection they felt. Occasionally their conversation paused, yet the silence between them felt natural rather than awkward, filled with unspoken possibilities. After their meal, Alfred gently proposed, "May I walk you to your door?"

"Yes, of course," Catherine agreed, and they strolled side by side in comfortable silence. The streetlights glowed faintly through the falling snow as the city settled into the quiet rhythm of the evening. Upon reaching her door, Alfred tenderly held her hand and kissed her fingers. "Until tomorrow morning," he said softly, leaving her with a promise of a new beginning.

The next morning, Catherine dressed meticulously for her first day at Alfred's firm. The pale morning light filtered through the curtains of her apartment as she prepared herself with careful attention. She chose a navy-blue Italian suit with a pencil skirt and a classic jacket that accentuated her eyes, complemented by an ivory silk blouse. After applying mascara and a touch of powder, she admired her reflection, pleased with her professional appearance. For a second she studied her own expression in the mirror, as if trying to recognize the woman she was about to become. Donning her blue coat to match her suit, she grabbed her keys and hurried out, filled with a mix of excitement and apprehension.

As she approached Alfred's building, a place she had never ventured close to before, Catherine reminded herself, "It seems rather safe as his company is working on the Olympics and has probably already been thoroughly checked by the *KGB*." The thought offered a fragile reassurance as she climbed the slight rise leading toward the towering structures ahead. With this thought, she steeled herself for the day ahead, stepping into a new chapter of her life.

Catherine, driven by a blend of courage and desperation, ventured into the realm of the forbidden towers. The massive high-rises loomed above the snowy streets like silent sentinels guarding a world normally closed to ordinary citizens. It was a typical Moscow winter day, with snowflakes dancing in the air and occasional blizzards whirling through the streets. She descended the hill cautiously, mindful of the black ice underfoot, and traversed the narrow highway that separated her familiar world from the unfamiliar territory of the high-rises. These towering structures were home to diplomats, journalists, and businessmen, a world apart from her own.

As she neared Gunther Huber's firm, her heart pounded with a mixture of excitement and fear. Each step forward felt like crossing an invisible border between two very different realities. The *militsioner*, Vasyli Ivanov, stood guard, symbolizing the boundary she was about to cross. His stern gaze fell upon her as she approached. "Lady citizen, where are you going? Your passport, please," he demanded. Catherine, suppressing her anxiety, presented Gunther Huber's business card as her passport to this new world.

On the other end of the line, Alfred Fuchs's voice echoed through the lobby. "Good afternoon—Herr Fuchs speaking." The Soviet official quickly relayed the situation. Alfred's response was swift and decisive, assuring the official that Catherine was expected and cleared for entry. The guard, flustered but compliant, allowed her to pass. For a brief second Catherine felt the tension leave her shoulders as the heavy glass doors opened before her.

Stepping into the building, Catherine took in the elegant austerity of her surroundings. The polished floors reflected the soft overhead lighting, and the quiet hum of the elevator machinery echoed faintly through the spacious lobby. The elevator ride to the seventh floor felt like a journey into another realm. The doors slid open, revealing Alfred Fuchs, smiling, and impeccably dressed in his business suit. He extended his hand, welcoming her into the office, their new shared space.

"Hello, Catherine." Alfred took Catherine by hand and led her into the office. "This is our office," he said.

The office was a haven of comfort and luxury, a stark contrast to the world outside. Leather furniture, wall stands adorned with souvenirs and books, and the subtle scent of cologne created an ambiance that was both welcoming and foreign. A large window overlooked the city, where the snowy rooftops of Moscow stretched endlessly toward the horizon. Catherine was shown to her new workspace, complete with a desk and telephone. Alfred's assurance of a special badge to formalize her role added a layer of legitimacy to her presence.

In this new environment, Catherine felt a sense of liberation mixed with trepidation. For the first time in years, the boundaries of her life seemed to shift slightly outward. She was now part of a world she had only dreamed of, a world that offered opportunities and challenges alike. As she settled into her desk, shuffling through papers, and acquainting herself with her new role, she couldn't help but wonder about the path that lay ahead. This moment marked a turning point in her life, a bold step into an uncertain future.

In the quiet office, Alfred Fuchs took a blank piece of paper and began to pen his thoughts, his handwriting a conduit for unspoken words. The scratch of his pen against the paper sounded unusually loud in the otherwise silent room, where even the ticking of the wall clock seemed cautious. "I do not know you well, but I am aware of the strict laws in this country. I realize that what you did by entering our office was quite courageous but may be risky for you. Our offices are bugged so we write notes when discussing important matters. We welcome you in our office and hope you will stay on board despite the risks involved." Catherine read the note; her understanding and agreement reflected in a silent nod. For a moment her eyes lingered on the words, absorbing not only their meaning but the quiet trust that lay behind them. The gravity of the situation was clear to her, yet the chance before her was too vital to ignore.

As the day progressed, the office environment relaxed with the soothing hum of the electric heater and the gentle melodies of records playing in the background. The faint crackle of the vinyl accompanied the music, filling the room with a warm atmosphere that softened the harsh winter pressing against the windows. Catherine diligently attended to her tasks, answering calls, and quickly adapting to her new role. Her voice grew more confident with each call she answered, and the rhythm of office work gradually replaced the nervous tension she had felt earlier that morning.

As the office hours wound down, Alfred, with a playful glint in his eye, inquired, "Catherine, are you a good cook? Do you cook very often?" He leaned slightly against the desk as he spoke, studying her reaction with curiosity.

Catherine responded with a light-hearted yet enigmatic reply, "Perhaps soon, you will discover what a good cook I am, good night, Alfred. Thank you for a wonderful day. See you in the morning." A faint smile appeared on her lips, leaving her answer balanced somewhere between humor and promise.

As they prepared to leave, the worsening weather prompted Alfred to offer her a ride home. Outside, the wind had begun to swirl snow across the streets, transforming the city into a blur of white under the dim streetlights.

Gratefully accepting his offer, Catherine accompanied Alfred to his car. The cold evening air rushed toward them as they stepped outside the building, and their breath formed pale clouds in the darkness. Upon reaching her destination, Alfred, ever the gentleman, kissed her hand, bidding her farewell. "Thank you for the ride, Alfred. I enjoyed it greatly," Catherine expressed her gratitude.

Alfred, in return, acknowledged their mutual enjoyment. "It was mutual, Catherine. Herr Gunther Huber, the company owner, is expected in Moscow tomorrow and will meet you. Good night." For a moment they stood beneath the soft glow of the streetlamp, neither quite ready to turn away. With these parting words, they each retreated into the night, anticipating the new dynamics the coming day would bring. The snow continued to fall quietly around them, covering the streets of Moscow as if concealing the fragile beginnings of a story neither of them yet fully understood.

Chapter 73

Catherine's Interrogation

Catherine's morning was abruptly disrupted by thunderous knocks at her door. The blows echoed through the small apartment like hammer strikes, rattling the thin wooden frame and shattering the quiet of the early hour. Her heart raced as she nervously inquired who it was. For a moment there was only silence beyond the door, heavy and threatening. The stern voice of a *militsioner* on the other side only heightened her anxiety. The sound of his voice carried the authority of the state, cold and impatient. She hesitantly opened the door to find a young, scowling *militsioner* who promptly barged into her apartment without invitation. His heavy boots left damp traces of melting snow on the worn floorboards as he stepped inside.

"Good morning," Catherine managed to utter, her voice laced with fear. Her fingers tightened nervously around the edge of the door as she tried to steady herself.

The *militsioner* introduced himself and immediately accused her of fraternizing with Alfred Fuchs, a West German citizen, reminding her of the strict rules against socializing with foreigners. His eyes moved slowly around the room, studying every detail of her modest apartment as if searching for evidence of wrongdoing. He demanded to know her workplace. Catherine quickly showed her work badge, explaining her role as a secretary and translator for Herr Fuchs's company. She held the badge carefully in her trembling hand, hoping the small piece of official paper might shield her from further trouble.

Despite her explanation, the *militsioner* looked at her suspiciously, his disdain evident. His lips tightened as he examined the badge, then returned his gaze to Catherine with a mixture of contempt and calculation. His harsh warning echoed in the small living room, "You are a Soviet citizeness and a refusenik. You cannot work for foreigners. Take this warning seriously!"

Trembling and pale, Catherine sensed the *militsioner's* underlying motive. Years of living within the Soviet system had taught her to read the subtle signals hidden beneath official words. It wasn't an arrest he was after; it was a bribe. Thinking quickly, she offered him a pair of new black silk stockings, hoping it would appease him. The delicate fabric glimmered faintly in the dim light as she held them out with cautious politeness.

His demeanor softened as he accepted the gift, a slight smile breaking through his stern facade. His fingers folded the stockings quickly before slipping them into his coat pocket with practiced ease. "Thank you, citizeness, for the gift."

As the *militsioner* left, slamming the door behind him, Catherine was left to ponder the implications of this encounter. The sudden silence that followed felt almost deafening. She stood motionless in the middle of the room, listening to the fading echo of his footsteps in the stairwell. The Soviet system, once unyielding and formidable, was showing signs of deterioration, with even its law enforcers resorting to petty bribery. The authority that once inspired fear now seemed strangely hollow, eroded by quiet corruption and desperation. It was a telling sign of the times, a crumbling facade that left its citizens to navigate an increasingly unpredictable landscape. Catherine slowly exhaled, realizing that survival in this world required not only courage, but constant vigilance.

Chapter 74

Coffee and Contemplation

Catherine, still catching breath from her frantic run, entered the office where Alfred immediately noticed her disheveled state. Her cheeks were flushed from the cold morning air, and small snowflakes clung to the edges of her coat as the door closed behind her. "Catherine, why are you out of breath?" he inquired with concern.

Leaning close to Alfred, she whispered her fears and frustrations. Her voice dropped to almost a breath, careful and guarded, as if the very walls might be listening. "I hate it here. I hate the Soviet Union," she confessed, her voice trembling. "They interrogated me about why I am working here. I had to give away my beautiful black silk stockings, the only thing I had, to avoid trouble. The KGB could have arrested me for being seen with you, a foreigner." Her words conveyed a mix of desperation and vulnerability. Her hands trembled slightly as she spoke, the morning's encounter still vivid in her mind.

Alfred, touched by her plight, offered her comfort and support. His expression softened, and he lowered his voice instinctively, aware of the ever-present danger of unseen listeners. "Wipe your tears and return to your desk," he advised gently. "Herr Huber will be here any moment, and I'll help you however I can."

As if on cue, Gunther Huber, a well-built, affable older man with a congenial smile, entered the office. The door opened briskly, allowing a brief gust of cold winter air to slip into the warm room. He exuded a sense of warmth and authority. Approaching Alfred, he shook his hand heartily. "Who is our new employee?" he inquired, his gaze drifting towards Catherine.

Alfred introduced Catherine to Herr Huber, who greeted her with a warm handshake. His handshake was firm yet friendly, radiating a calm confidence that instantly eased the tension in the room. "Good day! Welcome to our office! Fraulein—Miss, what a pleasure!" he said with genuine enthusiasm.

Catherine, maintaining her composure, greeted him respectfully. She straightened slightly, determined to appear calm and professional despite the turmoil of the morning. "Good afternoon, Herr Huber," she replied, meeting his handshake.

Herr Huber's presence was comforting. He was an older man compared to Alfred, dressed in a business suit and sweater. His demeanor radiated health, warmth, and quiet confidence. His steel grey eyes, tinged with blue, were expressive and thoughtful. When he spoke, his voice carried the reassuring tone of a man accustomed to leadership and responsibility. Alfred, too, was a handsome man in his mid-fifties, with a distinguished appearance and grey-blue eyes. Together, they were an impressive duo, commanding respect, and trust.

Gunther led them to the main room, lined with shelves filled with hardcover books. The polished wood shelves reflected the soft glow of the overhead lights, giving the room an atmosphere of quiet refinement. Catherine followed cautiously, aware of the importance of this meeting. Alfred guided her to the sofa, sitting beside her. The coffee table was adorned with an array of delicacies: thinly sliced salami, assorted cheeses, crackers, olives, and pickled mushrooms, all arranged meticulously with small silver forks for convenience. Crystal glasses sparkled beside the plates, and a faint aroma of freshly brewed coffee lingered in the air. The atmosphere was one of professionalism mixed with a touch of elegance, setting the stage for a significant discussion.

As the evening progressed in the sophisticated office setting, Gunther Huber invited Catherine and Alfred to indulge in the array of refreshments. He moved with the relaxed assurance of a host welcoming trusted colleagues into his private world. "Please, help yourself," he gestured towards the petite sandwiches and chocolates, adding a touch of continental charm to the atmosphere.

Gunther inquired if Catherine preferred brandy, speaking with his distinct German accent. Alfred and Catherine opted for their respective choices, Alfred sipping whisky while Catherine elegantly poured herself a glass of brandy from a finely crafted snifter. The amber liquid caught the light as she lifted the glass, its warmth a comforting contrast to the winter beyond the windows. The luxurious surroundings and the sense of quiet power enveloping the room seemed to captivate her.

Gunther, Alfred, well-acquainted with the perks of being accredited foreigners in Moscow, reveled in the privileges this status afforded them. From coveted Bolshoi tickets to lavish embassy receptions, their life in Moscow was rich with experiences akin to those enjoyed by the elite in the free world. In a city where most citizens lived modestly under constant scrutiny, these privileges created a rare bubble of freedom. Gunther, who preferred quieter, more intimate gatherings, often opted to entertain in the office.

Raising a toast to the friendship between their countries, Gunther initiated a warm and convivial atmosphere. The crystal glasses chimed softly as they touched. The three clinked their glasses, brandy and whisky enhancing the congenial mood. As they settled comfortably into the evening, Gunther opened about his business ventures, keen on sharing the story of his company's growth and success.

"I want to tell you about my firm," Gunther began, emphasizing the importance of understanding the company's background. He narrated his journey of establishing the company in West Germany post-war, building it from scratch without external investments. His voice carried both pride and quiet determination as he described the difficult years of rebuilding after the war. His entrepreneurial spirit had led the firm to flourish, expanding its presence into the Soviet Union and other socialist countries.

"We are purveyors of hygiene products," Gunther explained, "and our firm has been selected for the upcoming Summer Olympics in Moscow." Turning to Catherine, he sought her agreement to provide translation services for their interactions with business partners. His gaze rested on her thoughtfully, measuring her confidence and intelligence.

Catherine, seizing the opportunity, affirmed her commitment. The moment felt significant, as if the door to a new life had opened just slightly wider. "Absolutely, yes, I am. I thank you for this opportunity," she replied with gratitude.

Following the mutual agreement, the trio exchanged hearty handshakes, cementing their professional collaboration. Gunther, ever the busy executive, excused himself for another meeting, planning an early flight to Zurich the next morning. He glanced briefly at his watch, already calculating the schedule of his next journey. "Goodbye to you all," he said warmly, bustling out to continue his business endeavors.

***

Exhausted from their long day, Alfred suggested to Catherine that they have supper together, an invitation she gladly accepted. The office lights had grown dim, and beyond the tall windows the Moscow evening had settled into a soft veil of snow and amber streetlights.

"Catherine, we've had a long day. Would you partake supper with me tonight?"

"I would love to. It has been a long day."

They drove to the luxurious "Birch Tree" department store. The car glided slowly through the evening traffic, its headlights reflecting off the wet winter pavement as snowflakes drifted lazily through the air. Curious about the reason for their stop, Catherine asked Alfred, to which he replied with a hint of mystery, "You will see."

Upon entering the store and heading to the shoe department, a neatly dressed saleslady approached. The polished marble floors reflected the soft golden lights above, and the quiet elegance of the store contrasted sharply with the austerity of ordinary Moscow shops.

"May I help you, sir?"

"Yes, the lady has a small foot, no bigger than size 7. Could you please show us your latest arrivals of the Thierry Rabotin shoes? I will take one pair of your most elegant leather pumps, please." Catherine's eyes grew wide. For a moment she stood completely still, astonished by such unexpected generosity in a country where luxury was rarely within reach. She could not believe his generosity. And Alfred said, "May I invite you to my place for supper?"

"Yes, of course."

When they arrived at Alfred's residence, he greeted the guard, who let them pass without question. The guard nodded respectfully as they crossed the quiet lobby, the polished floors echoing faintly beneath their footsteps. Inside the dark room, Alfred and Catherine embraced and shared their first, deeply passionate kiss, marking the beginning of a romantic night. The city lights shimmered faintly through the window behind them, casting soft reflections across the room as the silence of the evening wrapped around them.

The next morning Alfred lamented having to leave after such an enchanting evening. A pale winter light filtered through the curtains, illuminating the quiet warmth of the apartment. "What a pity I must leave after such a divine night!" he said.

Catherine quickly made coffee and brought out buns and muffins, playfully asking Alfred to help her retrieve raspberry jelly from a high cabinet. The rich aroma of freshly brewed coffee filled the kitchen, blending with the sweet scent of warm pastries. They enjoyed their breakfast together, smiling and savoring the moment. Outside the window, the city was slowly awakening, yet inside the small apartment time seemed to pause for them. When it was time for Alfred to depart, Catherine coyly thought to herself: "Oh, this man shall be so easy to marry." With her striking beauty and clear intentions, she contemplated the potential of a future with Alfred. A faint smile crossed her lips as she watched him prepare to leave, already imagining the possibilities that might unfold between them.

Chapter 75

Tale of Love and Risk

Catherine's peaceful morning was suddenly disrupted by the ringing of the phone. The sharp sound cut through the quiet apartment like an alarm, echoing off the pale walls and startling her from her thoughts.

"Catherine, there will be some changes. I have been requested to leave Moscow immediately and fly back to Frankfurt. I will be calling you from Germany, and I promise I will make it right for you!" Alfred's voice sounded hurried, breathless, as if he were already moving through the chaos of departure. Then he paused for a minute and asked, "But I have something to ask you. I wish it were not over the phone, but I need to know … Will you become my wife? Sorry, I do not have a ring today, not even a bouquet of flowers, but life is moving so fast that we cannot keep up with the pace."

Despite the lack of a ring or flowers, and the rapid pace of events, Alfred's proposal filled Catherine with a mix of disbelief and elation. Her hand trembled slightly as she held the receiver, the words echoing in her mind as if they belonged to another life entirely. Her response was a faint, yet heartfelt, "yes."

"Catherine, dear! This makes me so happy! I'm sorry … we cannot celebrate tonight in person, it is very awkward to scramble our plans, but I must get on the plane today. I hardly have the time to do it, but I need to get to the airport in two hours. I am terribly sorry. Will call you as soon as possible. Do not worry! You will have a new life with me in Frankfurt or any city you desire."

The call ended quickly, leaving Catherine to process the whirlwind of changes in her life. For several seconds she remained motionless, the silent receiver still pressed against her ear, as if the conversation might somehow continue.

As Catherine passed the building's *militsioner,* Vasyli Ivanov, he sternly warned her not to return. This unexpected admonishment alarmed her, hinting that the authorities were monitoring her closely. His voice was low but unmistakably threatening, the kind of warning that carried far more meaning than the words themselves. Catherine chose not to engage and hurriedly left the scene, feeling the gravity of her situation.

Alone with Alfred's promise of marriage, Catherine found solace in the thought of their future together. The promise seemed almost unreal, like a distant light flickering somewhere beyond the heavy borders of the Soviet world. His words became her mantra, offering her a sense of security and hope for a new life as a West German national's wife. Despite her newfound optimism, she couldn't shake off the uncertainty of her situation. As she returned to her apartment, the quietness of the building and the memories of her former job weighed on her. She realized that her future in her homeland was over, and her only hope lay in the promise of a life with Alfred. Looking out the window, she saw signs of spring emerging, thin streams of melting snow trickling along the sidewalks and small patches of dark earth appearing beneath the trees, a fitting metaphor for the new beginnings that awaited her, contingent on Alfred's commitment to their shared future.

Catherine felt like a hostage. Her life had suddenly narrowed into a single fragile thread of expectation. In the evenings when she could not wander around, she sat by her phone waiting for Alfred to call her and remind her of his love and devotion to her. The apartment grew darker as evening settled outside, the only light coming from the small lamp beside the telephone. Suddenly the phone rang, and it was him. Ecstatically she picked up the phone listening to him as Alfred reinstated his initial promises to her.

"I am calling you from the airport," he said in his husky voice. Behind his words she could hear the distant murmur of loudspeakers and the indistinct noise of travelers moving through the terminal. "I will arrive in Frankfurt in a few hours. It will take me another hour to get settled, and I will call you immediately. Please, do not get upset. I know how you feel, Mein Liebchen—my beloved! Please, expect a call from my associate who will bring an envelope with cash for you. I want you to be comfortable and not have a worry in the world. We will get married soon even if it means more trouble for both of us. Have made up my mind. Ich Liebe dich! I love you!" and the line went dead a second later.

Alfred's words, filled with love and reassurance, comforted Catherine, but she couldn't shake off the feeling of uncertainty. The silence that followed the call felt heavy, almost ominous. His promises were heartfelt, but she knew that circumstances could change and were often out of their control. She clung to the hope of their future marriage despite the potential challenges it might bring.

As she hung up the phone, Catherine realized the necessity of secrecy in her life. In Moscow, trust was a dangerous luxury. She couldn't risk confiding in anyone, as any breach of trust could jeopardize her fragile situation. Her world had become a solitary one, where waiting and hope intertwined with the fear of the unknown. The telephone now sat at the center of her small room like a silent lifeline, connecting her fragile present to an uncertain future somewhere beyond the Soviet borders.

Chapter 76

Cryptic Connections

The phone buzzed again and when she picked it up, she heard a totally unfamiliar voice on the other end. The sudden sound made her heart jump; the quiet apartment instantly filled with tension.

"Hello," said the man in a deep voice. "May I speak to Catherine?"

The voice frightened her, but she needed to know who it was. "Yes." "How can I help you?"

"My name is Paulus and I have a message from your Aunt Natalie." Catherine worried— Can this man be trusted? Her fingers tightened around the receiver as she listened carefully. Paulus continued speaking Russian with a strong foreign accent. She assumed that the man speaking to her on the phone was probably from the Baltics where people never lost an unmistakable pleasant accent in Russian.

"Your Aunt Natalie asked me to call you. If you should ever need my help, here is my number. I have arrived from New York today and will stay in Moscow for a few days." Paulus continued after quickly ringing off the number while Catherine wrote it down. She grabbed the nearest scrap of paper and scribbled the digits hurriedly; afraid she might miss one. In case Alfred ever failed to marry her and get her out of the Soviet Union, she would keep Paulus's number and hide it in a safe place.

But for now, it was vital to be cryptic. She suspected that her phone was already bugged, and she would be better off to be always evasive. "How is my aunt? I would like to send a gift back to her with you, if possible." Her tone was deliberately casual, as though she were discussing nothing more than an ordinary family errand. There was no way she was ready for a lengthy conversation on the phone.

Paulus seemed to understand, and he set up a meeting place and meeting time. "I will be happy to meet you in the city center by the Bolshoi."

"Very well," said Catherine.

"We can meet at the Bolshoi at five p.m. Would that be OK with you?" Paulus asked. She was thinking that she should go and meet the gentleman, but what if it were a trap? The thought sent a chill through her. She contemplated and shivered.

"I will have a trench coat and a hat. What will you wear?" asked Paulus.

She thought for a moment, carefully choosing something distinctive yet ordinary enough not to attract attention. "I will have a black leather jacket with a white gardenia on the lapel. I will carry a book in my hand."

"Well, till five p.m., by the Bolshoi fountain."

"Bye, bye!" she said. She looked out the window. The late afternoon light flooded the street below; the sky was intensely blue with white clouds floating slowly by. For a moment the city looked almost peaceful, disguising the tension that ruled everyday life. She looked at her watch, and it was already 4 p.m.

Looking through her shelf of books, she grabbed a book, a pair of the black stockings that she would pretend was the gift if she were caught and rushed to the florist for a flower. Her movements became hurried and purposeful, as though time itself were pressing against her. What would happen to her if she had another encounter with militsiya? But she had to listen to her inner voice telling her to go. Catherine put on her big sunglasses and ran fast to the metro station. Cold air rushed against her face as she hurried down the street, the sounds of traffic and distant voices blending into a dull roar. She got on the train and took a seat by the window. The metro doors slammed shut with a metallic thud. The train started moving, and she closed her eyes.

She dreamed of Alfred Fuchs meeting her in Frankfurt and them traveling together in Europe. She imagined wide boulevards, elegant cafés, and the freedom to walk anywhere without fear. The whole world would be open to them. Is it possible? How can that dream become true given she was a refusenik? Nobody would give her those reassurances. Yet the fragile hope remained, flickering stubbornly inside her like a small flame refusing to die.

Chapter 77

Behind the Curtain

"*Revolution Square.*" The announcement from the train's loudspeaker snapped Catherine back to the present. The metallic voice echoed through the carriage, accompanied by the squeal of brakes and the slow shudder of the train coming to a halt. She disembarked and made her way to the street, her heart pounding with a mix of anticipation and anxiety. Cold winter air rushed into the metro entrance as people hurried past her, their coats brushing against one another in the crowded passage. As she approached the small square in front of the Bolshoi Theatre, her eyes scanned the area carefully, alert to every passerby, until they landed on a tall, lanky man wearing a Bavarian brown hat and an elegant overcoat. His distinguished western-style clothing and fine English leather shoes immediately indicated his identity. In a city where most citizens dressed modestly, his appearance stood out unmistakably.

"Good afternoon, Catherine!" Paulus greeted her with a warm smile, waving his hand in recognition.

"Good afternoon, Paulus!" Catherine replied, trying to mask her nervousness with a smile. Her voice sounded calm, though inside she felt the familiar tightening of fear that accompanied every risky encounter.

"You look just like your aunt described you. Young and incredibly attractive!" Paulus complimented her, to which she responded with a modest smile.

Quickly switching to English, Paulus said, "I have two tickets for the Bolshoi ballet tonight. During the intermission, we can go to the lobby, have a glass of champagne, and speak freely."

"I would be delighted," Catherine agreed, relieved at the opportunity for a discreet conversation. The proposal felt almost theatrical—an elegant cover for a conversation that could not safely occur anywhere else.

The ballet was a mesmerizing experience, the grand hall glowing beneath enormous chandeliers, the orchestra rising from the pit in waves of music, but Catherine's mind was elsewhere. Her eyes occasionally drifted from the stage to the audience, instinctively searching for any sign that they were being watched. During the intermission, they slipped into the opulent, heavily carpeted lounge. Crystal chandeliers cast warm light across polished marble floors while elegantly dressed patrons gathered in clusters, their conversations blending into a soft murmur. Amidst the crowd, they spoke in hushed tones, pretending to be engrossed in each other's company as though they were lovers, their voices barely rising above the surrounding noise.

"Your Aunt Natalie wants you to know that she fully supports you from New York and will help you in any way possible," Paulus whispered. "We hope you can make it through the iron curtain. It's best to say as little as possible over the phone; all lines are tapped." His words were calm, but the warning carried unmistakable gravity.

As the intermission ended, the ringing of a bell echoed through the corridors, and they reluctantly set down their champagne glasses and returned to their seats for the remainder of the ballet. The orchestra resumed with a dramatic swell of music as the velvet curtain slowly lifted once again. Before parting, Paulus added, “Remember my name and number. I won’t give you my business card for safety. If we come up with a plan, we’ll discuss it.”

After the ballet, Catherine hailed a taxi and headed home, her mind racing with possibilities and fears. The streets of Moscow were already dark, the theatre lights glowing against the cold night sky. Paulus waved goodbye and walked away, not looking back, disappearing into the evening crowd with the practiced caution of someone accustomed to remaining unnoticed, leaving Catherine to ponder the uncertain path that lay ahead.

Chapter 78

Distant Call

As Catherine stepped out of the taxi, she entered her apartment with a mind swirling in contemplation. The hallway smelled faintly of damp wool coats and old varnish, the familiar scent of the building that had suddenly begun to feel like a place of waiting rather than living. Before her whirlwind romance with Alfred, she had lived a reclusive life, deliberately avoiding any romantic ties. Yet the profound sense of loneliness had always lingered. Seeking a distraction, she picked up a book but found herself unable to concentrate, her eyes passing over the lines without absorbing a single word, her thoughts constantly drifting towards Alfred.

The late hour only intensified her unease, as the phone remained silent, sitting on the small table like an object of quiet authority, amplifying her dependence on the distant relationship with Alfred in a foreign land. Her thoughts wandered, oscillating between hope and doubt. She questioned the genuineness of Alfred's feelings and the solidity of his promises. Was his sudden proposal the impulse of a romantic evening, or the beginning of something real? Just as she began to feel overwhelmed by uncertainty, the phone finally rang, breaking the silence that had enveloped her.

Eagerly, she reached for the phone, which had become her sole connection to Alfred and her hopes for the future. The ringing sounded louder than usual in the stillness of the room.

On the third ring, she answered, "Hello?"

"Hello from Frankfurt," Alfred's voice came through, tired but unmistakable. In the background she could faintly hear distant voices and the muted clatter of an airport or office corridor. "I'm sorry, Catherine. Our flight was delayed, and things have been complicated here. But listen to me—I haven't changed my mind. I meant everything I said. I'm committed to us."

He switched to German, his voice softer now, more intimate.

"I should have my visa soon. Then we'll file the marriage papers. If everything goes as planned, in a few months we'll be married in Moscow. You'll be my wife." He paused. "Just… be patient. Please don't lose heart."

Relief washed over Catherine as she listened. Her shoulders slowly relaxed as if a great weight had been lifted from them. Alfred spoke of their future—of marriage, and of the West German visa she would apply for afterward. His words carried both apology and resolve. He urged her to be patient. These things took time.

Then the line went dead.

Catherine remained still, the receiver pressed to her ear. For a moment she heard only the faint static of the empty connection. Disconnections were common. Sometimes the lines failed. Sometimes they did not fail at all. In Moscow, even silence could carry meaning.

She replaced the receiver slowly, careful of what she had said—and what she had not. Every word spoken on a telephone could travel far beyond the room in which it was spoken.

The phone rang again. Her heart leapt as she answered.

It was Alfred. He apologized for the interruption and said he would call again the next day. His voice sounded hurried now, as if someone might be waiting nearby.

The line went silent once more.

Catherine stood there for a moment, holding the receiver in her hand. Outside, the distant rumble of traffic drifted through the window, reminding her that life in the vast city continued without pause. She clung to his words, though uncertainty lingered. In her world, hope required patience—and caution. Both had become necessary companions in the life she was now living.

Chapter 79

The Olympic Odyssey

The 1980 Summer Olympics in Moscow marked a historic moment as the Soviet Union hosted the prestigious event for the first time. For weeks the city had been preparing with almost theatrical precision. Streets were freshly painted, banners stretched across avenues, and enormous Olympic emblems fluttered in the summer wind. The grandeur of the opening ceremony was a testament to the Soviet Union's dedication to showcasing its athletic talent and cultural might. A spectacular display of artistry and skill honored Moscow, captivating audiences worldwide. Stadium lights illuminated the night sky while thousands of performers moved in perfect formation, their choreography symbolizing the power and unity the Soviet state wished the world to see.

Amidst the Olympic fever, Gunther Huber's office found itself inundated with work. The demand for their unique skincare products and perfumed soaps surged as the Olympics unfolded, making it their busiest season yet. Foreign visitors poured into Moscow, filling hotels, restaurants, and shops, all eager to carry home a small token of the Soviet spectacle. Gunther's return to Moscow was brief yet crucial, aimed at streamlining operations for the Olympic season. His deep understanding of the Soviet system, gained from years of experience, proved invaluable during this hectic period. He knew which doors required patience, which officials required diplomacy, and which conversations were best conducted quietly behind closed doors.

Gunther's familiarity with the Soviet Union traced back to the harrowing experiences of World War II. As a young man, he and his family attempted to escape the horrors of war by crossing into Switzerland. Unfortunately, their journey was cut short at the border, and they were detained by Swiss authorities. The bitter disappointment of being turned away at what they believed was the threshold of safety remained etched in his memory. Following their release, Gunther returned to Germany, where he was promptly conscripted into the army. He endured the brutalities of war, ultimately being captured, and sent to a Soviet POW camp. The endless winters, the harsh discipline, and the uncertainty of survival became the defining tests of his youth.

In captivity, Gunther's resolve to survive was fortified by his determination to maintain his health through meticulous hygiene and exercise. While others surrendered to despair, he forced himself into a daily routine—washing when water was available, exercising in cramped quarters, and disciplining his mind to endure the passing days. His efforts paid off when he was released and returned to Germany, only to discover the heartbreaking news of his parents' passing. They had mourned him, believing him dead, and had even erected a memorial in his honor. To them he had already become a ghost of the war.

Life, however, continued for Gunther. He married, had children, and built a life filled with love and generosity. The quiet stability of family life offered him a peace he had once thought impossible. His family became his sanctuary, a source of joy amidst the memories of war and loss.

In later years, as Gunther visited his Moscow office, he relished the freedom of driving his elegant Mercedes along the city's ring road. The polished car glided past endless Soviet apartment blocks and monumental government buildings, symbols of a system he understood but never fully belonged to. Each trip began with a ritualistic offering to his security guard, Nikolay—a pack of Marlboro cigarettes and Swiss chocolates—a gesture of appreciation and a reminder of his journey from a war-torn past to a prosperous present. Such small gifts were more than courtesy in Moscow; they were a quiet language of mutual understanding.

Gunther's story was one of resilience and triumph, a narrative that paralleled the spirit of the Olympic Games he now found himself intricately involved in. Like the athletes arriving from every corner of the world, he too had endured trials, defeats, and improbable victories. In many ways, his presence in Moscow—once the land of his captivity—was itself a remarkable symbol of history's unexpected turns.

Chapter 80

Unseen Ties

The decision of Gunther Huber to establish a representative office for his West German company in Moscow was more than a mere business strategy; it was deeply rooted in his personal history and experiences during World War II. Gunther's connection to the Soviet Union was forged in the crucible of his captivity and shaped his life in profound ways. For him, Moscow was not simply a distant market—it was a place where fate had once tested his survival.

As a young POW, Gunther found himself in a camp near Moscow. The endless forests surrounding the camp stretched toward the horizon, their dark silhouettes standing silent against the brutal winter sky. Surrounded by military guards of his own age, he rapidly became fluent in Russian, initially self-taught and later under the guidance of a language instructor. The language that had once sounded harsh and foreign gradually became familiar, a tool that would later shape the course of his life.

The Soviet military, recognizing his potential value, suggested a post-war arrangement. Gunther would maintain contact with Soviet agents, meeting them discreetly in various European countries. This arrangement, simple yet consequential, was facilitated by the relative ease of post-war travel across Europe. In the shattered landscape of post-war Europe, borders shifted, identities blurred, and opportunities often appeared where least expected.

Gunther's language instructor, Nikolay Soldatov, was an astute and cultured military officer with a barely detectable Baltic accent. Under Nikolay's tutelage, Gunther not only honed his Russian language skills but also earned privileges, including better food. The lessons often took place in a small wooden office near the barracks, where the smell of tobacco and ink lingered in the air while the two men discussed grammar, literature, and occasionally the uncertain future awaiting Europe. Despite the grim circumstances, Gunther felt fortunate and appreciated the opportunity to leave the camp unharmed.

Upon his release in 1947, Gunther was equipped with a new Dutch passport, altered to conceal his German identity, and provided with sufficient resources to start anew. His journey back to freedom began with a transition from his padded military coat to a civilian suit, symbolizing his rebirth as a free individual in a liberated Europe. The moment he first put on the suit, he felt as if an entire chapter of his life had been quietly closed. His destination was his hometown, where he hoped to reconnect with his past and build a new life.

Gunther's return to Germany marked the beginning of a remarkable journey. Leveraging his unique experience and connections, he ventured into business, focusing on the Soviet Union. While others saw the Soviet system as impenetrable, Gunther recognized its hidden corridors and unwritten rules. His company thrived, benefiting from the subtle yet significant support of Soviet authorities. Gunther's understanding of the Soviet system, coupled with his resilience and entrepreneurial spirit, made his business endeavors both profitable and sustainable.

For Catherine, Gunther Huber's presence in Moscow was more than just a business opportunity; he was a lifeline in her time of need. Although he may not have directly intervened in her personal struggles, his decision to employ her provided a sense of stability and protection under the auspices of his influential West German enterprise. Working inside a foreign company offered her something rare in Moscow—an island of relative safety within a tightly controlled world. Catherine's association with Gunther's company shielded her from the harsher realities of her situation, offering a semblance of normalcy in an otherwise tumultuous period of her life. Behind the office doors, she could briefly forget the constant vigilance demanded by life outside.

Chapter 81

Love's Embrace

Alfred Fuchs was gearing up for his imminent journey to Moscow. The usual bureaucratic hurdles and cumbersome visa procedures were a constant impediment. Every document required signatures, stamps, and endless waiting, the familiar ritual of navigating Soviet bureaucracy. He made it a point to call Catherine every other day, reaffirming his love for her. Each time Catherine responded, "Alfred, dearest! Do you love me? Do you still want to marry me?" And he answered her, "My love, who else would I want to marry and spend my life with? Every time we speak, I come to love you even more. I must dash to the airport. Barring any unforeseen delays, I shall be with you soon." Her smile lingered at the thought, everything unfolding as she had dreamed.

Arriving in Moscow under the cloak of night, Alfred presented the quintessential image of a successful West German businessman, donning a grey coat and hat. The runway lights of Sheremetyevo Airport shimmered in the darkness as the aircraft slowly taxied toward the terminal. After breezing through customs, he made his way to baggage claim. He couldn't help but admire the sleek, modern design of Sheremetyevo Airport, a product of late seventies West German craftsmanship, anticipating the influx of tourists for the Summer Olympics. The polished glass and steel architecture stood in striking contrast to the austerity that dominated much of Moscow. Shortly after, he headed for the exit, where his uniformed driver welcomed him and assisted with his luggage. Alfred, preferring solitude, merely nodded and settled in for the ride, eyes closed, as they drove past the dilapidated structures dotting the suburban outskirts of Moscow. Dim streetlights illuminated rows of aging apartment blocks, their gray concrete facades stretching endlessly into the distance.

Foreign regulations necessitated Alfred's stay in a hotel upon reentering Russia. That night, he found himself restless, yearning for Catherine's embrace. At the break of dawn, unable to resist the pull any longer, he swiftly dressed and ventured out to the parking lot. There, he approached a taxi driver with his rudimentary Russian, "Where might I exchange Deutsche Marks?"

"Hotel *Intourist*," the driver replied, gesturing to a nearby building.

"Please, take me there," Alfred requested, and the driver obliged. The hotel lobby buzzed with activity. Foreign journalists, businessmen, and Olympic officials moved briskly through the marble hall. Elegantly dressed single women roamed the area, their predatory gazes surveying the scene. Familiar with such sights from Frankfurt, Alfred couldn't help but smirk as he briskly made his way to the currency exchange booth.

Herr Fuchs greeted the clerk with a smile, exchanging his Deutsche Marks for rubles. He couldn't help but notice her perfectly manicured hands, adorned with a striking diamond ring. After a friendly wink, he left the booth, limping slightly on his left foot, a recent nuisance. The injury reminded him of the long journeys and constant travel his business required. He navigated through the throng of festive foreigners, eventually finding his driver waiting patiently outside.

"First, please, take me to the National Hotel," requested Alfred, and within five minutes, they arrived at the hotel's parking area.

Gratefully, he tipped the driver with a few extra rubles and made his way to the entrance, which exuded a classier aura compared to the previous hotel. The elegant façade of the National stood proudly opposite the Kremlin, its historic grandeur reflecting the prestige reserved for foreign guests. Once in his room, he showered and eagerly dialed Catherine's number.

Hearing her voice was a relief. "Hello!" she answered.

"Hello, Catherine. I'm here at last, ready to marry you and bring you to Frankfurt!" he exclaimed with excitement.

The news was both expected and startling for Catherine, leaving her momentarily breathless. Despite the uncertainty of Alfred's visits, plagued by the whims of the Soviet government and the complications of visa issuance, his constant declarations of love fortified her plans and hopes for a future together. Alfred had arranged for an associate to regularly deliver long-stem red roses and select delicacies from a hard-currency department store to Catherine, ensuring the flowers and gifts were of the finest quality. Each delivery brought a personal note from Alfred, endearing and heartfelt.

The prospect of visiting the West German Embassy now seemed within reach. "Alfred, dearest!" Catherine momentarily struggled to find words, repeating his name. Then, the realization that Alfred was serious about marrying her began to dawn on her. Sensing her astonishment and disbelief, Alfred reassured her, "Dearest, with your permission, I'm already planning our wedding date here in Moscow. I can't discuss more over the phone. We'll talk in person soon."

She was nearly overwhelmed. Could her dream truly be unfolding into reality?

"Alfred, dearest, my lifelong dream of being with you is becoming real. Where are you staying?"

"I'm at the National. My visa is only for a week, so we must act quickly. May I come to see you? I've missed you terribly."

"Please, do. Why even ask?" she responded eagerly.

"I'll be there as soon as I can, Mein Liebchen."

"Alfred dearest, I love you," Catherine finally said, and the call ended.

After hanging up, Catherine turned away, her face betraying a sly smile. Manipulating Alfred was effortless, especially given his profound love for her.

Alfred hastily quenched his thirst with a glass of mineral water before heading to the bathroom to splash his face with cold water. He looked wearied, his eyes bloodshot, squinting under the harsh bathroom lights. Before leaving, he took a final glance in the mirror, ensuring he still embodied the image of a successful businessman from Frankfurt. He picked up a bulky plastic bag filled with carefully selected gifts for Catherine: exclusive French perfume, champagne, chocolates, and an elegant Hermes scarf with a delicate design.

Exiting his room, he encountered the floor concierge, who greeted him with a "*Guten Tag*—good afternoon, her only German phrase. The lady seemed weary, her puffy face devoid of makeup. The time was past 1 a.m.; Moscow was enveloped in a quiet night, its streets dimly lit and devoid of pedestrians.

Alfred, limping on his left foot, chose to walk through central Gorky Street, enjoying the fresh air and scents of late Indian summer. A cool breeze carried the faint smell of asphalt and distant tobacco smoke through the nearly empty boulevard. He had deliberately avoided requesting a taxi at the hotel, weary of surveillance and wishing to spare Catherine any *KGB* harassment. Though he had noted a recent relaxation in Soviet intelligence activities, it was still September 1981.

Pausing in front of the Central Telegraph building, he checked the time: 1:30 a.m., with minimal traffic on Gorky Street. As he tried to hail a cab, a militsioner approached him, questioning his intentions. Alfred, in a panic, scrambled through his small dictionary, eventually finding the phrase "not much of anything!" to explain his situation. In a quick move, he handed a pack of Marlboro cigarettes to the officer, who, seemingly pleased with the unexpected gift, saluted and continued his patrol.

A taxi soon stopped for Alfred. It was an older model, possibly a Volga, a status symbol in the Soviet Union. The driver inquired about his destination in Russian, and Alfred, eager for a swift journey, settled in the back seat, hoping to soon be with Catherine.

Despite his annoyance at the Russian folk music blaring from the radio and the unnecessary detour past the Kremlin, Alfred chose not to complain. The illuminated towers of the Kremlin briefly appeared through the taxi window, glowing red against the dark sky. The taxi eventually slowed near Catherine's building, a unique high-rise resembling an open book, its white facade adorned with two navy blue vertical stripes. The surrounding landscape, eerily quiet in the early morning hours, reminded him of Swedish towns.

Relieved to leave the dirty car, Alfred paid and tipped the driver, then quickly approached the high-rise where Catherine resided. Notably, there was no security or concierge, and no cars were parked outside.

As Alfred prepared to see his beloved Russian bride-to-be, he reflexively smoothed his face with his hand, anticipating their reunion. The building's old elevator, its walls marked with scribbles, carried him slowly upwards. The elevator groaned softly as it climbed floor by floor.

Standing before Catherine's door, he knocked gently. The sound of swift footsteps approached from inside, and then the door swung open to reveal Catherine in her red peignoir, a piece Alfred had picked out for her at a boutique in Heidelberg. Embracing him tightly, she welcomed him with open arms, and he lifted her off the ground, carrying her into the bedroom.

As the clock chimed midnight, Alfred held Catherine close, believing his love for her would last forever as long as time existed. For Catherine, the chimes signaled a step closer to her setting her foot in the free world.

Chapter 82

The Engagement in Foreign Land

Morning arrived, the sun filtering through the bedroom shutters. Soft golden light spilled across the floorboards, illuminating the quiet room where the night's passion still lingered in the air. Catherine moved to the kitchen to prepare coffee and hot rolls. The park outside was serene, birds chirping audibly. A gentle breeze stirred the leaves of the tall trees beyond the window, carrying the faint scent of early autumn. As she brewed the coffee, Catherine contemplated the ease with which destiny seemed to be leading her to a new world.

Alfred entered the kitchen, playfully acknowledging her efforts. "Oh, you made breakfast for us!" he said with a wink. Embracing her, he heard her whisper, "I thought you might need some nourishment after last night... dearest."

"Thank you, Catherine. I'm so hungry. Famished, in fact," Alfred replied with genuine gratitude.

"Of course. I knew you would be," she responded, her voice soft and her smile gentle.

Reflecting on his journey to Moscow, Alfred marveled at how fate had led him to Catherine. The realization filled him with an unexpected sense of peace. He harbored a pang of regret for not having met her earlier in life. His previous marriage to a wealthy

German woman had been unfulfilling, and his subsequent affairs, though numerous, were devoid of meaning. Each ended with him compensating the spurned women. His travels around the world, initially filled with excitement, eventually left him jaded and longing for something more thrilling and adventurous. That longing had finally brought him to Catherine.

***

At the Moscow Civil Registration Department (*ZAGS*), housed within the ornate wedding palace, Alfred and Catherine found themselves in a room that radiated both stateliness and romance. Despite the austere portraits of Soviet leaders, the ivory walls with gold trim, white marble floor, and long windows created an atmosphere of elegance. Crystal vases filled with pink roses and other colorful flowers added to the room's charm. The setting felt strangely ceremonial—half romantic celebration, half bureaucratic ritual.

They were greeted by Vera Ivanovna, a woman in a black suit and white blouse, whose office was furnished with a mahogany table and chairs. Alfred introduced himself in his best Russian, and Catherine followed suit, looking radiant in her pale blue suit and lace veil, holding a small bouquet of white flowers.

Vera's demeanor shifted from suspicion to a more businesslike approach, aware of the delicate nature of a foreigner marrying a Soviet citizen. Her sharp eyes studied Alfred carefully, as if measuring the consequences of the union before her.

Alfred, despite his anticipation, felt uneasy due to his inexperience with such bureaucratic processes. He understood the political significance of the marriage, especially since it implied Catherine's dual jurisdiction under both Soviet and West German laws.

As Vera reviewed Catherine's Soviet passport, she remarked on their shared district residency. After a brief discussion on bureaucratic formalities, Vera returned the passport and provided her office number for any future needs. She then turned her attention to Alfred, instructing him to sign the marriage application documents.

Catherine translated the formalities as Alfred, somewhat nervously, signed the papers, not having the time to thoroughly review them. The scratching sound of his pen against the paper seemed unusually loud in the quiet room.

Vera then informed them of further formalities and steps to take.

"Now that you are a fiancé and a bride, you will have to put an apostille on all papers at the German Embassy. Only then, Catherine will be able to apply for a West German visa. If your husband insists on you leaving the Soviet Union, then it might take a couple of years to get the green light. I would advise you against it, Catherine. It would be better for Alfred to come to Moscow. You, Catherine, are a Soviet citizeness and shall be for your lifetime."

Vera threw a meaningful glance at Catherine.

Vera smiled at last and stood up from her chair, "I wish you both the best of luck!"

Vera hugged her and shook Alfred's hand who was ready by that time to jump out of his shoes.

Finally, she embraced Catherine and shook Alfred's hand, who by then was overwhelmed with emotion and relief. The couple had taken a significant step towards their future together, navigating the complexities of international marriage during a politically charged era.

***

"Dear Alfred and Catherine, if I may call you that, you may call me Vera. May I delay you a little longer? Please, be seated on the two chairs."

Vera pulled the two chairs by the small table. They sat down obediently.

Vera then snapped her fingers and from a rear door, a woman dressed as a servant with a crispy white apron and a black dress and a cap on her head came out with a silver tray with small Russian delicacies of pastry and cheeses.

She put it on the table and then brought out a lovely silver teapot filled to the brim with a fragrant hot tea.

Two cups were placed in front of the couple.

"May I serve you some tea," she asked as lovely porcelain cups were placed in front of them. "And please partake of the delicacies that the Soviet government has provided for you."

Much to their delight Catherine and Alfred drank a cup of tea and tasted a small piece of pastry.

The unexpected hospitality softened the earlier bureaucratic tension, transforming the formal office into something almost celebratory.

After this was done, they got up and profusely thanked the official for her graciousness and the country's cordiality.

***

They got into the taxicab happy and excited.

"Hotel National," said Alfred to the driver.

The first ordeal of technicalities was now over.

Alfred hugged her very tightly in the cab.

"I have brought a gift for you. A gift that I hope will last a lifetime."

She looked at him with a smile and great excitement. Alfred took out a velvet box from his coat pocket handing it to Catherine.

"Will you accept it," he said.

As she opened it, her eyes grew wide for all she could see was a sparkling diamond, quite a large and a beautiful one.

"Oh, yes, I will accept it."

Hardly able to breathe from excitement as he put it on her slender finger, Catherine became so excited she kissed the diamond.

Alfred looked at her and uttered, "What about kissing me?"

She threw her arms around Alfred's neck and kissed him also. But perhaps not quite as ardently...

***

Upon arriving at the National hotel, Alfred and Catherine, realizing their hunger, made their way to the restaurant on the first floor. They were seated at a charming table, where Alfred requested champagne and hors d'oeuvres, with dinner to follow in half an hour.

Anticipating that the champagne would help calm his butterflies, Alfred looked forward to celebrating their engagement.

The waiter soon arrived with an array of delicacies: red and black caviar, fresh white bread with butter, and a bottle of champagne chilling in an ice bucket.

With a skillful pop of the cork, the waiter served them, and Alfred raised his glass to Catherine, his official bride-to-be.

"Cheers!" Alfred exclaimed, clinking his glass with hers.

The light reflected off Catherine's engagement ring, creating a dazzling effect as they sipped their champagne.

***

In the expansive lounge of the Continental Hotel, Alfred led Catherine to the area where foreign currency stores, including the renowned birch tree store, were located.

Their first stop was a fine clothing shop, where Alfred expressed his intention to buy Catherine a wedding dress and other elegant attire.

“My love,” he said, “we are going to select a beautiful wedding dress for you, along with fine clothes and matching leather shoes.”

Catherine, momentarily closing her eyes, reassured herself that this was not a dream.

They then approached a department filled with fashionable foreign clothing, leaving Catherine in awe of the variety and style options.

Alfred smiled at another salesperson dressed in a neat black suit.

“Madam, we need a white satin wedding dress form fitting around the breast and slightly off the shoulder with lovely white long gloves…”

When Catherine went into the dressing room and put the dress on, the satin hugged her every curve.

Then the saleslady knocked on the door gently.

“Mademoiselle, would you like to try the veil on now?”

Catherine said, “I will.”

As she neatly placed the veil on her head, she felt like a queen.

It was trimmed with beautiful Alencon lace, and little sequins had been sewn into the veil giving it a gentle glow as she moved.

She looked stunning.

"Bravo, you are sparkling like your ring!" Alfred smiled with satisfaction.

***

"Do you have a German chocolate torte?" Alfred asked.

"Of course, sir."

When dessert was served and they took their first bites, Catherine compared it to sweet elegance.

The pastry was not of the dark chocolate variety, but milk chocolate instead, with white frosting braised in brown sugar. Chopped almonds were sprinkled on the top.

"Oh," said Catherine. "What a delicious confectionary. It is one I hope to have often."

What a delightful time they both had eating their chocolate delight and sipping their coffee.

As they savored their chocolate delight and sipped their coffee, Catherine looked at Alfred with seemingly loving eyes as she thought how easy it had been.

Internally, she marveled at how effortlessly everything was unfolding, basking in the moment and the promise of what lay ahead.

And yet, somewhere deep inside, a quiet voice reminded her that in Moscow nothing ever unfolded without consequence.

Chapter 83

Cracks in the Facade

The hum of activity in the hotel lobby had a soothing effect on Catherine. The low murmur of voices, the soft roll of luggage across polished floors, and the discreet movement of waiters and concierges created an atmosphere of elegant order. Amidst the whirlwind of events, she was exhilarated yet aware of the physical toll such a marathon of activities could take. She pondered the surprises Alfred might still have in store as they approached the elevators. The glass-enclosed elevators, a blend of artistic design and engineering marvel, captivated her as they ascended, offering a panoramic view of the grand lobby. From above, the chandeliers glittered like constellations suspended over the marble floor below.

Upon reaching their floor, Alfred led the way, reminding Catherine that they were now esteemed guests of the hotel. The concierge acknowledged them with a polite "*Guten Tag*," the traditional German greeting, as they made their way to their room.

Entering the elegant room, Alfred guided Catherine into the bedroom, where she was met with a breathtaking sight. Laid out on the bed was a stunning black evening dress, accompanied by satin high heels. The dress featured a black lace top with long sleeves that buttoned at the wrist, and a sheer black voile skirt. A matching black satin evening purse and a small box were placed beside the dress. Curious, Catherine inquired about the contents of the box.

"Open it, *mein Liebchen*—my love," Alfred encouraged.

Inside, she discovered sapphire earrings encircled by diamonds, complementing her blue eyes beautifully. For a moment she could only stare, unable to conceal her astonishment. Her gaze sparkled as she admired the earrings, then took Alfred's hand and led him into the rear bedroom where his imagination led to every ecstasy. Beyond the drawn curtains, the city lights shimmered faintly against the dark Moscow night.

The next morning, they awoke to bright sunshine and got dressed for breakfast. Sunlight poured through the curtains, softening the room's shadows and lending everything the unreal glow of a dream. In the breakfast shoppe, they each ordered a cappuccino, savoring the start of a new day together.

As they enjoyed their morning coffee, Catherine gazed dreamily at Alfred, seeking assurance of the reality of their experience. "Darling, is this true? Is this really happening to me?" she asked.

"Yes, darling," he said. "And there will be hundreds more beautiful times in our life together. I am so happy we are together," he replied.

Catherine, filled with happiness and gratitude, gently squeezed his hand, expressing her joy at being together.

In the hotel lobby, Alfred affectionately hugged and held Catherine's hand, openly displaying his affection. The bright lobby, with its polished brass fixtures and discreet elegance, seemed for a moment like neutral ground—an island of civility untouched by the city's harsher realities. As they approached the reception desk, their intimate moment was abruptly interrupted by two plainclothes men. They appeared almost soundlessly, as if they had been waiting for precisely this moment. One of them, without any preamble, demanded Catherine's passport in a harsh tone.

Catherine's complexion turned pale, sensing the danger she had long feared. A cold wave of dread passed through her, immediate and unmistakable. Alfred, taken aback by the demand, reacted indignantly and in a deep, commanding voice, declared his engagement to Catherine Yampolsky, embracing her protectively.

"Sir!" he spoke in English, another language he was fluent in and used for doing business with the Russians—as he mistakenly called all Soviet people. "My name is Herr Alfred Fuchs." He said, switching attention to himself. "I live in Frankfurt, and I do business with the Soviet Union. Here are my papers," and he handed them a stack of documents from his inner pocket.

"I am engaged to be married to a Soviet citizeness, Catherine Yampolsky. She is my fiancée, and we are formally engaged to get married."

The man in a black suit stared back and uttered in his gritty voice, "Herr Fuchs! You should know that your engagement is not the same as being officially married, and your fiancée, although engaged, is not yet married to you, and she had no right to spend the night with you at the hotel."

Alfred looked back at the man, evidently from the intelligence services, the ominous KGB. The second man did not intervene. He stood slightly behind his colleague, watchful and expressionless, like a silent witness who needed to say nothing at all. She kept silent. "Excuse me, comrade," his voice sounded indignant. "I will remember your reprimand about couples and will gladly spread the word across the business community that even though you are engaged to a Soviet woman, the Soviet state must give its blessings, and that one should not go to the Hotel Continental to celebrate." He loathed the *KGB* man and angrily added, "May I ask you, comrade?" he repeated sarcastically the Russian word throwing another furious look at the man. "Where and when exactly may we celebrate our engagement?"

The two men remained silent, offering no response to Alfred's challenge. Their silence was more menacing than any reply. Frustrated and defiant, Alfred led Catherine through the lobby and out onto the street. "*Auf Wiedersehen*, Moscow," he said bitterly, the familiar German farewell carrying none of its usual courtesy. The doorman opened the door for them, and the couple exited with dignity, Catherine carrying the bundles and boxes that symbolized their future together. Despite the unsettling encounter, they maintained their composure, walking away with a sense of pride and defiance against the oppressive oversight of the Soviet authorities. Behind them, the hotel doors closed with a muted thud, as if sealing off the fragile illusion of safety they had briefly inhabited.

Chapter 84

A Glimmer of Hope

Heading straight to the National Hotel, Alfred and Catherine's taxi swiftly navigated through Moscow's city center. The day was sunny and warm, with a gentle breeze rising from the nearby river and drifting through the wide boulevards of the capital. The streets were bustling with tourists and locals alike, and the Kremlin's golden domes shimmered in the sunlight. The city seemed alive with motion—streetcars rattling, voices echoing across the squares, and distant church bells faintly ringing above the traffic.

Arriving at the hotel in the early evening, Alfred tenderly clasped Catherine's hand and kissed her cheek, asking if she was happy. Her response, affirming her dreamlike joy, was met with another affectionate kiss, drawing surprised glances from onlookers. For a moment, the tension of the previous day seemed to dissolve into the warm evening air.

Inside the hotel, it seemed as if opportunities were opening for Catherine, both literally and figuratively. At Alfred's suggestion, they decided to dine at the hotel restaurant, requesting a private corner table. As they settled by the window, the waiter presented them with menus. Through the tall glass windows, the fading sunlight painted the city in soft shades of amber and gold.

They wanted a salad. The waiter then put a lovely large salad bowl in the center. "Would a Caesar salad suit you? Which I shall make freshly in front of you?"

"Oh, yes," they both said excitedly.

"A bottle of champagne, your best year," he ordered the drinks.

They were sipping on their champagne as their waiter mixed the salad personally for them. The ritual unfolded almost theatrically. First, he cracked two fresh eggs which he whipped and put into the fresh crispy lettuce. Then he poured the Caesar dressing over, tossing it around with practiced elegance. As the last part he put several anchovies at the top.

He then proudly said, "Madame, Monsieur, this is my own private recipe for Caesar salad."

After they had eaten to their satisfaction, Catherine then said, "That salad was divine, but I have a spot for some dessert. I think I want the lemon meringue pie with a small demitasse of coffee."

He had the same thing. Outside the windows, the evening deepened, and the lights of Moscow slowly began to appear one by one across the skyline. So ended a beautiful day.

"Cheers! To our health and happiness!" said Alfred.

They clinked long stem elegant glasses filled with bubbling champagne.

They were sitting at the table speaking softly to each other in hushed tones. As they spoke in quiet, intimate tones, the passage of time was marked only by Alfred's occasional glance at his watch. The golden hands moved steadily, reminding him that his departure was approaching.

"Will you see me off to the airport?" he asked softly.

"Yes, I will be glad to escort you," she said.

In the meantime, she pulled him into the dark hallway of the hotel where they gave each other a long lingering kiss. The corridor was quiet, the distant murmur of the restaurant fading behind them.

"This will hold you for a while," she said this with a wicked glint in her eyes.

Catherine, with mischief in her eyes, wondered if she could truly love him, hoping that she might.

"Mein Liebchen! We must finish up and pack my bags. I must get to the airport on time," Alfred reminded her, regretting that his stay in Moscow hadn't lasted as long as he had hoped.

Catherine responded with a provocative smile, both entering his room without any interference. The hallway carpet softened their footsteps as the door closed quietly behind them.

Alfred was eager to leave Moscow, frustrated by the tedious regulations and restrictions.

As Alfred organized his important files, ensuring no detail was overlooked, Catherine browsed through German magazines, contemplating her future. Glossy photographs of European beaches, cafés, and boutiques seemed to open windows into another life.

She dreamed of visiting places like Ibiza or Carlstadt or perhaps settling in Frankfurt and traveling across Europe. The thought of crossing borders freely—without permission, without fear—felt almost unreal.

Trusting in Alfred's care, she began to see herself as part of a union, soon to become husband and wife, embarking on a new chapter of her life.

Outside, the lights of Moscow flickered across the darkening river, while inside the quiet hotel room, Catherine imagined a future that seemed closer than ever—yet still separated by an invisible frontier.

Chapter 85

The Departure

Catherine was acutely aware that this day marked the end of her temporary tranquility. Alfred's presence had been a source of security for her, and time seemed to fly as he busied himself organizing his documents and belongings into his leather briefcase. Once his meticulous packing was complete, he paused to rest, checking his Swiss watch, the polished dial catching the afternoon light, his day's schedule meticulously planned in his head.

Alfred's affectionate gesture of kissing Catherine's hand was a reminder of her influence over him. He had the distinguished appearance of a Renaissance figure, almost as if he had stepped out of a portrait from another century, reminiscent of Albrecht Dürer's paintings, with his conservative dress, thinning hair, and metal-framed glasses accentuating his blue-grey eyes that sparkled in good spirits. His athletic build, despite occasional limping when tired, added to his aura of luxury and success.

Their departure was tinged with a sense of finality as Alfred embraced and kissed Catherine, holding her slightly longer than usual, as if parting for the last time.

By noon, they were on their way to the airport, the journey prolonged by heavy traffic. The taxi crawled slowly through Moscow's wide avenues, passing grey apartment blocks, crowded trolley stops, and endless streams of cars. Alfred's habitual punctuality proved beneficial under the circumstances.

Catherine, sensing his tension and preoccupation, tried to offer comfort.

Upon arriving at Sheremetyevo Airport, Alfred courteously thanked and paid the driver, who swiftly unloaded their luggage. Jet engines roared faintly in the distance as passengers hurried across the wide terminal plaza.

With Catherine by his side, Alfred, dressed in his beige trench coat and German hat, proceeded to the terminal, leaving her personal belongings in storage at the National Hotel.

At the airport, after checking in and obtaining his boarding pass, Alfred reassured Catherine that their marriage would be the key to her freedom.

"I will pray that everything goes smoothly," he whispered to her after he got his boarding pass and checked in his luggage. "Our marriage will bring you over the iron curtain."

Despite her outward smile, Catherine appeared lost in thought, prompting Alfred to hold her hand to ease her tension.

They stood at the final barrier separating departing passengers from their loved ones, a narrow checkpoint that seemed to divide two different worlds—a space reserved for travelers and a select few permitted to pass through customs and passport control.

Catherine clung to Alfred's hand, reluctant to let go.

Around them, loudspeaker announcements echoed through the terminal in Russian and German, while travelers embraced, waved, and hurried toward the gates.

Eventually, he gently released his grasp, promising to call her upon his arrival in Frankfurt and to seek assistance from his contacts at the German Embassy in Moscow to facilitate her visa.

After a passionate kiss and a whispered promise to call, Alfred disappeared into the line of departing passengers moving toward passport control.

Catherine remained standing where he had left her.

For a long moment she watched the place where he had vanished, until the crowd slowly closed the gap and the corridor beyond the barrier swallowed him completely.

Alone in the vast terminal, she was left to face the uncertainty—and the fragile hope—of their future apart.

Chapter 86

Threats in the Night

As Alfred was on the way to Frankfurt, Catherine found herself huddled in a taxi, sitting quietly in the back seat as the city passed by in blurred fragments of streetlights and grey buildings, seemingly seeking protection like a child.

Upon arriving at the National Hotel to retrieve her boxes and bundles from storage, she was confronted by two government agents in civilian clothing. They appeared suddenly beside the storage counter, their presence cold and deliberate. Their abrupt demand for her passport left her frightened and speechless, but she complied, handing over her passport after a brief fumble.

She froze for a moment and then opened her purse. She was so frightened that she couldn't utter a word. After fumbling for a few moments, she obediently handed her passport.

"Ms. Yampolsky, what business brings you here?" asked the older man sternly.

She answered quietly, "I am engaged to a German businessman, Herr Fuchs. Have just seen him off at the airport. I would like to pick up my engagement gifts from storage."

The younger man confronted her, using the usual scare tactics.

"You should drop your marriage plans. Your fiancé will not come back to Moscow."

His voice carried the cold certainty of someone accustomed to issuing threats without consequence.

After a few minutes of heated tirades, the younger man emerged from storage with her bundles and returned them all. The plain-clothed men obviously worked for the KGB and were used to intimidating people.

The older man handed her passport back.

"Do not forget that you are a Soviet citizeness for your lifetime!"

His words hung in the air like a sentence pronounced by an invisible court.

Back home, Catherine succumbed to exhaustion, falling into a deep sleep on her sofa.

She was roused by the telephone ringing.

Answering with closed eyes, she heard Alfred's voice, reassuring her that his flight had been uneventful and expressing his longing.

Catherine recounted her unsettling encounter with the government agents at the hotel, detailing their threats and aggressive behavior.

"Oh, I am so glad you called. I was accosted by two government agents when picking up your gifts at the National. They yelled at me and threatened me."

"Darling, my love, disregard those fools making empty threats. Just remember that you will soon become my wife."

Alfred, fully aware of the possibility of a wiretap, confidently dismissed the threats as mere bluster, reminding Catherine of their impending marriage.

"I would give a lot for us to be together tonight. Kisses and hugs. I must go. Auf Wiedersehen, Mein Liebchen," he said and hung up with a heavy heart and a promise of reunion.

Catherine slowly lowered the receiver and remained seated beside the telephone.

Outside, the Moscow night was silent and dark.

Somewhere far away, beyond the Iron Curtain, the man who promised to change her life was already flying toward Frankfurt.

Chapter 87

Race Against Time

In October, Catherine's routine was disrupted by a call from Alfred, the sudden ringing of the telephone breaking the stillness of her apartment. His voice bore a strain of concern. Greeting each other with affection, Catherine braced herself for unsettling news.

Alfred revealed the need for urgent action: Catherine must approach the West German Embassy to expedite their marriage process, as he was encountering formidable obstacles in obtaining a visa due to Soviet bureaucracy.

Catherine's response was marked by tears and a commitment to do her utmost. Alfred provided her with the embassy's contact details, but she knew simply showing up without proper documentation or cause would be futile.

Sitting silently after the call, she began to think quickly. In the Soviet Union, bureaucracy could delay anything—but certain circumstances forced the system to move faster.

She contemplated a plan to visit a gynecologist, hoping to acquire a medical note under the pretext of pregnancy—a legitimate reason to hasten the marriage registration.

The next day, Catherine visited a gynecologist. Alfred had left her some money, not a fortune, but sufficient to bribe the doctor into falsely declaring her pregnancy.

The doctor, upon examination, quickly surmised Catherine's true intentions and bluntly confronted her.

"What do you want from me? You are not pregnant," she said sharply.

Catherine then looked down and squirmed, and she said with a very nervous voice, "Doctor, I wish it written that I am four weeks pregnant so that my fiancée could marry me sooner and the date can be changed," she said with a trembling voice.

"Well, madam," said the doctor, "For a price I can do anything."

Her tone was cold and practical, the tone of someone accustomed to such requests.

After a tense negotiation over the price, the doctor acquiesced.

The pen scratched slowly across the medical certificate as the doctor filled out the form.

With the falsified medical document in hand, Catherine felt a surge of hope.

The single sheet of paper suddenly seemed more powerful than any passport or permit.

Her next step was to contact the embassy. She found a phone booth and dialed the West German Embassy, her heart pounding with anxiety.

The metallic smell of the telephone booth and the muffled noise of passing traffic surrounded her as she waited for the call to connect.

The embassy operator, Peter Schmidt, informed her that he did not handle civil matters and advised her to meet with the German consul.

He offered to schedule an appointment for her the following day at noon, instructing her to bring all necessary documents.

Catherine, relieved at this opportunity, expressed her gratitude, holding the receiver tightly as if afraid the chance might disappear if she spoke too quickly.

When she finally hung up, she remained inside the narrow booth for a moment longer, breathing slowly.

For the first time in days, she felt that the door to the West might open.

Chapter 88

At the Embassy Gate

Catherine needed every ounce of her courage to stand up to the government without the backing of her German fiancé. The embassy, a majestic old building, was her destination. Its tall iron gates and stone façade stood like a fragment of another world in the middle of Moscow.

As she approached, her steps were determined, leading her straight to the guards' booth. The guard inside eyed her with suspicion.

"Comrade *militsioner*, I have an appointment with the *consul* today," Catherine said, referring to the German diplomatic official, her voice steady despite the flutter of nerves within her.

The guard's response was immediate and dismissive.

"Go away and don't come back!" he barked, not even glancing up from his phone.

Retreating, Catherine's initial panic morphed into a steely resolve. For a moment she stood on the sidewalk, breathing slowly, refusing to let fear overwhelm her.

She made her way to a nearby telephone booth, shielded by trees, a quiet sanctuary from the harsh reception she'd just encountered. Inserting a coin, she dialed the West German consul's number, her fingers trembling slightly but her determination clear.

"*Guten Tag*. German Embassy," came the response, formal and distant.

"*Guten Morgen*—good morning," Catherine replied, switching to English with a slight quiver in her voice. "My name is Catherine Yampolsky. I have an appointment with the *consul*, but I've been turned away at the gate."

There was a brief pause as the secretary processed her words, then a polite, "May I place you on a brief hold?" followed.

Catherine stood in the booth, her heart pounding, clasping her hands together in a silent prayer for safety and success.

Outside the narrow booth, Moscow traffic moved slowly past, indifferent to the quiet drama unfolding inside the small glass enclosure.

Then, a new voice, calm and reassuring.

"Catherine, my name is Peter Hasselhoff. I am an interpreter. Please come back to the building. I will meet you at the entrance. Everything will be alright," said the German employee, his tone a balm to her frayed nerves.

"Thank you!" Catherine breathed out, a wave of relief washing over her as she hung up.

She stepped out of the booth, her resolve hardened, and walked back to the embassy, each step a defiance of the fear that sought to cripple her.

But as she neared, a chilling command stopped her.

"Stand down, citizeness! Do not step away, do not cross the street!"

The Soviet official's voice was cold, a sharp contrast to the hope that had just been kindled within her.

Yet Catherine stood her ground, frozen between the two worlds, the distant embassy doors now seemingly miles away.

Then, in a moment that felt suspended in time, the embassy staff emerged, walking quickly toward the gate, encircling her in a human shield of solidarity.

A Soviet colonel approached, his presence commanding yet oddly controlled in the surreal standoff that unfolded.

"I am at the embassy on behalf of my German fiancé," Catherine found herself explaining, the surreal nature of the situation making her voice sound distant to her own ears.

The colonel inspected her papers carefully. For several long seconds he said nothing.

Then, unexpectedly, his expression shifted. He instructed his men to assist her.

Once inside, the atmosphere was tense yet hopeful. Catherine, alongside two embassy officials, found herself in a sparsely furnished office, facing the *consul*, Peter Schmidt.

Her story, her reason for being there, spilled out not just in her words but in the quiet determination that had brought her this far.

Peter Schmidt listened, his expression one of understanding.

“Well, Catherine, I will do all I can to expedite your marriage. Good luck, and do not worry,” he assured, his words carrying the weight of promise.

As Catherine left the consulate, the chaos of the outside world seemed a stark contrast to the sanctuary she had found within.

The embassy gates closed quietly behind her.

The fear, the uncertainty, all seemed a little less daunting now.

She had faced adversity and, with a mixture of courage and desperation, had found allies in the most unexpected of places.

Chapter 89

Oktoberfest Revelry

Alfred Fuchs was at the heart of the *Oktoberfest* celebrations in a bustling beer hall in West Germany, surrounded by close friends. The atmosphere was lively, with the group enjoying large steins of beer and feasting on steaming knockwurst cooked in sauerkraut with apples, accompanied by traditional potato salad. Dressed in Tyrolean hats and jackets, they embraced the festive spirit of the season.

The hall was alive with waitresses in charming attire, consisting of white caps, fluffy skirts, and spotless white aprons, bustling about with trays of beer and hot food. Their golden braids, flirty blue eyes, and playful demeanor added to the vibrant setting. The local band, dressed in colorful Bavarian costumes, played continuously, filling the hall with lively music and laughter.

Patrons danced under the wide wooden beams in the center of the hall next to the band, boots stamping loudly against the floorboards. Even chocolate cake was served at this purely German festival, alongside endless mugs of foaming beer.

The event carried a certain rowdy energy. The beer flowed freely, and the mood grew increasingly uninhibited as the evening progressed. Men laughed loudly, slapping each other on the back, while the waitresses moved quickly between the crowded tables.

Alfred found himself seated next to a flamboyant woman whose peroxide-blonde hair and bright lipstick immediately drew attention. She flirted unabashedly, enjoying the attention from Alfred and another man at the table.

In their drunken euphoria, the two men pulled her closer, laughing loudly. She responded with playful laughter, enjoying the attention and the wild spirit of the evening. The noise of the band, the shouting of the crowd, and the constant clinking of beer steins blurred together as the night spiraled into intoxicated chaos. The night passed in Alfred's drunken oblivion.

When he finally awoke the following morning, he found himself in a dirty, grimy room. The hideous woman lay beside him on rumpled, disheveled sheets, as many a man had before.

"Oh, God, what have I done?" Alfred thought in horror. "I will never tell Catherine about it. It was a terrible error on my part."

The realization struck him like cold water. The drunken excitement of the night before vanished instantly, replaced by shame and dread.

He quickly dressed, avoiding looking at the woman beside him. Leaving some money on the small table, he slipped quietly out of the room, determined that Catherine must never learn of this disgraceful mistake.

***

Catherine, feeling a mix of irritation and concern, left a message on Alfred's answering machine.

She held the phone tightly as the automated message recorded by Alfred began to play.

"Hello, I am busy now. Please leave a message and I will call you back."

"Hello! I am very upset that I have not heard from you. I wanted to tell you that all went well at the embassy. Bye, my love—I love you!" she said irritably in faltering German.

He finally called her back later that night.

"Why have you not answered the phone for so long?" she asked anxiously. "Have you been out with another woman? I have left messages."

"My dearest, I adore you. I worship the ground you walk on," Alfred replied smoothly. "I ran into an old friend whom I had business with. We are making some new deals. I apologize from the bottom of my heart. You are the most beautiful woman I have ever met. And if we were together, there would be no parting of us."

"I love you very much. But may we please talk about the wedding date and what happened at the embassy?" she said, returning the conversation to what truly mattered.

"Of course, my love. Please tell me what the consul said."

Alfred listened intently as Catherine explained everything. He was impressed by her resourcefulness and her clever handling of the embassy situation. Though he wondered privately about the authenticity of her pregnancy claim, he chose not to raise the question over the phone, mindful that the line might be tapped.

Their conversation continued amiably, both reaffirming their love. Alfred privately admired Catherine's intelligence and beauty, while she found comfort in the security of their plans and the symbolic promise of her engagement ring. With her mind finally at ease, Catherine drifted into a deep and peaceful sleep.

Chapter 90

Seizing the Moment

Alfred, enjoying the tranquil routine of his morning walk with Wind, his Saint Bernard, found solace in the simple pleasure of a visit to a local café in Frankfurt. The crisp morning air carried the faint aroma of fresh bread and roasted coffee drifting from nearby bakeries. Indulging in apple strudel and *The Wall Street Journal*, Alfred began the day on a relaxed note, unaware of the pivotal phone call awaiting him at home.

Returning home, he found a message from Mr. Edward Horn, a partner at Gunther Huber's Moscow firm, inviting him to work there for an extended period. The offer intrigued Alfred, promising both new professional opportunities and the chance to reunite with Catherine. Mr. Horn emphasized Alfred's deep understanding of the local market, making the proposal all the more appealing.

The conversation ended with Alfred pondering the unexpected turn of events. For a moment he remained beside the telephone, reflecting on how fate seemed once again to be guiding him back toward Moscow. It was not only an opportunity to advance his career but also a chance to reunite with Catherine and finally carry out their plans to marry—perhaps this time with fewer barriers between them, if the authorities granted the necessary permissions.

Eager to share the news, Alfred called Catherine, already imagining their reunion and the wedding they had long planned.

The prospect of finally being together, overcoming bureaucratic hurdles, filled him with determination. His past pursuits of love, once unencumbered by commitment, now paled in comparison with his profound feelings for Catherine. Certain of his decision, he dialed the familiar number in Moscow.

The phone rang three times before her sultry voice answered, "Hello!"

"Hello," Alfred repeated, his heart skipping in anticipation.

"My love, do you know when you will be able to come here again?" she asked, her voice trembling with excitement.

"My dearest, I am about to receive my entry visa and will soon be on my way to you so that we can get the permission to marry. Please inquire at the Marriage Chambers if they can expedite our date. We will be in each other's arms again soon," he replied, his voice warm and steady, thickening the air between them with the weight of their impending reunion.

She responded with elation, her voice as fresh as morning dew.

"Dearest, we will be. I often dream of you. In my dreams, you smile and kiss me..." Her voice softened to almost a whisper. "I imagine us walking down quiet streets, your hand in mine, and the world seems to be created just for us. Every day without you feels like an eternity, and I count the minutes until your arrival."

Their conversation continued, each word warming their hearts and filling them with hope. Across the distance between Frankfurt and Moscow, their voices carried the fragile promise of a shared future. The invisible thread connecting them across thousands of miles seemed to strengthen with every moment spent apart, promising a reunion filled with love and happiness.

As they spoke of Alfred's imminent arrival and the possibility of expediting their wedding, a wave of excitement washed over them, bridging the physical distance with dreams of their near future together.

As Alfred prepared to depart once again for Moscow with his express visa, Catherine contemplated her impending escape from a life constrained by a totalitarian regime. She stood quietly by the window of her apartment, looking out at the grey Moscow streets below.

The promise of a new beginning with Alfred offered a glimmer of freedom and a future filled with love and possibilities. For the first time, the walls of the city that had long imprisoned her seemed to tremble slightly with the possibility of opening.

Chapter 91

Remaining Hurdles

Alfred, comfortably seated on his flight to Moscow, immersed himself in paperwork while the flight attendants moved about the cabin, offering drinks and snacks. The steady hum of the aircraft engines and the muted conversations of fellow passengers created a calm, almost hypnotic rhythm inside the cabin. Opting for a scotch, he allowed himself to drift into sweet memories and pleasant anticipation of reuniting with Catherine, eventually dozing off contentedly.

Upon landing at *Sheremetyevo Airport*, Alfred paused to gather his thoughts before calling Catherine from a phone booth. The familiar metallic smell of the airport telephone booths and the echo of distant announcements reminded him that he was once again inside the Soviet system. Her voice, vibrant yet slightly subdued, confirmed her excitement and relief at his safe arrival. Alfred's heart swelled with happiness as they exchanged brief but affectionate words.

Exiting the airport in the early evening, he was greeted by the chill of a windy Moscow night and the gentle fall of snow. The wind carried fine snowflakes across the dimly lit airport plaza as travelers hurried toward waiting taxis. Hailing a taxi, he provided the driver with Catherine's address, lost in thoughts of the warm and welcoming environment that awaited him at her apartment.

The journey through the dimly lit suburban streets was accompanied by the driver's curiosity and the soothing sounds of Russian folk music playing softly on the radio. Streetlights flickered past the taxi windows as the city moved slowly around them.

When the taxi arrived at the destination, Alfred paid the fare with rumpled rubles and stepped out into the wintry landscape. Pausing for a moment, he scooped up a handful of fresh snow, letting it melt slowly in his hands as he admired the quiet beauty of the winter night.

Making his way into the building and ascending in the graffiti-marked elevator, Alfred's eagerness grew with each passing moment. The elevator creaked as it climbed slowly toward Catherine's floor.

Upon reaching Catherine's door and announcing his arrival with a playful, almost poetic declaration, she swiftly opened the door. In an instant, he wrapped her in his arms, their reunion marked by a kiss full of warmth and passion.

"My love, it has been too long," Alfred whispered, overcome with a profound sense of belonging and love. The long-awaited embrace symbolized not just a physical reunion, but the merging of their dreams in the face of all they had endured.

In the morning, Alfred informed the embassy about his current situation and his new role at the firm. Later that day, he met with his American partner, Mr. Johnson, in Moscow. After concluding their business at the U.S. Embassy, Mr. Johnson invited Alfred for a coffee, seizing the opportunity to ask a pointed question.

"I must ask you a very personal question," Mr. Johnson began. "Naturally, Catherine is a woman of great beauty and charm. But do you believe she truly loves you? Or could it be that you're being used to help her leave the Soviet Union and become a West German citizen?"

Alfred, visibly taken aback, replied in astonishment, "Mr. Johnson, how could you even suggest that?"

Mr. Johnson pressed further, highlighting the harsh realities for single women in the USSR.

"Are you certain she isn't merely enchanting you?"

Frustrated by the insinuation, Alfred stood up abruptly.

"Excuse me, but I must attend to an important matter. We'll discuss business another time."

He hurriedly returned to Catherine's district, where they were finalizing their wedding arrangements. They planned to marry in early March 1983 and were about to meet with the Wedding Chambers' representative to confirm their date.

The following day was filled with the necessary preparations. Alfred and Catherine took a cab to the Wedding Chambers to officially set their wedding date for early March. They were informed of additional requirements: Alfred needed to provide more documentation for the embassy, and Catherine was required to submit a medical note confirming her supposed pregnancy.

Despite these tasks, the couple felt optimistic that their plans were progressing smoothly.

Yet beneath their optimism lingered an unspoken awareness that in the Soviet Union, even the smallest bureaucratic obstacle could suddenly derail the most carefully laid plans.

Chapter 92

Marriage of Convenience

The Soviet Union was passing through turbulent and uncertain times under the leadership of Yuri Andropov, the former chairman of the *KGB* who had recently become General Secretary of the Communist Party. The regime's oppressive nature was increasingly evident, casting a shadow over the lives of its citizens.

On March 1, 1983, a significant day for Alfred and Catherine, Alfred stood outside the Wedding Chambers, impeccably dressed in a tuxedo and white tie, his black shoes polished to perfection. The cold Moscow air carried the damp scent of melting snow as he waited anxiously near the entrance. He scanned every passing taxi, impatient for the arrival of his bride-to-be.

Catherine, in contrast, was at her home, adorning herself in a stunning white gown and veil. Before the mirror she carefully adjusted the lace along her shoulders, studying her reflection as though trying to recognize the woman who was about to change her life forever. She descended the stairs, her heart filled with anticipation and a hint of apprehension, as she prepared to meet Alfred. A taxi waited outside to take her to their wedding venue.

However, as she stepped outside, a chill wind greeted her, and raindrops began to fall, lightly dotting her veil. A shiver of fear passed through her, the cold gust stirring superstitious thoughts.

Was this an ill omen, a spectral warning of impending doom? What could it have meant?

As the drops of rain touched her veil, she felt a sudden unease. For a fleeting moment, beneath the grey Moscow sky, the joy of the day seemed to hesitate.

Shaking off these foreboding thoughts, Catherine composed herself and entered the taxi. Despite the ominous weather and her fleeting concerns, her resolve to join Alfred and begin their new life together remained steadfast.

Arriving early at the Wedding Palace, Catherine quickly found Alfred, who stood out among the crowd of grooms with his impeccable attire. Their reunion was filled with affection, as Alfred complimented Catherine's beauty.

"You are the most beautiful bride here. I love you so much."

Catherine replied softly,
"I love you too."

The lobby was bustling with couples, their families, and friends, all eagerly awaiting their turn to marry. The portraits of Soviet officials on the walls served as a reminder of the regime's presence even in these joyous moments. The brides, predominantly young, blonde, and blue-eyed, wore traditional white dresses and lace veils, while some grooms hailed from distant lands, symbolizing the union of cultures.

As the ceremony proceeded, Catherine and Alfred observed other couples completing their vows to the tune of Mendelssohn's wedding march, leaving the hall to cheers and celebrations.

Catherine's family, including her parents and sister, were present, sharing in the happiness of the occasion.

The couple's elegant appearance drew admiring glances from others. However, the solemnity of the moment was briefly interrupted when a stern Soviet official approached Alfred, demanding his German passport for registration. Understanding the futility of resistance, Alfred complied, making a brief call to the West German Embassy before returning to complete the necessary formalities.

With all procedures finalized, Alfred and Catherine were ready to proceed. They were called into the grand hall by a strict official, where they stood before a middle-aged woman who recited the timeless wedding vows:

"For better or worse, for richer, for poorer, in sickness and in health, in good times and in bad, and in joy as well as in sorrow. To love, support, honor, and respect, to cherish each other for as long as you live."

They stood there listening to the universal oath, simple and beautiful.

"Now, please exchange your rings."

Exchanging rings — a diamond-studded band for Catherine and a platinum ring for Alfred — they sealed their union with a kiss, marking the end of the ceremony and the beginning of their shared life. The simplicity and beauty of the oath resonated with them, symbolizing their commitment to each other in the face of any challenge.

A Mercedes provided by the embassy awaited the newlyweds, ready to transport them to their chosen celebration destination: the Continental Hotel, a place they had previously enjoyed for its elegance and luxury. With their official marriage status, they felt confident that they would not encounter any interference from secret service agents this time.

Arriving at the hotel, Alfred and Catherine checked in at the reception. Soft music drifted through the elegant lobby, including the romantic melody of Neil Diamond and Gilbert Bécaud's song "September Morn," filling the room with a gentle, nostalgic atmosphere.

Upon entering their room, 1314, they were greeted by a delightful box of luxury Swiss chocolates placed neatly on the dresser. The attentive bellboy also brought them an ice bucket filled with champagne. Adorning the room was a vase containing two dozen beautiful pink roses, adding a touch of romance to their celebration.

They collapsed onto the bed laughing like children, overcome by the excitement of the day. The tension of months of waiting dissolved into relief and passion, and they remained wrapped in each other's arms until morning.

When Catherine awoke, she saw Alfred already packing his bags.

"Would you like me to come with you to the airport?" she asked quietly.

He turned on some French music so that he could speak freely without being overheard, aware that the room might contain hidden microphones.

"No, my love," he replied softly. "I want you to rest and take it easy. Enjoy your hotel room for the week; it is all paid for. I love you forever. I have an important errand to run, and I will be gone for a week or less, so please, I do not want you to try to reach me under any circumstances, or you might endanger me and yourself, darling."

He took her hands gently.

"You know how much I love you, so trust me. I will be unreachable for some time. Enjoy it, My love."

He kissed her passionately goodbye.

She said nothing and quietly acquiesced to his request.

And off Alfred went on his errand, disappearing into the uncertain world beyond the hotel walls, not to be disturbed by anyone — not even Catherine.

***

Alfred had to leave immediately for business purposes. Later, he would have to attend to his parents' estate matters, but no longer free to delay his plans, he would first complete his international business mission and then return to bring Catherine home.

His parents had left him a beautiful residence in the German Alps, staffed with a butler, maids, and a cook. In Alfred's mind, Catherine's future was already secure — a life of comfort, elegance, and peace far removed from the harsh realities of Soviet life.

Next, he called his American partners. This time he knew he wanted to finish his business in Moskva once and for all. He thanked his former partners warmly in a letter sent to the headquarters in Basel, Switzerland, informing them that he was finally ready to retire.

Chapter 93

Waiting in Limbo

The next day, feeling quite alone, Catherine decided to visit the local militsiya office to obtain her travel passport bearing her new married name for the first time. She had to surrender her internal passport in exchange for the new travel document. Clutching her handbag tightly, she stepped out into the gray Moscow morning, the cold air stinging her cheeks as she made her way toward the government building.

Inside, she took her place in a short line of Soviet citizens applying for an exit visa. The wait felt like an eternity in the stuffy corridors of bureaucratic power. The walls were painted a dull institutional green, and the faint smell of damp coats and cigarette smoke lingered in the air. People spoke in hushed voices, careful not to attract unnecessary attention.

When it was finally her turn, she fervently prayed that her marriage to Alfred would make the difference between this new application and the previous one, which had been denied.

A young, uniformed female official stared intently at her from behind a small glass window.

"Your passport, citizeness!"

Catherine handed over her Soviet passport through the opening. The officer slowly opened the cover page and examined it with clinical indifference.

"Frau Fuchs, it is a requirement for a citizeness to change her last name to her married name," said the official.

"Yes, of course," Catherine replied obediently, trying to keep her voice steady despite the pounding of her heart.

"Please sign on the dotted line. Your application has been accepted by the Gagarin District militsiya unit," said the woman matter-of-factly.

For a moment Catherine could hardly believe what she had heard.

Overjoyed, she expressed her gratitude.

"Thank you!"

The official gave no response. She merely stamped the papers with a heavy metal seal — a dull thud that echoed through the quiet office like the sound of a small door opening somewhere far away.

The bureaucratic machinery had finally been set in motion.

After a week had passed, Catherine returned to her apartment and eagerly awaited both her passport and her husband.

But the apartment now felt strangely empty.

The silence of the rooms seemed heavier than before. Alfred's laughter no longer echoed in the hallway, and the flowers he had left behind were beginning to wilt on the windowsill.

Days stretched slowly into weeks.

Two weeks later, her passport application remained in limbo, and her husband was still away on his mysterious errand.

Each evening Catherine found herself standing by the window, staring down at the snow-covered street below, hoping to see Alfred suddenly appear from a taxi or step out of the shadows.

But the street remained empty.

Finally, realizing that patience alone would not move the machinery of the Soviet state, Catherine devised a clever plan to expedite the process.

If the system would not move for her, she would find a way to make it move.

Chapter 94

Risky Gambit

The West German Chancellor, Helmut Kohl, had scheduled an official visit to the Soviet Union in July 1983. The announcement reverberated through diplomatic circles in Moscow, quietly raising hopes among those seeking permission to leave the country. Reports that Chancellor Kohl intended to raise humanitarian concerns during his Moscow visit spread through the Soviet capital, reinforcing those cautious hopes.

Catherine decided to take matters into her own hands and wrote a letter, allegedly from Alfred Fuchs, petitioning Yuri Andropov, then General Secretary of the Communist Party, to grant his wife an exit visa to join him in West Germany. She knew that the letter had to reach Andropov well ahead of the West German Chancellor's visit, hoping that it would be elevated to the highest echelons of power.

While she hoped that her husband would approve of the idea, she faced the challenge of sending the letter without it being intercepted by Soviet authorities. All foreign mail was scrutinized, and sending such a letter through regular channels would almost certainly result in it being discarded, or worse, triggering unwanted attention from the security services.

Her only hope was a special diplomatic delivery arranged through friends with diplomatic status. The letter had to be sent from a foreign location, ostensibly by her spouse, directly to Yuri Andropov.

The letter's content was simple and direct: Alfred Fuchs was requesting permission for his spouse, Catherine Fuchs, to leave the Soviet Union and join him in West Germany, so that they could celebrate their wedding together in Frankfurt.

As she pondered how to accomplish this delicate operation, her phone rang one afternoon.

Hoping it was her husband, she answered eagerly, only to hear a dear old friend on the line—Doctor Kristof Svoboda, a department director at a renowned UN agency in Geneva, Switzerland. She was pleasantly surprised to hear from him and eager to catch up.

"I am in Moscow. Would you care to meet me at the National Hotel for lunch?" Dr. Svoboda's voice came through the phone. Catherine eagerly accepted.

"Sure! At what time?"

"Will 4 p.m. be good for you?" he asked.

"Yes, of course," she replied hastily, realizing that this might be her best chance to have the letter sent by someone she trusted.

"I will see you there," she added before saying goodbye.

Dr. Svoboda, an official from Geneva with diplomatic credentials, seemed like the perfect candidate to run this sensitive errand.

Catherine knew she couldn't show the letter at the National Hotel, so she devised a plan to hand it over discreetly in Aleksandrovsky Park, a place crowded enough to blend into the public flow yet open enough to avoid attracting suspicion. They finally met in the crowded lobby of the National Hotel. Her friend recognized Catherine immediately, hugged her warmly, and led her into the restaurant where they ordered a light lunch.

They began with casual conversation about trivial matters, carefully maintaining the appearance of two old friends simply catching up. Dr. Svoboda, in his late fifties, had a pleasant-looking face with intensely blue eyes that resembled the serene figures depicted in ancient Catholic cathedral frescoes. He dressed casually in light pants and a white linen shirt to avoid drawing attention.

After their meal, he suggested,

"Would you like to go for a walk?"

Catherine readily agreed, and they headed to Aleksandrovsky Park.

The park was lively with people strolling along the paths, tourists taking photographs near the Kremlin walls, and children chasing pigeons across the gravel walkways.

As they walked, Dr. Svoboda noticed Catherine's wedding ring.

"Catherine, how are you? I see there are some changes in your life. You have a very beautiful wedding ring. Did you get married recently?"

Catherine nodded.

"Yes. I am Frau Fuchs now, and my husband lives in Frankfurt."

Dr. Svoboda whistled softly, admiring the ring.

"You have changed a lot since the last time I saw you. You would easily fit into the horse-race crowd with a summer hat and this fine dress."

"Thank you for the compliment," Catherine replied. Then her expression grew serious.

"Now I want to ask you for a very special favor. I desperately need your help. Things are getting complicated here. I am struggling to obtain an exit visa so that I can be reunited with my husband in Frankfurt."

Kristof listened attentively without interrupting her. She continued quietly,

"I wrote a letter to Yuri Andropov, the General Secretary of the Communist Party. The letter must be sent from a foreign location. We must spare no time or effort and act immediately. It is dangerous for you to get involved in any nefarious business with a political twist, and I would never wish to tarnish your reputation. But my life and freedom are at stake."

He nodded slowly. "I have diplomatic credentials with a prestigious position," he replied thoughtfully.

Catherine could see that he was weighing the risks.

She continued, "This letter simply requests an exit visa to West Germany so that we may celebrate our wedding in Frankfurt. Alfred would have sent it himself, but he is involved in an important errand."

Kristof paused, then suddenly brightened. "I have an idea!" he said.

"I am flying out to West Germany via Finland. It would be very easy for me to send the letter from a local post office. Thanks to my diplomatic immunity, no one in Soviet customs would dare open my valise."

He smiled reassuringly. "I will be more than happy to do it for you."

Then he sought clarification.

"So, tell me if I understand correctly. This letter was written by you but should appear to have been written by your husband and sent from Frankfurt directly to Yuri Andropov in Moscow."

He sighed quietly, reflecting on his own past.

"In my lifetime, I had to escape from my native *Czechoslovakia* where I was born. Communism is evil. The devil always sends his servants to stir up fear and chaos among ordinary people. There is no personal freedom under communism. We must resist it to preserve our identity and pursue our dreams."

He looked at Catherine with compassion.

"I shall do everything I can to help you."

Catherine felt a profound sense of gratitude for having loyal friends like Kristof when faced with such dangerous circumstances.

For the first time in weeks, she felt that the frozen machinery of the Soviet state might finally begin to move.

Chapter 95

Summer Reveries

The summer of 1983 in Moscow unfurled like a masterpiece of nature, offering its residents and visitors a symphony of delightful weather. Days bathed in warm sunlight flowed into pleasantly cool nights, creating an enchanting contrast that drew countless admirers to the city. Tree-lined boulevards shimmered in the golden light of late afternoon, while open-air cafés and crowded parks buzzed with quiet conversations and laughter. Moscow, in all its splendor, played host to foreigners who reveled in the best it had to offer.

Catherine, however, held a bittersweet sentiment toward this radiant season. She hoped it would mark her final summer in Moscow. Her husband remained abroad, and the city felt both familiar and distant. While she cherished the frequent visits with her parents, George and Sonya, she keenly felt the absence of her beloved Aunt Natalie. Infrequent calls from her aunt in New York were moments of fleeting connection, always shadowed by the looming presence of surveillance. The rest of her extended family, ensconced in seemingly comfortable lives, remained distant.

Catherine often found solace in daydreams, her eidetic memory preserving every detail of this critical juncture in her life. She walked through familiar streets with heightened awareness, as if committing every corner of Moscow to memory before the moment of departure finally arrived. She knew that once she obtained an exit visa, there would be no turning back. Leaving her closest relatives behind, she needed to find someone trustworthy to watch over her cherished parents. Establishing secure lines of communication became her unfinished business in Moscow — a fragile bridge between the life she was leaving and the unknown future waiting beyond the Iron Curtain.

Her life in Moscow was intertwined with her sister's former marriage to a Soviet diplomat who had risen steadily through the ranks and acquired influence. This diplomat, Oleg Dobronravov, could potentially become her guardian angel and messenger.

In the summer of 1983, Oleg Dobronravov was stationed at his duty post in Vienna, Austria.

Late afternoon bathed the picturesque city in a soft golden glow, casting a tranquil ambiance over the historic streets. Horse-drawn carriages rolled slowly past elegant Baroque buildings, and the distant sound of a violin drifted through the warm evening air. Vienna held a special place in Oleg's heart, and he cherished the city's timeless beauty.

On this Wednesday, an air of monotony pervaded his office at the *UNCENTRALE.* Stacks of diplomatic reports and memoranda lay scattered across his desk, each document carrying the dry language of bureaucracy. Restlessness overcame him, and he decided to take a leisurely stroll back to his apartment. As he wandered through the city's central streets, he passed boutique stores and benches adorned with whimsical papier-mâché figurines, each exuding a touch of humor. Vienna was in the middle of hosting its annual music and theater festival, and the city pulsated with cultural vibrancy. Street musicians played lively melodies, and theater posters fluttered in the warm evening breeze.

By the time he returned to his comfortable apartment in one of Vienna's old districts, the day had waned, and the city had transitioned into the quiet serenity of evening. Oleg followed his familiar routine. He opened his mailbox and began sorting through the usual assortment of newspapers, bills, and official correspondence. Then he noticed an envelope bearing the unmistakable markings of the Soviet diplomatic service. Inside was a letter from the head office — a message that would alter the course of his life. The official correspondence bore a succinct yet weighty command: "Comrade Dobronravov, you are summoned to Moscow. Please inform us of your arrival date as expeditiously as possible."

Oleg read the line again slowly. In the world of Soviet diplomacy, such summons was rarely routine — and never optional. For a long moment he stood motionless in the quiet hallway of his apartment building, the letter still in his hand.

Somewhere behind the formal language of the message, he sensed that events far larger than himself were already beginning to move.

Chapter 96

Catherine's Secret Pact

The month of July in 1983 passed swiftly, leaving Catherine in a state of uncertainty about her future. The long summer days seemed to blur together, each one filled with the same mixture of fragile hope and quiet anxiety. As the days unfolded, a significant event loomed on the horizon.

In late July 1983, the Soviet diplomat, Comrade Dobronravov, who had previously been married to Catherine's sister, Maria, returned to Moscow in response to a summons. With a cordial friendship still intact, he extended an invitation to both Maria and Catherine to join him for lunch.

The gathering took place in a discreet corner of the restaurant inside the *National Hotel* — one of the few places in Moscow where foreigners, diplomats, and trusted Soviet officials could meet without attracting unnecessary attention. Oleg, after the meal, unveiled a bag filled with thoughtful gifts for the family.

The restaurant hummed quietly with restrained conversation. A few foreign businessmen sat at nearby tables while uniformed waiters moved carefully between them. In Moscow, such places were rare and closely watched, and everyone instinctively kept their voices low.

However, it soon became apparent that Oleg had more than just gifts on his mind.

He rose slowly from the table and turned to Catherine, his former sister-in-law, with a serious expression.

"Catherine," he began quietly, "I would greatly appreciate it if you could accompany me to the office building where you once worked."

Sensing the gravity of the situation, she swiftly collected her purse and followed him outside.

As they ventured away from the gathering, their path led them through a secluded alleyway that eventually opened onto the South-West highway. The summer air hung heavy over the quiet side streets, and the distant hum of traffic echoed between the tall apartment blocks.

Oleg slowed his pace and began speaking in hushed tones.

"You have my assurance," he whispered, "that you are on the verge of obtaining your exit visas. You will soon have the freedom to reunite with your husband in Europe."

He paused briefly before continuing.

"I have utilized every connection at my disposal to make this happen."

Concerned for his well-being, Catherine asked anxiously,

"But what risks are you taking, Oleg? Could this jeopardize you or your family?"

With heartfelt sincerity he replied,

"You are like a little sister to me, and I am compelled to help you. Let us not dwell on the potential consequences for me."

Touched by his devotion, Catherine declared softly,

"You will forever be my brother of the heart."

Before parting ways, Oleg outlined their future communication plan.

He handed her a small slip of paper containing a contact number.

"Please commit this number to memory," he said quietly. "You will assume the persona of Kat, Professor Angel's assistant, conducting research on international law for a book."

He glanced around cautiously before continuing.

"We will communicate using coded phrases."

He spoke slowly, ensuring she understood every word.

"'Jasmine is in full bloom in the local botanical garden' will signal that our meeting is arranged."

He continued,

"'Jasmine has faded in the garden' will indicate that I am unavailable."

Then his tone grew more serious.

"And if circumstances turn dire, I will say: 'The flower shop is closing. There will be no more deliveries.'"

The meaning was unmistakable. Danger.

Catherine, overwhelmed with emotion and questions, could only manage a quiet,

"Oh..."

She gazed at Oleg in silence, her gratitude impossible to fully express in words.

He embraced her in a brotherly farewell, planting a gentle kiss on her cheek.

Then, without another word, he turned and walked briskly away, his tall figure disappearing into the flow of pedestrians and traffic along the wide Moscow Avenue.

For several moments Catherine remained standing where he had left her, realizing that the quiet lunch meeting had just turned into a dangerous alliance.

***

Oleg Dobronravov was a consummate strategist in the intricate game of life, always anticipating events several moves ahead.

His relentless pursuit of excellence within the competitive and often treacherous landscape of the Soviet Foreign Ministry had propelled him to the prestigious diplomatic post in Vienna, Austria.

Now, as he gazed out over the sprawling city of Moscow from his temporary office window, his thoughts returned to Catherine, his former sister-in-law.

Oleg was a masterful chess player — not only on the board but also in the realm of politics and diplomacy.

His intellect, combined with a wide range of talents, had opened doors to a world of influence and power.

Yet beneath the polished exterior of a Soviet diplomat, his concern for Catherine was sincere.

He hoped she possessed the same resilience and strategic instincts required to navigate the dangerous path ahead.

While Oleg had climbed the social ladder and embraced the responsibilities of his prestigious position, he remained fundamentally good-hearted.

His actions were not driven solely by ambition, but by a deep-rooted desire to assist those he cared about.

As he contemplated Catherine's uncertain future, he held on to one quiet hope.

That her journey — fraught with risk, secrecy, and political maneuvering — would ultimately lead to freedom and reunion.

Chapter 97

Bound by Love, Liberated by Courage

On the crisp morning of July 27, 1983, Catherine approached her mailbox with a sense of trepidation. The hallway of her apartment building was quiet, the faint smell of dust and old newspapers lingering in the air. There, amidst the mundane letters and advertisements, she discovered a postcard bearing the emblem of *OVIR*, the Soviet visa processing department.

The message was brief but carried immense weight:

"You must report to the *OVIR* on the 28th of July. Bring your passport, four photos, and your marriage registration files attesting to your union with FRG citizen, Herr Alfred Fuchs."

Reality crashed upon her like a relentless wave. The moment had arrived.

Catherine now faced the painful realization that she would soon have to bid farewell to the life she had always known. Her cherished books and photographs — the small treasures of a life built in Moscow — would soon become distant memories. Every object in her apartment suddenly seemed to carry the weight of a farewell.

The thought of leaving her family and birthplace behind, perhaps forever, pressed heavily upon her heart. As she gazed at old photographs, memories of happier times with her sister Maria, her nephew Michael, and her parents Sonya and George flooded her mind. Their faces seemed to look back at her from another lifetime. Catherine knew there would be no turning back once she crossed the borders of the Soviet Union. Yet her resolve remained unbroken.

Her purpose had become clear: one day she hoped to help liberate her loved ones from the oppressive confines of the Soviet regime. These thoughts consumed her throughout that fateful day in July 1983.

Meanwhile, across the miles in Rome, Italy, Alfred's voice reached Catherine through the telephone. His familiar endearment — "My love" — resonated warmly in her heart as he spoke of their plans. He described a romantic hotel in Rome and the blissful honeymoon weekend awaiting them. The anticipation of reuniting with Alfred filled her with warmth and excitement.

"Rome, it sounds so wonderful," she said eagerly. "I can't wait to see you. I love you with all my heart."

The following morning, Catherine obediently presented herself at the local department.

The government building stood heavy and gray against the summer sky, its long corridors echoing with the quiet footsteps of anxious applicants waiting for decisions that could change their lives. A pile of registration papers awaited her. She signed each document with unwavering determination. With every signature, her identity underwent a profound transformation. She was no longer simply Catherine. She was now Frau Fuchs.

Finally, the moment of reckoning arrived when the official looked up from the papers.

"Frau Fuchs, report tomorrow to this office and hand over your domestic Soviet passport. Only then will you be issued a travel passport, and your exit visas will be stamped in your new passport."

With heartfelt gratitude, Catherine thanked the official and swiftly walked away, the rhythmic click of her high heels marking each determined step along the corridor.

The Soviets had granted her a temporary one-month exit visa — a fragile but priceless lifeline for someone who had spent years fighting for the right to leave.

Alfred, in his generosity toward his young bride, had left her with more than just money. He had given her the wings of freedom.

With the means to arrange her travel, Catherine stood on the brink of a new life, like a bird poised to break free from the bars of a long-closed cage.

The very next day she returned to the *OVIR* department, her heart pounding with anticipation. As she handed her domestic passport to the young official, she noticed the sour expression on the woman's face. It was as if the Soviet bureaucracy itself resented her departure. Without emotion, the official returned with a new document. It was her travel passport.

The cover bore the name:

Frau Fuchs. The pages were already marked with official stamps and instructions.

"You must have your passport registered at the Soviet Embassy in Frankfurt, West Germany upon arrival," the official said sternly. "Do not forget that you have a family you are leaving behind." She paused before adding another warning.

"You must report back to Moscow exactly on the date marked in your travel passport. Upon your return, you are expected to appear at the office to reclaim your domestic Soviet passport."

Then she added coldly: "Bon voyage."

Catherine felt a mixture of exhilaration and apprehension. The weight of leaving her homeland — and her loved ones — pressed heavily on her heart.

Yet she also understood that this journey marked the closing of one chapter and the uncertain beginning of another.

With her travel passport firmly in hand, Catherine made her way to the Alitalia office to purchase her first-class tickets to Rome.

This privilege was granted to only a select few Soviet citizens — those who had successfully navigated the endless scrutiny of the state.

As she secured her tickets, she reflected on the strange twists of fate that had brought her to this moment. Catherine had become one of the rare individuals allowed to pass beyond the Iron Curtain. And now, at last, her journey toward freedom was about to begin.

Chapter 98

Breaking Boundaries

The year was 1983, a time when very few Soviet citizens could dare to imagine the sweeping changes that lay ahead. The Soviet Union was mired in a period of stagnation, seemingly without hope of change. For *refuseniks*, those who longed to break free and start anew in Israel or America, the idea that their dreams might come true was beyond their wildest imagination.

In 1983, the notion that only a few years later a leader named Mikhail Gorbachev would step onto the stage and deliver a groundbreaking speech at the January 1987 Plenary session of the Central Committee of the Communist Party, accelerating a program of *perestroika—restructuring—and glasnost—openness,* was unthinkable. Political prisoners would begin to be released, some cleared of charges and gradually allowed to return to public life. The press would gain unprecedented freedom, and new political movements would emerge. Local and regional governing bodies would begin to acquire genuine powers. Gorbachev would fulfill his promise to withdraw Soviet troops from Afghanistan, and the Berlin Wall would crumble. The Warsaw Pact countries would undergo peaceful revolutions, paving their own paths toward a brighter future. Finally, in December 1991, the Soviet Union itself would collapse, bringing an end to the Cold War.

These momentous changes, however, would offer little consolation to the many *refuseniks* who had endured years of waiting and longing for a freedom that had remained beyond their reach.

With only a few days remaining before Catherine's early morning Alitalia flight to Rome, Italy—the ticket to her freedom—each moment became increasingly precious. She knew that these final days would determine whether she soared to the surface or got buried in the vortex of her choices. Every step had to be calculated, and time was of the essence.

Catherine and Maria spent time together, strolling through the city center and taking the metro along the circular line, passing by familiar subway stops whose marble halls and echoing tunnels Catherine had known all her life. As the days passed, Catherine felt the weight of the impending departure bearing down on her.

Returning home late after one of their downtown excursions, Catherine was acutely aware of the ticking clock. She needed to rest before embarking on her journey, leaving behind everything she had ever known and owned. Time seemed to race, reminding her of every minute spent in the Soviet Union.

On the 8th of August 1983, Frau Fuchs, armed with her new Soviet travel passport and visas, was set to leave Moscow. Her resolve was unwavering; she had no plans to return, despite any orders to the contrary. She carefully placed her beloved sapphire earrings in a black velvet jewelry satchel and proudly adorned her impressive diamond ring along with her wedding band, all gifts from Alfred. Tomorrow, she would don her golden pumps, aptly nicknamed her "freedom shoes."

In the early morning, her sister would accompany her to the airport, and Catherine found herself immersed in a whirlwind of thoughts as her new reality unfolded before her eyes. Suddenly, a loud and insistent doorbell disrupted her reverie. She rushed to answer the door, peering through the peephole to find her former student, Vadim Smirnov, standing outside.

Startled, she opened the door, and Vadim, in a desperate tone, asked for her help, requesting a hundred dollars. Catherine hesitated, knowing that unofficial hard currency transactions were considered crimes with severe consequences.

Regretfully, she replied, "I would have gladly helped you, but I only have three hundred US dollars officially exchanged for my trip. I'm afraid I can't be of assistance. You should seek help elsewhere. You must leave now. Good night." She escorted Vadim to the door and politely but firmly closed it behind him, acutely aware of the risks involved.

Catherine's apartment felt warm and comforting as she settled in for a brief rest. She had been exhausted and fell asleep immediately, awakening refreshed and ready to embark on her journey to freedom. With determination in her heart, she called for a cab, gathered her suitcase, and made her way downstairs.

As the cab arrived, she took her seat inside and calmly stated, "Sheremetyevo airport, please." Through the open window, she observed the city slowly awakening to a new bright and sunny day, the wide Moscow boulevards filling with early traffic as a light morning breeze moved through the trees.

Their first stop was Gertsen Street, where Maria and her son Michael, who had come to see her off, would join her on the journey to the airport. Catherine had bid farewell to her parents the day before, assuring them of a future reunion to avoid the emotional pain of parting. Their smiles, tinged with tears, conveyed their happiness and well wishes.

The driver guided them through the city center, allowing them one last glimpse of *Aleksandrovsky* Park and the iconic red brick walls of the Kremlin rising solemnly beyond the trees. It was as if even the city itself wished to ensure that Catherine's departure tugged at her heartstrings, prompting her return. The drive to the airport remained uneventful.

Upon reaching the airport, Catherine, accompanied by her sister Maria and nephew Michael, approached the Alitalia counter. She checked in and received her boarding pass. They remained together until they reached the last glass partition before passport control and customs. Catherine embraced her sister tightly, kissed her nephew, and felt Michael's tears as he asked her to bring back gifts—a toy bear and a car. She smiled at him, kissed his cheek, and then picked up her suitcase to continue her journey.

Turning back a few times to capture the image in her memory, Catherine approached the uniformed male official and handed him her Soviet travel passport. For a moment her heart pounded as she waited for him to examine the document. Anxiety filled her thoughts. What would happen at customs? Would anyone try to stop her from leaving?

The customs officer, quite amicably, asked her, "Did you pack your suitcase yourself? What exactly did you pack?" Catherine replied, "Russian books, my dresses, and a bottle of champagne."

The customs officer then inquired, "Are you bringing any jewelry?" She proudly displayed her engagement ring with a wedding band and revealed a pair of sapphire earrings. To her surprise, the officer smiled with respect and admiration, never requesting her to open her suitcase.

Boarding the plane was a blur for Catherine. This was her first time traveling abroad, and she felt a mix of excitement and anticipation as she prepared to depart for Rome, Italy, followed by Frankfurt, West Germany, in two weeks. Seated comfortably in first class, she welcomed the flight attendants' greetings in Russian, Italian, and English.

As she settled in, a flight attendant placed a pillow behind her back and kindly inquired about her choice of drink.

"A Martini would be perfect," Catherine replied as the flight attendant placed a small glass before her with two green olives resting at the bottom.

Peering out of the small window, she attempted to capture the last sights of Moscow for the final time. She knew that she would never dare set foot in this part of the world again. As the plane ascended, leaving Moscow and its suburbs behind, Catherine's heart brimmed with energy and joy, marking the beginning of her journey toward a new life filled with hope and possibility.

As the Alitalia flight soared away from her homeland, Catherine made a conscious effort to etch the scenes of Moscow deep into her heart. She knew that these were the sights she would never see again.

She watched the endless clouds drifting beneath the wing, wondering silently whether the invisible border had already been crossed.

As the flight attendant's announcement reached her ears, stating that they had crossed the border of the Soviet Union, Catherine couldn't help but shed tears of joy and triumph. She had defied the ominous words of the Soviet colonel who had declared, "You will never set your foot on foreign soil!" Her journey was a testament to her determination, resourcefulness, stubbornness, and the twists of destiny that had freed her from the chains that bound her.

The flight to Rome lasted four hours, and upon landing, the plane made a gentle thud as it touched down on the sunlit runway of Rome's Fiumicino Airport. Catherine and the few passengers disembarked, slowly moving through a long and seemingly dark passage. It felt like an eternity, but at long last, she emerged into the bright natural sunlight, greeted by a drastically new reality. Her tears had transformed into tears of liberation.

With her eyes adjusting to the sunlight and her mind adapting to her newfound freedom, Catherine proceeded to the baggage claim area. She collected her luggage from the carousel and made her way outside to the taxi stand. Her destination was *Piazza di Spagna*—the famous Spanish Steps—where she would reunite with Alfred. Somewhere beyond the airport roads lay Rome's warm evening air, the murmur of fountains, and the life she had dreamed of for years.

Having arrived in Rome, now married to a West German citizen, Catherine felt a deep sense of accomplishment. She had achieved her goal of escaping the confines of the Soviet Union and now stood at the threshold of a new life.

Outside the terminal, Roman sunlight flooded the pavement as taxis moved through the warm evening air, carrying her toward the Spanish Steps—and toward Alfred.

Chapter 99

The Roman Encounter

For the first time in her life, Catherine stood in a city where no one watched her, no one questioned her papers, and no one controlled where she could go. Rome felt impossibly alive—the air warm, the voices musical, the streets open in every direction. After years of fear and calculation in Moscow, freedom itself felt almost unreal.

Catherine settled her taxi fare with *liras* and stepped out onto the lively square as the driver pulled away. Standing in the middle of the bustling sidewalk, she marveled at the grand staircase rising before her, bathed in the early evening glow. Young women lounged on the steps, their loose skirts swaying as they enjoyed gelato. Her gaze traveled upward, where she spotted a handsome Italian man with wavy black hair, dressed in a crisp white shirt and casual beige slacks that accentuated his slender physique.

She felt someone step quietly behind her.

Suddenly, a soft voice whispered in her ear, "Madam, are you admiring that handsome fellow?"

She turned swiftly, and there he was—Alfred—embracing her tightly.

"My love, I already have one," she replied passionately, kissing him on the steps. "Where is our hotel, darling? I am rather weary."

"It is only down the street," Alfred assured her, and they set off for the *Nazionale Hotel* along the lively Roman street glowing with evening lights. Upon arrival, they presented their passports to the young concierge at the reception desk. A bellboy was summoned to carry their luggage to the second floor. He handed Alfred the room keys and said, "Signore, here are your keys."

"Thank you," Alfred acknowledged as he swiftly lifted Catherine in his arms to her delighted surprise. With a smile, he added, "Our honeymoon starts now," before extinguishing the room lights.

The following morning at 8 a.m., Alfred beckoned Catherine to the window. "Come see the most beautiful sky you have ever seen."

The upper sky was adorned in shades of pink, while the horizon glimmered with a golden hue over the rooftops of Rome. It was indeed the most breathtaking sky Catherine had ever witnessed.

Alfred picked up the phone and ordered a continental breakfast.

"A continental breakfast is a bit lighter," he said. "Rome offers so many culinary delights, and we don't want to fill up now."

They savored their coffee and nibbled on Danish rolls before calling for the table to be cleared.

"Sir," the waiter suggested, "there are some marvelous breakfast foods downstairs in the main dining room."

Feeling a slight pang of hunger, Catherine agreed.

"Let's have a look."

They descended to the main dining room, where guests filled the spacious hall, their conversations in Italian, French, and English blending into a cheerful morning hum. Sunlight streamed through the windows, glinting off polished silver trays and rows of white china.

Long buffet tables stretched across the room, laden with steaming café latte, espresso, and cappuccino. Brightly colored cereal boxes from America stood alongside baskets overflowing with freshly baked Italian bread and an assortment of pastries. Nearby, platters of thinly sliced Genovese salami and mortadella rested beside sizzling sausages fresh from the grill. Jars of spicy mustard completed the display, inviting guests on a culinary journey through flavors from across Europe and beyond.

Catherine looked around the dining room one last time.

"I could spend the whole morning here," she admitted.

"Then it's a good thing we have plans," Alfred replied, smiling.

She laughed and rose from her chair.

"Lead the way."

"Let's go," Alfred said. "We have a taxi waiting for us outside."

Leaving Rome, they embarked on a journey to Florence, the landscape slowly changing as the road carried them north through Umbria and into Tuscany, where rolling hills dotted with vineyards and tall cypress trees stretched toward the horizon. They arrived at a roundabout where a statue of Dante stood holding the *Inferno* in his hand. Catherine was in awe as she immersed herself in the wonders of Dante, Botticelli, Raphael, and, of course, Michelangelo. The beauty of it all was almost overwhelming.

Then Alfred suggested, "We haven't seen the real David. Let's visit the museum."

"But there are replicas everywhere," Catherine pointed out.

"No, I want us to see the original."

They entered the museum and walked slowly down a long gallery where sunlight filtered from above. At the far end of the hall, Michelangelo's David gradually appeared before them.

It was a magnificent seventeen-foot-high sculpture crafted from gleaming white marble, and every detail, from his head to his toes, left Catherine breathless. She couldn't help but remark, "When I see your naked body, I will always call you David," with a smile.

Alfred had more surprises in store. He mentioned, "We have another taxi to catch, one that will take us to the upper regions of Italy. There, we will witness something truly beautiful."

Off they went in the taxi, ascending the mountains of Assisi along winding roads overlooking the green Umbrian valleys below. They arrived at the Basilica of Saint Francis of Assisi, a breathtaking sight rising solemnly above the ancient stone town. The monastery featured numerous hidden doors adorned with wrought iron sculpted into winding scrolls. Across from these scrolls, Catherine noticed a lifelike statue of St. Francis. Then, as if in quiet blessing, a beautiful white dove flew from the garden and perched on St. Francis's hand.

"Alfred, is this a sign? An omen?" Catherine wondered aloud.

"My love, I don't know," Alfred replied. With these thoughts in their hearts, they concluded their tour and returned to their hotel. Exhausted yet invigorated, they found time for love and affection, their minds still filled with the beauty of David, the quiet hills of Assisi, and the promise of a new life together beyond the Iron Curtain.

Chapter 100

A Deadly Deception

The warm Roman air drifted through the open windows of the hotel restaurant as the city outside slowly settled into night. Alfred and Catherine sat across from one another, enjoying what seemed like another perfect evening in Rome. They had a marvelous dinner planned for 7:30 p.m., and Alfred decided to engage the young waiter, Louis, in conversation.

He asked, "What is your name?" The boy replied, "*Signore*, my name is Louis," using the Italian word for "sir."

Alfred asked, "What would you suggest for us to dine on tonight?"

Louis recommended, "*Signore,* the cook has just prepared the most beautiful roast beef. Perhaps it would please *Signora* as well."

Alfred agreed, saying, "Yes, I think that sounds very pleasant."

Louis offered, "I will bring you some sparkling water first. And then you may order a cocktail if you wish."

As the drinks arrived, they quenched their thirst and took in the surroundings of the restaurant. Catherine couldn't help but notice the well-dressed locals. Roman men wore elegant dark suits, starched white collars, silk ties, and impeccable brown leather shoes. Their quiet confidence contrasted sharply with the casual tourists in khaki trousers and wind-blown hair. Two respectable Roman ladies entered the restaurant, their brocade silk jackets catching the soft golden light, their hair perfectly coiffed.

The roasted beef was served promptly, and they hungrily indulged in the delicious meal. Within twenty minutes, Louis returned with a tray of artichokes, a culinary delight they had never tasted before. Another twenty minutes later, Louis presented Italian roasted potatoes. Though they were already feeling full, the temptation of the flavorful potatoes was too much to resist. After finishing their meal, it was now 11:30 p.m. Alfred expressed his desire to visit the bar for a drink.

The bar was dimly lit, its polished wood counter reflecting the amber glow of the lamps.

Two well-dressed men had similar intentions and sat on either side of him.

Catherine, seizing an opportunity, excused herself, saying, "Would you excuse me? I do need to go to the restroom for a moment."

She gave Alfred a quick kiss on the lips and made her way upstairs to the ladies' lounge.

Meanwhile, the two men engaged Alfred in a seemingly innocuous conversation.

"*Signore*, can we buy you a drink?"

"Will a double brandy be to your liking?"

Little did Alfred know that the casual conversation unfolding beside him was anything but friendly. As the bartender quickly brought the three double brandies to the bar, the man on the left of Alfred initiated a hasty conversation about the sights of Italy.

At that very moment, the man on the right discreetly opened a small vial and poured its contents into Alfred's drink. They all clinked their glasses together.

"Cheers!"

They downed their drinks in one swift motion. Within seconds, a strange bitterness burned in Alfred's throat. The room seemed to tilt slightly as the noise of the bar blurred into a distant hum. His head dropped to the bar with a dull thud. The man on the right quietly left the bar.

The bartender inquired, "*Signore*, what happened?"

The man on the left nonchalantly replied, "Apparently, the man cannot hold his liquor."

Then both men left the bar and disappeared into the bustling street.

Catherine descended the steps, surprised to find her husband in such a state.

She asked, "Alfred, are you tired?"

She nudged him and kissed the top of his head. Growing increasingly concerned by his lack of response, she tried to shake him gently.

"Alfred?"

She called out louder. Her nudge caused him to slump forward.

"Alfred!"

Panicking, she turned to the bartender and exclaimed,

"What is wrong? What happened here?"

The bartender responded,

"Apparently, he just cannot hold his liquor." He cleared away the three glasses and placed them in soapy water to be washed. Then he summoned Louis.

"Help this gentleman up."

As Louis attempted to lift Alfred, he realized that Alfred had become a lifeless weight.

Louis cried out, "*Madonna Mia*, he is dead!"

Catherine gasped. The bartender reassured her, "Only unconscious, Louis."

However, Louis had become hysterical and rushed out shouting,

"*Polizia! Polizia*!"

The police hurried to the scene and quietly planned for the body to be collected. They turned their attention to Catherine.

"*Signora*, who is this man to you?"

"He is my husband," she screamed.

"*Signora*, with deepest regrets, he is dead. Where were you, *Signora*, when this incident happened?"

"I was in the ladies' lounge!" she cried through her sobs. "The bartender can vouch for me. He was already on the floor when I came down. There were two other men with him."

The police insisted, "No. We saw nobody else."

"*Signora,* please come with us. When he is ready to be seen, you must identify him in the morgue."

Catherine was inconsolable and desolate, crying loudly as she accompanied the police to the morgue. The following days passed like fragments of a nightmare.

The West German Embassy arranged for Alfred's body and Catherine to be transported from Rome to Frankfurt for the funeral, where they would be reunited with the next of kin. Catherine appeared every bit the grieving widow she was. Amid her sorrow, she realized that she knew very little about Alfred's business affairs. Her own goal had been to escape the Soviet Union, and she had not delved into the intricacies of his financial matters.

After clearing the necessary formalities, Catherine was granted permission by the authorities to accompany her late husband's body on the flight from Rome to Frankfurt. The German family had kindly extended an invitation for their new daughter-in-law to stay with them for a week of rest in their spacious home in Frankfurt. Alfred's mother, overwhelmed with grief, stopped by Catherine's bedroom.

Knocking softly on the door, she said,

"Please, enter."

Catherine's red eyes bore witness to her tears.

"Dear Alfred," his mother lamented, the words escaping her like a broken refrain.

The mother-in-law, a gracious woman with an air of austerity, was elegant in every way.

She continued, "My dearest, I hate to disturb you in this time of sorrow, but we must meet with the lawyers regarding Alfred's estate. We will convene next week on Thursday at nine o'clock sharp. Please be prepared, my dear. I won't trouble you any further but try not to cry too much. I understand."

The lawyer had not yet disclosed the details of Catherine's share of her late husband's property but assured her that they would be in touch to ensure her contacts and arrangements were properly recorded. Later that night, alone in her room, Catherine sat quietly by the window overlooking the dark garden of the house.

The events in Rome replayed in her mind repeatedly.

Two men. Two glasses raised in a toast.

And Alfred collapsing only seconds later.

For the first time since the tragedy, a chilling thought crossed her mind.

What if Alfred had not died by accident?

Chapter 101

U.S. Consulate General Frankfurt, West Germany September 1983

A Turning Point

A police car left Catherine at the entrance to the American Consulate compound in Frankfurt, beneath a canopy of tall, shadowed trees. Clutching a small cabin bag filled with summer dresses, family photographs, and a few keepsakes Alfred had given her during their short time together, she stepped out into the heavy afternoon heat. She hesitated, looking toward the embassy doors. She did not know whether they would open to refuge—or another interrogation.

Emotionally drained and physically exhausted, she struggled to walk down the long driveway in the hot summer sun. Each step felt heavier than the last. When she got closer to the building, the sight of the American flag flying outside stirred in her a sudden, fragile sense of relief. She stopped walking, her eyes fixed on the flag as it moved slowly in the warm wind, as if confirming that she had finally reached a place where someone might listen. She approached the front door and was met by uniformed American military guards. In her best English, she said, "My name is Catherine Yampolsky. I am a Soviet citizen, born to an American father. My father, George, entered the Soviet Union in 1936. I want to talk to the American Consul."

Both guards hesitated, looking at her with suspicion and curiosity. They spoke to each other in low tones that she could not hear, their eyes occasionally returning to her as if measuring the gravity of her words, and then one guard opened the door and disappeared behind it. The remaining guard stood firmly in front of the door. Hungry, tired, and frightened, she forced herself to stand politely while she waited for whatever decision might determine her fate.

After a few minutes, the second guard reappeared, whispering something inaudible to his compatriot. The second guard very politely asked her to follow them into the building. They opened the door and gestured for Catherine to cross the threshold into the building. She immediately felt the cool, almost perfumed air of the building wash over her overheated skin.

They took her to the entrance of an elevator and slowly and methodically pressed the button. Almost immediately, the elevator door slid open. Again, the person who appeared to be the senior guard on duty courteously gestured for her to enter. After she stepped into the elevator, both guards entered with her and positioned themselves on each side of her. Catherine became acutely aware of their presence, the quiet authority of their uniforms and the narrow space between them making her feel as though she were already under careful supervision. Another button was pressed, and the elevator began to descend. Catherine looked up at the elevator display and saw the numbers slowly changing: 1 … B1. She wondered how far inside the building they intended to take her, the small, illuminated symbols glowing softly above the door as the elevator carried her farther from the bright summer sunlight outside. When the elevator stopped, the doors automatically opened.

One of the guards stepped out into a long corridor and motioned for Catherine to exit the elevator. She followed his directions, desperately hoping the journey would soon end and she could sit and relax. The second guard followed, and they slowly walked down the corridor in a single file, moving in perfect step as if there was a strange magnetism between the three of them. The sound of their footsteps echoed faintly along the polished floor. She walked with them until they reached the second door on the left. The guard on her right side opened the door and entered, gesturing for her to follow. She saw a large room dominated by a polished wooden desk with many chairs lined against the walls. The first guard walked to one of the chairs, slightly turning it towards her and motioning for her to sit. He returned to the door and spoke a few hushed words to the second guard, who exited the room quietly, closing the door behind him. The first guard positioned himself in front of the door, facing Catherine with the composed stillness of a sentry on duty.

As she sat, her eyes wandered across the wall, and she saw a framed picture of Ronald Reagan, the President of the United States. To the right of the picture of the president, there was a framed American flag. Catherine found herself studying the two images in silence, sensing that the quiet room, the guarded corridor outside, and the long journey that had brought her there were all somehow bound to the power represented on that wall. The two symbols seemed to radiate an almost solemn authority in the quiet room.

It seemed like hours passed although it was probably only minutes. She tried to be patient, knowing she was on the last leg of a similar perilous journey that her grandparents had embarked upon many years ago—only going the opposite direction—in September of 1936, a lifetime to many.

Time seemed to drag on, although it was likely only a matter of minutes, and the door behind the large desk opened. A tall man in a dark blue suit looked directly at Catherine and said, "Welcome to the United States, and welcome to freedom."

Chapter 102

The Consulate's Haven

Catherine was asked to take an oath, placing her hand on the Bible and solemnly repeating the words as instructed by an American consular officer. Her voice trembled slightly as she promised to speak the truth. Her nervousness was palpable as she vowed to tell everything she knew.

The official, a grey-haired man named Edwin, greeted her kindly and even addressed her in a few careful words of Russian, hoping to put her at ease. He began by asking her to recount how she had managed to escape from the Soviet Union.

Catherine proceeded to share the extraordinary story of her life—her years in Moscow, the suffocating atmosphere of surveillance, and the improbable chain of events that had finally carried her to freedom.

After the debriefing session, she had her fingerprints taken and was provided accommodation in a designated hotel occasionally used by the American Consulate. She had a phone by her bedside and was allowed a few short phone calls to a U.S. number.

Her first call was to Aunt Natalie in New York.

Despite the crackly connection and the early morning hour on the U.S. East Coast, Aunt Natalie's voice filled with joy when she answered the phone.

Catherine eagerly shared the news.

"This is me! I am in Germany!"

Aunt Natalie, shocked and delighted, exclaimed,

"My God! How did you do it? I never thought the Soviets would let you go!"

The phone connection crackled loudly, making their conversation difficult.

Catherine replied, still emotional,

"I didn't either," her voice breaking somewhere between laughter and tears.

"It's wonderful news," Natalie responded. "Now you are free. Be careful!"

She offered her well-wishes, and the line went dead, leaving Catherine with a newfound sense of hope and the quiet realization that her life had truly begun again.

The following day, Catherine returned to the consulate, where she was met by another American official. He escorted her to an inner office via an elevator.

The office was simple and modestly furnished, featuring a portrait of the sitting American president and an American flag.

The official introduced himself as Richard and explained that he would be conducting her interview.

Richard addressed Catherine in Russian, and she responded in kind with a greeting.

He continued, explaining that her case would likely involve the State Department due to her American parent, even though her father still resided in the Soviet Union. They would need to debrief her at length over the next few days.

During that time, she would remain under consular protection until further arrangements could be made, a precaution designed to ensure her safety while her case was being reviewed.

Despite the fear and uncertainty about her future, Catherine felt she had made the right decision. However, she couldn't help but miss her family and felt terribly lonely.

Richard advised her not to visit railway stations or travel far from the consulate for security reasons. Catherine, naturally cautious, followed this advice and stayed close to the consulate.

She was temporarily placed in a building resembling a small hotel. While the room lacked the luxury of a proper hotel, her security was paramount, and she felt vindicated after years of living under the constant pressure of the Soviet system.

In early September, she was transferred to another secure location in Frankfurt.

The city greeted her with sunny, warm weather.

She was shown her studio apartment in a modern five-story building with a view of a nearby city park. Catherine enjoyed the pleasant weather and beautiful surroundings.

She often walked in the early morning hours, smiling at passersby—something she had rarely seen people do in Moscow.

Her daily routine involved attending debriefing sessions at the embassy and spending quiet weekends near her residence.

Frankfurt was a beautiful city, and one evening she decided to try a local café.

The atmosphere was warm and welcoming, and a Mozart concerto drifted softly through the room.

Despite the uncertainty of her future, Catherine slowly began to embrace her newfound freedom.

***

Catherine sat in the café waiting for her order, studying the colorful menu. The waitress greeted her and asked what she would like.

Catherine decided on a slice of *Esterházy* torte, a delicate hazelnut layered cake and placed her order.

As she waited, her attention drifted toward the large television screen mounted in the corner of the café.

A news broadcast had interrupted the talk show.

The anchor was reporting on a tragic aviation disaster.

A passenger flight traveling from New York to Seoul had strayed off course and been shot down over the Soviet island of Sakhalin.

All passengers aboard the Korean airliner were presumed dead.

The Soviet authorities admitted that their military had destroyed the aircraft after it entered Soviet airspace. They claimed they had believed it to be an American military plane. The report sent a chill through the café.

Moments later, the broadcast turned to another disturbing story. Doctors were warning of a mysterious new illness called AIDS. The disease appeared to affect certain groups of patients, including gay men, drug users, and some recipients of blood transfusions. Little was understood about the illness, except that it was spreading and appeared to be fatal. Hospitals struggled to understand the nature of the disease.

Catherine watched silently. For a moment she realized how violently the world beyond the Soviet Union was also changing.

Yet she also understood something else. Had she not escaped when she did, the Korean airliner tragedy might easily have become an excuse for the Soviet authorities to close their borders even tighter. Her freedom had come at the narrowest possible moment in history.

***

As Catherine settled into her new life in Frankfurt, she continued meeting with Jeff, her primary contact, providing information about her students and her experiences in the USSR.

She described her students as brilliant and highly intelligent young people with a strong desire to learn languages in preparation for their future careers.

The atmosphere during these discussions was respectful and friendly, and the officials listened carefully to her descriptions of life inside the Soviet Union.

In her free time, Catherine explored the sunlit streets of Frankfurt, visiting cultural landmarks such as the rebuilt Old Town, the Städel Museum, the Alte Oper (Old Opera House), and smaller specialty museums.

Museums became a refuge for her—quiet places where she could disappear into art and history and forget the anxieties of the present.

***

Yet Catherine felt increasingly impatient. Her future now depended on the bureaucratic machinery of the United States government and the processing of her American visa. Still, she tried to enjoy the simple pleasures of life in Frankfurt.

When *Oktoberfest* festivities arrived, the city filled with music, laughter, and the aroma of roasted sausages and warm pretzels. Catherine joined the celebration. She ordered sausage with spicy mustard, a pretzel, and a beer.

She sat beside a cheerful middle-aged couple, clinking mugs with strangers and sharing in the easy camaraderie of the crowd. As the sun set over the river embankment, Catherine felt pleasantly tired but content.

The laughter and music of the festival felt worlds away from the gray silence of Soviet life.

***

Catherine often dreamed of moving to San Francisco and experiencing its free and easy way of life. She had read about California as a kind of modern paradise, and the idea of living there captivated her imagination.

One afternoon Jeff informed her that the debriefing process had finally been completed.

She was now free to move about as she wished.

While a few administrative details remained, her formal interviews were finished. Jeff also mentioned that she could now visit relatives if she wished. Then he explained the next step in her journey. She would soon be flying to New York and from there continuing on to San Francisco.

A congresswoman from California, Sala Burton, had advocated on her behalf and petitioned the State Department to grant her a visa. This support, combined with the presence of family members already living in California, helped open the path for Catherine's relocation to the United States.

Jeff reassured her that she would grow to appreciate the calm atmosphere and mild climate of San Francisco.

Catherine listened quietly. For the first time since leaving Moscow, the future no longer seemed uncertain. Her dreams of beginning a new life in California were now within reach.

And somewhere beyond the Atlantic Ocean, a new world was waiting for her.

Chapter 103

The Butterfly Café

The next morning, Catherine woke feeling refreshed and in better spirits. Sunlight filtered through the curtains of her small Frankfurt apartment, and for a moment she allowed herself to believe that the most dangerous part of her journey was behind her. She ventured outside and walked toward a nearby phone booth to make a crucial call.

Catherine dialed carefully and waited for the line to connect.

Voice on the Line: "*UNCENTRALE* headquarters, Comrade Petrov speaking."

Catherine replied calmly.

Catherine said in a confident voice: "My name is Kat. I am calling on behalf of Professor Angel. I would like to speak with Comrade Oleg Dobronravov, please."

For her own safety, Catherine did her best to sound like a professional research assistant. Her carefully rehearsed role was designed to protect Oleg—her former brother-in-law—from attracting the attention of Soviet intelligence services.

The voice on the line answered pleasantly.

Voice on the Line: "One moment, please. I will see if Comrade Dobronravov is available."

Catherine held the receiver tightly and waited in tense silence, hoping the first attempt would succeed.

At last, the voice returned.

Oleg Dobronravov answered: "Hello. Oleg Dobronravov speaking. May I ask who is calling?"

Catherine continued steadily: "My name is Kat. I assist Professor Angel with research on international trade law. We are preparing a study on how Soviet legislation adapts international conventions. I would be very grateful if you could recommend some Russian sources for our research."

Oleg did not hesitate. His voice remained calm and professional, as though such academic requests were routine.

Oleg Dobronravov replied: "Yes, of course. I would be glad to help. Perhaps we could meet in person so I may provide you with some references."

He paused briefly before continuing.

"I suggest the *Schmetterling Café*—Butterfly Café—on *Rosa Strasse* in the town of *Maria Enzersdorf*, just outside Vienna. It is about thirteen kilometers from the city. You may enjoy the train ride. The town is quite charming."

Then, almost casually, he added the coded phrase:

"By the way... the jasmine is in full bloom in the botanical garden."

Catherine understood the signal immediately and answered without hesitation: “That sounds lovely. I will look up the directions and most likely travel by train.”

Oleg added calmly: “Excellent. Tomorrow at three o'clock would suit me perfectly.”

Catherine concluded the conversation quickly: “Very well. Thank you for your help. Have a pleasant day.”

She slowly replaced the receiver, her heart still pounding.

***

The following morning Catherine set out for the meeting. Although she had already escaped the Soviet Union, years of caution had trained her instincts. With a lingering fear of being followed, she carefully scanned the streets around her.

She made her way to Frankfurt's main railway station and boarded the train to Vienna, choosing a seat where she could discreetly observe the passengers around her. Several hours later the train pulled into Vienna's central station. As an extra precaution, she deliberately chose the second taxi waiting outside the station rather than the first.

The driver carried her south toward the quiet town of *Maria Enzersdorf*, about thirteen kilometers from Vienna. Soon the taxi stopped on *Rosa Strasse*.

Catherine approached the *Schmetterling Café*—Butterfly Café cautiously. Through the window she could see a dim interior filled with conversation and the bluish haze of cigarette smoke.

She stepped inside. Her eyes slowly adjusted to the semi-darkness. Then she spotted him.

Oleg Dobronravov sat quietly at a corner table. He noticed her immediately but made no sudden movement, maintaining the composed demeanor of a diplomat accustomed to discretion. Catherine approached the table.

Catherine greeted him softly: "Hello… my brother."

Oleg responded calmly: "Hello, Kat."

Catherine lowered her voice.

"Professor Angel was very pleased when you agreed to meet with me."

A young waiter approached the table to take their orders.

Oleg ordered roast goose with dumplings, while Catherine chose apple strudel and coffee.

They spoke politely about academic matters while the waiter moved away.

To any casual observer, they appeared to be nothing more than a scholar and a visiting researcher discussing a harmless project.

While Oleg slowly sampled his goose leg, Catherine took a modest bite of her apple strudel.

Then, in a seemingly casual gesture, Oleg placed a pastry box on the table.

Inside was a slice of Vienna's famous chocolate torte, the Sachertorte, carefully wrapped in paper from the bakery. Oleg set the box gently on the table and spoke in a calm, almost casual tone.

"A small gift from a local bakery," he said quietly. "Please accept it."

After a brief pause, he leaned back slightly in his chair and added in the same measured voice, "Give me a little time, and I will gather the materials you need for your research. I believe you will find them… extremely useful."

Their half-hour lunch passed in carefully controlled conversation, blending effortlessly with the surrounding chatter of the café.

Yet beneath the polite discussion, their true communication occurred through brief glances, subtle gestures, and the careful choice of certain words. Neither wished to endanger the other. At last, the meeting ended. Oleg leaned slightly toward Catherine and whispered softly in her ear.

"I am very glad you are safe."

He paused.

"Your sister sends her love. I did everything I could."

Catherine felt a sudden wave of gratitude.

Oleg straightened his jacket, placed a few banknotes on the table, and rose from his chair.

Without another word he walked toward the door.

A moment later he disappeared into the quiet Austrian street—leaving behind the faint scent of tobacco smoke and the lingering sense that their brief meeting had carried enormous risks.

Chapter 104

Between Debriefings and Concerns

The following day, Catherine found herself once again inside the consulate's inner offices, located several floors beneath the bustling streets of Frankfurt. The underground rooms were quiet and windowless, insulated from the life of the city above.

Seated across from her was a man named Tom, an American officer fluent in Russian.

He leaned forward slightly and spoke in a calm voice.

"I know we said we were finished," he began, "but before you leave, there are a few more things we would like to understand. Tell me more about your students. What exactly did you teach them? And how old were they?"

Catherine answered carefully.

"I taught young adult students how to speak English," she said. "Most of them were preparing for advanced studies. Some hoped to continue their education in places like London, Cambridge, Oxford, or New York. Many dreamed of positions of influence in government, diplomacy, or international business."

She paused before adding,

"They were exceptionally bright students. Only those with very high academic scores were accepted into my classes."

Tom listened attentively and made a few final notes.

With that, the long debriefing process finally came to an end.

***

Later that afternoon Jeff approached Catherine in the hallway outside the consulate.

"Your U.S. visa application is still being processed," he told her. "That may take a little time. In the meantime, if you would like to take a short trip, that would be perfectly acceptable."

Catherine looked at him with quiet determination.

"Yes," she said. "I would like to travel."

Jeff nodded but immediately added a note of caution.

"Then you must be careful." His tone became more serious.

"For the moment, stay away from railway stations whenever possible. Try to remain within the central parts of the city near the embassy offices."

He continued, "Do not speak to strangers. If someone approaches you and asks questions, tell them you are from California and that you are busy. Keep moving."

Jeff studied her face carefully before adding,

"You should also assume that someone might be watching you."

Catherine listened without interruption. Such warnings were not new to her.

Jeff went on,

"If you ever notice the same man or woman appearing more than once—on the street, in a shop window reflection, or behind you on a tram—do not confront them."

He paused.

"Go down into the underground station and board the last car of the train. If necessary, change trains quickly. That usually shakes off anyone who might be following you."

The advice sounded almost routine to him, but Catherine understood its seriousness.

Jeff smiled faintly and tried to soften the moment.

"Think of it this way," he said. "Be like a summer breeze. Drift into a shop, buy what you need, and drift out again. Walk quietly through the city and return home alone."

Then his voice grew firm once more.

"Until you reach America safely, this is the best way to stay alive."

***

After a moment of silence Catherine asked a question that had been on her mind for days.

“Would it be possible for me to see Oleg once more while I am still here?”

Jeff considered the request.

Finally, he nodded.

“A family visit would not be a problem. If you wish to reconnect with him, you may call.”

He added,

“You might also prepare a small package—perhaps medicine, books, or something your family might need or enjoy.”

Catherine thanked him quietly.

But even as she spoke, a familiar anxiety returned.

She constantly feared hearing the coded message they had agreed upon long ago—

“Jasmine has faded.”

Those three words would mean that something had gone terribly wrong.

That Oleg was no longer safe.

Catherine said a silent prayer for her brother’s protection.

Somewhere beyond the borders of Germany, he was still living inside the dangerous machinery of the Soviet world.

And she knew that one wrong move could place him in grave danger.

Chapter 105

Signals and Setbacks

Catherine found herself making careful last-minute preparations for her second meeting. She purchased several boxes of fine chocolates, packets of coffee and tea, small bottles of essential medicines, and a charming toy for her young nephew, attending to every detail as if assembling a lifeline between two worlds.

Only after everything had been neatly packed did she sit down beside the telephone.

She dialed the *UNCENTRALE* office number in Vienna, patiently listening to the steady beeps until a man with a calm, resonant voice answered.

"*UNCENTRALE headquarters*," the man said. "Eugene speaking, Soviet Department."

Catherine immediately switched to English.

"Hello. My name is Kat. I work for Professor Angel. May I please speak with Oleg Dobronravov?"

There was a brief pause.

"One moment," the voice replied.

A few seconds later she heard a voice she recognized instantly. Oleg.

"Hello."

Catherine kept her tone measured and professional.

"Hello. This is Kat again. If you remember me, we met for lunch a couple of weeks ago. I am Professor Angel's secretary. The Professor sends his best regards. We would very much appreciate your kind help with our research."

She paused briefly before continuing.

"Perhaps we could meet again. I was thinking of Carlos's Bar in Vienna for lunch. Friends tell me it is an excellent place."

Oleg listened without interrupting, absorbing every word.

Finally, he replied, his voice calm but slightly guarded.

"Excuse me, Kat. Our line seems to be breaking up."

A brief pause followed.

"The news clips you requested are ready for you. I would be very happy to meet again and assist both you and Professor Angel."

Catherine understood the coded language instantly.

"Wonderful," she replied smoothly. "Please pencil in our luncheon date. Next Wednesday at Carlos's Bar."

Then she added deliberately,

"The train journey is rather long, so I may stay overnight at the *Schweizerhof* Hotel."

Her tone remained cheerful.

"Have a wonderful day. I look forward to seeing you."

The line clicked softly as the call ended.

***

On the following Wednesday morning Catherine boarded an early train departing Frankfurt for Vienna.

The journey lasted nearly seven hours, the landscape slowly changing outside the window as the train crossed southern Germany and moved toward Austria.

By the time she arrived in Vienna it was shortly after two o'clock in the afternoon.

She stepped out of the station, hailed a taxi, and gave the driver a simple instruction.

"*Carlos's Bar*, please."

The taxi wound through Vienna's elegant streets until it stopped near a quiet side street lined with old stone buildings.

Carlos's Bar was located a few steps below street level, tucked inside a cozy cellar-like space. Soft lighting reflected off polished wood tables, and a violinist played gentle melodies in the corner, filling the room with a subdued elegance.

Catherine chose a small table near the wall and ordered a modest glass of wine.

She sipped it slowly, keeping one eye on the door and the other on the clock.

Three o'clock passed.

Then three-fifteen.

The minutes stretched longer and heavier.

Oleg had not arrived.

A quiet unease began to grow inside her.

Finally, concerned that remaining too long might attract attention, Catherine stood calmly, placed several coins beside her untouched glass, and walked toward the exit.

The head waiter called after her politely.

"Madam, has your guest not arrived?"

Catherine did not answer. She stepped out onto the street, glancing quickly in both directions, searching the passing pedestrians for any sign of Oleg.

He never appeared. A cold realization settled over her. Something had gone wrong.

***

Confused and anxious, Catherine forced herself not to dwell on dangerous possibilities.

She knew that speculation could lead to panic.

Instead, she returned to the taxi stand and instructed the driver to take her to the *Schweizerhof* Hotel, where she had planned to spend the night.

Her room overlooked a quiet street, its lights glowing softly as evening descended over Vienna.

Catherine sat beside the telephone, watching it as if it were the only object in the room that mattered. Minutes passed. Then an hour. The silence felt unbearable.

Suddenly the telephone rang. The sharp sound made her heart leap. She grabbed the receiver.

"Oleg?"

His voice came through the line low and hurried.

"Catherine," he said, "I was briefly detained because of a traffic incident. It took some time to resolve. I cannot explain further."

There was a pause. Then his tone grew firmer.

"Listen carefully. Follow the plan exactly as we discussed. Wait for your U.S. visa approval and leave immediately once it is issued."

Another pause.

"When you arrive safely, find a way to let me know that you are all right."

Catherine opened her mouth to respond—

But the line suddenly went dead.

Catherine remained frozen for a moment, the receiver still pressed to her ear. Slowly, she lowered it back onto the cradle.

Relief washed over her—Oleg was alive.

But almost immediately another realization settled over her like a cold shadow.

Time was running out.

Chapter 106

Wings of Liberty

In November, Catherine finally received her American visa, granted after the intervention of a California congresswoman who had petitioned on her behalf, pointing out that a Soviet citizen born to an American father had managed to break through the Iron Curtain.

By mid-November the weather had turned sharply colder. Snowflakes drifted slowly from the darkening sky, settling over the streets of Frankfurt. Catherine was overwhelmed with joy that her visa had finally been approved. Yet even amid her excitement, she felt a quiet melancholy. Europe had given her the first taste of freedom she had ever known.

She had come to love West Germany — the orderly streets of Frankfurt, the quiet parks, the cafés where she could sit alone without fear. But now the time had come to move on.

On the twentieth of November she packed her suitcase and waited downstairs in the lobby. Soon a car arrived, sent by the American consulate, and the driver — an American serviceman — helped her place her bag in the trunk.

As the car sped along the autobahn toward Frankfurt Airport, Catherine watched the winter landscape glide past the window. Bare trees blurred against the pale sky; their branches dusted with fresh snow.

A wave of emotion rose within her.

She was leaving behind the continent that had sheltered her escape.

Yet ahead of her lay something even greater.

America.

At the airport she checked her single suitcase and received her boarding passes. Standing quietly in the departure line, Catherine felt the weight of the journey that had brought her to this moment.

Years of fear.

Years of waiting.

Years of careful steps through a world that could turn dangerous without warning.

Almost to herself, she whispered,

"It took me a lifetime to board this flight to JFK."

No one around her heard.

The line moved forward.

Flight attendants welcomed passengers aboard, guiding them gently to their seats.

As Catherine settled into her place by the window, she glanced around the cabin and wondered how many others carried stories like hers — travelers leaving behind troubled pasts, crossing an ocean toward an uncertain but hopeful future.

The aircraft began to roll slowly along the runway.

Catherine closed her eyes for a moment and let out a long breath.

Her childhood dreams were about to come true.

And somewhere in the back of her mind, she remembered the Soviet official who had once declared with absolute certainty:

"You will never set foot on foreign soil."

A quiet smile crossed her face.

It was almost Thanksgiving in America.

The thought lingered warmly in her mind as the aircraft climbed higher into the night sky.

She remembered reading about the Pilgrims who had arrived centuries earlier at Plymouth Rock aboard the Mayflower — men and women who had crossed the Atlantic in search of freedom, enduring hunger, sickness, and loss along the way.

Many had not survived that first winter.

Yet those who did had built something new.

Catherine found herself reflecting on how strangely similar her own journey had been — a passage through hardship toward a fragile promise of liberty.

Hours later the flight attendant's voice gently woke her.

"Ladies and gentlemen, we will soon be landing at John F. Kennedy International Airport in New York."

Catherine turned toward the window.

Far below, through the mist of early evening, she saw it.

The Statue of Liberty. Catherine pressed her hand gently against the airplane window.

The great figure stood in the harbor, her torch lifted high above the water, a silent guardian welcoming the weary and the hopeful alike.

For a moment Catherine could hardly breathe.

Her family's story — stretching from America to Russia and back again — had come full circle.

The *Lufthansa* aircraft touched down smoothly on the runway late that evening.

Passengers began gathering their belongings.

Catherine stepped into the vast terminal alone. No one was waiting for her. Her ticket allowed no stopover in New York, and she would continue her journey west to San Francisco without seeing her beloved Aunt Natalie.

That reunion would come later. For now, what mattered most was something simple. She was free.

When Catherine eventually arrived in California, she discovered more than a new country. She discovered a quiet purpose.

The peace she found there was not something the world had given her easily — it was something she had earned through endurance.

She had learned that one cannot confront a system of oppression head-on. Such machines are built to crush resistance and erase those who challenge them.

Instead, she had survived by moving around it — with silence when silence was necessary, and with truth whenever truth could safely be spoken. She kept records. She wrote down what others were too frightened to say.

And though she eventually found happiness, she never forgot the lessons of the world she had escaped.

For the violence of ideology, when left unchecked, can consume the soul of an entire people.

Her freedom was hard-won.

And she guarded it carefully — not only for herself, but for those who would come after her.

So that they would never forget.

And beyond the ocean, a new life was waiting — one no wall could ever imprison again.

For the first time in her life, the future belonged entirely to her.

Author's Note

Catherine's story does not truly end with her arrival in America—the land of the free—where she reconnects with her long-lost fatherland and, in time, with her beloved Aunt Natalie. The journey that carried her across continents and through the shadows of the Cold War was only the beginning of a life shaped by courage, uncertainty, and unexpected turns of fate.

The authors hope that readers who have followed Catherine through these pages will wish to accompany her further. Her life, and the lives of those closest to her, continued to unfold in ways that were no less dramatic than the events described in this book. Those later chapters may one day be told in a future volume.

Hostages for Life is a work of historical fiction partly inspired by and partly based on real experiences and historical events. While some characters and episodes draw directly from those experiences, others have been imagined or adapted for narrative purposes.

Historical Notes and Terms

1. ***Militsioner*** — A uniformed officer of the Soviet *militsiya*, the civilian police force responsible for maintaining public order in the Soviet Union.

2. ***Amtorg*** — The American Trading Corporation, a Soviet state-controlled organization established in New York in 1924 to facilitate trade between the Soviet Union and the United States.

3. ***Torgsyn*** — A Soviet chain of special state stores in the 1930s where goods could be purchased only with foreign currency, gold, or precious metals.

4. ***NKVD*** — The People's Commissariat for Internal Affairs, the Soviet secret police and internal security organization during the Stalin era, responsible for political surveillance, arrests, and the administration of labor camps.

5. ***Gulag*** — The Soviet system of state-run forced labor camps used primarily during the Stalin era to imprison political prisoners and other detainees.

6. ***Moskvich*** — A compact Soviet automobile manufactured in Moscow and widely used throughout the Soviet Union during the mid-twentieth century.

7. ***Refusenik*** — A person in the Soviet Union who was denied permission to emigrate abroad, often because the authorities considered them politically sensitive.

www.ingramcontent.com/pod-product-compliance
Lightning Source LLC
LaVergne TN
LVHW100500110826
845146LV00002B/463

* 9 7 9 8 9 9 3 0 1 6 7 7 1 *